Forgotten Bones

WHITBY'S FORGOTTEN VICTIMS

Wes Markin

About the Author

Wes Markin is the bestselling author of The Yorkshire Murders, which stars the compassionate and relentless DCI Emma Gardner. He is also the author of Whitby's Forgotten Victims, the DCI Michael Yorke Thrillers set in Salisbury, and the Jake Pettman Thrillers set in New England. Wes lives in Harrogate with his wife, two children, and his cheeky cockapoo, Rosie, close to the crime scenes in The Yorkshire Murders and Whitby's Forgotten Victims.

You can find out more at:
www.wesmarkinauthor.com
facebook.com/wesmarkinauthor

By Wes Markin

DCI Yorke Thrillers

One Last Prayer

The Repenting Serpent

The Silence of Severance

Rise of the Rays

Dance with the Reaper

Christmas with the Conduit

Better the Devil

The Secret Diary of Lacey Ray

A Lesson in Crime

Jake Pettman Thrillers

The Killing Pit

Fire in Bone

Blue Falls

The Rotten Core

Rock and a Hard Place

The Yorkshire Murders

The Viaduct Killings

The Lonely Lake Killings

The Crying Cave Killings

The Graveyard Killings

The Winter Killings

Whitby's Forgotten Victims

Forgotten Bones

Forgotten Lives

Forgotten Souls

∼

Details of how to claim your **FREE** DCI Michael Yorke quick read, **A lesson in Crime**, can be found at the end of this book.

This story is a work of fiction. All names, characters, organizations, places, events and incidents are products of the author's imagination or are used fictitiously. Any resemblance to any persons, alive or dead, events or locals is entirely coincidental.

Text copyright © 2024 Wes Markin

First published 2024

ISBN: 9798329453898

Edited by: Candida Bradford

Published by: WFM Publishing Ltd

All rights reserved.

No part of this book should be reproduced in any way without the express permission of the author.

For Jo

Chapter One

Following a six-day tempest, seeing the morning sun in a clear sky had to rate as the highlight of Sam Farnsworth's week in Whitby.

And not because of the picture-perfect scenery. Yes, that was great, but not having to wrestle Ella, eight, and Ollie, five, into waterproofs before exiting the cottage, well, that was a dream come true.

It was also good to see Eliza in a better mood, too. She was an Aussie, and always felt she had to pass comment on English weather. So, when she'd thrown back the curtains this morning and declared, 'That's more like it!' he finally felt that their break was about to get going. On this, the last bloody day!

There were a few people up on the West Cliff, but it wasn't busy at all. Not only was it out of season, and drastically early in the morning, but everyone was still tentative regarding the weather. The BBC warnings were still in full flow.

Ollie and Ella were first to the famous whalebones.

Through the bony frame, you could see the majestic abbey half a mile or so away on the East Cliff.

Eliza tugged his sleeve. 'Phone, picture, quick.'

Just like her to introduce panic into an otherwise tranquil situation!

He handed his phone over. Sam, by his own admission, was useless at photos. Not that an admission was required, not when you had Eliza around, who was always happy to mention it.

His wife was also talented at forcing back the frustration in her tone of voice as the children, inevitably, came out of the perfect pose before the camera was ready to go.

While she worked her magic, he gazed out over the North Sea, breathing in the tangy, salty air. For days, it'd been a frenzied monster, but this morning it sat calmly, turning Whitby into the seaside town he remembered visiting as a child with his parents.

Sam recalled his father's jolly demeanour, ever present, come rain or shine, and then felt guilt over his own dour mood these last days. He returned his gaze back to Eliza, who was still failing, inevitably, to capture a perfect digital memory.

He looked at the whalebones again, feeling a moment of inspiration.

His father used to prance around them when he was a kid, captivating him and his sister, Lucy, with tales of Whitby's maritime history. The memory sparked him into life, and he rode a sudden wave of enthusiasm, right up to the whalebones and his children.

Standing between them, dead centre of the fifteen-foot-high arch, he pretended to hold a harpoon. He deepened his voice. 'And having ventured far into the chaos of the North

Sea, the brave sailor finally sights his catch.' He realised his voice was loud, but he forced back any feelings of embarrassment, the tang of self-consciousness bitter on his tongue. His father would have gone to town on this dramatic reconstruction. Time to take a leaf out of his book. He pointed the imaginary harpoon at the North Sea. 'A colossal leviathan rising from the depths.'

He noticed Ollie turning and wandering away towards the Captain Cook memorial, which stood tall about twenty metres away in the direction of the cliff edge.

He's five; maybe to be expected.

He glanced at Ella, who was grimacing, and then let out his breath in a long sigh.

She didn't look like she was buying it either.

'And,' Sam continued regardless, 'knowing that the whale oil and bones would fetch him a pretty penny, he did what needed to be done—'

'Dad, please,' Ella hissed. 'This is embarrassing.'

She turned and walked away to the memorial.

'Okay, go and check on your brother then!' He stood up, shaking his head, stunned by how badly he'd crashed and burned. A group of tourists, readying themselves for their turn with the iconic jawbones, offered him sympathetic looks.

He shrugged and smiled at them. 'Different world. I'm not YouTube.' He waited for a polite laugh, which didn't come.

The confused tourists spoke to one another in an unfamiliar language, forcing him to consider the possibility that those looks hadn't been sympathetic, after all, but rather, looks of concern.

As he approached his wife, who was laughing, he

shrugged. 'Well, I have to say it worked on me as a kid.' He checked on Ollie and Ella, who were now staring up at the Captain Cook memorial, and then turned back. 'Wrestling that whale to its death out in—'

'You see, that might be the problem,' Eliza said, taking his hand.

'Eh?'

'Bit barbaric. Ollie loves animals, and Ella, well, she's savvy enough to know that you shouldn't be celebrating something that brutal.'

'Hardly celebrating,' Sam said. 'Just trying to stir up some enthusiasm. I love whales, too. I'm glad we don't hurt them any more.'

He looked back at his children, who'd moved further away and were now playing on a grassy patch lined with benches where people could sit and gaze off the cliffs at the staggering views.

'Ella... Ollie... that's far enough!' he called out.

They seemed to be happy where they were.

Sam turned back to his wife, smiling. 'While we've got this free second...' He leaned in for a kiss.

'Unheard of,' she said, and met his lips.

After Eliza pulled back, Sam sighed with his eyes closed. 'I've missed that.' His eyes snapped back open, the blissful moment shattered by her next words.

'Shit,' Eliza said. 'They're off.'

'Bloody hell,' Sam said.

Together, Eliza and Sam jogged past the memorial and onto the grass. 'Ella... Ollie...' he shouted. 'Stay where you are!'

The heavy, rushing wind coming in off the ocean seemed to be drowning out his shouts. *Shit!* The kids must have been ten metres or so from the corner of the Pavilion Drive car park. 'Don't you *dare* go to that bloody car park!'

Ella was eight! Surely, she wouldn't be that bloody stupid?

Sam took Eliza's hand and they sprinted, but their children, just before they reached the corner of the car park, swerved right, towards the fence that separated off the cliff edge.

Christ!

'They won't climb it... they aren't that silly—'

Sam's breath caught in his throat, the metallic taste of fear flooding his mouth. They didn't need to climb it. The fence was broken, and they were through.

Sam let go of Eliza's hand and threw everything into the last couple of metres.

Ollie screamed.

Panic clawed at Sam's insides. 'Ollie!'

He saw Ella on the other side of the broken fence, stationary.

The cliff edge proper was still a fair way from them. Ollie couldn't have gone right to the edge... it was too far.

So, where the hell was he? His heart pounded wildly. 'Ollie!'

Ella was lowering herself to her knees.

Sam's mind whirred as he slid through the broken fence. His footing was no longer steady; recent storms had chewed up the unkempt undergrowth and the mud on this side, but he had to stay on his feet. 'Ollie!'

He heard a familiar sound. Relief flooded his body. Ollie crying. His distressed boy was lying, unmoving, on the ground at Ella's feet.

He glanced back at Eliza, noticing how far they'd come

from the whalebones. *Horrendous parenting skills*, he thought, *and the most terrifying moment of my life.* 'He's okay, hon!'

Sam jogged around some scattered rocks and crouched next to Ollie, who was on his side, crying, holding his knee up to his chest.

'Did you slip, son?' Sam said.

'No... he went over this rock,' Ella said, pointing.

Eliza came alongside him and leaned over to scoop their five-year-old up.

'More like a boulder.' Sam's hand settled on a half-a-metre by half-a-metre rock. He then glanced left at Eliza, who was lowering Ollie's trousers to look at his leg.

'His knee is red, but I think it's okay,' she said loudly, over her son's wails.

Sam looked over his shoulder to see if anyone had noticed what was going on, but there was no one. The whalebones and tourists were some distance from here, nobody was occupying the benches, and the car park beside them was almost empty.

Sam used his hand on the rock to give himself leverage as he rose from his haunches—

It wobbled, throwing him off balance. 'Shit!' he said, trying to right himself. No good. His feet tore through soggy mud, and he was on his arse. 'Shit!'

Ella giggled over his bad language and put a hand to her mouth.

Sam looked over at his wife. 'Sorry.'

Eliza shook her head and refocused on Ollie's knee.

He turned his head and smiled at Ella. 'You going to help me up or what?'

'No,' she said and giggled again.

He adjusted himself into a squat and then attempted to

rise a second time, seeking no help from loose debris this time. Rubbing his backside, which was damp with mud, he looked down at the rock with annoyance.

'You're covered in mud,' Ella said, poking Sam in the leg before joining her mother and brother to walk back in the direction they'd come from. Ollie was looking more settled now. He'd locked his arms around Eliza's neck and his head was pressed against her chest as she carried him back in the direction of the car park.

Sam looked down at the rock again. *Piece of shit.* He put the tip of his boot against it and pushed.

The rock slumped over onto its side.

Wow. He rose an eyebrow. *Unexpected.*

But, in a way, it wasn't, really. A storm over a coast knew how to chew up a place.

He looked down into a shallow groove in the ground revealed by the falling rock and then took a deep breath. *What was that?*

'Come on, Sam,' Eliza called.

'Okay,' he called back, but didn't turn. 'Just a moment.'

He knelt again, and peered into the hole, squinting.

Something was clearly poking out from the dirt.

He pressed his fingers down on the mud, and around whatever the object was. He identified a handle…

Then he located curves… It was some kind of container.

'What are you doing?' Eliza said. She was standing just behind him again, having returned.

His two children came alongside him, too.

'What you found, Daddy?' Ollie asked between sniffs.

Sam sighed and smiled at his son, whose face was red from the tears. 'I don't know. A suitcase, perhaps?'

He put his hands in again and worked his hands around the contours. 'Yes… a suitcase. Buried upright and' – he nodded at the rock – 'sealed in with that.' He could now feel the cool metallic teeth of a zipper. 'It's closed.'

'Is it a time capsule?' Ella asked.

Ella was no stranger to time capsules, having built one as part of her Year 3 project. A project that was repeated yearly. The fields around her school must have been overflowing with them.

Sam shrugged. 'Rather big for a time capsule.'

'Can we dig it up?' Ella said. 'Can we?'

'What with, honey?' Eliza laughed.

'I've a spade,' Ollie said.

Sam laughed too. 'That's for the beach and sandcastles, matey. It won't cut it here.'

'What if it's money?' Ella said.

'Well, if it is, it goes to the police, anyway. So, we may as well tell them and let them break their backs by digging it up rather than us!'

'Break their backs?' Ollie said.

Sam felt Eliza prodding him. 'Sam!'

'Not literally break their backs, son. It's an expression. Means work hard. Anyway, let's leave it to the experts.'

'But if there's a lot of money,' Ella said, 'we could go to Disneyland.'

'Honey, we've already discussed what we'll do if we find anything valuable.'

Ella sighed.

'If you want to live in a world where your lost things find their way back to you, then you need to be part of the process.'

'But will the police really give it back to whoever it belongs to?' Ella said. 'They may just keep it for themselves.'

'The police wouldn't do that,' Sam said. 'Anyway...' His

finger was tracing the zip the other way now. And then the tiny, orderly metal teeth just stopped. 'Hang on a tick…' He leaned forward. 'There's a hole. It's burst.' He wriggled some fingers in, then leaned a bit more. 'I can get my entire hand in—'

'Careful,' Eliza said.

'Not like anything will be alive in here,' Sam said.

'I was more worried about you getting stuck.'

His fingers met something cold and firm. 'Something here…' He moved his own fingers until he could clutch onto—

He snatched his hand out. 'Shit! Shit!'

Ella giggled again.

'Sam!' Eliza said. 'Stop swearing, will you?'

Sam scurried backwards, stopping against his wife. He was looking down at his mud-encrusted hand. He was certain he'd just taken hold of a bone. A finger or a toe. He'd felt the knuckle.

'Sam? What's wrong?'

He looked up at her, his eyes wide.

Her eyes widened, too, as his panic became infectious.

'I… I…' He moved his eyes between his children, who were now looking concerned. He stopped himself, took a deep breath, the earthy smell of mud filling his nostrils. 'Just a worm… a long one.' He closed his eyes. 'Disgusting.' He gulped and opened his eyes, reaching out for his daughter.

Giggling again, Ella backed away. 'Ugh. Don't touch me.'

He heard Ollie moving as he said, 'Let me see.' Then he was scrambling for the shallow hole.

Sam looped his arms around him. 'The case doesn't belong to us, Ollie. It belongs to someone else. It's important that the police find out who.'

'So they can get their worms back?' Ella said and laughed.

No, Sam thought, standing and leading his family away, *so they can ask them why they've buried a body on this cliff edge.*

Chapter Two

It had been a long and brutal night.

Frank Black was sitting up straight in his oak chair.

Its high backrest and attached velvet cushion made it his favourite chair. No other chair he owned could support his ageing spine to the same degree.

He did everything in this chair. Ate, watched television, read the newspaper... and guarded the bedroom behind him.

Technically, he didn't need to be on guard. The bedroom door, like his sturdy chair, was solid oak. And, even before malnourishment, she'd been slight. No chance she'd have the strength to break down this locked door.

Still, he remained.

He *needed* to be here.

Every long and brutal night. Listening.

As the week-long storm holding Whitby in its savage grip had intensified, so, it seemed, had her pain.

And his.

Nothing made you feel as if you'd descended into hell

faster than screaming winds outside your home, combined with wailing agony within.

But despite the living hell, he remained.

Each morning, he left his home with barely any rest, only to return that evening to do it all over again.

Every long and brutal night. Sentry at his post.

It was hard to measure, but Frank felt as if last night had been the worst yet.

Because, at one point, there'd been complete silence within, while the ear-splitting cracks of thunder raged outside.

He'd managed thirty minutes before he could handle it no longer and went in to her, terrified that her heart had given out.

Thankfully, no.

She'd given signs of life by spitting in his face.

Frank looked at his watch. It was early. He wasn't working today, but he planned to go food shopping and wanted to beat the late morning crowds.

Pulling himself away from the sound of her sobbing was another agony he endured.

All day, the guilt would gnaw at him, and doubts would consume him.

Frank *knew* he should let her go. *Knew* this wasn't right.

And he'd always *known* better.

But sometimes the line between what you knew you should do, and what you felt compelled to do, well, it just blurred. He'd seen it so many times in others. In those he'd brought to justice.

So, with the line blurred, she'd stay, and he'd sit here and suffer *every long and brutal night*, and eventually, in the moments in which exhaustion claimed her and she slept, he may allow himself a moment to cry.

And if the crying ever became too overpowering, and his sobs too loud, he'd retreat quickly to his bedroom.

Because he just couldn't believe she'd enjoy that. Hearing him suffer.

What he believed, *really believed*, was that the longer he kept her, the longer she endured this torment, the more chance that she'd come to love him again.

Because she'd loved him before. Once upon a time.

And love like that could never really die, could it?

Frank's phone rang. He recognised the number.

He stood, stretched out and groaned. It may be his best chair, but that didn't mean it solved his back problem.

He was sixty-four, and ready for the scrap heap.

He answered his mobile phone in the kitchen.

'It's my day off,' he said.

'I'm sorry, Detective Chief Inspector, but we've recovered a body.'

Chapter Three

Like most coastal towns, Whitby was no stranger to a good battering from Mother Nature. Severe weather, such as the storm this week, rising sea levels and strong tidal currents ensured regular cliff erosion. And it certainly wasn't unusual for bodies to come out in the wash.

Still, DCI Frank Black couldn't remember a single discovery of human remains that had amounted to anything. Most were hundreds of years old.

However, for Chief Constable Donald Oxley to ring him personally, and assign him an assistant, it suggested that someone, somewhere, didn't consider this usual.

'This isn't a washed-up mariner from the eighteenth century, then?' he asked Donald.

'The remains are in a suitcase.'

'Maybe someone threw him overboard in it?'

'This is a modern suitcase, not something from the eighteenth century.'

Frank had, of course, been joking. However, his superior didn't appreciate humour; he didn't appreciate socialising in any regard, truth be told, so Donald moved swiftly on to tell him that a new kid on the block was assisting him. 'Geraldine's only just joined us. Go easy. You've read the memo about her?'

'Aye,' he lied. 'I'll go easy.' Also, probably a lie.

Frank drove to the Khyber Pass and parked by one of his favourite cafes.

Sherlock's did a great coffee. Frank was feeling ragged from almost two weeks of sleeping in a wooden chair, and it was tempting as anything. But he had a new DI who was only thirty-two. Practically a bairn in his eyes! And if she was already there, keen as mustard, who knew what damage she was going to be delivering onto his crime scene.

And Sherlock's wasn't going anywhere. He'd grab a couple of espressos after doing his duty. *That,* he concluded with a smile, *was elementary.*

The smile over his shit joke lingered, but quickly fell away halfway up the steps to the North Terrace on West Cliff. 'Bloody hell.' He paused, grabbing the iron railing with one hand, coughing and sucking air into his ageing lungs. He looked at the roll-up in his hand, then down at his large gut.

Where to start?

He chucked the roll-up and continued.

At the top of the steps, he encountered the blue-and-white cordon and an officer manning a logbook. The young male officer looked nervous to see Frank.

Wasn't unusual. Frank had a reputation as being rather fierce.

Not that anyone should be nervous around him at this precise moment. He could barely breathe! Maybe the lad was just worried about potentially having to issue CPR.

'Sorry lad,' he said, stumbling over to a bench. He sat down and caught his breath, the salty sea air filling his nostrils. When he did, he looked back up, and the young man still looked nervous.

'Are you all right, sir?'

'Aye.' Frank stood again. 'Just stay off the fags, and maybe don't bother getting to sixty-four.' He reached for his badge.

'Don't worry, sir.' The lad pointed at his logbook. 'I've got you.'

Frank gave a thumbs-up, turned and headed along the brick path towards the whalebone arch. As he walked, he looked to his right. Off in the distance, approximately fifty metres away, between the edge of the Pavilion Drive car park and the cliff edge, he glimpsed the tent, and movement.

When he was parallel with the Captain Cook memorial, he turned off the path and started his journey over grass, passing between two of the benches which were organised in a semi-circle.

'Aye, aye, then boss...' Detective Sergeant Reggie Moyes said, stepping out from behind the memorial.

He was only ten years Frank's junior, but the epitome of health. Marathon runner, and a man who enjoyed throwing weights around. His glow seemed designed to make Frank feel worse than he nearly always felt.

Here's what you should have done with your life, Frank... instead of letting yourself deteriorate into... He opted not to finish that thought.

Still, Reggie was more irritating than Frank could ever hope to be. He was always in a jovial mood. And everyone knew that when you were always that jovial, it just had to be an act.

Are you masking some deep sadness, Reggie?

'How do, Reggie,' Frank said, staring past him over to

the whalebones. He recalled bringing his daughter, Maddie, here many times when she was a bairn to gaze on in awe. Strange to think that the bones were older back then than they were right now. In 2003, they'd been replaced with the bones of a fin whale from Alaska.

He sighed over the memory of bringing his daughter here. It was so long ago now. Back before he'd lost everything. Back before he'd struggled to climb sodding steps. *Shit!* Back before he even smoked roll-ups.

He looked back at Reggie and gave a sigh. *Maybe I'd have been the marathon runner if things had turned out different, eh?*

'What are you thinking, boss?' Reggie said.

'I'm thinking: which bastard's gone and ruined this bonny little spot, then?'

'Exactly what I thought. Do you think this body will be something, then?'

'Well, a body's always something.' Frank nodded at a small crowd forming outside the Royal Hotel about forty metres away on East Terrace. 'And they certainly seem to think it is.'

'Press just being cautious. Maybe that's all we're doing, boss, being cautious?'

Frank nodded. 'Maybe.'

'Surely, there's a better place to bury a body than near this landmark?'

'Probably. Still a body there, though, isn't there? And' – Frank pointed towards the tent – 'there's still a fair distance between it and the landmark. If it were dark... few people about... you could dispose of a body secretly over yonder, I guess?'

'I guess.'

'We'd best stop guessing, though,' Frank said. 'The both

of us. Because unless those SOCOs over there tell me the bones are plastic, and the local science teacher twenty years back has been fly tipping old props from his room, we're going to have to find some answers. Have you seen the new detective inspector then?'

Reggie laughed.

Frank raised an eyebrow. Reggie stopped laughing. 'Sorry, but you won't like it.'

'Eh?'

'She's young.'

'So?'

'Very young.'

'Happens. Even I was young once.'

'But different because of it.'

'Different because of being young?' He raised an eyebrow. 'Or different because she's young and also a female?'

Reggie flushed and looked over both shoulders, fearing that Frank's words might offend someone. No one was close enough to hear, of course. 'No. Of course not. Not what I meant at all!'

'All right, Reggie. But you'll have to give me more than bloody young!'

'Dunno. Just different like. Didn't you read that memo? About working with her? How to approach her and such?'

'Why do I have to read a memo about working with someone? I'm not a schoolteacher. I work with adults who can take care of themselves!'

'It's not like that, just more of a heads-up. A be-patient kind of memo. Well, you'll see, anyway.'

Frank sighed. 'So, back to my original question, which wasn't: what's she like? But: where is she?'

'Over with the SOCOs.'

Frank sighed again. 'Already flying around my crime scene, keen as mustard?' Too late to stop her from destroying the scene now. *Might as well have stopped for that coffee at Sherlock's, after all.*

Reggie shook his head. 'Not flying, no. She doesn't strike me as a person who flies about.'

'Calm, then?' Frank nodded. 'I'll take that. An old man like me needs calm in my life.'

He instructed Reggie to hang back for now and keep his eye on the crowd over by the hotel in case they grew in confidence and moved closer; then, he began the march toward the tent. The ground was uneven and muddy underfoot, so he took care. He'd prefer to approach his next set of colleagues with dignity, rather than how he'd approached the lad with the logbook.

As was always the case on these cliff edges, the sea breeze was strong, and whipped at his face. He glanced over the sea, remarking the unusually calm waters. The worst of the weather may be behind them. At least for a day or two. It never stayed away for too long.

Frank paused before the corner of the car park and watched the white-suited scenes of crime officers moving in and around the tent on the other side of the broken fencing. He wondered if the new DI was within that crowd.

Someone noticed him and raised their hand in the air. He waved back, and waited, only realising that it was Chief Forensic Officer Helen Taylor when she was much nearer and had peeled off her mask.

She came armed with a bagged white suit and a smile for him.

He and Helen went back a fair way. It'd been a while since they'd last seen each other, though. And he could tell from the look in her eyes that she was stunned by his size.

She opened her mouth to say something, but then stopped herself. After a quick shake of the head, she looked away.

That bad?

'Come now, Hel... you were going to compliment me, weren't you? But you stopped, concerned that it may come across as inappropriate.'

She smirked and met his eyes.

He smirked back. 'Look.' He pointed at his hair, which, like the rest of him, was in need of some care and attention. 'The rest of me may have already gone to shit, but I still have all my hair.'

She glanced down, the smirk fading. 'It's not my business, Frank.'

'Never stopped you from speaking your mind before.'

'Maybe. It was easier back then.'

She was, of course, referring to when Frank's wife, Mary, had been around. Helen and Mary had been close friends since their schooldays.

'Okay, imagine it's still back then, Hel. What would you have said?'

'Really?' She raised an eyebrow. 'That what you want?'

'Aye. Home truths. Go for it.'

She sighed. 'I would've asked you what's going on.' She stared at him sadly and shook her head. 'I mean... look at the state of you.'

Frank couldn't help but laugh. 'Wish I hadn't asked. I'm pretty sure you never unleashed it both barrels back then!'

'Not sure I needed to use both barrels in those days. So, what's going on with you, Frank?'

'The usual. Personal matters. At home.'

'But you live alone?'

He nodded. 'Aye... making the matters very personal,

indeed.' He gestured at the tent about three metres past the fence. 'Shall we get to it?' He took the white suit from her. 'Is DI Geraldine Carver over yonder, too?'

'She was.' She pointed behind Frank at the car park. 'Before wandering off that way a few minutes back.'

'Did she have much to say?'

'Not that I noticed. Quiet. Observant.'

'So, I hear. Anyway, what're you thinking?' He nodded at the tent. 'About the body.'

'That it's been there a while.'

'Apart from the obvious?'

She shrugged.

'Is this where you point me toward a forensic anthropologist?'

'Roughly around that point, yes.'

He tried to work his way into the white suit. She'd gone for a large one so as not to embarrass him, but it still didn't seem big enough.

There goes the dignity again.

After finally succeeding, he said, 'So I'm here with world famous Helen Taylor, and I'm simply getting shrugged shoulders... Well—'

'Don't say it, Frank.'

'Hell's bells?'

Hell's bells. Frank's nickname for the hunches Helen liked to offer at a crime scene. She'd an excellent reputation for striking gold firing up an investigation.

'Not today, I'm afraid,' Hel said.

'Something... anything... owt? I promise to get myself in better shape for the next time we meet...?' He fluttered his eyelashes.

'Don't try for me! Do it for yourself, man! Look, okay, take this with a pinch of salt, though, a *big* pinch. You need a full analysis. But I'm thinking female. Women usually have a wider, more circular pelvic inlet, and broader hips. Their brow ridges are less pronounced, too... but still, a long way to go yet. Age is tricky. Not old. There's little wear in the teeth and bones that I can tell.'

'Okay... the pathologist in there at the moment?'

'Yes.'

Frank nodded and followed her through the break in the fence.

Just before the entrance to the tent, Helen nudged him and pointed over to a suited woman walking around the edge of the car park.

'My DI?' he asked.

'Young, eh?'

DI Geraldine Carver had already taken her white suit off. She was staring in their direction but seemed to look right through them at the sea behind, rather than at them.

'Thirty-two,' Frank said. 'And away with the fairies, by the looks of things.'

'Thirty-two. Jesus... get me some of *that* product.'

'You think it'll work for me, too?'

Helen grinned.

Frank watched the DI for a moment, waiting for her to stop looking through him and acknowledge his arrival. At that point, he'd go over to introduce himself before looking at the body.

However, her head suddenly dropped. She then lifted her mobile phone and began typing away.

How could you bloody miss me, DI?

Not having it, he started forward, away from the tent now, back through the fence, and into the car park, eyes on her. The DI, of modest height and build, was now pacing back and forth, typing into her mobile phone.

Even when Frank got to within two metres of her, she didn't look back up.

Irritated and bewildered, Frank coughed.

She stopped and glanced up. *Bingo!* He raised a hand in greeting. *Here we go...*

Her eyes fell again, and she resumed pacing while tapping on her phone.

You can't be serious?

He marched to within a metre of her. 'You're Detective Inspector Geraldine Carver?'

'Yes.' She continued typing on her phone. 'A moment, please.'

Shit! And people always have me penned down as the most ignorant detective in town. She's literally swept the trophy from my hands in the blink of an eye.

'I'm Frank Black...'

She held one palm up to gesture for patience while keeping her eyes down. Then she lowered her hand and continued typing.

'That'll be *DCI* Frank Black,' he continued. '*Your* superior. I'm sure you know that I'll be the SIO if this case has legs?'

She nodded and kept up with the ignorance.

'Meanwhile... somewhere yonder... off in the great beyond...' Frank said, suddenly feeling amused rather than frustrated. 'My new DI is texting who?'

'I'm not texting,' she said, finally stopping.

Hallelujah!

She slipped the phone into her pocket and glanced up, again, only briefly, before looking back down.

'Well, Geraldine, that's good, I guess. Contacting the husband to arrange a dinner at a crime scene probably isn't the best use of time.'

'I'm not married, sir.'

'Okay...' He nodded. 'Not prying, you understand. Just making a point.'

'Point? If I'm not married, how can there be a point to what you said?'

'Just saying we're at a crime scene, and you're the assistant SIO. Surely, it'd be best for you to just focus on the task at hand?'

She glanced up at him and then looked away quickly. 'I'm focused, sir.'

'Aye, *certainly* looked that way.'

'I was typing in notes.'

He rose an eyebrow, but she didn't see it. 'All right... fine... let's start afresh.' He observed her. She wore a neat, black suit. It looked tailored and clean. Yet, despite the formality and cleanliness of her suit, which most certainly surpassed his own, there was a noticeable lack of attention given to her hair. She tied her hair tight, but it remained uncombed and frazzled.

'You saw the remains, I believe? And made a lot of notes in your phone.' He tried to keep the sarcastic tone from his voice. Knowing she wasn't looking up, he rolled his eyes, though. 'So, what are you thinking?'

'Sorry sir, but I don't like to share notes.'

'Why not?'

'I like to vet them first.'

'But they're notes.'

'I don't feel comfortable being judged by brief notes.'

'For pity's sake, don't worry about it. We'll be working together. Go on. You were in the tent. Tell me what you scribbled down?'

'Sorry, sir, I just said I don't like to share notes.'

Lord, give me strength!

Different, Reggie? Different? I feel like I've just landed on another bloody planet.

'Forget the notes, then. Just tell me what you thought, Geraldine.' As she wasn't making eye contact, he couldn't gesture at the tent. So, he simply added, 'In the tent?' instead.

'Can you call me Gerry please, sir?'

'Of course, if you call me Tom,' Frank said, realising how poor his icebreaker was, but he was feeling rather awkward now, and that was when desperate behaviours crept in.

'Tom?' Another brief glance before averting her eyes. 'I thought it was Frank, sir.'

'It is Frank. It was a joke. Tom and Jerry.' *Christ!* 'Never mind, you mightn't have heard of them. You're a young lass, and I'm a creaking old bas—'

'I know Tom and Jerry, sir.'

Obviously not amused then. You probably get on just fine with Chief Constable Donald Oxley. He doesn't laugh at my shit jokes either. 'Look, don't keep calling me sir. You can call me boss or Frank... I *just* can't abide sir.'

'Okay, which one? Frank or boss?'

'Whichever, I don't mind.'

'I'd like you to state your preference, please.'

State your preference! 'Frank, okay... I think it's best if I look at the body now. Hang on, sorry... I *still* don't have your initial thoughts.'

'I prefer not to give thoughts either, Frank.'

Frank nodded. 'Of course you don't.'

'Just what I know.'

'Well, that sounds good. What do you know, Gerry?'

'I know that's a woman in there.'

'Hang on...' He creased his brow. 'So Helen told you it was a woman, too?'

'No. No one did.'

'Do you have a qualification in forensic anthropology?' Frank asked.

'No.' She didn't pick up on the sarcasm. 'I've read up on the matter. The pelvis... the hips... even the shape of the skull. There were too many linking factors. The probability of the body being female is far too high to be a simple suspicion, or a *thought*, Frank, as you suggested.'

Shit the bed!

'Go on then, any more of this grand knowledge?'

'I've two more things.'

'Two!' Frank nodded and raised his hands. 'I'm warming to you now.'

She glanced up at him, before rapidly dropping her eyes again. 'One. I noticed the concentric fractures on the skull, indicative of blunt-force trauma.'

'A qualification in pathology, too. I'm impressed...'

'No, why would you—'

'Okay.' He waved her on. 'I'm just implying you're a jack of all trades. Number two, please?'

'Second, I recognise the case someone folded her up and forced her inside. It's from the 1980s.'

He raised his eyebrow, not from the graphic description, but from how precise she was. 'So, you studied the history of suitcases?'

'No. My mum had the same suitcase when I was little. Twenty years she had it for. She bought it in 1981 for £34.'

'How could you know that? You wouldn't even have been born.'

'Correct. I was born in 1992. I know because I asked her on my eighth birthday when it broke. We were in

France. The handle snapped. Thirty-four pounds was a reasonable amount of money for a suitcase in 1981. High-end. Those were the words she used. Anyway, bar a different shade on the interior, it's the same case.'

Shit the bed again!

'You've got an excellent memory.'

Gerry nodded.

'No need for me to look now.' He snorted. 'What could I hope to achieve after that?'

She glanced up at him and turned away. 'If you'll excuse me, Frank, I'd like to get back to Rylan.'

'Rylan?' *Who the hell is Rylan?*

She didn't respond as she walked away over the grass.

'Gerry, who's Rylan?' he called after her.

Gerry stopped and spun back. 'Rylan is my dog.' Then she was off.

Really? 'I'll see you in Scarborough then,' Frank called after her.

She didn't respond. Maybe it had to be framed as a question to warrant a response?

Shaking his head, he turned back to the tent, both unnerved and impressed by what he'd just witnessed. Something very different, that was for sure. Almost like a walking computer. A machine of facts. God, he often felt obsolete, but right now, that took the biscuit.

And she must have met his eyes for two seconds, tops!

It seems social skills weren't important any more to their role.

Mind you, some, if not most, would argue that Frank Black had never really had social skills either.

At least, not *pleasant* ones, anyway.

Chapter Four

Frank didn't forget to pick up his double espresso from Sherlock's.

However, sitting in the front of his 1980s Volvo Estate, he didn't know if he could stomach it. He swirled it around the bottom of his coffee cup, watching it while it went cold.

Even the roll-up hanging from his mouth was making him nauseous, so he wound down the window and chucked it.

He took a deep breath and faced the obvious: what he'd just seen had disturbed him.

Up on West Cliff, close to Captain Cook and the jawbones of a fin whale, someone had buried a young woman after smashing the back of her skull in.

Swirling the coffee, he closed his eyes and took himself back to the tent.

The two SOCOs parted, allowing him access to the remains... a skeleton folded and squeezed into a case. Behind him, the sea breeze whipped the canvas walls.

He knelt, craned his head, and stared into hollow sockets. Then, he drew back, took a deep breath, and panned his gaze over yellowing bones, willing himself back through the fabric of time, back to when this person lived.

Who are you?

How old are you?

An adolescent finding yourself, maybe?

Older perhaps? Early twenties? Enjoying the liberty and adventure youth bring?

Or older, still? Thirty-something? A life partly built? The impetuousness of youth over, responsibilities and concerns for others now the order of the day?

Frank exhaled.

The answers were ambiguous, but he'd one conclusion already.

Here was a life cruelly snatched away.

He opened his eyes in the car and drank his cold coffee in one mouthful.

It'd been a long time since this job had hit him with something like this.

Who are you, lass, and why are you here?

Chapter Five

Before heading to HQ in Scarborough, Frank popped home to check on her.

He stared at his front door, wondering whether this was such a good move. Did he risk unsettling her even more?

Last night had been ferocious. More so than normal.

There'd been one hour in which she'd shouted and screamed almost continuously.

Her choice of words – if it was fair to say she'd made a choice in the state she was in – had been aggressive.

Maybe he should leave her be? Let her rest?

Henrietta Timber watched him from her window next door.

He couldn't resist a smile. *Who needs police when you have Henrietta?*

After he delivered the nosy seventy-five-year-old a wave, she retreated into the shadows.

In fairness, he must have looked quite the oddball, sitting outside his own home.

The church bell of St Mary's clanged the half-hour over on East Cliff, and Frank left his car.

Chapter Six

Although she was unlikely to eat it, Frank made fresh toast. He set it on the chair he'd spent the night on, and then knocked on her door.

She didn't answer, but he'd already checked on her before leaving the crime scene and so wasn't too concerned.

He gave another knock and warned her he was coming in. He unlocked it, opened it, and keeping it wedged ajar with one foot, he reached down for the tray, groaning as his back informed him it was not flexible enough for such a manoeuvre.

A couple of years back, a younger colleague had suggested Pilates. However, a curious Google search had quickly informed him that it was a suggestion best ignored. Paracetamol was faster, cheaper, and, most importantly, easier. He wondered now, briefly, if he'd made the wrong decision.

He slipped into her room. 'Room service.'

She was curled up on the mattress in her bra and knickers with her back to him, shivering. Having kicked her duvet away, it lay scrunched up on the floor.

He looked down at the toast, and then the bucket by her double bed, which, judging by the sour, pungent smell, she'd recently used, and decided there was no chance of her eating.

After depositing the tray on a table beneath the barred window, he glanced back at the door that he kept locked nearly twenty-four hours a day, and suddenly felt overwhelmed with guilt.

He was taking such a risk. What if there was a fire while he was out?

After circling the bed, he checked the five small bottles of water on the bedside table. He picked up two empty ones, knelt, stifling a groan, and slipped the bottles into the bin beneath the table, gently, not wishing to wake her. His back clicked as he straightened.

From the corner of his eye, he caught her turning her head, directing her face upwards towards him.

In this moment, she was the spitting image of Mary.

Sighing, he placed his hand on her pale cheek.

She shivered, and he snapped his hand back.

Let her sleep.

Recalling the bucket, he started towards the foot of the bed again, intending to circle it.

'Daddy?'

He froze.

'Daddy, I'm cold.'

Gulping, he glanced back.

His daughter was looking right at him with bloodshot eyes.

He filled his lungs slowly with air, tasting the staleness in the room.

Daddy.

How long had it been?

Twenty years?

She was now thirty-two.

'Maddie?' His questioning tone would suggest that he was only seeing her now for the first time in a while, although she'd been here for weeks.

He reached down for the duvet on the floor and covered her. 'It won't be for much longer, lass. Cold, like. It'll be over soon. Just keep drinking the water and, if that runs out and I'm not here, there's more over yonder in the top drawer. There are also snacks there for when you get your appetite back.'

Before he'd finished, her eyes were closed again.

He took another slow, deep inhalation, recalled the bucket that needed to be cleaned—

'Daddy. I'm cold. Mummy isn't here. Can I sleep with you?'

He exhaled.

She must be dreaming. Hallucinating, perhaps?

Or maybe it was he that was dreaming?

Maddie hadn't done this since she was a child, when, so often, he'd feel a tap on the shoulder in the middle of the night to dismiss him from the bed so she could curl up with Mary. And, if Mary was away, visiting her sick mother, as she often had been, then she'd ask to be with Frank instead.

'Can I sleep with you?' she repeated, eyes still closed.

It's really you, isn't it?

He wiped tears away with the back of his hand and circled to the other side of the bed. 'Aye,' he said, lying down on the double bed next to her.

Staring at the ceiling, he kept close to the edge, so there was ample space between them. He'd be lying if he said this didn't feel awkward. She was a grown woman, and it'd been a long time since he'd been emotionally close to his daughter in any way whatsoever.

He let his head drop to the left, so that he was looking at her upper back, which poked out from the duvet he'd placed over her. His eyes moved over familiar blonde hair...

She could have been her mother.

He closed his eyes and smiled as he remembered stroking his daughter's hair as a child, helping her drift off back to sleep. The memory lifted the awkwardness. But Frank held back, ignoring an intense longing to touch her. He feared unnerving her, bringing her from this dream, causing the situation to end.

'I'm still cold, Daddy. Can you hug me?'

That was too much for Frank. His hesitations collapsed. He turned onto his side and let his arm fall around her, over the duvet.

Then he felt her gripping his arm, and he squeezed his eyes closed to force back tears.

He was unsuccessful.

I've missed you, he thought. *Both of you.*

Then, he pressed his nose against the back of his daughter's soft head and breathed in the faint scent of her shampoo.

Sleep Maddie.

I've got you.

Chapter Seven

SCARBOROUGH HQ MANAGED operations based in and around Whitby in North Yorkshire. It had modern incident rooms equipped.

Unfortunately, it also came equipped with Chief Constable Donald Oxley.

A humourless cubicle farmer who'd no time for dinosaurs of Frank's ilk.

Frank couldn't help but feel telepathic every time they conversed. The bastard's thoughts always found a way into his head. *Why aren't you retired yet?*

He wasn't about to grace the pedantic pen-pusher with an answer, but if he did, it'd probably go something like this. *Because with no wife, I'm pretty much useless to anyone without this job.*

Of course, since the return of Maddie, things had altered somewhat in that regard.

After embracing Maddie back home for fifteen minutes, he suddenly felt inclined, for the first time, to tell Donald to stick his job where the sun doesn't shine. After all, someone finally needed him. He was on the verge of doing just that when Donald had pointed him towards Incident Room 7, and a cocktail of frustration and disbelief immediately intoxicated him.

IR7 was tiny. A converted office. Little more than a broom cupboard. Donald leaned back in his chair, his expression nonchalant.

'Earlier you were champing at the bit to get me out there, sir,' Frank said.

'Yes, but on reflection, we've a lot going on at the moment.'

Frank furrowed his brow. 'It's a body, sir. A potential murder victim.'

'*Potential.* Look, until we know the remains are significant, then we should proceed gently. Let's assess the severity first.'

'Severity?' Frank's eyes widened. 'Helen suspects blunt-force trauma! Is that enough severity?'

'Let me finish, DCI.' He held up a hand, his tone firm. 'We can't free the personnel. Things are tight—'

'Sorry...' Frank shook his head. 'I'm stuck here! You just implied that the remains of this woman are insignificant?'

Donald sighed, leaning forward and clasping his hands together. 'We can't even be certain it's a woman yet. Listen... I know the press are interested, which is kind of why I allowed the large show of force earlier, and with such a weighty start, I know that you'll be able to work out who this person is. But, Frank, the reality is that they're insignificant until we know how old this body is. If there's no one out there, alive, hankering over justice, it's a use of valuable resources that we can't spare. Bring me the identity. If the relatives are still living, then we'll throw the door open.'

'Meanwhile, I'm locked in the dungeon?'

'I've just had all the IT equipment upgraded in there.'

'There's one computer.' Frank's expression was deadpan.

'Two now. And there's a fan.'

'It's not warm.'

'It will be in summer.' Donald shrugged, a hint of a smirk on his face.

'Well, with such meagre resources, I'll still be there!'

Donald leaned back into his chair and recovered the same nonchalant expression he'd started the conversation with. 'It's the way it is.'

It's the way it always seems to be these days.

Frank stomped away, regretting not getting to the point and retiring.

Chapter Eight

In fairness, there'd been a slight makeover to IR7.

Although it still wasn't fit for purpose.

There was a large table in the centre of the room which could sit about six; an untouched whiteboard beside it and two desks, complete with computers, at the back.

DI Geraldine Carver was in the far corner of the room at one of the computers. 'Hello, Frank,' she said without looking up.

Blow me down like a feather... She'd acknowledged his existence!

'How do, Gerry?'

'I want to apologise for earlier. I wasn't calm at the scene. If I'm not calm, it affects my ability to converse.'

He started into the room – what there was of it.

'Don't worry. It's hard to be calm after seeing that. Let's start afresh.'

'Break the ice?' She delivered her question with very little enthusiasm.

Already, their second interaction was developing, at an

alarming rate, into something peculiar. 'No need.' *The ice is already broken.*

He stopped dead and stared wide eyed at her feet. 'What the bloody hell is that?'

'Rylan,' she said.

A medium-sized golden dog regarded him.

'You've got an animal in the incident room?'

'Rylan's a dog.'

'I know what it is.'

'*He* is,' she corrected. 'That's why I'm calm, Frank. He's a therapy dog. Without him, it'd be difficult for us to break the ice.'

You just smashed the ice into bloody pieces!

'He's a Lab Retriever.' Gerry had her hand on Rylan's golden back. 'He's well behaved. You don't have to worry about his presence.' Rylan was sitting upright, perfectly still.

Frank wished he'd read that memo. He shook his head, unable to get right with it. 'But a dog... in the incident room... aye, I get it's IR7... his kennel is probably cleaner, but—'

'He doesn't sleep in a kennel. He sleeps with me.'

Frank suppressed a sigh. *Seriously, what was the point?*

'He goes everywhere with me,' Gerry said. 'Apart from into a crime scene and someone's home and an interview room.'

'So, basically, just into the incident room?' He stared into Rylan's eyes as he asked this question. The Lab's eyes, like the rest of him, were calm and composed, and seemed to regard the world around him with remarkable understanding.

'He won't cause a problem.'

'Aye,' Frank said, completely stunned by what he was

seeing. 'It's just that in my experience, dogs like to beg. Do I have to keep my sarnies out of reach?'

'No. He's a service dog. Perfectly trained. He won't beg. He won't show you any affection unless you show him affection first.' Before Frank could think of a response, she added, 'You seem surprised about Rylan. Someone should have notified you.'

'Aye... I was notified.' *In my unread memo, no doubt.* 'Could I ask why, though?'

'Of course. Throughout my life, I've never operated for any significant length of time without one. I become distant and lost. You may have noticed some peculiarities earlier?'

Just earlier?

'Although those circumstances were stronger than the norm,' Gerry continued. 'Usually, I last longer without comfort, so I'm normally okay to attend interviews and make house calls without him.'

'I see. Okay...' Frank thought, biting back a sigh. *This is a new world, old man, accept it or piss off.* 'He's a handsome dog.' The scent of Rylan's fur lingered in the air, a comforting, earthy aroma.

'Yes. He's young still. Four. Before that, I had Ronnie until he was eight.'

'Eight?' That sounded young for a dog to die. 'I'm sorry you lost Ronnie so young.'

She looked confused. 'I didn't lose Ronnie. He retired. The older they get, the more attention they need in return, so they're retired and given to a suitable home.'

'I see. So, you visit him?'

She still looked confused. 'No. Why'd I do that?'

'I dunno, maybe you liked...' Frank broke off in time, taking his glasses from his head, before running a hand through his unkempt hair. He really wasn't the best person to have these discussions with. Also, he didn't like surprises! Although, to be fair, this surprise was his own fault for ignoring his emails. He replaced his glasses on his head. 'If he's harmless, then no problem.' He looked around at the empty room. 'Not like we've anyone here scared of dogs who can object, anyway.' He walked past Rylan, who barely moved and paused behind Gerry. 'So, what're you bidding on?'

She scrolled the eBay screen down.

There was an image of the same suitcase they'd seen earlier at the scene.

'Someone has bid sixty quid?' Frank shook his head. *People bought just about anything these days.* 'Why not just buy a new suitcase?'

'These Samsonite hard-shell suitcases were durable and popular.'

'In 1980… it's 2024!'

'Yes.'

'Time has moved on. Technology has moved on.'

'Not everyone likes to move with technology.'

'Fair point,' Frank said. 'So, what year was this one manufactured?'

Gerry highlighted the year on the screen. 1982. She then reopened another tab that listed a range of other similar-looking suitcases. There was some information at the bottom, which she highlighted. The 1980s saw a transition to different materials for luggage. Vinyl came into fashion because of its durability, flexibility and water-resistant properties.

Frank raised an eyebrow. 'Someone has created a webpage on the history of luggage?'

'Yes,' Gerry said, without a hint of surprise in her tone. 'But even though this body must have come after 1980, until we've a forensic analysis of the bones and the luggage, it's impossible to say how long this case has been buried.'

Frank nodded. 'But, if this proves it was after 1980, can we print it out, and hand deliver it to Donald?'

'Why not just email?'

'I like the personal touch,' Frank said, grinning on the inside.

'Also...' She opened an Excel spreadsheet. 'A list of names of people reported missing after 1980 in a twenty-five-mile radius of Whitby, working chronologically, starting with women aged between fifteen and forty. I'll continue until 1990, and then move back to 1980, and open the search for men. I'm 90 per cent sure the victim will be female and young, but at least we're prepared when facial composites and forensic data come in.'

'Have you already searched for people reported missing close to the whalebones, in particular?'

'Yes. It was the first thing I did. I'm cross-referencing a lot of information from the database as I go. I find this preliminary research always helps.'

Seems like a needle in a haystack to me, Frank thought. But it was very early doors, and they didn't have a great deal to go on. Plus, background research was a conscientious approach, so he let her forge ahead. 'Okay, if you print that stuff for me.'

He noticed a picture of Gerry standing in front of an older couple on her desk. They were all in wetsuits. He pointed to the picture. 'Your parents?'

'Yes,' she said, opening the print screen.

'They look happy.'

'Yes.'

'Where you at?'

'Robin Hood's Bay, near our cottage. Sailing.'

'Never tried sailing. Enjoy it?'

Gerry hit print and then glanced up at him. She made eye contact with him for the longest period yet and nodded.

He then took her number so he could contact her with ease and, as he was leaving the room, he heard her call out, 'Frank. I'm sorry. Are your family happy too?'

Frank stopped and turned. Strange question to stop him with, but at least she was considering his existence now. *Happy? How to answer that?* 'I have a daughter. Name's Maddie. She's thirty-two.'

'That's the same age as me.'

'I know,' Frank said and left the room.

Chapter Nine

On the way to Donald's office, Frank took a phone call from Helen.

'Bloody hell,' Frank said. 'That were quick. I can usually squeeze in a few birthdays between forensic results.'

'Who said anything about results?'

'Figures.'

'Got something interesting, though.'

He looked at Donald's door and the papers in his hand, a smug smile on his face. *Is it as interesting as what I'm about to do?* 'Go on.'

'We found two items in that suitcase other than those remains. They'd slipped behind the inner material, which had torn slightly. A red plectrum and a key.'

'Right, I'm listening.'

'The plectrum is rather standard, but the key has an interesting blue fob with a black triangle on it.'

'A logo?' Frank asked.

'Hmm... it's very basic to be a logo. Almost looks hand drawn. I'll send an image over. Once we've the key cleaned up, we'll give you more. There may be markings or identifiers on it.'

After thanking her and ending the call, he looked back down the corridor, knowing that he needed to give Gerry a heads-up on the new findings. It was a reasonable walk back to IR7. Thoroughly off the beaten track!

His wife, Mary, used to celebrate ten thousand steps a day with her watch, whereas he'd spent most of his life trying to keep his own daily number of steps as low as possible. It'd clearly backfired on him and his waistline, but today didn't feel like the day to break trend with tradition.

He phoned Gerry, explained the findings, and then made a request. 'On account of the plectrum, ensure you include budding guitarists on that super list of potential victims you're knocking together.'

'The Excel spreadsheet?'

'Aye. That's the one.'

After the call, Frank saw Donald and placed the information that Gerry had printed out in front of him. 'In black and white, as requested, sir. Gerry recognised this type of case, as you knew, but here's the evidence that they started manufacturing them at the beginning of the eighties.'

Donald grabbed the information and threw it in his tray. 'Thanks, I'll look shortly.'

'I can wait,' Frank kept a straight face, determined not to betray his smugness.

'No, I've an appointment now.'

Disappointed, Frank stood.

As he was leaving, he said, 'You'll let us know?' He paused at the door, his hand on the handle, hoping for a more definitive response from Donald. The dismissive attitude was grating on his nerves, and he could feel his frustration building.

'After I look and make a few calls, I'll give you my assessment.'

Chapter Ten

Frank was a fan of winter. Mainly, because there were far fewer tourists.

After stopping home and attempting to feed Maddie, who ate very little, he headed to the old town and one of his favourite haunts, the Black Horse Inn.

On the way in, he noticed Dave, the miniature schnauzer, mingling with some other visiting dogs. He made a mental note to tell Gerry about this place; she may like to bring Rylan here. The warm, inviting scent of pub food wafted through the air, making his mouth water.

As he ordered from the bar, he struck off the mental note to talk to Gerry.

Gerry in a local pub? Not a chance.

To save himself a return journey to the bar, he grabbed two pints and ordered a Yorkshire cheese board from the Yapas menu. Yapas, of course, referred to the little-known selection of Yorkshire Tapas. He also bought himself some Wilson's snuff. Since smoking had become outlawed indoors in 2007, Frank had become fond of this source of nicotine.

As always, he gulped the first beer before gently inhaling a pinch of snuff through his nostrils. It'd been over a month since he'd experienced the sharp sensation, and he had to force back a sneeze. The rich, nutty flavour lingered on his tongue, complementing the bitter taste of the ale.

Feeling suddenly alert, he took out his phone and stared at a photo of the missing person's bones unfolded on a white mat. He took another pinch of snuff, drank from his beer and then zoomed in on those hollow eyes.

What are you?

The blunt trauma to the back of the head suggested that she may not have seen the fatal wound coming.

He sighed and switched off the phone.

He looked around the bar at all the customers. Older couples, youngsters; the pub brought quite a mix of punters. Yorkshire's way. A heady mix of generations and walks of life.

It'd been Mary's favourite pub.

She'd always opted for a homemade kipper pate from the Yapas menu. Washed down with Whitley Neill Gin. She'd been more refined than her cheese-guzzling, ale-swilling, snuff-snorting husband!

Too refined, maybe?

Opposites attracted, he guessed, until they didn't any more...

He ate his cheeseboard, drank four more pints, made himself feel green on snuff, ignored locals who recognised him and tried to say hello, and caught a taxi to see Mary.

Chapter Eleven

The driver said nothing about dropping him off. It must have seemed odd. The locked gate of Whitby Cemetery at ten at night?

He stepped out the taxi. It wasn't warm by any stretch of the imagination, but after seven days of storms and torrential rain, it was tolerable. He was also six pints to the good, which always helped with discomfort.

After the taxi had driven away, Frank attempted to scale the low wall to access the cemetery. He impressed himself by getting on top of it, albeit with no elegance whatsoever.

The sodden ground took his feet away and he landed on his backside. 'Shit.' He was still in his work suit, too.

He felt positively elated about being in the dark corner of a graveyard, where no one had to watch him drag his fat arse up.

It wouldn't have been a pretty sight.

Dusting himself down – although the caked mud on the back of his trousers would require more than a quick dusting – he set off into the graveyard.

It didn't take him long to locate Mary's grave. He'd been here several times a week for five years, after all.

He always tried to come sober, and not late at night. But it'd been a taxing fortnight with Maddie, and now, with the body of a woman, considered insignificant by his cubicle farmer of a boss, calling out to him across time, he felt frayed.

While he sat by Mary's gravestone, he brought her up to date.

Knowing he wouldn't be too wide of the mark, he envisaged her responses. Thirty-three years of marriage had given him this skill.

As he explained his plan regarding Maddie, Mary provided rapid-fire nods to show agreement. No matter the risks, she considered this the right way, too.

'I hope she's almost over the worst,' Frank said. 'From everything I read, she should be. Just a little longer...'

A slower, gentle nod also expressed agreement, but after, she raised an eyebrow at him. She was suggesting he shouldn't get ahead of himself. He agreed. It was best to be cautious with his optimism.

'She called me Daddy.' He looked up into the sky. 'Can you believe it, eh? Long time since I heard myself addressed like that. Bloody hell!' He saw the flashing light of a plane. 'This time we'll get there, love. This time.' He looked back down at the grave and winked.

Still, that same slow nod from Mary. 'Keep at it, darling,' he imagined her saying.

'Aye. This time.' *Because last time, and the times before, she didn't call me Daddy. She didn't let me hold her as she trembled.*

He changed the subject to the unidentified remains.

'Crammed in a suitcase, Mary. Buried in the mud. I've seen some things but... she was thrown away.'

His wife gave him a knowing look.

'Aye, you're right. *Maddie*. It's all I could think about, too. What if it'd been her? What if she'd never come back? But that makes me more determined. If it'd been Maddie, I'd stop at nowt for the truth. So, why should it be any different with this lass?' He then told her about Gerry. 'I glanced back at the memo. She's autistic. Not that I really get what that means. I don't think I've ever known anyone that's autistic, never mind worked with someone that is. Reggie just referred to her as different. Not politically correct, I know. Mind you, how many of us dinosaurs are PC? Don't worry, love, I'll put him straight if he says it again. You know she has a therapy dog! A therapy dog, aye! Rylan. A Lab Retriever. Sitting in the bloody incident room! Different! Different world more like. Still, don't fret... I may not be able to help the thoughts, but I won't say them. You know, love, I've been giving retirement serious consideration. What with Maddie being back and everything. Plus, I don't know how much longer I can go without punching Don.' He thought about the roll-ups in his suit pocket but stopped himself. Mary had never been a fan. 'Mind you, I expect to be getting a few more officers tomorrow, and out of the dungeon, too, so I may be able to hold off punching the dickhead a while longer...'

He broke off and took a deep breath. Like clockwork. Fifteen minutes into his visits, the same thought always occurred to him. The one which sent him into a guilty spin.

Do I speak to you more now than when you were alive?

He sighed. 'Anyway, thought I'd stop by. And don't worry, I'm giving Gerry a chance. Like you'd expect. I'm just figuring her out, you know.'

His wife smiled.

'Ha. Aye. I'm sure she's figured me out already. I mean, there's not much to work out, is there? Oh, before I forget, I saw Helen today too. She thinks I look like shit. Obviously, didn't tell her I've hardly slept for over two weeks.' He pressed his fingers to his lips, walked alongside the grave, and placed a kiss on the headstone. 'Good night my love.'

Frank turned, knowing his best move was to return home now.

But that wouldn't happen.

It was late. It was desolate. And it was a perfect opportunity to see him.

Chapter Twelve

'How do, Nigel?'

Up against Nigel Wainwright's headstone were some fresh flowers.

'Your wife been to visit, eh?'

Frank inhaled deeply through his nose and looked up again. This time, he could see stars poking through the darkness. 'Storms have gone and cleared it up yonder, eh? You must be happy to have a night not being pissed on.' He looked back down at the gravestone of the man who'd ruined his life. 'Can't be having that, can we?' He undid his fly and urinated on Nigel's grave.

Chapter Thirteen

Back home, Frank stood over his sleeping daughter.

She was no longer shivering.

He longed to kiss her forehead, reconnect with her again, like earlier, and he desperately wanted to tell her he'd just spent some time with her mother, and that he was confident – more confident than ever before – that they could overcome this nightmare together.

But he didn't want to disturb her while she was sleeping so soundly.

He could smell salt and vinegar and noticed an empty crisp packet beside her. His heart warmed, knowing that she'd eaten some food.

After he locked her door, he drew the chair across, readying it for the night ahead. Then, he headed through to the kitchen, took a glass from the cupboard, and turned on the cold water—

His breath caught in his throat.

A hooded figure was outside, in the darkness, staring through his window.

Heart pounding, Frank unlocked the door, and was out in the garden in time to watch the figure scale the fence.

'Oi!'

Frank looked up at the outside light that should be lit.

How long have you put off replacing that bulb, you daft sod?

The figure swooped both legs over and disappeared.

Frank swore under his breath. No point in going over that fence. He'd struggled with one half the size at the graveyard tonight!

Still, there was hope.

He knew who the hooded figure was.

And he knew exactly what he had to do about it.

Chapter Fourteen

After Frank had done what needed to be done, he sat in his chair and tried to sleep.

Maddie had a much better night, only waking twice.

There was little shouting and nothing like the usual: 'You killed her! Mum would be here if not for you! How could anyone suffer such a miserable bastard as you?'

She wasn't far wrong, but she didn't need to sacrifice her rest to remind him.

He was content that she was coming out of the other side.

For this reason, Frank really should have slept much better, too.

But that scrote in his back garden had put an end to any chance of that.

Chapter Fifteen

Frank had to dig around in his wardrobe for a pair of old work trousers. It'd been foolish of him to forget to blast the other pair in the washing machine last night.

He regarded the old pair with a shake of his head.

Do you really think you'll make it through the day without splitting them?

What option did he have?

Going in wearing jeans would piss Donald off, and it wasn't the best time to do that. Not when he needed him to see sense and give him an actual team and a better room.

With a sigh of resignation, Frank pulled on the worn trousers, grimacing as he felt the fabric stretch tightly across his thighs. He silently prayed that they would hold up throughout the day, knowing that a wardrobe malfunction was the last thing he needed on top of his already frustrating work situation.

At work, he discovered he was to remain in IR7, and that he still made up half a team of two. Even though Donald had assured him the assessment of his evidence was done! 'It just needs approval.'

'But surely, if the assessment is done, that means you've already approved it?' Frank asked.

'Approval requires a secondary process of checking.'

How ridiculous!

Donald continued, 'I need to ensure that all North Yorkshire operations being currently run from Scarborough are being suitably managed before reallocating—'

Frank held up his hand. 'Right, I get it. A missing person from the eighties is still not enough to warrant serious attention.'

'It's not that. Not at all. Look. No one is actively looking for this missing person. If not for the press, this wouldn't be a priority. Our budget demands conservative use of labour until we've a name. Until then, we've assigned a DCI, your good self, which will keep the press happy for the moment.'

Does everything have to be a PR exercise these days?

'Whatever,' Frank left the room, calling over his shoulder, 'I'll have a name for you by the end of the day.'

In the incident room, Rylan was enjoying a kibble breakfast at his owner's feet. 'How do, Gerry?'

'Fine, Frank. How are you today?' Gerry asked. She offered him a smile and a fleeting glance. It looked rehearsed.

'Not the best.' *But then, what does "the best" feel like? I've no memory of it.* 'Still no approval for expanding the team. Any news on your end?'

'Nothing definitive as yet.'

Frank came around behind her and looked at her screen. 'Good lord!'

It was a mass of information. Column after column, row after row, a multitude of colours.

'How many rows?'

When she told him, his eyes widened. He thought the

same as he'd thought yesterday. It was a needle in a bloody haystack. 'Did you get any sleep?'

'Four hours.'

Practically a lie-in for me these days. Still, that wasn't enough sleep by any stretch. 'You must be exhausted, Gerry.'

'Four hours is optimal for me. Any more, and it works against me. I can become less focused.'

'I see.' Frank nodded. 'Fancy that.'

She looked up at him. 'I noticed when you walked in that your suit jacket and trousers don't match.'

He grinned. 'Does it bother you?'

'A little.'

'Oh.'

'I sometimes struggle with clothing combinations. Inconsistency. Colour clashes.'

'Gotcha. Would you prefer I took the jacket off?'

'No, it's okay... It's something I've learned to manage.'

Why bother telling me then?

Frank's phone beeped. 'Excuse me.'

He went over, logged onto his computer, and opened a secure email.

It contained several images of the recovered key and its blue fob with the small black triangle. He phoned Helen. 'What am I looking at?'

'The key after we cleaned it up. Go to the close-up of the key itself, not the fob.'

Frank clicked. 'Right... an arrow pointing to the "u" on the key?'

'The "u" in a circle. It most certainly belongs to the company who manufactured the key. Although the key hasn't been coded, the manufacturer has stamped it, which isn't uncommon. There's also a serial number. I suggest getting someone from your team to look.'

'Ha! Team? There's two of us.'

'Shit. Really?'

'Uh-huh. Victim has no name. No name, no game, you know how it goes.'

'You'll get a name, soon.'

'Damn right I will.' He looked over at Gerry, who bashed away on the keyboard, and smiled. 'Got a feeling about the other half of this team.'

Chapter Sixteen

While Gerry went to work on the circled 'u', Frank organised the whiteboard.

It didn't take long. Pictures of a key with a fob, a plectrum, a Samsonite suitcase, and the skeletal remains.

Today, he thought, looking long and hard at the victim again, *is the day we find out who you are... right?*

He went over to Gerry and noticed Rylan looking at him, so he went into a crouch.

'Come here, lad,' he said, holding a palm out.

Rylan didn't move.

'He doesn't like to be addressed as "lad".' Gerry tapped the keys harder.

Who'd have thought it, eh? Does he prefer man? Master? King?

Frank nodded. 'Fair play. Rylan, come here.'

Rylan's eyes widened. He rose and moved closer to Frank.

Frank smiled. 'Good lad... Rylan.'

How did a therapy dog work then? He reached out a hand. *You see, if ever someone was in need of TLC, that'd be me right now.* The Lab leaned forward, ever so slightly, and brushed Frank's palm in a gentle greeting.

Frank worked his hand into Rylan's soft, warm fur. 'You really are a handsome devil, aren't you?' He caught the Lab's scent. It reminded him of long walks in the countryside with Mary.

Rylan came closer and nuzzled his neck.

Frank laughed, nodded and rose to his feet.

You know, Rylan, in a way, that really worked. I feel better already!

'Got it,' Gerry said. 'I've an address for the key manufacturer.'

And now, Frank thought, looking over at Gerry, *your owner has me feeling positively elated.*

Chapter Seventeen

Oliver Bancroft, owner of Unlock-Utopia Key Services, was a busy man. He was out of breath when he answered the phone and apologised each time he put Frank on hold to deal with customers.

'Right, DCI Black, I'm back,' he said for the third time.

'Your keys are clearly in demand, Mr Bancroft,' Frank said.

'Since the competition around the corner upped and left, it's barely let up. I'm going to have to take on someone new at this rate. Anyway, I've flipped the sign and locked the door. I'm all yours this time, I promise.'

Frank explained why he was phoning.

'I was still at school in the eighties. Back then, it was my father's business.'

'Would it be possible to get in touch with your father?'

'He passed eight years back.'

Shit! He looked over at Gerry with a disappointed expression. Pointless. She wasn't looking at him. How was she not curious? 'Sorry to hear that. Were these keys logged at all? There's a serial number.'

'There were handwritten records. But there was never a real need to convert them to digital in the nineties, so the records have gone I'm afraid.'

He glanced over at Rylan, who was, unlike his owner, looking right at him. *Hang about, fella, I'm going to need some of that therapy.*

'Can I send it over to your email, Mr Bancroft? Let you look... see if it rings any bells? Like I said, the fob is distinctive with its black triangle.'

'Of course.' Oliver gave out his email.

'Thanks for your help.'

After the call, he sent the image to Oliver's email and wandered over to Gerry to give her the bad news. She nodded and reached down to stroke Rylan's head and then turned back to her whizz-bang database.

Frank wondered if he could get away with bringing his own therapy dog to the office.

'Off for a coffee. Want one?' he asked.

'I don't like coffee.'

'Rather you than me. What drink do you like instead? Tea?'

'Yes.'

'How do you take it?'

'With lemon?'

He paused. 'Not sure we can do that. Would milk be right?'

'No. But I'd prefer it if you didn't make me drinks, anyway. I only ever prepare my own.'

'I see.' *Suits me, means I can carry two back for myself.* He shook his head on the way out the door.

Chapter Eighteen

As Gerry didn't require a drink, he slipped out to the car park to smoke a couple of roll-ups and deal with another pressing situation.

Smoking, he strolled over to the car-charging parking spots. Between all the modern electrical cars, his 1980s Volvo Estate stuck out like a sore thumb. As he opened the door, it creaked. A young man he didn't recognise was plugging in his Tesla two cars down. He glanced at Frank with an irritated look on his face.

Frank returned the unfriendly look. 'You know how it is. I can't bear to see a space go to waste, fella.' He believed he had a point. Since they'd installed this long row, it was only half-used, while everyone else struggled for a space.

The young man looked away, probably intimidated. Frank was good at that. He'd a reputation for it.

Frank reached into his Volvo and checked the firm cushion he kept on the driver's seat was central. Either that or he'd sink into old upholstery, and risk being unable to rise again.

After sitting and closing the door, he worked down the

window manually – which now required both hands – prepared and lit a roll-up and got out his phone.

Last night, he'd recognised the lad with the hoodie who'd come into his garden.

A year back, Maddie had called him out of the blue. She was back in Whitby, at rock bottom, and desperate to get clean. The usual yarn. Still, it didn't stop Frank biting hook, line and sinker. Maddie told him she was in Pannett Park. It was late, and dark, but that didn't stop the desperate father bounding in there to help her. Maddie wasn't there, but that scrote was. He blindsided Frank and clobbered him with a rock before swiping his wallet. Being the old-school pillock he was, there'd been a fair amount of cash in it, too.

Since then, he'd only carried cards.

The most painful thing about the situation wasn't the cut on his head, it was that his daughter had obviously set him up.

Maddie rang him several days later to apologise. Lying that she'd nothing to do with it. That the scrote had chucked her in the back of his car around the corner, before lying in wait for some easy money.

Frank had told Maddie he believed her, just so he could keep her on the phone. He'd pleaded with her to come home. The usual, 'It's what your mother would've desperately wanted,' was as unsuccessful as always. Maddie had the money now. So she'd been ready to disappear again for another year.

Last night, after recognising the scrote in his garden, Frank had headed to his kitchen drawer, where he kept his old receipts and bills. Beneath these, he'd hidden Maddie's phone the day she'd returned two weeks previous. It was reasonably old, but Frank was relieved to see it carried fingerprint recognition. He slipped into her room, where she slept, and used her finger to open it. Then, perched on his oak chair, he accessed her contact list and wrote down all the male names and their numbers on a sheet of notepaper. Ten in total. After that, he read through Maddie's text messages. Most were to three of the ten males. Reading through the messages had made Frank's heart sink. Most were about scoring drugs. Eventually, he got to an exchange with a lass called Sarah. She'd been in some kind of bother with an abusive boyfriend and Maddie had been a shoulder to cry on.

It was also evident from some affectionate messages that Maddie was in a relationship with a lad called Bobby. She'd sent him images that turned Frank's stomach.

At one point, he'd gone through to the kitchen and thrown the phone away, before sitting, for over an hour, with his head in his hands.

Later, he'd retrieved the phone from the bin, switched it off and hid it back in the drawer beneath the loose papers.

Now, in his Volvo, he finished his roll-up, threw it from the window, and retrieved last night's notepaper from his suit jacket pocket. Checking his phone was set to 'do not display caller ID', he called Bobby first. The one Maddie seemed to be in some kind of relationship with. As the phone rang, he winced over the thought of the images he'd seen last night.

'Hey, who's this?'

'A friend.'

'Eh?'

'Well, I'm assuming you're a friend as you came into my garden last night?'

'Eh?'

'Last night, dickhead. My garden?'

'Eh?'

'Can you speak?'

'Who are you, man? Why are you phoning me?'

'Just told you, Romeo, you came into my garden last night. I wondered if you'd like to hook up.'

'I don't have a clue what you're—'

'Your ugly mug up against my window, that's what I'm talking about.'

'Watch your mouth.'

'If I see that mug again, I'll tear it from your skull. Do you understand?'

'You can try.'

'I'll do more than try. And after the tearing, I'll post these nude photos of you all over the internet.'

'Eh?'

Frank hung up.

He'd seemed genuine surprised. Maybe the scrote in his garden hadn't been Bobby.

Next, he reached out to a lad named Brad who sounded stoned out of his mind. He also came across as completely surprised. Frank concluded that this level of astonishment would be hard to fabricate in his current state.

Last throw of the dice... 'Hey Rez, my man!'

The phone went silent.

'Rez, my man?' Frank tried again.

'Who's this?'

'Take a guess.'

'Piss off, fool. I'm putting the phone—'

'Got a good look at you last night through the glass, Rez, ruining my flowerbed.'

'Ah... Fat Daddy, isn't it?'

'What were you doing there?'

'Who said I was?'

'You just admitted it.'

'I never.'

'Fat Daddy? You've obviously seen me.'

'Or a lucky guess? You sound like a fat daddy. A fat old daddy.'

'Three out of three. That's some guess. Hey, was it you a while back? Blindsiding me in Pannett Park?'

'Don't know what you're on about.'

'You fancy hooking up again? Except, this time, no ambush?'

'Wouldn't want to hurt you.'

Frank narrowed his eyes. 'Listen, Rez. Notice how I'm using your name. Rez. Did my daughter tell you I was a police officer? Probably not. Anyway, I am, and it won't take me long at all to find you.'

He laughed.

'What's so funny?'

'Course I know you're a pig... that makes it all the better! What you going to do?'

'Well, if you listen, gobshite, you'll know that I'm prepared to do more than you realise. I'm about to retire... what with being a fat, old man, and everything. No need to worry about my job. Pension secure. Listen, Rez, this is your only warning. I see your disgusting face near my window again, or anywhere near my daughter again, for that matter, then—'

'You'll do what?'

Frank told him. It was detailed, and it certainly wasn't pretty.

'Creative.' Rez laughed before he hung up.

Aye, and I meant every word.

Frank smoked another roll-up, and after, closed his eyes for a time, taking deep breaths.

He needed to calm himself down. He didn't want to be

taking this in to Gerry.

When feeling more collected, he made a quick phone call to an old colleague of his, gave over Rez's phone number, and the limited details he had, and asked if he could dig out an address. It was heavily frowned upon, but his friend had never been risk averse. Besides, he owed Frank.

Afterwards, his phone beeped. He looked down at it and saw that an email had come to his work account from Oliver of *Unlock-Utopia*.

He slid his glasses down from his head and read the message. *Bloody hell.*

He phoned Gerry. 'Come outside, now. I'm driving. Unlock-Utopia came good.'

'What car are you driving?'

'I'm just charging it now,' he lied. 'It's bright orange.' At least that part was true.

Chapter Nineteen

Gerry stood at the open passenger door of his Volvo, white knuckles glowing on the hand holding Rylan's lead. She stared in with wide eyes. 'I'm not getting in there.'

'Ha! Understandable,' Frank said. 'When I first bought it, early eighties, my missus didn't want to get in it either. But you'll grow to love it, you know? Bertha has her own personality and' – he turned around to the spacious back seat, brushing off empty take-away cartons, and tapes – 'if I pop the seat down, it'll be like Rylan's own castle!'

'I only ever get taxis,' she said.

'Right, I won't be offended.' He tapped his dash. 'Bertha might be though... Look, I'll drive slowly. You'll be waiting, what, fifteen minutes for a taxi?'

She looked down at Rylan, deep in thought. She knelt and patted his head. 'Okay, we'll try.'

So, once Rylan was king of the castle, Gerry clicked her seatbelt on. She was still nodding to herself, almost certainly rationalising the situation in her head. He guessed she must face such challenges regularly and had established techniques to allow herself to adapt.

Eventually, he explained the contents of the email. 'The black triangle on the fob meant nowt to Oliver Bancroft. Why would it? The key predates him. Fortunately, for us, he's overrun with customers and his mother had to come to lend a hand. She recalled the symbol. Her late husband used to cut keys for a company called North Sea Nook Beach Huts. It's very relevant to her as the company gave them a key to a beach hut at a discount for their services.' He started the engine. The car made a horrendous sound, and Gerry flinched. 'Sorry, that's the worst it gets, I promise. You may wish to crack the window a bit... sometimes the smell of burned oil can be overwhelming.' He needed to get to the point of his discovery before driving as it was hard to talk over the car's incessant rattle. 'You know the colourful chalets that sit on the concrete pathway at the foot of West Cliff?'

'Yes,' Gerry murmured.

'Well, they're council owned until much further up the beach. Then, you reach a privately owned cluster available for hire. North Sea Nook Beach Huts has since changed hands and is now called the Whitby Wavefront Cabins. The new company doesn't get the keys from Unlock-Utopia; hence, Oliver was none the wiser. You ready?'

Another murmured, 'Yes.'

Frank reversed out. Incredibly, he could hear Rylan's whine above the rattle. 'You'll get used to it, fella. And you will too, Gerry. If my missus could get used to Bertha, then anyone can.' He smiled. Long before the shocks went, Mary had completely fallen for Bertha. This was one of the reasons he was struggling to get rid of it.

But how long did Bertha have left? Realistically? He sighed. She was surely on her last legs. But to kill Bertha would be to kill another part of his past with Mary.

However, he reminded himself, *two weeks ago things had changed*.

Now, there was a possibility, hope, that Maddie may come back to him.

Not just physically, but emotionally.

He made a deal with himself as he drove Bertha.

When Maddie completed her recovery, and started anew with Frank, he'd put Bertha to rest, and join the other robots in buying something he could plug in.

Chapter Twenty

They didn't talk for the entire journey.

It wasn't because of Gerry's nerves, or Frank's distractible mind, which was flitting between two women – one who'd been abandoned in such a grotesque fashion; and another, who wasn't discarded, but could just as easily be gone in the blink of an eye. No, they didn't talk because driving this Volvo was like driving a horse-drawn wagon piled with bottles.

After stopping in the car park, he looked at Gerry, acknowledging that this was the first time someone had been in his car since Mary and, judging by the colour of her face, probably the last.

Anybody with an ounce of pride would have felt some embarrassment.

Not Frank.

They exited the car and took the steps down to the concrete walkway that crested the beach. He expected going down these steps to be remarkably easier than going up the steps to the crime scene yesterday. Of course, he was right, but it didn't stop him from getting out of breath.

He considered the importance of sorting his health out if Maddie was back for good. Last night's feast of six pints, Wilson's snuff and a cheese board probably wasn't the best route to success on that one. Catching his breath, he contemplated a hell of diets and step counting; then he reached into his suit pocket for a roll-up he'd prepped earlier. After lighting it, he led Gerry and Rylan to a row of vibrantly coloured chalets, crisp and welcoming, a stark contrast to the tumultuous, intimidating sea only metres away.

As it always was, the sea breeze was brisk, and despite being fatigued by the descent, Frank felt some invigoration and energy creeping back into his old bones, although there was the argument that it may have been coming from the nicotine he was flooding his bloodstream with.

'Here.' He pointed to a small, glass-fronted shop that marked the beginning of the row of beach huts. Above the front was the sign: Whitby Wavefront Cabins.

'Dog friendly.' Frank nodded at the sign on the door. 'Like many places in Whitby. You'd struggle in London, eh?'

'I've never been.'

He looked back at her. 'Really?'

'No.'

He shrugged and turned back. 'Don't blame you.' He tossed his roll-up and went into the shop.

A man rose from an office chair behind the counter. He wore a brightly coloured shirt, as vibrant as the lick of paint on the cabins.

'Mr Barnaby Rose?' Frank held up his badge. 'I'm DCI Black. I rang not so long ago. This is DI Carver—'

'An absolutely stunning Lab!' Barnaby came around the

counter, his eyes suddenly glowing. He knelt and stroked the therapy dog. 'What's his name?'

'Rylan,' Gerry said.

'Well, Rylan.' He stood, went round his counter again, reached down and lifted a plastic container onto the surface. He unscrewed it and freed a large dog biscuit. 'How does this look?'

'He doesn't eat biscuits,' Gerry said.

Frank watched the glow in Barnaby's expression diminish. 'I see...'

'So, no thank you.'

'Bless him! Bad stomach?' Barnaby asked.

Ha. I'd let it go, fella.

'No,' Gerry said.

'Right... so nothing is wrong with him. I'm sure a biscuit would be fine,' Barnaby persevered.

'I feed him twice a day. It keeps his weight optimal, and his stools solid,' Gerry said.

Frank coughed. 'Anyway, Mr Rose. Have you looked at the email I sent after our call?'

'Yes... it's bad news, I'm afraid.'

Frank stifled a sigh. 'How so?'

'Well, like I said, I used to work for the last owner, back when it was North Sea Nook, and the key were indeed ours. Each fob had a symbol on which correspond to a different block of chalets. The one on the picture you sent me had a triangle. Now, if I remember correctly, that corresponded with the second block along. Aye... that's right. The first block was a circle. Now, if we still had the logbooks, the serial number itself would tell us which cabin it was. We used to avoid putting the cabin door number on the key itself in case it got lost. But, alas, all the details went when the business changed hands.'

'How many beach huts made up a block?'

'Eight, I recall.'

'Well, that's something. Where're they?'

'Ah... I'm sorry, but the original cabins are all gone. They've been rebuilt, you see. The North Sea and our weather can make a right mess of them. In fact, they're rebuilt regularly.'

Shit. And he'd felt so close. Frank plucked his glasses from his head and ran a hand through his hair, trying not to look too disappointed. 'Does anything remain from that time?'

'Afraid not.' He looked down at the dog biscuit he was still holding, looked at Gerry rather sheepishly, and slipped it beneath the counter.

'Do you have lost property?' Gerry asked.

Frank looked at her.

'Sorry?' Barnaby said.

'Do you have lost property?'

'Well, yes, of course! Doesn't everyone? People are forever leaving things in these chalets. Most of it is junk, like.'

'Where do you keep it?'

Frank regarded her. *Nice idea, but is a box full of unmatching gloves, and some discarded Y-fronts, going to help here?*

'Behind this office, and the next three chalets, we've some storage cabins, which are just old beach huts. Now, they're old, and really are due to be taken away, but they're serving a purpose, I guess.'

Frank raised an eyebrow. 'Old... how old?'

'Good question.'

Frank nodded, feeling the first jabs of adrenaline. 'Were

they here when North Sea Nook Beach Huts was operating?'

'Oh yes. They're on their last legs.'

'Which of the three cabins do you chuck your lost property in?' Frank asked.

'Well...' He lowered his head, rather embarrassed. 'They're all about full. I've been meaning to get to cleaning them out for years. But, you know, whenever someone leaves something behind, these days, I bung it in one of them, and that item ends up at the front of all that chaos. So, then I panic about emptying everything into the skip in case a recent customer comes back for something. I know. Poor system, eh? Anyway, I've a skip ready. It's going to happen soon.'

Frank looked at Gerry, who was, at this moment, looking down at Rylan. No emotion on her face.

He looked back at Barnaby, feeling hopeful again. 'Do you want help to clear them out, fella?' Frank could almost taste the stale air that must be lingering inside those abandoned cabins, a reminder of the forgotten relics they might contain.

Chapter Twenty-One

Frank's reservations about DI Gerry Carver were waning. Communication was an issue, yes, but she'd an impressive skill-set. Smart beyond belief, insightful, able to bend the information on the internet to her will, and now, here she was, barely breaking a sweat, dragging out box after box of shite from the cabins.

Frank, on the other hand, managed a box or two before he was on his knees, waiting for his heart to decide whether enough was enough.

Gerry was as fit as a butcher's dog! On four hours' sleep a night too!

She had him speechless. A remarkable achievement.

At the beginning of the grind, Barnaby was twitchy, regarding some of the more recent pieces of lost property at the front of the cabins. He requested they went into separate, newer boxes he had ready. However, any junk pushed back a foot or two in the old cabins was fair game, and that could be chucked into a skip he'd had alongside it for almost a year now. 'What're you looking for, exactly?'

'Good question,' Frank said. 'Guess we'll know when we know.' *If at all.*

Barnaby could have at least offered to muck in. But he was happy to stand back. Hypocritically, barking instructions to keep things orderly, even though he'd not made any effort to do so before today.

There was no way that this man was getting his colourful shirt dirty.

Although irritating, it was probably for the best. The dog-biscuit-wielding manager may end up chucking away something relevant.

Together, Gerry and Frank emptied boxes onto the ground, and rustled through scarves, towels, trunks, and other junk. They would then throw it all back into the boxes again, before lugging them over to the skip.

Occasionally, they came across stuff that may have had a place in a charity shop. Old books, swim goggles, toy cars and the like. Again, these found a separate box, as Gerry, rather than Frank, was keen to recycle.

Several hours into the task, Frank was running on empty, but Gerry maintained her intensity. Dust and grime covered them from head to toe. Frank also noticed that he was starting to smell a bit ripe.

Another hour went by as Rylan watched on inquisitively and Barnaby drank tea. Frank decided that if he survived this intense workout to see another sunset, he'd be a very lucky man.

This is useless... a waste of time.

It wasn't the first time Frank had concluded this a failure. In fact, he must have been in treble figures by now.

Although he believed it a failure, whole-heartedly – who wouldn't? – he carried on, fearful that this could be their last hope of getting a name to that arrogant prick Donald Oxley by the end of the day.

When they'd an hour of sunlight left, Barnaby told them he was closing soon and reminded them again that they needed to leave the cabins in some kind of order.

Frank, who was exhausted, and more pessimistic than ever about finding anything, stood up straight, wondering if he'd enough energy to swing a punch.

He was about to call it a day when Gerry emerged from the second cabin along, holding a guitar case.

Frank thought of the plectrum, and his tired heart sparked back into life.

Gerry put it down on the ground and they gathered around.

'The things people leave behind, eh?' Barnaby said.

'You've some gloves?' Frank asked Barnaby and then edged closer to the find.

'I'll have to take a—'

'I've some.' Gerry reached into her pocket. She pulled out a sealed plastic wrap, tore it carefully and slipped on the gloves. She knelt and unclipped the hinges on the guitar case.

'Can't be much of anything if they left it behind and never thought to claim it back,' Barnaby said, drawing closer.

Fair point, Frank thought, but that didn't kill his sudden burst of optimism.

'Do you play guitar, DCI?' Barnaby asked.

'Used to.' *Hell of a lot. Back in happier times.*

Gerry opened the case. He worked his way round the back of her so he could look inside. Just being this close to a guitar made his fingers itch, but like Barnaby had just pointed out, it'd probably be a worthless piece of junk that would crumble to pieces when—

'Jesus wept.' His eyes widened. 'Jesus...' He knelt next to Gerry. His trousers split. '...Wept.'

'What?' Barnaby asked.

Frank linked his hands behind his back, fighting the urge to touch the Sitka spruce top of the guitar and stroke the solid East Indian Rosewood sides. 'A bloody Martin D-35.' He looked up at the other two as if they might know what he was talking about. They clearly didn't. 'Bloody lovely sound. Played one once. In a store.' He looked down at the beautiful instrument again. 'And they cost a small fortune. No way I was buying it.'

'How much did it cost?' Barnaby asked.

'A couple of hundred if I remember right.'

'Not that much.'

Frank looked up at Barnaby. 'Then! A couple of hundred then! They manufactured these guitars in the seventies. Now, it'd set you back a fair few thousand.'

Barnaby rose an eyebrow.

Ha! I can hear loud and clear what you're thinking, Barnaby, but you may as well stop. 'Whoever left this behind didn't leave it behind by accident.'

'What do you mean?' Barnaby asked.

'I'm saying no one loses or forgets a Martin D-35, not if they know anything about guitars. Whoever owned this guitar had a reason for not coming back for it.'

'Such as?'

Frank didn't want to say. He hoped his serious expression would do the talking. 'Are the old owners still alive?'

'No, I'm afraid not,' Barnaby said.

Frank sighed. 'A shame. I reckon they would remember

finding this and slipping it into lost property. I mean, it's not a forgotten tennis ball. Gerry, was it in a box?'

'No. It was standing on its own. Far right corner.'

'Right, let's look there, and then scour the area immediately around where it was. We'll scrape the dirt up with our fingernails if we must... What are you doing?'

Gerry was lifting the guitar out by its neck.

'Careful now,' he said, almost envious that she was touching it, but also concerned that it could be potential evidence.

There was a clunking sound.

Gerry stood and tilted the guitar back the other way. It clunked again.

'There's something inside it,' Frank said. He could almost taste the anticipation, a sour tang on his tongue as his heart raced.

She laid it back down in the case.

'We need to call this in.' Frank took his phone out and called Helen.

Barnaby was still standing there with his eyebrow raised. 'And if it isn't evidence for anything? Then what? You return it?'

Frank looked down at the guitar as he waited for Helen to answer.

'It's evidence,' Gerry said.

'I see... but how do you know that?' Barnaby didn't want to let this potential cash cow go.

Because I can hear her, Frank thought. *She's speaking to me, and I can hear her.*

Chapter Twenty-Two

Frank paced outside the forensic lab, recalling Mary's obsession with step counting.

You'll be proud of my count by the end of today, he thought, recalling his busy afternoon going in and out of old beach huts.

Gerry had waited outside in the car with Rylan. Apparently, there was no place for a therapy dog in an establishment that strived to be as sterile as possible.

Which begged the question...

He looked at his reflection in the glass window. Two-tone suit, ripped trousers, belly hanging over a belt, hair a dishevelled mess, unshaven.

How the hell had he made it in?

Rylan was country miles ahead of him in terms of appearance and hygiene!

Times were changing, though. He'd need to get his act together for Maddie. He winked at his reflection. *We'll get you sorted in no time, old man.*

Helen opened the door.

He stopped dead. 'And?'

'And… suit up and come in.'

Inside, ahead of him, Roger, Helen's suited colleague, said, 'Quite the haul, DCI,' and stepped to one side, revealing a yellowing, scrunched A4 envelope on the table.

Helen pointed at it with tweezers. 'This was what you heard thudding around inside the guitar. There were two items in this envelope.'

Frank put on his glasses and leaned in. 'That's a C on the front of the envelope?'

'I'd agree with that,' Helen said.

'So, is the letter addressed to "C" do you think?' Frank asked.

'You're the detective.'

'Someone has scratched a line under it, yes? That's what you do when you write a Christmas card or something, isn't it? Write the name and scratch a line under it?'

'I do,' Roger said.

Frank took a deep breath. *Okay… good… C… I'm listening…*

'Over here.' Helen led him to another table and pointed at a TDK cassette. 'Takes me back.'

Frank didn't feel it necessary to add that he still had a whole heap of them in the Volvo. Although he never used them any more, as you couldn't hear the tinny speakers over the shocks.

'What's on it?' Frank asked.

'Good question. We have arranged for the equipment to come over. It'll be here within the hour. We'll digitise it for you.'

'The top ten singles chart, perhaps?' Roger said. 'There was a time when I recorded it every week.'

'Wouldn't be a bad thing,' Frank said. 'It'll give us a clearer sign of the year. Anything written on the white bar?'

'Not on this side, but...' She flipped it. 'This side.'

'Most of the ink has gone.' Frank squinted through his glasses.

'Indented writing analysis gave us a word,' Helen said. 'Broken.'

Broken... The name of a song? An album?

'You said there was a second item?'

Helen nodded and led him to a third table.

Frank leaned closer to an old polaroid.

The image was grainy. There were two young individuals, male and female, propped up against the bar, smiling. They had their arms around each other in the picture, and looked a couple, although they could just have been close friends. There was enough scenery there for Frank to recognise the place. 'Is that the Mariner's Lantern?'

'Yes,' Helen said. 'Took me right back, too.'

'Care to enlighten me?' Roger said. 'Not from around here.'

'Popular local boozer. You won't find many locals who didn't buy their first drink from this place...' She stared off wistfully. 'Or met their other half there.'

'I don't fit into either bracket, as I didn't move here until I was twenty-six,' Frank said. 'Mary dragged me here from Leeds after we married in '86. Was a little older than most of the clientele in that place if I recall, but I remember stopping by for an afternoon bevvy occasionally.'

'Where's this pub then?' Roger asked.

'Gone,' Frank said. 'A fire in the nineties. There's a new pub in its place now... The Saltwick Sailor.'

'Still not heard of it.'

'Near to the whalebones,' Helen said. 'Along East Terrace, past the Royal Hotel. It's not as popular as it once was. Used to be renowned for serving kids back in the day.

Remembered I was only fifteen when I had my first drink there! The world has moved on considerably since then.'

'Thankfully,' Roger said. 'I have a seventeen-year-old daughter.'

'Oh, when I was seventeen...' Helen said.

'Not what I want to hear,' Roger said.

Ignoring them, Frank leaned forward, his eyes focusing on the young woman in the photo. She was taller than the boy beside her, but that wasn't what made her so striking. The partial afro, framing her face elegantly, caught Frank's attention. As did her mixed heritage, which brought radiant skin and a perfect canvas for those bright, expressive eyes.

Now then, C, is that you?

'How old do you reckon she is, Helen?' Frank asked.

'Anywhere from sixteen to nineteen, perhaps?'

Frank looked at the young woman again. It wasn't just the rich tapestry of her ancestry that made her so captivating; he could already see inside her personality. He looked closer. Those eyes, before they became hollows, sparked with vivacity. Before some bastard squeezed her into a case, she had a confident posture. A sense of grace and strength. He looked up at Helen. 'It's her.'

Helen nodded. She didn't confirm whether this was an agreement, but he didn't need her to.

'Let me show you the back.' She flipped the polaroid with tweezers.

Written on the back: C + DR, 1987.

'C... again. She was alive in 1987.' Frank felt his body filling with adrenaline. 'Now, then, who's DR?'

'A doctor? Maybe, just initials?'

'Flip it back, please.'

Using the tweezers again, Helen did.

'Do you recognise that lad, Helen? 1987...'

'In 1987, I would have been...' She thought about it. 'Twenty-two. At that point, me, and Mary were drinking much further afield.'

'What? Scarborough?' Frank rolled his eyes.

'Among other places.'

'So, you don't recognise him?'

'I don't recognise either of them.'

Frank nodded. 'Okay.' He looked down at C again. 'Well, at least the starter gun has been fired.'

Chapter Twenty-Three

Frank and Gerry passed Donald's office on the way to the broom cupboard.

'Maybe we should update him? Smug bas—' He broke off in time, unaware of how Gerry would respond to profanities. He'd not heard her use any herself and he doubted he ever would.

So far, he'd been well-behaved with his language. He'd brought up a little girl, or at least had a considerable part in it, and, when push came to shove, he knew how to keep a lid on it.

'I want to check my spreadsheet first.'

'Eh? You think you've something?'

'After you finished updating me, you immediately started the engine. It isn't possible to converse. Also, with all that noise, I felt too on edge to access the spreadsheet on the cloud—'

'Okay, you've made your point regarding Bertha... so, what do you think you found?' he asked as they continued to the incident room.

'I'm only 80 per cent sure. Over the night, I processed a

lot of information. I need to check the database before I get any hopes up.'

'They're already up.'

And what was with the percentages? How accurate could they be? Could she really attach a number to her level of surety?

Either way, she'd made good on nearly everything she'd touched so far, so he followed her eagerly to the dungeon. 'Okay, but only if you promise we can take Rylan into Donald's office to crap in the corner later.'

'No. He defecates twice a day, Frank, at specific times, and not on command.'

Chapter Twenty-Four

Gerry's hands flew over the keyboard.

He started pacing again as he'd done back at the lab.

Anyone else would have been unnerved by this small elephant pounding the floor.

But Gerry was an enigma. She appeared unaware of his presence, and completely absorbed by her process.

Finally, she said, 'Yes. I did remember accurately.'

'God love us.' He marched towards her. 'What do you have?'

'I have a young musician, mixed race, last seen with her guitar. Her first initial is C. It all correlates with a girl reported missing by her mother in Middlesbrough. September 18th, 1987.'

'Middlesbrough? That's far afield...'

'Yes, but her last known location was Scarborough, see?' She pointed at the information. 'So, it fell into my radius. After you mentioned the plectrum last night, I narrowed the list using a connection to music. Yes, tenuous, but her name is Charlotte. We have the initial on the photograph, *and* her mother's report stresses that she had a guitar in her possession.'

Frank steadied himself against the back of her chair and slipped his glasses down so he could see the screen. Gerry's nimble fingers danced across the keyboard at an unnatural speed.

'Here,' Gerry said. 'Charlotte Wilson. Date of birth, 1 March 1969, making her eighteen years old at the time of her disappearance. And...'

Frank rubbed at his chin, wondering if a heart fatigued from hours of scrabbling through the cabins could survive these continuous blasts of adrenaline.

Gerry zoomed in on an extract from a Middlesbrough-based newspaper. Frank leaned forward, squinting through his glasses. The heading read: *Charlotte Wilson, 18, missing four months.*

A small sigh left his lips when he regarded the black-and-white photograph of a girl in a school uniform, smiling.

It was the young woman in the polaroid taken in the Mariner's Lantern.

Slightly younger but unmistakably her.

He placed his hand on the top of the monitor. 'Hello Charlotte.' *Are you ready?*

He took a deep breath.

Shall we begin?

Chapter Twenty-Five

MIDWAY THROUGH THE SESSION, David Roberts leaned forward just enough to present an air of unwavering attention.

He'd been doing this for over thirty years now, so he knew what came next.

Sylvia Morris took a deep breath and moved her recount starkly forward, straight into her most traumatic moment – the moment that had eventually led to these sessions.

'The silence. *Immediately* afterwards. That's when I felt it the most.'

'Not uncommon,' David said. 'In the calm after the storm.'

'It felt anything but calm.'

David nodded.

'I *felt* caged. Trapped. Lost in guilt. What had I done so wrong? Was this all my fault?'

David offered his most well-rehearsed, empathetic expression. 'Quiet moments after intense encounters can often be the worst. Sometimes, the encounter is so noisy that you can't think, but in the silence, you can suddenly hear those thoughts... those doubts. This is when everything can become... *loudest.*' He sat back now, and rubbed his chin as if deep in thought, but he knew exactly what he was going to say because he'd said it a thousand times before. 'So, you *must* remember, daily, when it is silent, and you're feeling guilt-ridden... that you did nothing, I repeat *nothing*, to deserve such treatment from Wilf. The storm was never your doing... that's the thought that's most relevant in the silence.'

Sylvia welled up. She reached for a tissue and dabbed at her eyes. No mascara to smudge. She'd known she was going to cry today. She'd known that a session here with him would offer a purge.

No one could ever accuse him of being bad at his job.

'Easier said than done...'

'Oh, I know. That's why you're here. With me.' He smiled. 'But I see you making progress all the time, so be kind to yourself.'

She giggled and continued to dab her eyes. 'But how do I move past it completely?'

He offered her a well-practised, reassuring smile. 'Rather than force your way past it, you gently reclaim these moments. Fill them with something new... something that's yours. Write... sing... meditate... whatever you like to do. One of my former patients took up a new sport. Rowing, would you believe?'

'I'm too old for anything like that.'

'How so? She was older than you.' He smiled again.

Another giggle.

'When you reclaim them, then you'll have the opportunity to heal.'

'But they'll come back. Those memories. The physical

pain in my jaw... my shaking hands... the plates smashed all over the kitchen... it all comes back.'

'I won't lie. Yes, it does. And then, Sylvia, you can, gently again, of course, remind yourself that you've moved beyond this place. It no longer truly exists. It's expired. You've moved on from the silence. Taken control of the silence. Taken *control* of your life.'

She nodded and looked down. 'A journey.'

'Precisely,' David said, carefully adjusting his tone. 'Always the journey. That's how we started. Talking about the journey, and that's how we'll finish today, by reminding ourselves of that same journey. And I'll also remind you that you're not alone in any of it. Together, we'll journey past the trauma, and one day, the moments of peace you feel sporadically will become more regular.'

Afterwards, he led her out of his therapy room and into reception. He noticed that she was already walking with more purpose. It was amazing how an hour with him could alter a person's gait so significantly.

Sylvia was David's last appointment. He'd let Maggie, his receptionist, leave early, so he block-booked Sylvia for six more sessions, took payment, and then showed her out.

Afterwards, he sat in his office and surfed the internet for holidays.

At fifty-five, he wasn't getting any younger. He'd like, very much, to get some skiing in before arthritis or any other nasty ailments settled in.

Hanna despised skiing, and she especially despised the cold, so he'd pick up a bottle of wine on the way home to make her feel better about the fact that it was happening.

Hopefully, it'd ward off any moaning. In fairness, it'd been a difficult time for her. Her mother had passed earlier in the year. Worse still, that had led her to spending more time with her interfering sister, Briony.

Now, there was a woman who'd a view about everything!

Never a helpful view though...

Still, a bottle of wine, followed by some gentle reminders that it was *him* that paid for everything, usually did the trick. She'd been able to knock nursing on the head at fifty, after all! Sometimes, you just had to refresh her memory of these details.

And she always saw things the right way after some gentle encouragement.

He plucked his American Express card from his wallet and booked the ski trip.

Chapter Twenty-Six

Paul Harrison couldn't believe what he was hearing.

'Tonight?' Paul asked.

'Sorry, but—'

'Tonight! *Shit!* You know what tonight is!'

'I know, but Charlie's seconds away from going into surgery. *Seconds.*'

'Can't his father look after him?'

'No. *My son* is having his appendix out. He's *twelve.*'

'I get that... but...' He broke off and rubbed at his temples. *Hold back, lad... hold back... this is the worst possible news, but don't cross any lines you can't get back over...*

'I don't think you're hearing me properly, Paul. This is a big deal,' Jess said.

'Yes...' Paul slumped back in his office chair. 'You're right.'

This was precisely the reason he'd never had children.

Not that the option had ever presented itself. Almost fifty-five years of age, and he'd had only two long-term relationships. Neither had reached a year. He didn't class the fling that he'd had with Jess as a relationship, because she was still married, so there'd been no strings.

'Look... I understand,' he said. 'And I'll manage.'

Or not.

'I'm sorry. Listen, the kitchen knows your menu. Inside out. And Ray is ready. He's desperate, too. He'll see you right.'

No. There's a mistake in Ray. I know there is. You can see it in those over-eager eyes. Too desperate to impress all the time.

But Jess trusted Ray; he'd been her *special* project for a while now.

He took a deep breath. 'Go to Charlie, I'm sorry. Ignore me. I'm panicking.'

'You'll smash it, Paul. I've no doubt.'

And then Paul Harrison's sous chef was gone. *And with it my hope and dreams?*

He looked up at the bottle of single malt whisky on his shelf. A Macallan eighteen-year-old sherry oak. Three hundred and fifty pounds they cost. A Christmas present from the shareholders of his restaurant after a stellar opening year.

It was unopened.

He'd come close to rectifying that before, but never closer than *now*.

But stumbling into his kitchen half-cut wouldn't rectify any disasters.

He looked at his watch. *Stop turning it into a catastrophe, you dick! You've come through worse...*

Nothing with this much at stake, though.

Standing up and stretching out, he took a deep breath. *You got this. Time to trust Ray.*

He headed for the door of his office with his chest puffed out.

This evening, some of the wealthiest investors in North Yorkshire were coming to the Cliffside Culinarian, and Head Chef Paul Harrison was desperate to knock their socks off even without the only person in the world he'd ever really trusted.

He looked and pointed upwards. 'I'll make you proud, yet.'

Chapter Twenty-Seven

EARLIER, dental records confirmed that the body did indeed belong to Charlotte Wilson, so Donald assigned three more officers. Frank diligently set up the more spacious and impressive Incident Room 3, all the while showering his colleagues with compliments. 'If not for you, Gerry, we'd still be operating out of a Travelodge rather than the Hilton.'

Gerry, as to be expected, was rather nonchalant around compliments and equally indifferent to the upgrade in the room. Having a powerful computer and her obedient Lab at her feet brought her contentment enough it seemed.

He wondered, briefly, how other members of the team would take to her.

He knew DS Reggie Moyes, marathon runner extraordinaire, wouldn't be a problem. A people-pleaser, Reggie was desperate to be liked. It fed his vanity.

On second thoughts, that could be a problem. If he tried too hard with Gerry, he could very well make her uncomfortable.

The other two members of his team were a mystery, as he'd yet to meet them.

It was hard to be confident in Donald's choices. He didn't seem motivated by this case at all.

Still, there was no real need to worry about Gerry. She'd already shown that she could handle herself. He laughed to himself when he thought about her putting Barnaby in his place with that dog biscuit. He was starting to warm to her.

Frank returned to IR7, alone, to make the phone call he was dreading.

This was his second attempt at calling Laura Wilson, and like earlier, he felt a cold sweat break on his forehead as he chewed his bottom lip. Earlier, he'd felt some relief when she didn't pick up. Which, of course, made no sense, because it caused the sense of dread to escalate over the next hour as he waited to make his second attempt.

Half-expecting her not to pick up, he flinched with shock when the ringing stopped. 'Hello?'

'Hello. Sorry about calling late. I'm DCI Frank Black of the North Yorkshire police. Is this Laura Wilson?' He waited for her to respond, but the phone was silent. 'Sorry, ma'am, but am I talking to Laura Wilson?'

'Yes... How can I help?' She spoke slowly. Hesitantly.

Frank suddenly regretted making the call.

Laura was seventy years old.

He should have just told her in person. *Such an idiot.* 'Ms Wilson, are you alone?'

'Why do you ask?'

Struggling with regret now, Frank tried to backtrack. 'It may be best if myself and a colleague drive out this evening to speak to you? It's just with it being late, I didn't want to come unannounced.'

Silence.

Now you're just making it obvious that this is dreadful news.

Idiot.

'Is this about Charlotte?' Laura asked.

Frank's breath caught in his throat.

She'd been reported missing thirty-seven years ago.

Thirty-seven years!

Longer than both Maddie and Gerry had been alive.

And *considerably* longer than Charlotte had lived.

But wasn't it to be expected? Frank rubbed his own eyes and thought of Mary. Thought of how Maddie had been front and centre of her thoughts, and his, when she'd run from them over twelve years ago.

Front and centre.

Every day... all the time...

'You've found her, haven't you?' Laura asked.

Twelve years... thirty-seven years... it didn't matter. The longing, the desperation, the despair – none of it'd ever end.

'Ms Wilson, I'm sorry. I really am, but we found some remains in Whitby. Dental records suggest the remains belong to Charlotte.'

The phone went silent again.

'Ms Wilson, I—'

'I understand.'

'I'm sorry, I truly am.'

'Thank you for telling me.'

'Please, may I come to see you? Tomorrow?'

'Of course.'

Frank paused, waiting for her to ask questions. She must have hundreds. Thousands. He was prepared for the barrage and was prepared to give her everything he knew. She deserved that. He wouldn't withhold any information.

But there was nothing.

Not a single question.

It seemed odd... was odd... but was it anything to read into? People processed things differently. He couldn't imagine how he'd respond in her situation.

'Ms Wilson?'

'Yes.'

'You can ask me questions.'

There was a long silence before she asked, 'Did Charlotte suffer?'

Frank closed his eyes. *Of all the questions. Ask me a question I can answer. A question that doesn't rip the heart from my bloody body.*

Frank considered the blunt-force trauma. The pathologist believed it'd have killed her quickly, as it was at the back of her head. She may not have seen it coming, but was it too early to guarantee that? *Bugger it,* he thought. *She needs something.* 'A blow to the head. We suspect she didn't suffer.'

'An accident?'

'We don't believe that to be the case. I'm sorry.'

Although Laura would know soon enough, he really didn't want to tell her that someone had folded her up and buried her in a suitcase like she was nothing... an inconvenience...

'Okay,' Laura said. 'Thank you, again.'

Frank expected her to burst into tears. Or maybe he was hoping she would? It could be cathartic for her. Bottling it up often came to no good.

'Is there anyone that could come and stay with you tonight?' Frank asked.

'No need.'

He inwardly sighed. 'I think it'd be for the best.'

'Okay, I could ask Margaret. She'll be happy to.'

Good. Laura was clearly in shock. No more questions. No demand to see her daughter's body. Her response seemed disproportionate.

'I'll try to get to you for around ten tomorrow morning, if that's all right?'

'Thank you.'

Stop thanking me. I've done nothing. And even when I've found the truth, which I will, don't thank me then either. You've lost so much. So, so much.

'Tomorrow, then,' Laura said. 'I look forward to it.'

Such a strange thing to say. The shock must have her spinning. 'Make sure you call Margaret, please.'

'I will.'

He expected her to put the phone down, but he could hear her breathing.

After a couple of seconds, he said, 'Ms Wilson?'

She sighed. 'I always knew...' And then she was gone.

After the call, he couldn't help but recall the look in Mary's eyes the morning of the first-year anniversary of Maddie's disappearance. Her twenty-year-old daughter. Not knowing if she was alive or dead. Twelve months. Three hundred and sixty-five days.

It'd broken her.

Broken him.

And their relationship.

Ironically, at that point, his phone pinged, and he saw Helen had sent him the audio file lifted from Charlotte's TDK cassette labelled 'Broken'.

Feeling subdued, he returned to Gerry and together they listened to three songs.

'Her voice is incredible,' Frank said. 'Genuinely.'

Gerry didn't respond to his opinion. That was okay. He knew she'd be deep in thought.

On their second listen, Frank noted how fantastic the Martin D-35 sounded. 'That isn't someone who just learned to play. She's been playing her whole life.'

Realising that he was speaking about her in the present tense, his heart dropped.

Her angelic voice, her skilful guitar playing, all of her, gone.

He gritted his teeth. He wouldn't allow the story of her life to end simply with a buried suitcase.

On the third listen, he scribbled down snippets from the song, trying desperately to hear her. *Really* understand who she was.

Her lyrics were riddles, and he knew so little about her. It'd be a daunting task even with more background information about who she'd been. But still he tried.

He paused and wrote:

A melody lost in the air... a memory I can't resume...

Did you lose someone, Charlotte, someone close to you?

A face I knew... then disappeared.

A friend, a boyfriend... a father? Who gave you that guitar? Hard to believe your mother could have bought you that. Could she have afforded it? Really?

A child's laughter no more.

Did something happen to you as a child? Is this when you lost someone?

He scribbled as many questions and ideas as he could. Tomorrow, at ten, he'd be with Laura Wilson.

There'd be background there for these song lyrics. Context.

Many of Charlotte's lyrics concerned music, and how it'd acted as a glue in putting her back together again after being broken. It wasn't the most sophisticated, admittedly, and there was too much overemphasis, but she'd only been eighteen. Eighteen and writing that! Combine this with a natural blossoming talent in both singing and guitar playing, and you'd a special, talented young woman.

One with a bright future.

All three demos covered the same themes. This was what had driven her to write music after all. Something she lost. Something she craved. Something she could only find through the melody.

She'd been young, and *this* collection of songs had been a starting point.

But what a starting point it had been.

He wandered over to his whiteboard and looked at the picture of Charlotte in her school uniform, and then moved his eyes down to the polaroid of her, looking older, with her own sense of style, standing in the Mariner's Lantern, while a lad had his arm around her.

'DR' according to the scribble on the back.

Initials? A doctor? He looked young to be a doctor.

He took a deep breath and closed his eyes.

I'm starting to hear, Charlotte.

Keep on singing.

Chapter Twenty-Eight

It was a whirlwind.

All around him was agitation and breathless activity.

And him, the conductor in the middle, with everything on the line.

And yet, all Head Chef Paul Harrison could think about was the bottle of Macallan eighteen-year-old sherry malt on the shelf in his office.

This was out of the ordinary for Paul. Accuse him of being a workaholic? Then yes, he'd hold his hand up.

But an alcoholic?

No. That had never been him.

It seemed having one of the wealthiest men in North Yorkshire sitting in your restaurant, combined with the loss of his sous chef, Jess, was taking its toll.

Roy Thomas, the man he was determined to impress, was no stranger to fine dining. People of such wealth rarely were. Their palates gave new definition to the word 'refined'.

A5 Wagyu beef was Jess' speciality. She could cook it

better than him. When it'd found its way onto tonight's menu, there'd been no talk of her being unable to show.

But now, her kid, Charlie, was having part of his appendix plucked out, so it was down to him.

It shouldn't be a problem. He was, of course, the best chef in town. But the unexpectedness of it all, the sudden change in rhythm, had him more on edge than ever before. In fact, his hands were shaking, and this was something he'd never experienced previously.

While he waited for the Wagyu to be prepped, he swooped for the next order slip and bellowed to the kitchen, 'Two orders of the spiced lamb.'

No one responded.

'I don't hear a "Yes, Chef".' His voice was louder than it needed to be. His tone, also, more aggressive than necessary.

He was a wreck.

'Yes, Chef. Prepping now, Chef,' Louis shouted.

'Bloody hell, you serious? None prepped?'

'That last table swooped up eight, Chef,' Ray shouted, as he shifted some monstrous prawns around the grill, monitoring the change in colour with wide, unblinking eyes.

Credit where credit was due. Ray hadn't put a foot wrong tonight. He was stepping up. It seemed another good call by Jess, but that didn't stop Paul from being pissed off. He clapped his hands. 'More careful bloody monitoring then, yeah?'

'Yes, Chef,' Ray said.

'And those prawns, lad... they're ready.'

'Sorry, Chef.' Ray took the pan off.

Ray would wonder how Paul could tell that from this distance.

'I don't need colour, lad, I just need the smell.' *Been doing this a long bloody time.*

'The Wagyu is prepped, Chef,' Polly called out.

'You angel, Polly.' He smiled, but inside he was shaking like a leaf.

Snap out of this Paul, you've done this a thousand times.

Still, easier said than done when this meal could be the difference between several millions of investment and a kingly retirement, or potential bankruptcy when three more competitors popped up next year.

Panicked, he exited the kitchen at a pace. He passed the Maître d'.

'Are you okay, Chef?'

'Fine, Kristoff! A quick toilet break before I get stuck into the Wagyu.'

'Well, make sure you wash your hands!' Kristoff said.

In his office, Paul checked the blinds were down, plucked the Macallan from the shelf, twisted the lid, breaking the seal, and then gulped from it. Twice.

His throat and stomach burned.

He shook his head. Gulping from a £350 bottle like a wino!

He took a deep breath, screwed the lid back on the bottle, returned it to the shelf.

You got this, Paul.

He marched back to the kitchen, remembering what Arthur Barclay, his mentor, used to say... *Silent moments of struggle will lead to your greatest masterpiece.*

In the kitchen, he washed his hands and winked at Sam, who manned the dishwasher. 'Our invisible hero.'

The eighteen-year-old glowed over the words.

Arthur had often said that to Paul when he'd first started in the kitchen at sixteen. Then, Paul had been the dishwasher, and Arthur, the head chef.

Paul weaved around servers, bringing in orders and

empty dishes while the door swung continuously behind them. He saw the door as the kitchen's mouth, drawing in the oxygen, keeping it alive.

Whereas I'm the beating heart.

He stood next to the hot pans, clapped his hands, and whooped, 'Bring it on! The Wagyu, please.'

He knew they'd all be looking at each other with raised eyebrows. *Chef has lost it again!*

But, sometimes, you just had to lose it.

No one wanted to work for a robot.

Suddenly, he felt great. The whisky had done its job.

Let's do this.

The Wagyu hit the pan.

Greatest struggle.

He tossed the Wagyu, took a deep breath, cranked the temperature for a couple of seconds and...

Greatest masterpiece.

He carried the plates to Elsie and Lawrence.

'Marbled, tender and rich.' He handed them over. 'Bring home the bacon, my two lovelies.'

Chapter Twenty-Nine

DAVID ROBERTS SAT on the edge of his bed alongside his wife, Hanna, and watched her.

As she cried, she kept her head turned from him.

This was her default manoeuvre after every disagreement.

In the same way that David remained patient in his therapy sessions, he stayed patient here, too.

After all, he had the experience. This marriage was thirty-three years old.

So, he continued to maintain his distance of approximately half a metre. If he came in too quick, she'd flinch, and delay the process.

The next step was to remind her about everything that was good in their life. *The expensive house... her early retirement that he'd funded... the time he'd allowed her to spend on her artwork.*

Then he moved into praise. Although he often admitted that her version of art – all her wavy lines and use of conflicting colours – was beyond him, now was not the time for that. So, he talked about how wonderful it'd be to see it all on display next month when the nearby library hosted a local art display.

As he followed his process, he moved closer. Almost imperceptibly. A tiny wriggle at a time. Until their sides were touching. Then he kissed her head and apologised. 'And tomorrow, I'll send you some dates. Find us a week in the sun. You've my permission to grab my credit card. Top drawer in the office. Book it and then we get the best of both worlds, eh? The cold skiing trip and some sun worshipping!'

She was still quivering, but the tears had stopped. *Good.* 'Does that sound okay?'

She didn't respond. He slipped his arm around her shoulders and pulled her tighter against him. 'Okay, my love?'

She nodded. 'Yes.' She rested her head on his shoulder, and he stroked her hair. 'And now... when you're ready?'

She sniffed but didn't respond.

'I *need* to hear it, Hanna.'

'I'm sorry.'

'Good... it's okay, my dear... Sometimes, in the heat of the moment, we forget things. And you forgot, and that's okay.'

They lay back on the bed together. She turned to face him. Her right eye was swollen. An accident. He hadn't expected her to hit the shelf after he'd slapped her.

But that was the heat of the moment for you.

She knew better than to start arguments with him.

That even something as simple as: 'Do I ever get a say in anything?' was enough of a trigger.

There was no point in wishing it wasn't so, because it was, and always had been. Also, it always would be. No amount of therapy would solve that!

So, it was imperative that Hanna simply knew better. And reminders were never a bad thing, were they?

Chapter Thirty

Seeing Maddie, his daughter, sitting up in bed, smiling, had to rate as one of the most significant moments in Frank's life.

In fact, he was so taken aback by the experience, he spun from the room, apologising, and disappeared into the bathroom.

He didn't know how she'd respond to his tears.

It's taken too long to get her back, and Mary wasn't here to witness it. But the relief and hope he now felt was like nothing he'd ever experienced.

He cleaned himself up in the mirror and gave himself a swift nod.

This is your last case, fella. It's time to be there for your daughter. Time to put right the things you got so wrong in the past.

Then, a coldness spread throughout his body.

He'd left Maddie's door unlocked!

Charging from the bathroom, he glanced at the front door, half-expecting it to be open, banging in the wind. Relieved it wasn't, he marched back into his daughter's bedroom, and steadied himself against the barred window, out of breath.

'Are you okay, Dad?' Maddie's voice was weak, still, but that smile was still there.

That smile.

When was the last time I saw that smile?

'Yes... sorry... just been a heavy day at work. Tell me how you feel?'

'Almost clear-headed. First time in a while. It's strange, I thought I'd died at one point.'

His heart sank. To hear such things from your own flesh and blood? 'But getting better?'

'Definitely today, I feel... like I said... kind of clear? It's hard to explain.'

He saw the empty crisp packets everywhere. *Good.* She was eating. Now it was time to get some goodness into her. He thought of his empty fridge.

But a take-away would be better than crisps, wouldn't it?

He edged forward. 'Do you need food? I—'

'Dad. Please relax. I'm still tired. I want to sleep, but first...' She patted the bed. 'Can you just sit?'

'Of course.' Frank sat on the edge of the bed. He rubbed his hands together as he looked at his child, whom he'd always cherished, but seeing now a woman he barely knew. He struggled to maintain eye contact, but tried his best to do so, and returned her smile.

'Are you cold?' Maddie asked.

'No... why?'

'Your hands. You keep rubbing them.'

'Oh yes, just had a cold drink,' he lied. It was nerves.

They chatted some more about how she was feeling. Slowly, but surely, he could extend his eye contact with her as his mind grew accustomed to the facts.

This is her.
Your daughter.
Your Maddie.
She's back.

'Your mother would be proud of you.' Frank nodded. 'She knows. She knows you came home and fought to get well.'

Welling up, she looked down.

'I'm sorry,' Frank said.

'No... Dad. That was nice.'

After a minute's reflection, she said, 'Thanks for being here. I remember very little. Desperation... but it's hazy. I know I was lost, and I needed you.'

He understood this. Sometimes when Frank was lonely, and at his lowest, he'd think about his own parents. No matter how old you got, when you felt lost, you always remembered those that loved you more than anything.

'I'm sorry I locked you up,' Frank said.

'I said you could.'

'Yes, to start with...' He broke off. He didn't want to make her feel bad.

'It's like a nightmare, but I remember. I shouted at you to let me out. I'm sorry. Did I say horrible things?'

Water under the bridge. He skirted around the question. 'Look, we need to get you to a doctor. You wouldn't go before, but now you must.'

'I know.'

'I'll be with you, you know? Every step of the way. I'm an old man now, so retirement beckons.' He winked. 'We've got this.'

She nodded and yawned. 'Can I sleep now?'

Frank nodded and stood.

'Listen, Dad, leave the door open now… And I don't want you sitting outside the room all night monitoring me.'

Frank felt another cold sensation bubble in his stomach. 'You sure? I don't mind. It's better for my back in that chair, I think.'

'Dad. Trust me. I asked you to lock me in and now I'm asking you – with a clearer head than I've had in years – to leave the door open. You must at some point. It's time. You can trust me. I promise.'

Frank nodded. 'Okay.' But it felt anything but okay.

'And, one last thing, did I give you my phone? I can't remember.'

He recalled the images she'd sent to her boyfriend; the messages about scoring drugs; and that horrendous scrote in his garden that had come looking for her. 'No. You didn't. I'm sorry.'

She sighed. 'Shit. It's not in any of my pockets.'

'No problem.' Frank edged towards the door. 'I'll get you a new one.'

'Thanks, but it's just… well…' She shook her head. 'It's okay.'

'Tomorrow. I'll bring one home after work with me – is that okay?'

She smiled. 'Good night, Dad.'

'Good night, Maddie.'

He closed the door and looked down at the lock. He rustled in his pocket for the key, pulled it out and stared at it. Then he looked at the keyhole.

Listen, Dad, you can leave the door open now…

He moved the key towards the lock. She'd hear.

You can trust me. I promise.

He nodded and drew back.

Later, while he was in his own bed for the first time in

eight days, he listened to Charlotte Wilson's demo tape over and over.

She'd the voice of an angel.

I'm sorry you never had the chance to heal before someone took you, Charlotte.

He wished that she could have felt like he did right now.

Like everything was coming back together.

Chapter Thirty-One

Julie Fletcher struggled to get the key into her lock.

She batted away the hands working at her blouse beneath her coat. 'Steady, man, need to get the sodding key in.'

Ron obliged.

'And I told you to hold off until I was ready, didn't I? I've a thirteen-year-old son in there.' She continued trying to jab the key into the lock, failing every time.

Maybe she shouldn't be too harsh on the sex pest next to her for his wandering hands. Rum was having a major say in matters, and it'd been Julie that had persuaded him to drink more than he could handle.

'Thirteen?' Ron said. 'Bloody hell. How old are you?'

'Thanks. It's nice to hear I look too young to have a kid.'

'Yes... I... well, I didn't—'

'Don't get all embarrassed on me now, you daft sod. Winding you up. I had him when I was forty-two... You think fifty-five is too old to have a teen boy?' She looked at him with a raised eyebrow.

He shook his head. She wondered if he was red-faced

from embarrassment, or lust; the wandering hands had let up for the moment, which suggested the former.

'Or do I look older than fifty-five?' She laughed. She pinched his flabby cheek and shook it. 'Don't sweat it. At least we're both old enough to know what we want.'

She tried the key again, and this time, she dropped it. 'Shit!'

He knelt, groaning.

'Watch you don't put your back out, Ron.' She stared down at his bald spot as he rustled on the ground for the key.

Eventually, he grabbed it, and lifted his head. 'Let me.' He looked so proud of himself!

God, I know how to pick them!

Not that it'd last long, anyway. The men she dated always seemed to like the idea of a woman who enjoyed drinking too much. But when they realised the baggage that came with, interest quickly waned.

Ron would last a month at the most.

In a way, though, it got easier to jump to the next, the older she got. Older men gravitated towards her; they usually lacked confidence approaching anyone younger than them. It was a new world. They probably feared the judgement and wrath that came with coming on to someone from a younger generation.

But it was a win-win for her. Older men tended to be far wealthier than their younger counterparts, especially the married ones. Divorced ones had often been taken to the cleaners already.

She wasn't stupid. She knew she'd a drink problem, but at least it wasn't costing her to service it. This allowed the money she earned in the day job in Morrisons to go on raising Tom. Her son.

'You're a gentleman.' Julie edged to one side as Ron attacked the door with the recovered key. 'And remember, best behaviour. It's past eleven so Tom will be up in bed, but' – she put her finger to her mouth – 'if he wakes, you're not coming in. You're not meeting him at his hour.'

'I'll be like a bloody mouse,' he said, rather loudly, before slipping the key home.

'Oh, I should also warn you about—'

The door opened before Ron turned the key.

'My dad,' she finished.

Arnold Fletcher stood in the doorway with that familiar, stern expression on his face.

Despite being eighty-five, Arnold had kept most of the height he was blessed with from his younger years. And despite his arthritis, still held himself upright into a commanding posture, albeit supported with an especially long walking stick.

Ron looked back at Julie, his mouth falling open.

Feeling like a rumbled teenager, she couldn't help but giggle. She hadn't expected him up after eleven. He rarely roamed around this late. And to be honest, he knew about her many partners and tried to stay out of the way. Judging by his face of thunder, though, something was on his mind.

Julie stepped alongside Ron. 'Dad, this is—'

'I don't care,' Arnold said.

Her father still possessed that same air of authority he always had done, but there was a notable difference in how she responded to it now than in her teens and even her twenties. Back then, she'd crumbled under this familiar gaze and command; now, she was long in the tooth, too, and ground down with years of disappointment, misfortune, and alcohol, she hadn't the energy to respect his old-fashioned ways.

That didn't negate the fact that she *needed* him.

His pension kept the household ticking over.

But he *also* needed her.

Without her, he'd be in a nursing home and living out his ultimate fear. Watching others around him of the same age, or younger, letting go of life.

Arnold was a self-proclaimed man of dignity. He'd most certainly make that clear to Ron if she didn't intervene.

Arnold said, 'Young man, I—'

'Dad, he's not young. You're just ancient,' Julie said.

Arnold ran his fingers through his shock of white hair, and his face reddened. He stared at Ron. 'It's better you go now.'

'It's my house!' Julie said.

'It's okay.' Ron held his palms up, and glanced at Julie, looking awkward. 'It's best I go.'

Arnold nodded.

Thanks Dad, Julie thought. *That was the fastest one yet to bite the dust, and he's got his own yacht... or so he said, anyway.*

She rolled her eyes. Was she that bothered? *Was* it worth an argument with her dad? And potentially waking Tom...

Ron turned, smiled at Julie, made a gesture of placing a phone to his ear.

Bollocks... 'Get back home to your wife,' she said.

'I'm not...' He broke off when he caught her raised eyebrow. Knowing it was pointless, he scarpered.

She couldn't resist another giggle. *God, it really was like being a rumbled teenager. The terrified boy running off with his tail between his legs.*

When she turned back, her father hadn't moved, or changed his expression.

'Funny?' he asked.

'In some ways,' she said.

'And you don't think any of this is disgusting?'

'Well, you do. You tell me often.'

'Your mother—'

'I know! Would turn in her grave... except we had her cremated.'

His eyes widened. He lifted his stick and pointed it at her. 'Don't you dare, young lady. Don't you dare mock and joke.'

She took a deep breath, forcing back another retort. It was the alcohol. Causing an escalation with an eighty-five-year-old man was pointless. It wouldn't solve anything. They both needed each other and would continue to suffer each other. She walked past him. 'Surprised you're even up.'

'I wasn't.'

'Oh...' She turned. 'So that loudmouth woke you?'

Arthur's expression softened. He shook his head, turned and closed the door. He stood there for a moment, so the silence stretched long enough for Julie to hear a noise from upstairs.

'Tom?' she asked.

He sighed.

She listened. She could hear her son weeping.

Her father turned back. 'Nothing to do with your adulterer out there. I'm up because Tom did it again. He's in your bed. Good job I intercepted before you dragged that lout in there with you!'

Julie felt her heart drop. Her son had wet the bed again. 'Shit.' She looked up the stairs. 'I'll go to him.'

'Why bother?' Arnold asked.

'Not now... don't be nasty, Dad. You know what'll happen.' She often lost control of her temper.

'I'm not being nasty, Julie. I'm just asking, why you keep doing this? You cause these problems, don't you? All you do is solve the issue and then do it again.'

'Do what? I'm allowed a life, too, you know.'

'Different men all the time? Drinking? Hangovers? You think a thirteen-year-old boy isn't affected by that?'

'Like you ever cared about your family. You only ever cared what other people *thought* of us. Our emotions were always secondary to you. How many times did I piss my bed?'

He nodded, looked down, and sighed.

'You were rarely even there,' she continued. 'You always chose your political chums over your own family. Councillor Fletcher!'

He sighed again. 'I loved you... still do. And I love Tom. He's our priority. *Your* priority.' Using his stick for support, Arnold walked past her, down the hallway, keeping his head held upright, as if he was auditioning for a parade. It looked like an act, but of course, it wasn't. If he didn't force himself, rigidly, into the posture he desired, he'd start to fold and hunch.

She waited until his door was closed and then went up to her son.

Chapter Thirty-Two

'*Chef!*'

Paul Harrison, who was just praising Ray on stepping up to the plate, almost jumped out of his skin.

He spun, pressing a hand to his chest and fixing the Maître d' with a stare. 'What've I told you about that?'

Kristoff came round the counter, breaking the sodding rules by leaving his hands unwashed, and gripped Paul's shoulders. 'Chef... they... they...'

'Loved it?'

'*Bloody* loved it.'

'Of course they did,' his stand-in sous chef said, coming up alongside Paul. 'Because it was a sodding masterpiece!'

Paul smiled at Ray. He'd already imparted Arthur's mantra onto him at the beginning of the session. *Greatest struggle... greatest masterpiece...*

Paul shook off Kristoff's hands and threw an arm around Ray's shoulders. He leaned in and kissed him on the forehead. 'Team effort.'

'Jesus, Chef!' Ray wiped his brow.

'Not quite.' Paul grinned. 'But almost, by the sounds of it.'

'They want to see you,' Kristoff said. '*Now*.'

'Who can blame them?' He was riding a wave of confidence and euphoria. He took the towel off his shoulder, threw it onto the counter, turned to his kitchen, raised his hands and clapped his team as he backed towards the door.

To the background cries of 'Go, *Chef*!' Paul followed Kristoff out onto the restaurant floor.

The Thomas brothers and a group of around six people stood up from the biggest table in the restaurant's corner. Roy Thomas, the elder of the two at seventy-three, and by far the richest, made a clapping gesture. When Paul was close enough, Roy said, 'Bravo, Chef... knocked it out the park.'

Paul smiled. 'Thank you, sir. But I must mention a team the envy of every restaurant in North Yorkshire back in the kitchen.'

'Modest,' Phil Thomas, the younger brother, said. 'But bask in the glory, Chef! What you've done here is nothing short of incredible. I mean, don't get me wrong, as a young man I loved the crab shack they'd set up here, and when I heard you were getting the bulldozers in, I considered taking a hit out on you, but—'

He couldn't finish his sentence; everyone was laughing too hard.

'Glad I didn't. Turns out you made the right call with your demolition crew. A crab shack is one thing, but we want this restaurant to be pulling in crowds from all over the country.' The Thomas brothers looked at each other. 'A timely boost for tourism, too, I feel, following the last five years!'

Paul nodded. 'I'm grateful for your confidence.'

Roy waved him away as he sat. 'Come off it, Chef! No one cooks like that without balls full of confidence. Your balls are big enough without ours!'

More laughter filled the table as Roy and Phil sat, followed by their entourage.

'Can I get you another two bottles of Sassicaia?' Paul asked.

'Only if you drink a glass with us,' Roy said.

'One!' Phil said. 'Typical Yorkshire man... can't share.'

More laughter.

'Have as many glasses as you like...' Roy smiled. 'Just this once!'

'Ha! I would, but I've work to do!' *Plus, I've already slipped back into my office for several more glugs of whisky.*

Paul turned. Kristoff was staring at him from the kitchen doors, ready to make a move when required. Paul summoned him over. The Maître d' approached and met him halfway on the restaurant floor. Paul didn't wish to disturb everyone's meal with this unfolding show, but the customers didn't look put out. They appeared more than happy to watch. Paul himself was a bit of a local celebrity, and the Thomas brothers were seriously big news. 'Two more bottles of Sassicaia.'

Kristoff's face fell.

'Don't...'

'Sorry, Chef, but—'

'Okay, do we have any other Super Tuscan in?'

'Ornellaia.'

'Okay, two of them will do. They'll be okay with that, and—'

Paul's blood froze over. He clutched Kristoff's arm.

'Chef?'

Surely not?

Paul squinted. The woman dining alone at the far end of his restaurant was familiar.

God... no...

He gulped. Even though he only had a profile, and she'd aged considerably since he'd last seen her, the likeness was undeniable... terrifyingly so.

Was it her? His stomach turned. What the hell was she doing here?

'Chef... are you okay?'

Paul opened his mouth to speak, but no words emerged.

'Chef, *talk* to me.'

'Don't look now. But over there, at the back, do you recognise that woman?'

He glanced over, then looked back, shaking his head. 'No...'

But why would Kristoff recognise her? He'd never have met her.

'Get me her name,' Paul said.

'Give me a tick.' Kristoff went over to Lyndsey at the hostess stand.

'Is everything okay?' Roy had approached him from behind.

Paul swung. He smiled, trying to mask the cold sensation threatening to bring him to his knees. 'Fine... out of Sassicaia, but we've Ornellaia.'

Roy clapped a hand on his shoulder. 'No problem then, eh? And trust me, when this place gets its first Michelin, you won't be running out of any decent bottles of plonk again! I assure you.'

Paul tried to focus on Roy's words and slow his breathing, but it was a tall order. In fact, he could feel his respiration speeding up, and his heart was thrashing so hard now that he thought it might just come out of his chest.

'Come on then, Chef.' Roy turned back towards his table and led the way.

As Paul followed, Kristoff came up alongside him.

'Who is it?'

When Kristoff said her name, his stomach turned again, and he stared ahead at the smiling investors, who could have bought a small country, awaiting him.

He was going to lose control.

She couldn't be here. Surely, it wasn't possible. And if she was. Why? *Why come?*

Was he imagining things? Her profile. Kristoff's words. Was his mind exhausted from stress, alcohol, and Wagyu beef perfection?

He glanced back.

And now she was standing. Staring *dead* ahead. At him.

Nothing had ever felt so surreal.

He turned back to the smiles of his potential investors and felt Kristoff clutching his arm.

Glancing right, he saw Kristoff wasn't there, and the clutching was, in fact, a cramp.

A cramp becoming progressively worse.

Not that...

He grabbed his numbing arm.

Anything but that...

The pain spread quickly over his chest, and then he was falling.

Chapter Thirty-Three

In the darkness, Julie Fletcher lay beside her thirteen-year-old boy. Tom had been sobbing when she'd climbed into her bed beside him, but after turning onto his side and looping his arm over her, he'd drifted quickly back off to sleep.

Now, over an hour later, the tears were in her eyes instead.

Other kids Tom's age, with single parents living this life, may have gone off the rails and been very vocal that change was imperative. Tom, however, had toiled away under a black cloud of anxiety that was causing him night terrors and bedwetting, and never challenged her.

It was selfish of her. Was she causing this? Was her father right?

Tom had always differed from many of his friends.

He'd had severe hearing issues until five, and his language and development had been delayed considerably. And although his hearing was back on track, the development was taking an age to catch up. Tom was still very childlike, and not at all like some of his teenage friends, who were already breaking curfews, and showing an interest in girls.

He was happy with computer games, Marvel films and, to her bewilderment, being with his mother.

But he certainly wasn't happy at school.

Sometimes, she'd have to pick him up early, because of his anxiety, and drop him off with her father, Arnold, while she went back to work.

She should be helping him, not making everything worse.

What kind of shitty person am I?

She kissed Tom on the forehead.

I'm sorry...

She ran her fingers through his hair.

Her heart sank when she considered the path her own anxiety had taken her on since childhood.

I won't let you become me, Tom. I won't let you find the answers in the wrong places. She kissed his head again. *I won't let it happen.*

I can't.

Tom needed her now. More than ever.

So, as the alcohol took Julie to sleep, she vowed to take control of her life.

But then she dreamed about drinking, dancing and sex, and when she woke the next morning, she felt as she always did.

Trapped in that same spiral.

Chapter Thirty-Four

Frank had slept better than he'd done in almost a fortnight, but it still fell a long way short of perfection.

He'd been out of bed at least ten times to check on her, every time breathing a sigh of relief, before returning to bed and falling asleep with a single thought on his mind: *she's still here.*

Only to wake again thirty minutes later in a cold sweat.

In a way, he was glad when it turned five, and he could break away from the loop.

Before leaving for work, he stared over at Maddie from her door, weighing up whether to approach and kiss her on the forehead or not. Deciding against waking her, he headed outside.

He almost made it to his car before suffering another cold sweat, and a sudden increase in his heart rate.

Turning, he looked back at his home, considering that unlocked bedroom.

No, Frank. Leave her. Trust her.

He turned and opened the door of his Volvo, grunted and nodded.

She'll come good.

Chapter Thirty-Five

Frank thought it was impressive that he made it to IR3 for a quarter to six until he saw Gerry, hard at work on the computer. Rylan was asleep at her feet. He clearly wasn't an early riser like the rest of them.

'Did you get your four hours?' he asked Gerry as he approached.

'No. Rylan's been sick.'

Frank knelt, wincing over the usual stiffness in his back. He stroked the Lab's head. 'A tummy bug, eh?'

'No,' Gerry said. 'Barnaby gave him a dog biscuit...'

'Bloody hell... after the warning you gave him?' *Takes some balls that.* 'My father always said not to trust a man with a flowery shirt.'

'Why?'

He shrugged. 'Good question. He always had a distrust, or rather distaste, for the flamboyant. Anyway, how can you be sure it was Barnaby's biscuit?'

'When I collected my bag late afternoon, before he closed, I saw the jar was open again on the counter. He'd put it away earlier after I refused the biscuit. He also told me he'd had no customers at all that day.'

Jesus, you're observant. 'Why didn't you say something?'

'By that point, it was too late. Flagging it up would serve no purpose.' She shook her head. 'Anyway, sleeping *less* than four hours is better than sleeping longer, so I should be okay.'

'You know yourself well.' *Best way to be, rather than like old muggins here, stumbling around in the darkness for most of his life...*

He walked over to the board.

I'm better with an obvious purpose.

He looked up at Charlotte Wilson's school photo.

Chapter Thirty-Six

FRANK WANTED to be open-minded about the detectives that Donald had chosen. But he just couldn't shake an image of a smiling Donald waving the V sign at him from his mind. A completely unrealistic image of course. Donald never smiled.

To be honest, Frank was probably being unfair to these detectives. He knew little about the two youngest ones, Detective Constable Sharon Miller, and Detective Constable Sean Groves. There were no memos on them as there'd been with Gerry. If there had, he'd have read them. He wasn't about to make that mistake again.

He resolved himself to be positive. Sean and Sharon could yet turn out to be great.

Detective Sergeant Reggie Moyes, on the other hand, was a foregone conclusion. Frank knew Reggie well enough. He was currently listening to the plonker telling Sharon and Sean that he preferred to be called Reggie rather than Reg. Frank had heard it a thousand times before. He'd used to provide a reason for this request. 'Reg makes me sound like an old man!' However, ten years back, an outspoken youngster had seen fit to quip that he *was* an old man, and Reggie had broken trend as a loveable rogue to make a formal complaint and get the upstart disciplined.

Frank and Reggie couldn't be any more different. Frank had little desire to be liked. At least, little desire to force people to like him. He found it peculiar that excessive vanity, a false interest in others, laughing at things that weren't funny, and smiling when it was raining, earned you boatloads of friends. Whereas moaning and being down to earth earned you nothing but contempt.

He believed in truth and honesty, not performance.

Reggie was currently over-celebrating Rylan having a place on the team like it marked the most important shift in society since Rosa Parks had taken that seat...

'And why not?' Reggie asked. 'About time this archaic institution caught up with the times. I saw an article about therapy dogs in schools. Changing lives. Good on you, Gerry, for pushing these agendas through.'

Frank watched Gerry's response. He was trying to figure out if she was impressed with Reggie's compliment, or repulsed, as he was, by his constant need to please. But to be honest, it was impossible to tell if she was even paying attention.

'Look Gerry, you ever need me to take him for a walk, grab some food, whatever, let me know. I love dogs, always have. Got one at home I like to run with. Sandy. She'll easily do five miles.' Reggie winked, although Gerry wasn't looking to see it. 'She can almost keep up with me.'

Frank rolled his eyes as Reggie laughed over his own joke, which, of course, wasn't really a joke, because he most certainly believed it.

'Anyway. Shall we get to it?' Frank said. 'I've got to get to Middlesbrough.'

Reggie nodded and smiled up at him.

Shit... no way your teeth should shine like that at your age.

'Okay, no HOLMES 2 operative, so thank you Gerry for taking on the honour. Let's keep everything thorough. These old cases have a habit of getting messy and tangled. Thanks for joining us, Sharon and Sean.'

The two colleagues, obviously acquainted with one another, sat together. Whereas Sharon had a youthful glow and an air of confidence about her, helped along by long, striking red hair, Sean looked pale, hunched and not at ease. Frank wondered if he'd got wind of his reputation. *All exaggerated. I won't bite, young man. You're better off being wary of the better dressed senior in the room, sitting close to you. He'll stab you in the back at the drop of a hat.*

'Most of the images on the board are in the pack in front of you, and I know you'll have all read up on it last night.' He moved his fingers between images. 'The remains... the close-up on the blunt-force trauma... the suitcase. Now, it seems strange that whoever buried her chose to do it in the vicinity of an iconic landmark, but it was sixty-four metres away from the whalebones, on the other side of the fence which runs alongside the Pavilion Drive car park. If it'd been the dead of night, the car park may have been empty.' He traced an enlarged map with his finger. 'Several metres from the start of that fence, and we have the spot where she was buried. Not the most secluded place in the world, but low risk, I guess. A woodland would've been better though. So, I suspect Charlotte must have died somewhere near to this area, making quick disposal a necessity. I'd be surprised if this was a planned murder.

'It's also significant that the public house the Mariner's Lantern is close by on East Terrace. The photograph recovered from the guitar case shows she was in there at some point with a young man of a similar age. Look at the initials on the back. C + DR, 1987. I suspect the initials on the back, DR, refer to the young man.

'After the Mariner's Lantern burned down, it was replaced with the Saltwick Sailor, which you may or may not be familiar with.'

'*Too* familiar with,' Reggie said, rubbing his forehead extravagantly, 'from what I remember! I'd like to volunteer for that gig, though. A trip down memory lane. A hazy trip, mind!'

No one laughed.

Read the room, dickhead. Nervous kid, a young lass rolling her eyes, and Gerry, who, by your own admission, is different, remember?

Oh, and me.

Frank locked his eyes on Reggie. 'I'd like to keep this quick so I can get off to Middlesbrough, right?'

Another nervous smile and flash of white teeth from Reggie.

Frank looked between the eyes of his other colleagues now. 'And, of course, we've got the tape. I'm assuming you've all listened to the recordings. If not, make that a priority. I've had a go at transcribing some lyrics. Rarely go in for the metaphorical myself, all too airy for me, but there was something very personal driving this lass.' He threw a quick glance at Charlotte on the board and nodded. Then, he turned back. 'Obviously, we'd like a bigger team, but this is what we've got… for now, anyway. So, I've tried to break down today's approach into four. First, family. Now, unless something changes in our information, we've one living relative. The mother. Laura Wilson. Now, I'm going to stress that again… for you all… *the mother*. Think of her loss. This was 1987, folks. Three of you weren't even born—'

'Spring chickens you lot!' Reggie said.

Frank glared at him. *One more interruption, and I'm going to bloody lose it and embarrass both of us in entirely different ways. The difference being, I don't give a shit about being embarrassed.* Reggie lowered his head.

Frank pointed at the image of Charlotte with the young lad. 'In 1987, Laura Wilson lost her only child. It's a long time. Charlotte was eighteen. *Eighteen.* The pain Laura Wilson feels now when she wakes every day will be the same as she felt almost forty years ago. I want you all to understand that. Not knowing what happened to her would have been awful. Now that she knows Charlotte's never coming home, she's got to start her grieving process properly. There's a lot of time, a lot of pain and trauma...' He glanced back at the team. 'If we can give Laura Wilson something back, then we will do. Charlotte would've been fifty-five. That's a lifetime. That's marriage... children of her own. Someone took that from her. Took it, and when that wasn't enough, took any hope of Laura moving on with her life, by making it a secret that would stay buried forever. Thanks to the Whitby storms, we've been given a chance to right that wrong. So, we begin where it will eventually end, with compassion for the family. *I'll* visit Laura.'

He paused and took a deep breath. 'Charlotte disappeared on September 18th, 1987. There was an investigation. So, our second line of enquiry involves speaking to those involved in the missing person's case. Let's find out what CID got up to and found out, and why they gave up. Are you okay with that one, Sharon?'

Sharon nodded, eyes widening.

'In between her own tasks, Gerry can support you on

that. Reggie, you get your wish. I'd like you to take Sean and go to the Saltwick Sailor and speak to the landlord, Marvin Hails. But take your chuffing water bottle. No drinking on duty! The Saltwick Sailor is a different pub to the Mariner's Lantern, I know, but connections *could* remain. Meanwhile, Gerry, if you continue with the evidence we already have, as well as dragging up everything you can find on the Mariner's Lantern's history and demise. We'll reconvene here around four.'

He looked up at Charlotte again.

All right, lass, let's see your mother.

Chapter Thirty-Seven

Sensing he was being watched, David opened his eyes.

Hanna, sitting upright in bed, stared down at him.

Her swollen right eye had darkened overnight.

Disappointing. She'd have to be careful in conversation with others over the next week or so.

'Good morning.' He smiled.

'Good morning.' She looked away.

No smile. Unusual.

He wondered if she'd break behaviour patterns further and mention last night's incident. Hopefully not. He'd early appointments and wanted to get a move on.

Last night, she'd been contrite for triggering him. And it was important that his loss of control, that *small, rather insignificant moment*, was water under the bridge. Besides, as he'd explained to her, that she'd the potential to trigger him, when no one else ever really did, actually showed how strong his feelings for her were. 'How much I love you.'

David reached up and stroked her cheek on the undamaged left side. 'Do you want to go out for dinner this evening?'

'That would be nice... David?'

'Yes.'

'Do you regret not having children?'

He took a deep breath, sighing internally. It seemed, unfortunately, that there were some lingering aftereffects of last night's conflict. 'Why are you asking that now?'

'I was just thinking about it the other day.'

He sat up. 'I thought you were preoccupied with all the painting?'

'I've had a bit of a lull.'

He put an arm around her shoulders.

'I keep thinking that we missed out on something,' she said.

He kissed the side of her head. 'Honey... really? The life we lead! We can do whatever we want when we want!' – he thought better than to mention the holiday home he was eying up on a ski resort for now – 'And when I retire, there'll be no time for either of us to regret anything.'

'Still... when I look at Maisie, she seems so *excited* when she sees her grandson, and Lucy, so *happy* when she has her granddaughter over—'

Feeling a flicker of irritation, he tightened his arm around her shoulders. Only a little. She'd notice, but it wouldn't cause discomfort. 'And when my friends talk about divorce, and younger women, am I then supposed to question the life I built?'

'It's different—'

'How so? What have I told you about looking at others for answers?'

'Yes, I know, but it's all they talk about—'

'No, Hanna. I want you to repeat what I've told you again and again.'

'I don't—'

He tightened his arm; it still wouldn't hurt, but it should be convincing.

'Don't look at other people to judge your own happiness,' she said.

'Yes. And?'

'You don't know what's really going on. They could be deeply unhappy and choose not to tell you about it.'

Almost word for word, now. The pride of her learning soothed his irritation and he loosened his grip. Still, best she knew that enough was enough. 'You know how many times a day I tell others not to use friends and family as a yardstick to measure their own happiness? It gets tedious.' *As it does here, too, my love.* 'Are you happy, Hanna?'

'I'm not saying—'

'It's a simple question.'

'Yes. I'm happy.'

And he believed her. Despite their difficulties, and the way she sometimes looked at him in the aftermath of his loss of control, they'd a close bond. He knew, deep down, she felt secure.

'It was because of me, though.' There were tears in her eyes now. 'I couldn't give you children, and ... I feel...'

He pulled his arm away and swung his legs out of bed. 'Hanna... really? Honestly?' He stood up and stretched out. 'You couldn't have children. I never longed for them before. Why would I suddenly want them now?' He headed to the wardrobe for his clothes. 'I've no desire to look after grandchildren like Maisie and Lucy, instead of heading off on a cruise.' He took out an ironed white shirt.

'I don't know... I wonder if you...' She broke off.

He swung, holding the shirt by the coat hanger. 'Go on.'

'I don't know.'

'Go on.' He slipped the shirt from the hanger.

Hanna looked away. 'I'll make us tea.'

'Finish what you were going to say, love. I insist.'

She looked back at him.

He smiled, trying to be reassuring as he put his shirt on.

'Well, I wonder if you would have been different if you'd had children.'

'Different?' He buttoned his shirt while he stared at her. 'Different how?'

She shook her head and stood. 'I don't know. I'm just confused.'

David turned and plucked a tie from the cupboard. He tied it beneath his collar. 'No, I'm listening. Different *how*, my love*?*'

She didn't respond.

He turned and sighted her heading for the door. '*How?*' he called, fixing his tie.

She paused and looked back. 'Less focused on... well... other things. More open, and caring. Less...' She broke off again.

'Less *what*, Hanna?'

The colour drained from her face. 'I don't know.' She turned back, near the door now.

'Less focused on myself?'

She opened the door. 'No.'

'Less controlling?' And there it was again. That word. That trigger. Except he'd said it this time. But had she thought it? She *had,* hadn't she? How dare she! The bitch!

He gritted his teeth and squeezed his eyes shut.

In this moment, he saw that rotten woman.

Weak from the cancer.

Instructing him, in her last days, to change.

To be different.

To cast off his real self like a disgusting, slimy snakeskin.

My own mother... ashamed... not willing to accept me—

'You're too controlling, David.' It'd been the day before her death. 'Expecting us, everyone, to do what you say. You must change. You can't live like this. You can't keep hurting others.'

He could feel that anger again.

Out of nothing.

Red mist from somewhere inexplicable.

When he opened his eyes, Hanna was gone.

He looked at his clenched fists and then swooped for an empty coat hanger from the wardrobe.

He snapped it in half.

Chapter Thirty Eight

'You gave me quite the scare,' Jess said.

'I gave myself quite the scare, too.' Paul sat up in his hospital bed. 'Was certain I was a goner. Panic attack, they reckon. Except, I've never had one in my life before.'

Jess took his hand. He sighed and closed his eyes. Feeling her skin against his was always remarkably pleasant.

'Much better than a heart attack,' she said.

'Yes.' He looked down at their joined hands. Then, he raised his head and winked. 'Every cloud has a silver lining...'

She slipped her hand out of his. 'No more sympathy.'

He smiled and nodded, respecting her decision. Their affair had ended ten months ago. She'd opted to make it work with her husband. At first, he'd felt devastated, but he knew his place. If he wanted to keep her as his sous chef, and by God he did, then he'd have to suck up the rejection.

Besides, he was fifteen years older than her and was an absolute car crash with long-term relationships. It'd never have lasted. And no way was he putting Jess through that. He adored her too much.

'What do you think caused it?' Jess asked.

'Stress... alcohol... yes, I know, what a dickhead, eh? Started hitting the Macallan.'

She drew back, widened her eyes. 'Yes, you really are a dickhead! I thought you were saving that for us.'

'You said that we were never to drink together again!'

'Good point. Can you think of anything else that may have caused the panic?'

He sighed. 'Some delusions?'

'Eh?'

'Thought I saw someone from the past. Someone it couldn't possibly be. I'm fifty-five.' He touched his head. 'Maybe it's falling to pieces in here.'

'Not sure that it was ever in one piece.'

'Ha! I thought you were here to make me feel better. Anyway, tell me... Charlie... all good?'

'Surgery went fine. They caught it all early. Pretty routine, the surgeon reckoned.'

'Sorry for being a dick last night.'

'Used to it. Don't worry. I *know* what it's like when you're in the zone. Turns you into a selfish, gibbering wreck!'

She always grinned to herself when she was being sarcastic. Enjoying this familiarity with her, he watched her closely. If there'd been anyone, anyone at all in his life he could settle down with, it was her. *Banish those thoughts, Paul. You won't do that to her. You won't destroy your relationship.* 'Take the night off,' he said.

'*So* understanding.' She grinned again. 'Hey, that doesn't mean you're going in, does it?'

He shrugged.

'No chance,' she said.

'Bollocks. Heart like an ox, the doctor just told me.'

'You passed out in the middle of your restaurant.'

Paul cracked his knuckles. 'I won't have the Thomas brothers sizing me up tonight though, will I? And I won't be drinking...'

'Bloody hell, you're a nightmare. One night off, at least?'

'I'll think about it.'

'Go in and I'm done. *Resigning.*' She widened her eyes.

'Shit, Chef. Best listen then, hadn't I? One night off.'

He reached over for a glass of water on the bedside table. His mouth and throat felt permanently dry, probably because of the panic and anxiety of the previous evening. As he drank, he watched her texting. 'Your husband?' he said, after swallowing.

She didn't grace him with a response. 'So, who's this person you imagined?'

He flinched as he recalled seeing her in profile. Alone, eating, nonchalant, her presence a complete oddity. Unsettling... unnerving. 'A scary lady from long ago... when I was practically a kid.'

'Go on.'

'A teacher who used to make me sit in the corner of the room,' he lied.

'Can't blame her.'

He took another mouthful of water and placed it down. Now, he recalled his *delusion* standing there, staring at him, older than he remembered her. Yet, *still* her. Eyes full of judgement and condemnation.

The woman who'd once tried to kill him.

Impossible.

It had to have been a hallucination.

'I've to go... are you sure you're okay?' Jess asked.

'I made a complete tit out of myself in front of the Thomas brothers, so, not really, no.'

'Behave. They still love you. I mean... that looks like a nice whisky they've sent over for you...'

By his belongings, over by his door, was a bottle of Glenlivet Archive 21. It'd sit nicely next to the quarter-drunk Macallan.

Paul nodded. 'Yes. Thanks Jess.' He took her hand this time. 'I couldn't have done it without you.'

'Behave. I wasn't even there.'

'No... we built that together. I'd say grab that whisky and toast new beginnings... except, wait a second, your no-drinking rule?'

'I'm sure we can make an exception when the deal goes through,' she said. 'And there're no doctors present.'

There was a flash in her eyes as she said that. *Was she flirting?*

He turned away. *Don't even think it...*

'Did you hear what they found up by the whalebone arch?'

Paul turned his eyes slowly back to Jess. 'No... what?'

'Human remains.'

He took a deep breath and closed his eyes.

For a brief second, he was eighteen, back working in the restaurant Captain Cook's Galley, next to the Mariner's Lantern on East Terrace. Often, he'd take a break and a short stroll up to the bones to smoke. Sometimes alone. Sometimes with someone else.

He closed his eyes and recalled *her* smile.

She'd had such a beautiful smile.

Heart beating faster, he reached over, squeezed Jess' hand again, and opened his eyes.

Chapter Thirty-Nine

Julie sat in the cramped office. Opposite her, her manager regarded his notes.

Usually a jovial fellow, his serious expression concerned her.

She'd been here before, several times, and, on those occasions, the atmosphere had been remarkably different.

In fact, the last time she was here, she'd won employee of the month!

Customers liked her. In five years of working here, she'd only had one customer complain. And Judy Teller was infamous for complaining about everyone. No one in Morrisons had escaped her wrath.

'Everything all right?' Julie asked.

Lionel looked up at her. 'I'm sorry, Julie, but I'm going to have to suspend you.'

Her stomach felt full of rocks. 'What? Why?'

'We've CCTV of you around the back of the store on your break and—'

'How? What? Why was I being watched?'

'Random equipment checks... nothing untoward. It was just one of those things—'

'Is that even allowed?' She took a deep breath. 'Anyway... everyone goes around there to smoke!'

'I know, but it's not about smoking...'

She put her face into her hands.

'It's about the drinking.'

'Please... shit...' she murmured into her hands. 'Please.'

'I...' He broke off.

An awkward silence lingered.

When she dropped her hands and looked up, tears ran down her face. 'Please?'

He flushed and adjusted his spectacles on his nose. 'I'm sorry... Julie... but you're to be suspended pending an inquiry.'

'After which you'll sack me!'

'No one is saying that.'

'But I will be!'

He shook his head. 'I don't know.' He was clearly lying. 'Look, I wish I could do this differently, but—'

'Then, do it differently, Lionel!' She wiped tears away with the back of her hand. 'I've a bloody kid to support... and an ageing father, too, mind.'

'I know and I'm sorry... but it really is out of my hands.' To be fair to Lionel, he looked like he was going to burst into tears. Still, sympathy wouldn't help her. Not one bit.

This was going to leave her in a right mess.

Jesus, how had she let this happen? She was a high-functioning alcoholic, so she didn't suffer from hangovers, and when she took swigs of vodka on toilet breaks and lunch, she ensured she was careful to conceal all evidence of doing so.

Those bloody cameras!

Her drinking wasn't even a revelation to these people. Most of the people she worked with, including Lionel, knew she drank too much, but her ability to keep it away from her working life – at least, in their eyes — combined with job efficiency, had bought her years she should probably never have had.

'Who saw the CCTV footage?' Julie willed herself not to throw up.

'It doesn't matter,' Lionel said.

'*Who?* Mason?'

Lionel gave a swift nod.

Julie and Mason, the security guard, had never had a problem; actually, they got on like a house on fire.

However, he values his job... and did the right thing. Maybe, if I'd valued it more, I wouldn't be in this mess.

'If he reported it to you,' Julie said, feeling desperation grow, 'then the decision lies with you still?'

'Julie, please...'

'I've a growing boy.'

'Like I said, I know.'

'So?'

'So, if I let this slide, and Mason speaks to someone. Then what?' Lionel asked. 'I also have children.'

'Please... Lionel... there must be something you can do?'

She could tell that he was on the edge of tears. 'It's too late, anyway. It's formal. Julie, I'll do whatever I can. You've been exceptional in the workplace, and I'll fight your corner—'

'But I've got no chance, you know that!'

He lifted his glasses off, took a deep breath, and tried to look serious, despite his watery eyes. 'We can be positive... I'll try my best.'

'Bollocks! I'll never find another job!' She rubbed her

damp face with trembling hands. *CCTV? Random checks? Sounds like spying to me. This is bollocks...* She looked up. 'There's someone else involved, isn't there?'

Lionel flinched.

That was all she needed.

'Lionel?'

'Look, I...'

'Come on, at least give me the truth. There's a reason Mason watched that footage of me, isn't there? Someone reported me, I bet.'

'Julie...'

'Who was it?'

Lionel sighed.

'Who was it?'

He lowered his head.

Cassie...

Of course.

'Cassie?'

Lionel looked away.

'God, it was, wasn't it? That bitch hates me.' Julie stood. 'Do you know how screwed I am, Lionel? Because of Cassie? *Do you?*'

Lionel shook his head. 'I didn't say it was Cassie! Anyway... here is some paperwork. It'll discuss the next steps and you should consider getting in touch with this union—'

She kicked the rolling chair. It flew across the room and crashed into the wall.

'Thanks for nothing, Lionel. My kid's thirteen. My old man's eighty-five. And now we'll all have to live on his pension.' She turned.

'Wait... Julie... Mason must walk you out. It's policy—'

'Fuck off.' She stormed out.

Mason, tall and smartly dressed, was awaiting her. He looked sheepishly down. 'Julie, I—'

'Don't...' She waved him away. 'Not if you value your bollocks.' She stormed past him.

As she walked across the shop floor, weaving among customers, ignoring those who greeted her, and flashing angry looks at those who tutted when she blocked their view of the shelves, she felt everything teetering on the edge.

Not an unusual feeling for her, admittedly, but that didn't make it any more welcome.

When she reached the tills, the enormity of what was happening here finally sent her falling over the precipice. She scanned the tills and saw Cassie's eyes on hers.

Was that a smile?

Smug bitch.

Julie approached.

Yes... something about those eyes... pride? She'd heard Cassie slagging many people off behind their backs and always knew how insidious she could be. No one had ever been safe with her about. Julie's mistake had been to call her out one time over it. She hated gossips.

The bitch had cost her this job...

She hovered behind her at the till. 'Cassie—'

'Are you here to take over? I've still got fifteen minutes.' Cassie ran a block of cheese over the bar-code scanner.

Beep.

Julie looked up at an elderly couple packing bags at the front of the checkout.

Beep.

Then up at a regular customer, a middle-aged man, who dressed better every time he shopped, and always had a smile and a glint in his eye for Julie.

Beep.

Today, however, there was no glint. His eyes were lowered. He was able to sense her fury.

Julie hissed in Cassie's ear. 'I've a kid, you horrible bitch.' She grabbed her by the hair and dragged her screaming from the chair.

Chapter Forty

Frank couldn't resist stopping home on the journey to Middlesbrough.

Despite his concerns, Maddie hadn't upped and left.

He gave her an excuse about having forgotten his wallet.

Back outside in his Volvo, he wondered, *Am I forever doomed to worry?*

Nosy neighbour, Henrietta Timber, was questioning his presence with an enquiring peek out of her window.

After giving her a little wave, he clattered off down the road in Bertha, leaving a black cloud behind him.

En route to Middlesbrough, he considered playing Charlotte's demo again through his phone, before realising that you'd have more chance of listening to it to the backdrop of machine-gun fire.

Was he most disappointed that he couldn't fill this dead time by listening to those lyrics for clues and insights again? Or was it simply because he liked it so much?

He was a sucker for melodic guitar playing, and a female voice that could reach such a range.

He hummed instead, despite not being able to hear himself.

Broken.

That was the song that really had him by the throat.

And one line in the second verse that he simply couldn't get out of his head.

A child's laughter no more.

Chapter Forty-One

ON THE JOURNEY to Laura Wilson's, Frank couldn't help but think back to the disappearance of his own daughter.

It had stripped the happiness from his home.

For such a long time, there'd been no laughter. And when they had started start to laugh again, the guilt that followed those moments reached a whole new level of torture.

Still, Frank knew that he was one of the lucky ones. For a long time, he'd had Mary to share the pain with. Laura Wilson had been alone.

He parked outside her home and sighed.

Frank had also been lucky in that Maddie had come home to him. Laura would never experience that with Charlotte.

He left the Volvo, knocked on the door, and mentally prepared himself for a broken and dishevelled woman.

The lady who opened the door stood tall with her chest puffed out. Her hair was grey and cut into a bob, adding to a sophisticated look. She wore a blouse and a black skirt, looking smart, as if she was expecting distinguished guests, and not Frank, whose suit was long overdue a dry clean; combined with his excessive weight, he was as far from distinguished as a human being could be.

She was so different from what Frank had imagined, he wondered if this was, in fact, Margaret, the friend Laura had insisted she'd call last night to come and stay with her. However, when she spoke, he recognised the voice from their telephone call. 'DCI Black?'

'Aye.' He confirmed it with his identification. 'Thank you for seeing me, Ms Wilson. I'm so sorry for your loss.'

She nodded. 'Years back, your colleagues wanted me to believe Charlotte was out there. Wandering, free-spirited, happy in some kind of escape.' She smiled. 'They wouldn't listen to me when I told them that just wasn't possible. We were close. Very close. My daughter would never have left me that way.' She took a deep breath. 'So, thank you, DCI Black.'

'I've done nothing. I—'

'Nonsense,' Laura said. 'It's been thirty-seven years. She's coming home because of you.'

'I wasn't the one who found her, ma'am, I—'

'No, you misunderstand. My daughter *chose* you, DCI Black. To find the truth. And it's only right that I thank you for that. So, sincerely... thank you.'

No pressure then. Frank gulped and rolled his shoulders back.

Chapter Forty-Two

FRANK SAT in Laura's small lounge. It was quaint, rather than flashy. The television was a modest size, and the sofas had seen better days. The pictures of Charlotte that adorned the walls, and the mantlepiece, added to a warm, homely feel.

Frank thought of the many photographs of Maddie that Mary had put up around the house. Of course, they were all still there. Frank hadn't redecorated since Mary's passing and had sometimes wondered if he ever would do.

He wondered what Maddie thought of all those pictures of herself. Would she consider it overkill? He wondered if she'd want to help him upgrade the place.

'Tea, one sugar,' Laura said, entering the lounge and handing him a cup.

He preferred *three* sugars, but there was no time for change like the present; he'd a life-threatening waistline to take head-on.

'Wonderful photos,' Frank said. 'I never had an eye for a decent pic myself, not like my wife, Mary. You clearly have that same eye, Ms Wilson.'

'Please... Laura. You didn't need an eye for a picture when it came to Charlotte.'

Because she was beautiful. He stopped himself short of saying this, for fear of sounding inappropriate. 'She was very photogenic.'

Laura nodded. 'Thank you for saying so, DCI Black.'

He regarded how smart she looked again. She'd dressed specifically for this occasion. She really held Frank in high regard for setting this in motion. And now, she'd everything pinned on him. All her hopes for closure.

'Hey, if it's Laura, it's Frank, all right?'

'Okay, Frank. Can I admit to fibbing to you last night?'

He thought about it. 'Right... Margaret... aye. You didn't phone her, did you?'

'Once the shock settled, I had a brandy, and looked through some old albums and I felt a strange sense of peace.' She looked down at her cup of tea and then up again. 'When can I see her?'

The questions that Frank had expected last night on the phone were beginning. He was prepared for them and had considered his answers before arrival. He'd already promised himself that he'd be completely honest. To sugar-coat it would do her a disservice.

Frank leaned over and put his cup on the coffee table. 'That's something you can expect if you wish, Laura. But I think it best I make some things clear to you first. Charlotte's remains are... well... remains. I don't think that you'll find what you're looking for, or even see Charlotte through the process of viewing them.'

'So, she's a skeleton?' Laura gulped after the question, and her face twisted slightly, as if she couldn't believe she'd asked.

He nodded.

'And Charlotte's head... her *skull*... is it intact?'

'Yes. Her body, too,' Frank said. 'And if viewing her is something you genuinely wish to do, then I can arrange it.'

'Of course, I'll have her remains back for the burial, won't I?'

'Eventually,' Frank said. 'Once we get to the truth of the matter.'

Laura nodded. 'Yes, that's what she'd want. For me to know the truth. That's why she found you, Frank.'

Aye, so you keep saying. 'And we'll get there.'

'Last night you told me she didn't suffer.'

'We believe she died after a blow to the head, and so suspect it would have been quick.'

'Where?' Laura touched her forehead.

Frank touched the back of his head. 'Here.'

'Ah, I see. So, she may never have known?'

'That may have been the case. I certainly hope so.'

'Okay, I see. It sounds better to wait until *after* you find out what happened, and then I can have her remains taken and organised for burial.'

He nodded.

'There's one thing that I'd like, though. No negotiation, Frank, do you understand?'

He nodded. 'Go on...'

'That you take me to where you found Charlotte. I want to see where she's been resting all this time.'

Frank felt a flicker of surprise at her request, but he understood the need for closure, the desire to connect with a lost loved one. 'I'll have it organised.'

'And it must be you, Frank. I want you to take me.'

The weight of her trust settled on his shoulders. 'That won't be a problem.'

Laura looked up at the mantlepiece at a row of

photographs and smiled. Her gaze lingered there for more than a minute, and Frank merely kept his eyes lowered, giving her the time and space she needed.

He tried his best to keep his mind from the lyrics of 'Broken', but again and again, he found those same words in his mind.

A child's laughter no more.

There'd been happiness in this house. A lot. Surely.

What'd taken it away?

Who'd taken it away?

'Ask your questions, Frank. I'm ready,' she said as she stared at Charlotte's picture. 'In fact, I've always been ready.'

Chapter Forty-Three

Frank scribbled down Charlotte's father's name, John Asante, in his notebook.

Laura continued to talk about him. 'He was a good man, a kind man. He was Jamaican. Charlotte put him on a pedestal, and I did nothing but encourage that. Still, we were young, *so young*, when we had her, and I don't think there was ever any future for me and John. Not really.

'I was born in Ireland. My parents were devout Catholics. We emigrated here when I was five. They were, understandably, horrified when I became pregnant at fifteen. I'd lost my faith for a time but regained it after my parents forgave me. John's parents were religious, but he believed that religion took away independence. He was free-spirited and laid back... to be honest, we were complete opposites, which was probably what excited me. Charlotte was just like him. Try as I might, I could never steer her towards faith, but, you know, I'm okay with that. I liked her wilful attitude. Still, I didn't want her to make the same mistakes I did... so, I often warned her about boyfriends and getting pregnant too young.'

'How did you meet John?' Frank asked.

'He was playing guitar in a pub.'

Frank's pen nib paused on the notepad. Guitar player. *Like father, like daughter.*

She smiled. 'The Original Oak. Lots of younger people. Those interested in music rather than the other idiots getting hung up on ethnicity, which could be an issue for him back then. I was fifteen and in a pub! Even saying it now sends a shiver down my spine. My mother and father always thought I was staying at a friend's, revising. When the truth came out, their world came crashing down. I wasn't the best daughter... like I said, I lost my way a little back then. Underage drinking... it isn't just the current crop of kids who like to rebel!'

'Very true.'

She sighed. 'The world was going crazy for Bob Marley and here was John, Jamaican, a whizz on the guitar... incredible voice. He caught my eye.'

Frank nodded. 'From the missing person's report, I saw Charlotte was playing open mic nights at various pubs around North Yorkshire? I take it John taught her to play?'

'He didn't just teach her!' Laura's eyes widened. 'He gave it all to her. His talent.' She grinned. 'And then some! She was something else.'

Aye... I've heard her.

He was yet to mention the Whitby Wavefront Cabins, or rather, North Sea Nook Beach Huts, as they were named in 1987. He felt it was time to mention some of his early findings now. 'We recovered her guitar.'

Laura put a hand to her chest.

'A Martin D-35 acoustic guitar.'

She opened her mouth to speak, but nothing came out.

'Was it her father's?' Frank asked, trying to help her along.

She nodded. 'Yes... He gave it to her when she was eleven and he knew he was dying.' She chewed her bottom lip for a moment and then said, 'Was it with Charlotte?'

'No.' He leaned forward. 'Did you know about a beach hut in Whitby?'

Laura shook her head, her brow creased with confusion.

'We suspect Charlotte, or someone close to her, may have hired one long term, perhaps at a place called North Sea Nook Beach Huts. That's where we recovered her guitar.'

'A beach hut?' She shook her head 'No. She never told me about that'. She broke off, and Frank suspected she'd just recalled her own words from before. *It isn't just the current crop of kids who like to rebel.*

'Did you know she was visiting Whitby regularly?'

'Yes. But she was visiting other towns, too. Anywhere that would let her play open mic, really. Or, if she got lucky, paid gigs. She was obsessed. How long did she hire this beach hut for?'

'We're not sure at this stage. Records are difficult to recover from that era.'

'But where would she get the money for a beach hut? Those open mic slots she kept signing up for paid nothing. She got a few paid gigs, but it was a pittance.'

'A boyfriend, perhaps?'

Laura sighed. 'If she had a boyfriend, I knew nothing about it.'

Frank nodded, making notes. 'You said her father John used to gig at the Original Oak in Middlesbrough?'

She nodded.

'Is the pub still there?'

She shook her head. 'No, it's been gone a while now. It's derelict.'

'Did Charlotte ever gig there too? When she was old enough?'

'Not that I remember. She was on and off buses and trains all over North Yorkshire.' She looked over into space. 'I used to go out of my mind with worry, but she was eighteen. I trusted her and thought her responsible. She always let me know what time she'd be home and, if she was staying out, what friend she was staying with. That's how I knew she was gone, Frank. This wasn't a girl that ran away.'

Frank thought, *I never saw Maddie as a girl who would run away either.* 'Do you have any names of these pubs?'

She shook her head sadly. 'Not off the top of my head. But if I look through some lists, then maybe something will jump out?'

'We can arrange that.' Frank made another note.

Laura leaned forward, paling slightly. 'Should I have been more mindful, Frank? Was it a mistake to think I could trust her?'

Frank looked at her with sympathy. 'She was an adult, Laura. A young adult, but an adult. You weren't wrong to trust her; we must let them make their own way.'

Even if it backfires on you... as it seems to have done for both of us, Laura.

'Do you have children, Frank?'

'A daughter. Maddie. She's thirty-two.'

'And did you trust her?'

'Aye.' *And now I've got her back, I'm finding it difficult to do that again. You know, only this last week, I kept her locked up.* 'What happened to your daughter is no fault of yours. And when we get to the truth, I'm sure we'll discover that she was everything you believed her to be.' *At least I hope so, Laura. I really do.* 'So, you were always aware of where she was?' Frank asked.

'Yes… she'd tell me where she was going, and then, if she stayed with a friend, often through missing the last train or bus, she'd call me from a payphone. That's how I first knew something was wrong on that day. September 18th. She didn't call. That was the first time she didn't call.'

'And where did she tell you she was headed that day?'

'Scarborough. Although I can't remember the name. So, again, that list of pubs may help?'

Frank nodded. 'Can you remember how many calls you took from Whitby?'

'A fair few. We used to visit Whitby when she was a child, as you do. She knew I loved the sea. I remember one time her describing the sound of the sea and the smell of the air to me when she said she was staying at her friends. She mentioned those whalebones, too. Maybe the payphone was close to those whalebones?'

Frank wrote payphone and a question mark.

'You say a "fair few". How many times roughly do you think it was?'

'It was one of her most popular destinations. Once a week for a good couple of months? Maybe longer?'

He nodded. 'Any chance you can remember who Charlotte said she'd be staying with on the nights she phoned from Whitby? Any names?'

'I'm sorry. She never gave names. And I never pried. I never asked if there was a boyfriend, so I never knew. She was eighteen, remember? I was always conscious of smothering her. And I knew she thought I was slightly paranoid about her getting pregnant, so I didn't want to make her feel awkward about telling me until she was ready.'

He wrote 'boyfriend' and 'beach hut' and circled both.

'What happened to John?'

'He died when she was twelve. Cancer. It was a brief illness. Six months. We weren't together, but he visited regularly until he got too sick, and as I mentioned before, she had him on a pedestal. He encouraged her music to no end. It meant the world to her that guitar. She took it everywhere. I'm so glad you found it, Frank. I *must* have it back.' She looked up at a picture of her daughter again. 'She'd want that.'

Frank choked back a sigh. 'It's evidence... for now, Laura.'

She nodded. 'Then you must keep it.'

'How hard did her father's death hit her?'

'If you're suggesting she went off the rails, she didn't. She continued working hard at school, and then at college. She got her qualifications, but she threw herself entirely into her music. Obsessively so. I guess as well as a passion, it was almost her tribute to John. I always encouraged it. John deserved to be the centre of her life before and after he was gone...' She broke off and flinched. 'Her life.' She sighed. 'Do you need another drink, Frank?'

'No, thank you. I'm alright, but if you do, or you need a break, please, let me know.'

She reached over for a tissue on the table beside her own chair.

Now, for the first time, Frank noticed tears.

It'd been remarkable how long she'd held herself together.

'John never got to hear the songs she wrote for him,' she paused, welling up further. 'They were special... so special.'

'Laura...'

She nodded, dabbing her eyes.

'I've heard the songs.'

She dropped the hand holding the tissue to her lap and widened her eyes. 'How?'

'We recovered a tape along with the guitar and—'

'"Broken"?'

Frank nodded. 'Aye...'

'Oh my. Really?'

'Aye.'

She shook her head.

He nodded again, helping her to comprehend that it was so. 'Laura, I agree, the songs, they're special.'

Laura buried her face in her hands and cried heavily.

For a moment, Frank saw Mary sitting there, during those rare moments when she'd lost control and folded.

Frank rose and moved instinctively towards the bereaved mother.

Over at her chair, he placed his hand on her shoulder.

'I'm sorry,' she said between mouthfuls of tears.

Don't you be sorry now, lass. Don't you dare.

He rubbed her shoulder firmly, letting it move over her back, trying to reassure her, like he used to do with Mary, that she wasn't alone.

'I want to stay in control for her. This is important. This is her moment. Her time,' Laura said.

Frank knelt. She dropped her hands from her face and looked down at him with swollen eyes. She sucked in breaths between tears.

Instinctively, he took one of her hands, unconcerned about the damp tissue squashed between their palms. 'Aye, but it's your time, too. It belongs to both of you.'

She considered this and then fixed Frank with a stare. 'The tape... the music... it's safe?'

'Aye. And it's beautiful,' Frank said, now sandwiching

her one hand between both of his own. 'You should be so proud.'

'It was the only one. The only one she made. Since I lost her, I've never heard her voice again. Not once.'

No other copies? Surprising.

'Her voice. Her beautiful voice. You have it with you?' Laura asked.

'I do.'

She folded forward and Frank rose onto his haunches, fighting the agonising strain on his back to embrace her.

He moved his hands around her back and clung to her. 'We'll listen to it now and then, later, I'll make sure you get a copy. I promise.'

He backed away, reached into his pocket, and took out his phone so she could hear her daughter's voice.

Chapter Forty-Four

Frank placed his hand against Charlotte's closed bedroom door and sighed, acknowledging again how fortunate he'd been.

Although driven half-mad by her own demons, Maddie was back, occupying that same space she grew up in.

Laura hadn't been as fortunate. Charlotte would never occupy her room again.

He thought of Mary, too; who'd died without ever knowing if her beloved daughter would come home.

Charlotte, Laura and Mary. Frank, the fortunate one, had an obligation to fight with everything he had on behalf of all three of them.

He opened the door and stepped inside.

Before heading into the kitchen to make another drink, Laura had informed him that the room remained exactly as Charlotte had left it, despite being cleaned weekly.

Why wouldn't it be? Why would you have ever stopped hoping that she'd return to it?

His eyes fell first to a worn acoustic guitar standing in the room's corner. He didn't recognise the model of this one, and assumed this may have been the one she started out on, prior to her dying father's gift of a Martin D-35.

A memory I can't resume... Her voice, her lyrics, moved through his head as he walked into the room.

Posters of legendary guitarists adorned the walls. The poetic Bob Dylan; Joni Mitchell, whose lyrics, like Charlotte's, had spoken of love and loss; James Taylor, whose tunes could soothe.

A melody lost in the air...

In one corner, a small, framed photograph of a Jamaican man with dreadlocks. The resemblance was unmistakable. Gentle eyes. An easy manner. A guitar slung over the man's back.

John Asante.

A face I knew... then disappeared.

An untouched bedspread. Teddies; each one a guardian of Charlotte's innocence and dreams. Up on a shelf was an array of music biographies: Leonard Cohen, Bob Marley and Janis Joplin were some standouts.

The room was full of music and stories.

This life had been so sharply interrupted.

A child's laughter no more.

He looked over at the guitar again and thought of Charlotte's remains folded into that suitcase.

An unfinished song.

When he looked up, Laura was standing at the door. Her face was red and puffy. She'd cried for a long time after hearing her daughter's demo. 'You must have more questions,' she said.

Frank nodded. Too many to count. *But we'll do what we can, Laura, to piece together the final chords of your daughter's story.*

Chapter Forty-Five

Frank and Laura sat beside each other on Charlotte's bed.

'What can you recall of the investigation into Charlotte's disappearance?'

'It's hazy,' Laura said. 'Feels like a nightmare that you can only remember glimpses of? Does that make sense?'

'Perfectly.'

'I'm worried that some of it's disappeared, but I *know* it's all buried in here somewhere. I can feel it, you see. Boiling away. I'm already recalling moments. Don't you have all the details of the investigation?'

He wondered how DC Sharon Miller was getting on with the flimsy case file. 'Only some. We'll have more later. How did it all start?'

'As I told you before, Charlotte would never stay away from home without ringing me. It was September 18th, 1987. Hot. Balmy hot. I remember sitting by the telephone, sweating, terrified, while it got later and later.'

'And when did you last see her?'

'Early. Ten in the morning. She told me she was

meeting friends for lunch in Scarborough, and then she'd be going to a pub in the evening for a gig. I waved her off.'

'Which friends?'

'She never said. The pub was The Lance. I phoned them and they told me she'd never got there. In fact, there was no open mic that night, nor were there any bookings for gigs, and they'd never expected her. I think this gave the police the ammunition they needed to say she was deceitful and had simply run away.'

Frank nodded and looked over at the row of music biographies on the shelf. 'Could you think of any reason she lied about having that gig?'

'Well, I realised she *must* have been in some kind of trouble. She just wasn't like that. We were close. She may not tell me everything, but she'd never lied to me. As far as I knew. The police wouldn't have it though. An eighteen-year-old lying to her mother? Common enough. She was obviously just off partying somewhere.'

'Do you think she actually met with those friends in Scarborough?'

Laura shrugged and adjusted some teddies lying on the bed beside her. 'I don't know. There was a confirmed sighting of her at Scarborough train station around eleven, but then the trail went cold. Eventually, the police put some effort into it with a press release and going door to door around shops and cafes but came up empty-handed. I couldn't tell you how hard they tried. I trusted them. What more can you do?'

'Nothing. You did everything the right way, Laura.'

'And only now do I know she ended up in Whitby.' Laura picked up one of the teddies she'd just adjusted and held it at arm's length as if examining it for damage. 'I didn't know she was heading there that day.'

Also, Whitby isn't walking distance, so that leaves the train, bus or taxi.

He resisted the temptation to sigh. Today, with ANPR and extensive CCTV use, they'd have a fighting chance, but this had been 1987. He wondered if any taxi driver, bus driver or rail attendant had ever come forward. *How hard did my predecessors try?*

Did someone see her in Whitby on that day? Was her killer really the only one who knew she'd arrived there? If she'd made it to the Mariner's Lantern and played there, wouldn't someone have reported it?

If someone killed her at the whalebones, which was more than likely, then why had she been there? Was it someone she'd met there? Or a cynical, random act of violence?

He suspected she must have died before eleven; otherwise, wouldn't she have used this payphone on East Terrace to reassure her mother? It seemed she never failed to do that.

'What did she take with her that day?' Frank asked.

'Her father's guitar... that was a given. Also, on that day, I remember spotting her favourite plectrum by the sofa. Another gift from her father, and she always used it for luck. I chased her down the road with it and she was stunned that it wasn't in the guitar case she was holding.'

He reached for his phone and showed her a picture of the recovered red plectrum.

'That wasn't her special plectrum. That one was pink and had Bob Marley's signature on it. Something John had acquired on a visit home to Jamaica.'

Frank made a note and then considered.

The guitar didn't confirm that she was ever in that hut. The killer could have taken it there afterwards and left it, but it made little sense. Why would the killer risk leaving that kind of evidence behind? They'd have been better off throwing it over the cliff edge.

The more Frank thought about it, the more convinced he was that Charlotte stayed in that beach hut on the nights she stayed in Whitby and, following her death, the stuff had been left abandoned. Wouldn't the person who owned North Sea Nook Beach Huts have known it was Charlotte, though? And following the press report, contacted the police? It was possible she gave a false name, but was that enough to conceal her tracks? More likely then that someone else rented it out, and let Charlotte use it, but then never returned there. A lover, perhaps? A married man who didn't want to associate himself with an affair? Or, maybe, it was just the killer, after all, who stupidly left the evidence rather than risk being seen there again? Frank let out an internal sigh when he realised that he'd come full circle with his considerations.

While Frank had his phone out, he pulled up a picture of the suitcase that had contained her bones. 'Do you recognise this?'

Laura shook her head. 'I'm sorry. No. Why? Was she *in* that?'

'Aye.' Frank softened his tone. 'I'm sorry.'

'She only ever travelled with a small backpack and that guitar.'

They'd recovered no backpack. Was it possible that it was still among the debris in the lost property at Whitby Wavefront Cabins? He took a description of the backpack from Laura so he could contact Barnaby and ask him if he could double check.

Next, he moved onto the picture of Charlotte in the

Mariner's Lantern standing alongside an unidentified young man.

Laura stared at it and sighed.

'Do you recognise him?'

'No. I guess he's handsome. Or was. Hard to believe that this is thirty-seven years ago. In my mind, she's still this age. Beautiful. Her father's eyes, skin, his easy manner...'

Frank nodded. He showed her the image of the writing on the back of the photo. C + DR, 1987. 'If C is Charlotte, do you've any idea who DR is?'

She shook her head. 'Doctor?' she said with a raised eyebrow.

You're not the first to say that... and won't be the last...

Following another half an hour of questions, Laura led him downstairs. At the door, he told her he'd be in touch about viewing the place where Charlotte had been recovered and sending over the audio file of her demo.

Outside, he turned back and smiled at her. 'Laura, I know you're doing well. You're strong and I respect that. But there's no shame in asking for help. I think contacting Margaret is still a great idea.'

'I will.'

She didn't sound convincing in the slightest. He said, 'Otherwise, you've my number; phone me any time, day or night, all right?'

'You wouldn't want me on the phone in the middle of the night, surely?'

'Me and sleeping don't have a great relationship these days. Seriously. Please phone me whenever.'

'Yes... and thank you.'

'And about this thanking. Please stop, Laura. *We* let you down in 1987. We aren't worthy of any gratitude.'

'It wasn't you, Frank. You're different. I know you're going to put an end to it.'

He smiled. *I hope I can live up to your expectations.*

'And if you can hurry with that audio, I'd be so grateful.'

Frank nodded. 'I'll put the call in now.'

'Good...' She smiled. 'And then I'll text you another thank you, Frank. Because of you, I get something I never believed I'd have again. My angel's voice.'

Chapter Forty-Six

Usually, wild horses wouldn't keep Paul from work, but the combination of his promise to Jess, last night's panic attack and the news of the remains close to the whalebone arch made a compelling argument for rest.

While watching a movie, he'd received a call from Kristoff. He'd already texted his Maître d' to tell him that Jess would have it in hand this evening, but it seemed he wanted to check up on Paul himself. Fair enough. They'd worked together for a long time.

After assuring Kristoff he was fine, he said, 'Sorry for being a delusional mess.'

'Behave, Chef! We're just over the moon that you're all right. You gave us a right scare. When I gave you that customer's name, and I saw that look—'

His blood ran cold. 'Sorry, what?'

'Yes, you asked for the name of a customer. Remember? You didn't say why and—'

Paul leaned forward. He was hyperventilating. *Not again.* 'I didn't realise...' He broke off and closed his eyes. *It'd happened.*

'Chef?'

'Sorry, I must go. I'm fine... someone at the door,' he lied.

He hung up.

She'd been there!

Trying to regulate his breathing, he placed a hand on his chest. He'd been so convinced it'd been a drunken, stressed delusion... a mistake.

But Kristoff was right. Paul recalled it clearly now. Kristoff's voice in his ear, 'Fiona Barclay.'

Which meant that she really had stood and stared at him with judgement in her eyes.

The chickens had come home to roost.

Chapter Forty-Seven

Julie listened to the conditions of her bail for common assault.

Barmy! For pulling someone's hair?

She wasn't allowed anywhere near work. Which made no difference, really, as she was already suspended. She was also required to report to the station three times a week. The last condition was a real body blow. A ban on alcohol! They'd seen the footage of her drinking at work, and that'd gone down as the trigger for her violent behaviour.

Walking home, she considered the solicitor's warning that a six-month prison sentence was possible. However, he remained positive that a fine for a first-time offence was more likely if she stayed out of trouble.

Breaking bail by getting drunk would be a weak and foolish move.

But weak and foolish was how she felt, so she headed into her local off-licence.

She requested the cheapest vodka in stock from a young man reading a newspaper at the counter. While he was grabbing the bottle from the shelf behind him, she saw the whalebones and turned the newspaper around.

The headline was stark: *Remains Found.*

Julie took a deep breath.

'This is the cheapest we stock,' the server said.

She pushed a ten-pound note over the counter towards him, keeping her eyes, and focus, on the image of the whalebones.

She closed her eyes.

Over on the East Cliff, under the bright moon, the abbey shone. Before her, on the West Cliff, the whalebone arch towered, reaching up, touching the stars.

She looked down at her hand, which was held by another.

'Your change,' the server said.

Her eyes snapped open. She took the change, requested a bag to hide the vodka from inquiring eyes, and headed home, thoughts of the whalebone arch, a moonlit night, and *that* hand in hers, on her mind.

When she arrived at her house, Arnold and Tom were sitting in the kitchen playing chess.

They both regarded her, especially her father, whose eyes immediately went to the plastic bag in her hands. 'I thought your shift was until seven?'

'Don't feel so good.'

He was about to say something, probably about her excessive drinking last night, but stopped himself. Instead, he turned back to the board, moved his queen, and took one of Tom's rooks.

'Grandpa!'

'Told you to slow down, young man. *Think* ahead. Three moves.'

'But how can I think ahead three moves when I don't know what moves you're going to do?'

Arnold smiled. 'Anticipation. Putting yourselves into the shoes of the enemy.'

Tom sighed.

Julie went over to her son and kissed him on the crown of his head. 'Love you.'

'Love you Mum.' He continued staring, narrow-eyed, at the chessboard.

Her father regarded her plastic bag again and then his eyes went back to the chessboard.

She went and grabbed a glass from the kitchen cupboard, stood behind her father, lent down and kissed him on the back of his head. 'Love you, too, Dad.'

'Eh? What's going on?' He sounded confused.

She smiled. 'Can't a daughter tell her father she loves him?'

He looked up at her with a creased brow.

She took her glass, the bagged vodka, and headed up to her bedroom.

After settling herself down with several shots, she scoured the internet for information regarding the remains on West Cliff.

Sources suggest the body could be decades old. Potentially, from the eighties.

She locked her bedroom door, looked at her hand, closed her eyes, felt the other hand clutching hers, and cried.

After that, she drank until she passed out.

Chapter Forty-Eight

Having planned his day to the second, David watched the second-hand sweep around the clock face on his Rolex until the minute ended, then he threw back the sheets and climbed out of bed.

'Something I said?' Freya asked.

David grabbed his underwear from the chair and slipped them on. He glanced back at his patient, Freya Green, who was, despite the tone in her voice, smiling. 'It obviously wasn't something I *did*.' She winked.

He turned to face her as he dressed. She lay on her side, naked above the sheets.

At thirteen years his junior, she was older than most women he slept with these days. She'd her figure to thank for that; at forty-two, she was in unbelievable shape.

'I'm never late for an appointment.' He fastened his trousers.

He turned, finished dressing and when he looked back again, she'd already slipped beneath the sheets. He headed towards the ensuite.

'Everything okay at home? With Hanna?'

He stopped in the doorway.

'I'd prefer it—'

'If I didn't mention your wife. I know the rules. Is it hard to live by so many rules?'

He turned and looked at her. It was a shame. Attachment. It always reared its ugly head, eventually. He sighed. 'Not for me. For others, maybe.'

'Sounds selfish! So, what're you leaving me with today? A same time next week? Or will I be fortunate to get a late night at the office phone call?'

That confirmed it. Attachment. Yes, a real shame. But any sign that it'd get out of hand was a sign to end it immediately. He'd made the mistake of leaving it too long in the past once before.

Not again.

'Me and Jake are through by the way,' Freya said.

David nodded. *Hardly surprising. Especially if you've become attached to me.* 'That could be a mistake. He's considerate, gentle... everything Mark wasn't.'

'Yes, but I told him about us...'

He sucked in a deep breath and leaned against the wall. The world seemed to tilt. 'That was a mistake.'

'Relax! Ha! I didn't tell him about us in *that* way. What do you think I am? A home wrecker? I told him I'd booked some sessions with you. That was enough to offend him because he knew I had therapy with you while I was with Mark. He walked.'

He exhaled. *For a moment there...* 'Look, we need to take a break, anyway. Talk to Jake. Iron things back out.'

'A break from the sessions? I block-booked ten!'

'No, not from the sessions. From this.' He moved his finger between them. 'You understand.'

'I *understand* you're being paranoid.'

Am I? I work so hard to avoid paranoia.

He went into the bathroom to use the toilet.

When he emerged, she was reading something on her phone.

'Listen to this. Whitby made the news. They found some remains up by the whalebone arch.'

He took another deep breath, and the world tilted again. This time, he didn't steady himself; instead, he stepped over towards her, holding his hand out for her phone. 'Let me see.'

As soon as he saw the image of the whalebones, he was an eighteen-year-old again, walking past that iconic scene, framed by the tumultuous sea and the dark clouds.

Back home. To his father's pub. The Mariner's Lantern.

His poky bedroom.

His poky life.

He scanned the article and saw a claim that the remains could date back to the eighties.

'You look like you've seen a ghost,' Freya said.

'Why would you say that?' He looked at her. 'I'm fine.'

She shrugged and he continued to look through the article. Afterwards, he said, 'Lots of remains in the ground around these parts; bet it turns out to be nothing out of the ordinary.'

'Sounds out of the ordinary to me.'

'Whatever.' He threw her phone onto the bed. 'I've got to get back.'

'Make sure you call,' she said as he left the room.

He didn't respond. His mind was elsewhere.

Chapter Forty-Nine

FRANK STOPPED by Middlesbrough town centre to pick up a new mobile phone for Maddie.

He gravitated towards CeX, where he knew there'd be an adequate range of second-hand models to select from. En route, though, he saw a Vodafone store.

What the hell!

He was so proud of his daughter for what she'd been through of late. A shiny new boxed iPhone was the least she deserved after all that turbulence.

His idea of gifting her a phone excited him; the actual price of the product didn't. However, he figured he could shake off the pain of the expenditure. After all, he'd no mortgage payments following his wife's passing, an enviable salary, and his diet lacked all nutrition, so was very cheap. Still, knowing that he was spending six hundred pounds was akin to getting a tattoo – a sharp needle over the skin.

He dreaded to think what psychological turmoil he'd endure when he finally got round to buying a new car!

Was it something to do with his age?

Young men and women threw their money around all over the place without batting an eyelid.

Well, that's how it seemed to him, anyway.

After setting Maddie up on a pay-as-you-go, he thanked the sales agent who'd spread him on toast like melted butter and devoured him in a single mouthful, and headed back to HQ in Scarborough.

Before beginning the briefing, he went over to see how Gerry was. He nodded down at Rylan, who was eating. 'Back on his grub, then?'

'Yes. He managed to get the last of that biscuit out earlier.'

Nice.

While turning, something occurred to him. 'What do you do if he, you know, goes in here?' He pointed at the floor of IR3, before catching sight of the bin beside her desk, hoping and praying that he was barking up the wrong tree...

'He's three years old.'

'All right, of course.' He turned. 'Thing is, what does that mean?' he swung back. 'I never had a dog.'

'It means he goes outdoors. If it's an emergency, he'll let me know.'

He glanced at the bin, relieved. 'Good to know.'

Frank took centre stage, and his eyes immediately fell to Sharon. There was a rather pissed-off look on her face as she shuffled through her notes. *You really don't want to be here, do you?*

His eyes then swept between the vacuous Reggie, whose jokes, as per, weren't finding the right audience; Sean, the pale copper that looked like the terrified new boy at school, pissing in his pants; and his genius DI in the corner, tapping away on her computer, unaware that there was a human race to engage with.

Thinking about it again, who could blame Sharon for not wanting to be here?

After Frank called everyone to attention, he went through everything he'd found out from his discussions with Laura. Gerry tapped away as she listened. Her typing speed was impressive. Frank asked Sean to get together a list of all pubs trading in 1987 around North Yorkshire for Laura to see if they could jog her memory over any Charlotte might have visited. He tasked Reggie with investigating the old payphone that was on the East Parade used by Charlotte to contact her mother on the nights she stayed out. He already knew call logs from BT were out of the question for a catalogue of reasons, ranging from legal implications over the retention of data past a few years to a lack of technological advancement. Still, it was worth verifying the payphone's existence so they could take it from there. He asked Sean to dig into John Asante's background, including his passing from cancer. Could her laid-back guitar-playing father's life hold any clues about what caused his daughter's premature demise? He mentioned the special plectrum, the pink one with Bob Marley's signature, and the backpack; both of which could still be gathering dust in one of Barnaby's lost-property-stuffed cabins. He almost asked Gerry to make that call, but recalled the 'forbidden' biscuit, and decided it wasn't worth risking a spiky interaction. Mr Feel Good, Reggie, was the man for that.

He closed his notebook.

'Sharon? Was the investigation in 1987 better than we hoped?'

'Not really. Firstly, DI Carver and I went through the detail in the case file. "Detail" is a generous word. Were investigations always this vague back then?'

'I'd like to think mine weren't,' Frank said. 'Go on.'

'We could only get in touch with one of the investigators. DS Harry Tyne. He's retired now.'

'Is that it? One investigator?'

'There was another,' Sharon said. 'But he's dead. DI Roger Roland.'

Now that was a blast from the past. 'I remember him well, can't say I was his biggest fan. Found him narrow-minded and unapproachable. Mind you, could say that about many of them way back when...'

In fact, you could probably say that about me, Frank thought.

'Okay, so what did DS Harry Tyne have to say for himself?' Frank asked.

'He remembered the case well.'

Frank snorted. 'I'm glad to hear that he noticed.'

'He was short with me on the phone, boss. Very short.'

That could explain Sharon's worsening mood. 'Sorry to hear that.' He stopped himself short of saying: *You think there's a smattering of dickheads in the force now? Well, back then, there were enough to fill most of the country clubs in England.*

'At least they recorded the necessaries... public appeal, door to door... but there were things not followed up on. And there's no mention of Whitby, outside of Laura's statement that her daughter visited there regularly. When I flagged these inconsistencies up with Harry, he claimed to be unable to recall all the specifics. He snapped regularly about not having the same resources available then as we do today.'

'Not the same, no.' Frank exhaled. 'But hardly an excuse for not using the ones you do have.'

'Apparently, they did. Or so Harry said, after I questioned how thin the case file was. He said the emphasis on logging every little thing was unheard of back then.'

'Bollocks. They just weren't held to bloody account as often. So, they were lazy. Daft bastards.' He looked over the wide eyes of his team. 'Apologies for the language.'

'Harry reckoned the investigation was sharp,' Sharon said.

'Did he mean short?' Reggie asked.

'He referred to Charlotte as...' Sharon broke off, clearly not comfortable.

'It's okay,' Frank said.

'Half-caste.' She shook her head. 'I pointed out that it was an outdated, politically incorrect term. For that, I received a snort, and a further indignant response that at least he tried, whereas most of his superiors at the time didn't consider,' – she broke off again and sighed – 'coloured folk a priority. Again, I tried to correct, but I realised I was winding up an eighty-plus man in a nursing home and gave up.'

'He had a point, I guess,' Frank said.

His entire crew looked up at him in horror; even Gerry stopped typing.

'No.' He waved them away. 'No, not about the terminology. What do you think I am? Thick? No, just saying this was 1987. I remember some of my superiors. Most of them still had attitudes from a bygone era. A bygone century truth be told. No chance we'd be looking at a file this thin if Charlotte had been a wealthy white lass. That she was mixed race worked against her and that, folks, is just not cricket. Make sure you type all of that up accurately, Gerry.' He didn't want to be hauled over the coals for that misunderstanding!

He looked at Sharon. No wonder she was glum.

Listening to those who used to represent her profession being so dismissive and rude must have been demotivating.

'When I informed Harry about Charlotte's body, he refused to believe they'd let her and her mother down,' she said. 'First, it was: "Are you sure?" Followed by: "Maybe it happened years later?" He was adamant that everything pointed to a young woman doing a runner back then.'

'Okay, thanks Sharon, we'll look at your notes after. Reggie and Sean? The Saltwick Sailor?'

Reggie opened his book. 'Interesting chap that landlord, Marvin Hails.' He leaned over and clapped Sean on the back, who didn't look so happy about the physical contact. 'This young man here kept it together well. Kudos to him. Few times, I felt myself teetering, you know. Marvin, the daft sod, kept asking if he thought the discovery nearby was going to boost takings! I kid you not.' He looked around the room, meeting eyes with everyone – apart from Gerry, who stared at her computer screen. 'I know, what an idiot! Sean kept it respectful though, didn't you son?' He clapped Sean on the shoulder again. He looked even unhappier this time. 'Anyway... Marvin was friends with the previous landlord, Graham Roberts, and his wife, Carrie. Following the burning down of the Mariner's Lantern, Graham collected the insurance, but rather than rebuild himself, he sold what was left to Marvin at a modest cost. Marvin was of wealthy stock and had no problem setting up the Saltwick Sailor, which is a snazzy affair. Graham and Carrie have since passed, but this is where it gets interesting. Marvin remembers Charlotte.' He looked down at his notes. 'Said she could really play. And sing, too. He said no one else could silence the Mariner's like Charlotte Wilson. He waxed lyrical for a while. Said no one could forget anyone able to hold an audience like that.'

'Did he not notice the disappearance then? Hear the public appeal?' Frank raised an eyebrow. 'And think to say something?'

'He said he heard about it and was stunned. He used the word "devastated".'

'Yet didn't respond to the appeal?' Frank shook his head.

'He said he hadn't seen her in over a month, and he knew for a fact that she'd not played on the night that was on the public appeal. He said that when he heard it, he checked the diary. Marvin used to help with bookings back then, and he said that all the acts were logged, on account of them getting a free drink if they played! A tick by their name meant they'd claimed the freebie. Marvin was adamant that he checked in 1987 following the appeal, and there was no record of Charlotte playing that night.'

'Did you enquire after the logbook?' Frank asked.

'Destroyed in the fire.'

'Okay,' Frank said. 'Even if she didn't play on September 18th, I still believe she went back to Whitby that night. She didn't phone Laura after eleven to tell her she was staying out. This had never happened before, suggesting she died before she got the chance. Okay, what else did Marvin cough up, Reggie? Acquaintances, boyfriends?'

'She never hung around the pub too long, he reckoned. Said she seemed kind of shy. She often just turned up, played the open mic, had her drink, and then left. He said blokes often tried to chat to her, but that she never seemed interested. Not stand-offish like, because she was always polite, just not that engaged with their advances. He said he even tried a few times himself. His words were: "Would've been rude not to!"'

'Charmer,' Frank said.

'Yes, said he quite fancied her, but admitted that nearly every other fella did, so he never figured himself having much of a chance. That's about all, boss.'

'And the photo? Did he recognise the lad in the photo?'

Reggie looked at Sean. Sean didn't meet his eyes and made some notes instead. Reggie's face paled. 'Shit.'

'Oh, for the *love* of God.' Frank rolled his eyes. 'I printed it for you.'

'I know, boss, but I left it in the car.'

He leaned over his desk at the front and took a deep breath. 'So, why didn't you go back and get it?'

'Sorry... I got distracted. Look, I'll handle it.' He stood.

'Jesus wept.' Frank shook his head. A deathly silence fell over the room. He sighed. 'Okay, no damage done, Reggie.' *You're just slowing things down as per.* 'Go out, use the office over the hall, phone him and email him the photo.' *You daft 'apeth!*

'Okay, boss.' He left the room.

Everybody was now looking down, apart from Gerry, who was still typing away, her expression unchanging.

'Okay, Gerry, the evidence so far? Anything to add?'

'Yes.'

'Go on, then.' He tried not to get his hopes up. She'd worked miracles before, but again? So soon? *Unlikely*.

'I've two people of interest here,' Gerry said. 'And the sooner we can talk to them, the better for this investigation.'

Two!

Rylan gave a small yap.

Everyone looked at the Lab and then at Gerry.

Good. Otherwise, they'd have witnessed his jaw hitting the ground...

Chapter Fifty

Bang, bang!

Julie groaned and opened her eyes.

Bang, bang!

Her vision swam.

The next bang felt like it was inside her head.

Someone was knocking on her door.

'One moment.' She rubbed her forehead and sat up. Alongside her was the half-drunk bottle of vodka the police had forbidden her to drink. It was fortunate she'd screwed the lid back on before passing out. She lifted back her bedsheet and slipped it under.

Bang! Bang!

'Coming!'

She opened the door. Her father, Arnold, stood there with his walking stick raised, ready to knock it against the door again. He lowered it and shook his head.

'I drifted off,' she said.

'Your eyes are bloodshot.'

'Tired...'

'Day drinking now?'

'Look... not now. I can't take any more—'

'What's happened?'

She thought about telling him. But then there'd be more judgement, more scathing comments, more damage to their already fragile relationship. 'Nothing's happened. *Nothing!*'

'Your son could hear! Keep your voice down.'

'Sorry,' she said. 'But not now, please.'

He looked down and sighed. 'I haven't always been there for you... but I've tried over these last years. So, please tell me what's wrong and I'll do what I can...' He looked back up.

She rubbed her temples. 'Stupid. I was suspended. I was caught on camera drinking and...' She stopped short. *And I've been arrested for assault, bailed, and could go to jail for six months. Also, there're remains by the whalebones...*

Arnold shook his head. He didn't look angry, just disappointed.

'I'm an idiot.'

'Listen... Tom keeps asking after you. He wants you to come down for dinner. I'll tell him you're sick... okay... then we'll chat later?'

She nodded. 'Thank you.'

'But, please, I'm begging you, don't drink any more.'

'I won't.' As she said it, she wanted to believe herself, but deep down, she knew it was a lie.

She closed the door and went back to sit on the bed. She reached behind herself and felt the lump of the bottle through her sheet.

Hold off, you stupid, stupid bitch. Hold off it. Don't spiral further.

Her eyes panned the room, desperate for something to distract her.

The guitar.

Untouched for so long.

She wandered over, picked it up, and returned to the bed. She plucked the plectrum from beneath the strings, readied it between her fingers, and tuned the guitar.

Then she lay back and stared at the ceiling with the guitar on her chest. She strummed. It'd been a long time. That, and the alcohol, meant it took her a while to find her rhythm, but eventually she did.

She closed her eyes and thought of that hand in hers.

Thought of the whalebones.

And then she sang, '*A melody lost in the air... a memory I can't resume.*'

How long has it been since I was last happy?
How long has it been since I was broken?
'*A face I knew... then disappeared.*'

Chapter Fifty-One

David's last two patients, Ian and Dan, were both in their late forties, living lives immensely troubled by childhood events.

David cruised through his session with Ian on autopilot. Ian had experienced severe bullying at school to the point where he flat out refused to attend. Ian's father's reaction had been none too helpful. He'd dragged him kicking and screaming through the school gates. Embarrassing Ian had not only intensified the bullying, but had swollen the trauma he now lived with, or tried to live with, tenfold.

Autopilot was slightly more difficult for David in his session with Dan.

Dan had experienced intense feelings of failure in childhood because of his mother. She'd continually compared him to his older brother, who seemed to succeed at everything; eventually, it'd destroyed Dan's self-confidence and, therefore, self-worth.

The similarities between Dan and David were clear. David's mother had also judged him, but for different reasons. He'd been academic and successful, but she'd considered him too selfish, too devoid of empathy, and had hit his feelings of self-worth, too.

That the most emotionally charged conversation he'd had with her was on her deathbed hadn't helped.

'David, you must change. It hurt me and it hurts your father so much. When you're older, and we're both gone, I fear it'll hurt you significantly more.'

But has it, Mother?

I'm healthy, successful, wealthy. Yes, sometimes I upset Hanna, but she's rather forgiving and understanding of what you did to me with your judgements.

Despite the difficulties attached to the second session with Dan, David made it through.

Heading home, he felt unsettled.

Not because of his own baggage, because he'd long made peace with that. He knew he craved the approval of women because of his mother's condemnation and eventual rejection. Starting illicit affairs with vulnerable women seemed to be the cost of this.

And, despite knowing that it was his role as therapist which caused patients to become infatuated with him, and knowing that it would most certainly lead to no good, he couldn't stop himself.

Freya wasn't the first who'd desired him because of the therapy, and she wouldn't be the last.

Eventually, however, as was the case with Freya, they always became too clingy, and that placed his career and marriage under threat.

Not that Freya concerned him. He'd dealt with others before her. Usually with threats. The promised divulgence of revealed secrets. David was careful. He always made sure, before the affairs began, that those secrets carried serious weight and substance.

For example, Freya had slept with her sister's boyfriend and her best friend's husband.

Wow! Two life-destroying secrets for the price of one.

If Freya attempted to destroy him, she'd destroy herself.

So, the discontent he felt didn't come from his baggage, or Freya, and the threat she posed.

Those remains. Up near the whalebone arch. That was what was firmly on his mind.

Along the way, he parked on the new side of Whitby, wrapped up, and strolled over to the other side of the swing bridge. There, he walked down Church Street until he got to the Duke of York, ducked behind it and onto the Tate Hill Pier. He walked to the end, happy to see a lack of tourists in this darkening hour, and gazed out over the sea.

He closed his eyes, thought of the kiss he'd enjoyed on this pier and touched his lips.

That hadn't just been validation; that had been something else.

Something he'd never felt before and never felt since.

Something he believed he wasn't designed to feel, but had been given a short, sharp glimmer of, before it was snatched away.

He walked over to the post that they'd both carved their names into. His fingers traced down the wood to the spot where their names should have been.

But, of course, they weren't there. There was merely a deep groove. He recalled Hanna's confession that she'd observed them, and then approached afterwards to scratch out the memory with a stone, so aggressively, she'd pulled away a sizeable chunk of the rotten wood.

David stroked the indented wood, which was furry and moist from the never-ending sea breeze.

Chapter Fifty-Two

Gerry didn't rise from behind her computer. Neither did she take her eyes off the screen. She did, however, at least stop typing when she addressed the incident room.

Gerry didn't appear anxious, yet Rylan stood and rested his chin on her knee, offering comfort. Frank wondered if there'd been a signal imperceptible to the human eye. Maybe it was a subtle change in her tone of voice, her posture, or, who knew, her body temperature? Something that Rylan was attuned to.

Everyone listened with bated breath as she explained the rationale behind the two persons of interest.

Frank's eyes widened. Her attention to detail was beyond anything he'd ever witnessed before. Usually, when he listened to these analytical types, you couldn't make head nor tail of what they were saying, but it seemed so different with Gerry. She may have been socially awkward, but she was intelligent and skilful enough to adjust to her audience. He imagined that the years of masking her emotional turbulence had allowed her to develop this skill-set. He couldn't imagine it came easily to her, though. She'd surely have to exert a large amount of mental effort.

She was currently discussing the backing vocals on 'Broken'. 'You may have heard them and assumed they also belonged to Charlotte?'

Aye, I did. I guess you're about to tell us something different.

'The backing vocals were slight. Turned all the way down during post-production. Even at that volume, I could hear a subtle difference. Using some music software on my Apple Mac perfect for this, I isolated the track. Would you like to hear, or should I just summarise?'

'Summarise please.' Frank was eager to get to the point. He put his hands on the desk and leaned. His back was aching, but there'd be no way he could sit still when listening to a mind like Gerry's at work. It was something to behold.

'The software confirmed that the backing vocals weren't Charlotte's. I completed an analysis to try to place the accent regionally. North Yorkshire was a certainty, but that wasn't enough. So, I compared the backing vocals to as many accent varieties as I could, locking in a twenty-mile zone, which included Whitby. I used that to run my next search for recording studios that were in operation in the eighties. I found quite a few, but I figured I'd start with one I found in Whitby and work outwards. Turned out to be the right move. Ron Michaels used to run a recording studio out of his soundproof cottage in Whitby.'

Frank nodded. 'Aye... I know Ron. He still shows up at local events to play the blues. He's getting on quite a bit, like. Must be well into his eighties. Few people around here would have a bad word for that man. The music studio has been the starting point for many a local band, looking for cheap production and a chance to get on that terrifying ladder up into the industry. I'm assuming you contacted him, Gerry?'

'Yes. He remembered Charlotte Wilson.'

Frank felt himself stiffen all over; even in parts of his body that he never knew existed.

'And he knew *this* backing singer, too.'

Bloody hell!

'Julie Fletcher. He said we were lucky. That he'd recorded thousands and thousands of aspiring artists, but he remembered Charlotte and Julie well on account of how beautiful the song was. He even remembered the name. "Broken". He spoke at length about her voice, and guitar playing, recalling how he used to let them come and practise for free. He recalls it was in 1987, because that was the year he lost his father, and that Charlotte was very sympathetic with him. Maybe because she'd lost her own?'

Frank nodded. 'What do we know about Julie?'

'Lives in Whitby. Fifty-five years old. Same age as Charlotte would've been. She lives with her father, who's in his eighties, and her son, thirteen.'

'Remarkable, Gerry. This really is. So, the second person of interest?'

'Oh, that was much easier. Ron told me a young man used to tag along with them to watch them record. He assumed he was Julie's boyfriend because he caught them kissing between rehearsals. He told me that this lad made quite a name for himself. Almost a celebrity around these parts. A chef, apparently. An extremely popular one.'

At that point, Reggie came back through the door, looking rather excited. His mouth was halfway open, and he was clearly desperate to unleash something before basking in the glow of some kind of success.

As curious as Frank was, he needed to hear Gerry out, and nothing gave him greater pleasure than saying, 'Park it, Reggie, just getting to the good bit.'

Gerry rubbed her dog's head and then looked around her audience for the first time since her remarkable revelation began. 'His name's Paul Harrison. And he's also the same age. Fifty-five. Childless, single...'

'And rolling in cash. Ha! I know him.' Frank nodded. 'He's not a gentle old musical soul like Ron Michaels, either.'

'A driven entrepreneur is what he is,' Reggie added.

'That's a polite term. I prefer to call them sociopaths,' Frank said. 'I don't know what to say, Gerry. Well done.'

He caught Sharon looking around at the awkward DI, nodding. Clearly impressed. Sean still looked nervous, but had straightened up in his seat somewhat, and looked more tuned in. Even in his anxious state, he'd have realised that Gerry putting together Charlotte's social group from 1987 was a thing of wonder.

He quickly filled Reggie in on what he'd missed.

'So, judging by the way you were licking your lips as you flew through the door, I'm assuming you can top that, or at least match it?'

'Dunno, but I think it may earn your forgiveness.' He smiled, all teeth.

Don't bet on it.

'Marvin Hails recognised the lad with his arm around Charlotte in the photograph.'

Again, Frank stiffened as the adrenaline rushed through him. *For the first time in your life, Reggie, you have my attention.*

'He was the son of the landlord. He lived above the pub.'

Reggie, I may just be warming to you.

'David Roberts. And get on this... His initials are—'

'DR,' Frank interrupted. 'Reggie, this is one of your finer moments. As there haven't been many of note, we'll bank this one for now, and see if we can push for another, eh?' He winked. 'Do we know anything about him?'

'I've just searched for him,' Gerry said. 'He's a psychiatrist and has his own practice. Married. Also, the same age as our others – fifty-five. I'll have more shortly.'

She was lightning, this one.

Frank looked around the room. 'Well, team, three people of interest! Looks like we've got a busy day ahead of us. Let's get some rest and interview them tomorrow.'

Looking between the faces of those in his meagre team, he thought of Donald Oxley.

There was a reason Donald had assigned him the detectives he hadn't asked for.

You never believed I'd a snowball's chance in hell with a case that was almost forty years old, did you?

So, you palmed me off with detectives no one else wanted.

Well, lad, it seems your stupidity has served me, and that lass, Charlotte Wilson, very well.

Very well indeed.

His team must have seen him smiling, but no one had the confidence to ask him why.

A good thing. He was a man of honesty and would probably just give it to them straight:

Despite expectations to the contrary, you lot are delivering.

Chapter Fifty-Three

PAUL FILLED his whisky glass with the Glenlivet Archive 21 gifted to him by the Thomas brothers.

It wasn't the first glass of the evening, and it was unlikely to be the last

Fiona Barclay.

He burned his mouth, throat, and stomach with a large mouthful.

Why now? After so long?

Had she known that it was the most important night of his professional life?

A coincidence?

Surely not.

After another couple of mouthfuls, he closed his eyes and let his head swim.

Thirty-seven years since the night Fiona had stood opposite his eighteen-year-old self, slicing the air with a knife.

Thirty-seven years since the moment in which he'd thought he was going to die.

Fiona Barclay.

She must be what? Early seventies?

Yet, here she was.

Kristoff had seen her name in the bookings. He couldn't deny it any more.

He opened his eyes and finished the glass. The alcohol warmed his fractured mind, but didn't heal it. Elbows on the kitchen table, he put his head in his hands.

He remembered the moment just after he'd hit the floor. That terrifying day in 1987. Fiona kneeling over him, knife poised, on the verge of striking the killer blow.

His phone rang. He dropped his hands and saw it was Roy Thomas. He answered. 'Hello Roy.'

'How's our future Michelin-star chef?'

'On the mend,' he lied. He twirled the bottle of Glenlivet. 'Thanks for the gift.'

'You can wash the antibiotics down with it.' Roy laughed.

Antibiotics? Where had he got that from?

Roy would've noticed the silence. 'Yes, sorry, Paul. We spoke to Kristoff at the restaurant; he told us all about the infection. A rare one. Working that magic with a high fever, too. Can't imagine what delights you'll cook up when you're back to normal.'

'Oh yes.' *Good thinking, Kristoff.* It wouldn't do to tell the cash cows that they were banking on a man riddled with anxiety. Paul laughed. 'Giving me time to sit down and plan some new menus, at least.'

'Look, I'd like to pin down a meeting for next week if that's okay?'

'Suits me.'

'Fantastic. I'll get Mandy, my PA, to put something together. How's that sound?'

'Great. Make it a late one so I can pick up where I left off with the Ornellaia.'

'You never bloody got started. Ha! You're a card, Paul. Get well, mate.'

The phone went dead.

Paul put the phone down, sighed, and rubbed his temples.

'Next week...' He smiled, poured himself another glass, and drank. *Next week is a long bloody way away. Anything could happen before then.*

He closed his eyes.

He recalled the knife close to his throat in 1987 while he lay on the floor. Arthur, now alongside his wife, Fiona, his hands clamped to her shoulders. 'What did I tell you?'

'But ... you know what he's done! I can't just watch him walk away. I just can't.'

'After everything I said to you. Everything we discussed. Unless you stop this now, Fiona, it'll be me walking away.'

Paul remembered the tears in Fiona's eyes and her quivering lips. Both of which he was certain were caused by anger rather than sadness.

She'd stood and stepped away from Paul. 'Get out. If I ever see you again, my husband won't save you.'

The doorbell tore him from his memory.

His blood ran cold.

It wouldn't be... it couldn't be...

He rose to his feet, looked at his kitchen drawer, considering arming himself as she'd done in the past.

You're being ridiculous, Paul. Why would she come here?

He turned and walked to the front door.

Probably just a late delivery.

When he looked through the peephole, he took a deep breath.

'If I ever see you again, my husband won't save you.'

And he wouldn't because poor Arthur Barclay had died eighteen months earlier from a stroke. Someone close to them had brought him the sad news.

Paul shook his head. *You're being ridiculous. She's in her seventies, and you're not a terrified eighteen-year-old any more! Snap out of it!*

He opened the door to find out what Fiona Barclay wanted.

Chapter Fifty-Four

David pulled into his driveway and sensed Hanna's absence.

The curtains were the driving force behind this concern. Granted, the day was down to its last dregs of sunshine, but it was still too early to have them closed.

Also, when he'd left this morning, they'd been closed, which suggested she'd never opened them.

This was unusual. Her absence caused him displeasure. She knew not to do this.

But last night and this morning, she'd been behaving out of character. He sighed, suspecting the situation was going to get worse before it got better.

He had to hope it didn't spiral too much. It'd be hard, if not impossible, to find someone so biddable again. They'd been together since they were fifteen, and despite their difficulties, she understood him, functioned correctly around him, and didn't ask too many questions about the times when he was overly busy or away.

He sighed a second time as he exited the car.

Briony.

Her sister was a meddling irritant! A well-paid asexual creature who'd too much time on her hands.

A bitch who would tell Hanna, time and time again, that she was better off away from David.

Well done, Briony. Seems you finally got your message over!

David reassured himself that he'd still have Hanna's mother, Sue, in his corner. And that woman could talk a car salesman into buying back an old banger he'd just sold for twice the price!

And Sue was a realist, too. Her marriage to Hanna's father had lasted fifty years. Sue would know that these minor blips were minor and not worth ending a marriage over.

He went into the house, positive that he could halt the spiralling.

Then he saw the note she'd left him in the bedroom.

He sat on the bed and read it again and again.

This was new. Unusual.

He screwed up the letter.

That black eye had been a mistake, and was, for the first time, really challenging the control he had over her.

At first, he praised himself for holding back his temper, but then he decided it'd do him good to release some of it, so he smashed Hanna's dressing-table mirror.

Chapter Fifty-Five

When Frank arrived home, it was dark.

His street was quiet, or at least was, after he'd killed Bertha's engine.

Henrietta Timber's curtains twitched on cue.

He grabbed the mobile phone, which probably cost the same as a human organ on the black market, and headed up his drive. On the way, he threw a wave at Henrietta but couldn't see her well enough to tell if she waved back.

Every light in his place was off, so he assumed, at first, that Maddie must have slept through sunset. He trod quietly. Withdrawal was nasty, and despite the recent green shoots, she wasn't out of the woods yet. Last thing he wanted to do was wake her.

Excited as he was about giving her this new phone, he could hold off until the morning.

Still, before he squirrelled himself away in the lounge with water (yes, the diet had begun – beer was out of the question) and a film to ease him out of the turbulent waking world, he'd at least look in on her.

He slid around her half-open door, breathing the bitter

tang of this morning's vomit. Expecting her to be in her bed, a sudden chill spread through his body when he saw she wasn't. He backed out of the room and looked left toward the toilet where he hoped she'd surely be.

The door to the bathroom was open, and the light was off.

Maddie wasn't there.

Chapter Fifty-Six

Having slipped in through the back door of his restaurant, Paul plucked the three-quarter full bottle of Macallan from his shelf and sat it down on the desk.

He was yet to turn on the office light, but the glow from the kitchen slipped beneath a closed door, and down the corridor, giving him enough visibility.

He poured himself a glass and took a mouthful.

If he carried on drinking like this, he wouldn't be able to think straight for much longer.

Although, that sounded appealing!

After all, what was there to think about? He was absolutely stuffed.

Simple as that.

If what Fiona Barclay had said was true, and he'd no reason to doubt her, he really was out of options. She wasn't interested in money.

In fact, he almost wished now she'd come at him with a knife, like she'd done in 1987. Finished the job. Put him out of this bloody misery.

He closed his eyes and drank.

No. This was worse. Far worse.

This was torture.

His demise would be slow and drawn out.

Someone opened the door and hit the light switch.

Jess, in her chef whites, slammed a hand to her chest. 'You scared the living shit out of me!'

'Sorry.' Paul took another drink. 'Get used to it. The apologies. You're going to be hearing it a lot over the current weeks, months... years.'

'You're pissed, Chef.'

'I'm not working; drop the Chef.'

'Did you drive?'

'Do you want the truth?'

'You're a dickhead.'

'Agreed.'

Jess closed the door behind her. Her face suggested she wanted to slam it, but she was sensible, and wouldn't want to draw attention to the state of their boss. 'What's wrong? Why am I going to be hearing a lot of apologies?'

He held up his hand. 'My sweet Jess... you know that you're the best thing that's ever happened to me.'

She narrowed her eyes. 'Get to the point before I empty that liquid gold down the sink.'

'Ha. It's over, Jess.'

'What's over?'

He refilled the glass and pushed it across the table to her. 'Everything. Or at least *I'm* over.'

She looked at the whisky and screwed her face up. 'I don't want any. Talk to me.' She rolled a chair towards the desk and sat opposite him.

He nodded at the whisky. 'You'll need to drink some of that first.'

She took a mouthful and winced. 'Okay... happy? Now talk to me.'

'There's no one I'd rather talk to. It's always been that way. Not sure I'm telling you something you didn't know already.'

'Stop now... that's enough. Get to the point.'

'The point is that you've always been the point.'

'Fucking hell.' She took another mouthful.

'Okay, you ready? 1987. I was eighteen. Bloody hell, a kid! Thirty-seven years ago, and it's only now I'm going to be held to account. Still, I can remember it well enough. I mean, I did it. It was me. Can still see it all in here,' – he pointed at his head – 'clear as day.'

Her brow creased. He could see the panic entering her eyes. 'What did you do?'

'Isn't it obvious? I killed someone.'

The colour drained from her face 'Bollocks. You're pissed... talking nonsense.'

'Oh, I'm thinking straight. And by this time tomorrow, I'll be in custody.' He reached back over for his glass. 'Just let me drink. Dissolve everything into a blur.' He took a mouthful. 'Still, best we talk about damage control. This restaurant. You deserve it. We need some kind of plan.'

Jess shook her head. 'Who did you kill, Paul?'

Chapter Fifty-Seven

Frank was still at the heart of his bungalow, turning in circles, disorientated, unsure of where Maddie was and what to do about it, when he heard the key turning in his front door.

He stared at it, mouth agape, as it swung open.

Maddie walked in, wearing a tracksuit and one of Frank's long winter coats. She was holding a bulky paper bag.

Flicking a switch by the door, she flooded the hallway with light.

She jumped, almost dropping the bag. 'Bloody hell! What're you doing, Dad?'

Thank God. He leaned against the wall and ran a hand through his straggly hair. 'Just wondered where you'd got to.'

She held up the bag and smiled. 'Guess what?'

'I know, I can smell it from here.'

'Magpie fish and chips. Your favourite. Remember when you used to say the smell made you close your eyes...

put you right there on the pier, listening to the waves, dipping—'

'Dipping the chips in the homemade tartar. Aye, I remember.' He smiled. His breathing was returning to a regular speed.

'I didn't know what time you'd be back, but I was going to keep it warm in the oven and wait.'

'Thoughtful.' He paused. 'Except, where did you get the money?'

'Yeah, about that.' She looked down and bobbed her head. 'I kind of borrowed some.'

'From who?'

'You. There was a twenty-quid note by your bed. I wanted to surprise you. Plus, I needed a walk. Honestly, I feel better than I've felt in ages.'

He was about to say, *I just wish you'd phoned me to tell me you were going out,* when he remembered. *She doesn't have a phone, dipshit.*

She closed the door behind her and nodded at the bag in his hand. 'What's in there?'

'Let's eat and I'll tell you. Twenty quid for two? These days? Sounds cheap! If you tell me you skimped on mushy peas, you're going to have to put me into the recovery position.'

'As if!' Maddie reached out and patted his stomach. 'They took pity on me.'

'Why?'

'I said Frank Black was my dad, and they insisted I take whatever I needed.'

'Figures.' He grunted and then smiled.

Chapter Fifty-Eight

'Not the best start to my diet,' Frank finished his fish supper and patted his stomach.

'Why are you going on a diet?'

Frank raised an eyebrow. 'No need to be polite, dear.' He gestured down. 'Can you not see how far I'm sitting from the table? I wasn't joking before. If you carry on like this, you *will* have to put me in the recovery position one day! And imagine that. Isn't going to be easy. Can barely move myself up a flight of steps these days... *And*, I haven't had time to enjoy any of my pension. Do you know how bloody hard I've worked for that? Not going to pop my clogs yet. Not on my watch.'

And I have you, Maddie, now, remember? But you don't need to hear that. Because you know. You saw my face when I thought you'd gone.

'Anyway,' Frank said. 'I usually have two or three beers a night with my take-away. So, if I stay off the beer tonight, then isn't that a big leap forward in calorie reduction?'

Maddie laughed.

Frank reached over for her plate and stood.

'Dad?'

He stayed where he was, hovering over the table.

'I've something to admit to you...'

An icy sensation crept up his spine. 'Go on.'

She sighed. 'I smoke.'

'Oh,' he said, the icy sensation evaporating. *Is that it?* Her heroin addiction had preoccupied most of his waking thoughts for as long as he could remember. Nicotine dependency barely registered. 'I do too.'

She smiled.

'More than ever. Something else that I need to knock on the head.'

'I've been worried about telling you. I remember when I was a kid you used to harp on about it. You said you'd be annoyed if I ever took it up.'

'I remember.' *But now, in retrospect, if that had been as bad as it got, I would've been over the sodding moon.*

'I'd have got some while I was out, but I didn't have enough change...'

'Behave. I'll roll us both one up. Mind you, there's one rule here. We only smoke in the garden. That was your mother's demand, and I see no reason to change it.'

He turned towards the sink with the plates.

'Dad?'

'Yup?'

'Maybe it's time to talk about Mum and what happened?'

Inwardly sighing, Frank put the plates in the sink and stared at the wedding ring on his finger as he twisted the tap. When the washing bowl was full, he turned around. 'There's another rule in this house. Never have a serious conversation when eating, drinking, or smoking.'

She laughed. 'That's all the time with you!'

'Aye.' He smiled. 'That's why I'm still alive. Those three hobbies are my well-earned breaks from the stress, which they say is the biggest killer of them all...'

Chapter Fifty-Nine

THE CAT on his fence turned its green eyes between the two smokers and scarpered.

'Usually hangs about does Tabby,' Frank said. 'You got her all jealous.'

'You always hated animals.'

'Not true. My DI has a dog at work. Rylan. Taken a shine to him, if you must know.' Frank nodded and took a drag.

'A dog at work?'

'A therapy dog; she's autistic.'

'I see. That's modern. How do you find working with them?'

Frank regarded her. 'What're you suggesting?'

'Nothing.'

'I may be old-school, but I'm not totally narrow-minded, love! And credit where credit is due concerning Gerry. This lass is a genius. Me... the old guard? Ready for the scrap heap!'

They smoked and stood a while, listening to the seagulls, watching the stars flicker, breathing in salty air between bursts of tobacco.

Maddie said, 'Are you sure you haven't seen my phone anywhere?'

Frank shook his head but didn't make eye contact. Lying set his insides on fire, but how could he give her a phone loaded with scrotes?

The king of whom, Rez, had already visited this garden.

'I got something for you in the house.'

He killed his roll-up and went back in to retrieve the mobile.

He handed it over. 'Ready to go, love. Loaded up with a new SIM. It's pay-as-you-go, but I put about thirty quid on. Look... if you need more, let me know, I'll sort it.'

She wiped tears away with the back of her hand as she stared at the box.

'You right?'

'I don't deserve this.' She threw her roll-up on the ground. 'I don't deserve you.' She embraced him.

He closed his eyes. Feeling the arms of his daughter wrapped around him was indescribable. How he'd longed for this moment for years.

Mary, too, God rest her soul, had often dreamed about this reunion and woken up in tears.

He rubbed her back. 'Don't be silly, love, least I could do. So now you can let me know when you go out for a walk. I've already put my number in.'

The embrace ended, and she wiped tears from her eyes, sniffing, and nodding. She turned the mobile phone box over in her hands. 'It's miles better than the old one.'

'All good then,' Frank said, glowing a little now after successfully supplanting the old, malignant mobile.

'But the reason I wanted the other phone back wasn't to

contact anyone. It was for the photos. I never backed them up on a cloud.'

Good, he thought, recalling the photo exchange he'd seen with Bobby. 'I know, but—'

'Dad. I made friends, you know, while I was on the street. Sarah was my best friend. She was fifteen. I was like a mother to her. There were a few others, too. As much as I'm glad I'm here now, with you, I want to keep those memories. Want to hold on to them. As scary as it sometimes was, it was part of me, and now always will be. I want to remember Sarah and the others. They deserve that. So, is there a way of recovering the old one? Can the police do anything?'

'I'm not sure they can, love.'

Her face dropped.

'But I'll try.'

She embraced him again.

No part of him could ever allow her to have that phone back again.

Those numbers? Those horrendous images?

There was only one place for her old device.

He'd destroy it when he had the chance.

His stomach turned as he wondered if his deceit would come back to bite him on the arse.

Chapter Sixty

AFTER THE BRIEFING, Frank asked Gerry if she'd be okay without Rylan for most of the day. Interviewing three people of interest was no small task.

'I'm fine at the moment,' Gerry said. 'I can't guarantee I will be for the rest of the day. I can only assess my state of mind at any one particular moment. The triggers are hard to swerve. If I feel overwhelmed, I'll inform you right away, as mentioned in the profile you received. I wouldn't put the investigation in any jeopardy by working without full cognitive control.'

'And are you okay with my car?'

'No. Not at all. But that's all arranged. I signed out a new car for you to drive us in... we can pick the key up at reception.'

Charming. 'That's going to hurt Bertha's feelings.'

She smiled. 'Excellent use of humour.'

'He's been working on his routine!' Reggie laughed. He was a metre away, petting Rylan. 'You need to take your routine on the road, boss.'

He looked between them both, working out who most deserved to be told to piss off.

By the time he'd decided, Gerry was already halfway out of the room, and Reggie was playing tug of war with Rylan.

So, he exited IR3, wondering how Julie, David and Paul were going to respond to today's impromptu visits.

Chapter Sixty-One

Frank wasn't used to driving a car that literally purred.

A growling motor took away the need to converse, which could be rather pleasant.

These new vehicles demanded voices to fill the silence.

'So, sailing, eh? How did you get into that?' Frank asked.

'Since childhood, my parents were keen sailors. So, they trained me from the moment I could understand instructions.'

'I imagine you could understand instructions from a very young age.' Frank smiled. 'You must be made up with this Whitby investigation then. The place has a lot of history? Mariners and the like.'

'Why? The similarities are limited. I don't sail to hunt.'

'Of course.' He nodded, wondering why he bothered trying to be sociable. 'Whaling wouldn't be your thing.'

Mid-journey, she said, 'Can I ask you something personal?'

'I'm not the best with personal conversations.'

'You just asked me about sailing. I think it's appropriate to be interested in your life.'

I was being polite! I wasn't genuinely interested in your response. He suppressed a sigh. *Whatever!* 'What do you want to know? Best case? Worse case? My biggest standoff with top brass?'

'No. I've researched all that already.'

He regarded her out of the corner of his eye. 'Come again? You were poking around in my history?'

'When I start a new job, I always research my new colleagues.'

'Why?'

I want to make the transition into my colleagues' working environments as gentle as possible. In the early days, some people felt unsettled by me. I felt that by learning about those I was going to work with, I'd feel less anxious, and if I was less anxious, I'd be less inclined to upset them. Understanding the tolerances of others can lead to a calmer workplace.'

'I get it. When I first started the job, you were measured on how many pints you could drink in the pub on a Friday.'

'I struggle to see how it's the same.'

'Getting the measure of someone?' He sighed. 'Never mind. Was a simpler life back then, you see. Anyway, you still haven't asked me this question.'

'Are you lonely, Frank?'

He almost veered off the road. 'Sorry?'

'Lonely. Are you lonely?'

Bloody hell! He took a deep breath. 'There's personal and then there's personal. I asked about a sodding hobby!'

'I'm sorry. The degree to which something is personal can sometimes be a little difficult for me.'

'Why did you even ask that?'

'Your wife, Mary, died.'

His eyes flew to the Sat Nav. Only six more minutes! *Hang tight, Frank.*

'I was sorry to hear about that,' Gerry said.

'It was a while ago.'

'Yet, you haven't remarried, so maybe you're lonely?'

'How did you reach that conclusion? Maybe I enjoy my own company? Maybe I've met someone else, and I'm fulfilled without a wedding ring?'

Gerry shook her head. 'No. You were married for most of your life. That suggests you prefer company, and so will miss it. As for another partner, no, again. I asked Reggie. It's well known amongst your colleagues that you live by yourself, go out to drink and eat alone… He said no one has ever seen you out and about with anyone else at all…'

His hands tightened on the steering wheel. 'What does it even matter if I'm bloody lonely?'

Gerry didn't respond.

'Eh? Why?'

Still no response.

'Could you answer?'

'I can't. I detected hostility and—'

'Look, forget it, I'm calling time on it, then. I feel we're acquainted enough now. I'm sorry to swear, okay?'

Gerry nodded. 'Apology accepted. Still, if you ever need to talk about anything, Frank, then…'

'We just did. It didn't go so well. Let's whack a line under it now. Move on.'

'It's considered usual for close colleagues to open up to one another. I'd like to develop that side of myself.'

'I'm close to retirement and I don't think I've ever opened up to anyone but my wife.'

'I sensed that. This was why I asked in the first place—'

'And when did we become close?'

'We should aim for that.'

He shook his head. 'You sound like you're quoting from some kind of manual.'

'Not a manual, no. The internet. I research conversations, interactions, relationships. I try to vary sources, but overall, there're generic strands that feature in all these contexts. The most difficult thing is to interpret the situation I'm in and adjust to that person. Therefore, I'm always learning.'

Christ!

He thought about 'opening up'. At least she was trying. In her own peculiar way. More than anyone else had ever done since Mary. 'Okay, I'm not that lonely. Feeling better than ever.' He glanced at her. For once, she was looking at him. 'Because my daughter came home.'

'That's good news,' Gerry said. 'I read she was homeless, and I suspect that made—'

He held his hand up and cut her off. 'I've lived it, Gerry. It's unnecessary to hear what's available in an internet domain somewhere.'

'So, she's home. How is that? Is she still a substance misuser?'

'Lord have mercy!' He shook his head. 'Is this actually happening? Look, Gerry, when you're questioning witnesses, is there anything I need to be aware of?'

'You've read my file. Nothing that isn't reported in there.'

'Aye – but remind me. You seem very straight to the point. Should I be wary of anything?'

'People have praised my questioning technique for its directness. In my last posting, my DCI asked that the team observe me and take notes.'

'Okay.' *I'll believe that when I see it.* 'We'll see. Try to leave it to me in these first instances, all right? Just until I've the lay of the land regarding your capabilities.'

'Of course. You're my superior, so if that's what you want. It seems a waste of resources, though.'

'Well, just watch Julie closely, okay? Analyse her reactions. All right? That'll help.'

'I can do that.'

'And just so you're clear...' He indicated to come off the carriageway. 'My daughter is no longer a... what did you call it? A substance misuser?'

He half-expected her to say something like 'the evidence shows that once an addict has developed a dependence, then...' so he spoke before that could happen. 'At least she's not using at the moment.'

'I *also* know how your wife died, Frank.'

Fucking hell.

He hit the brakes hard outside Julie's home. 'Saved by the job.'

'It was good to get to know you better,' Gerry opened the door.

I'm glad you enjoyed it. Frank exited the vehicle, gagging for a roll-up but knowing it was better for appearances not to have one outside Julie's home.

However, he reached into his suit pocket, pulled out the tin of snuff, and took a blast up each nostril.

Riding the nicotine rush, he hit the path, and switched his attention back to Charlotte Wilson.

And the life she never got to lead.

He looked up at the house. *And was that anything to do with you, Julie Fletcher?*

Chapter Sixty-Two

A TALL, elderly man answered the door. Frank showed his ID. 'Sorry to disturb you this early. I'm Detective Chief Inspector Frank Black, and this is Detective Inspector Gerry Carver. Are you Mr Arnold Fletcher?'

'Can I help you?'

'Is Ms Julie—'

'Ha!' Arnold's eyes widened. 'Are you serious? Over pulling a lass's hair! Not as if she scalped her?'

Frank forced back a grin. Arnold was a retired council man; he'd obviously great experience in delivering his views with strident wit. 'No, sir. It's not about the common assault charge.'

Which is a real charge for breaking the law, Arnold, but let's not get into semantics and your dogmatic views right now.

Arnold creased further his already wrinkled brow. 'Then what's it about, young man?'

Frank couldn't recall being referred to as a young man in a very long time, but he guessed next to this eighty-five-year-old, who loomed large and strong despite the support of a stick, he was comparatively young. Young enough to be his son!

Fancy that! Young enough to be someone's son!

'Is she home?' Frank asked.

'Answering a question with a question, eh?'

You'd know all about that as an ex-politician.

Frank could see the staircase behind Arnold, and the two pink slippers on the top step.

Bingo.

He leaned in, not enough to unsettle Arnold, but enough to see the lady in the dressing gown on the top step. 'Ms Fletcher?'

Keeping her hand on the top of the banister, she stared down at Frank. She didn't move or speak.

Now, how's that for an initial reaction, Gerry?

'We're letting all your heat out here, Ms Fletcher. Probably best if we came in? We've shown your father our identification.'

She chanced a couple of steps, sliding her hand down the banister as she came. 'Of course.' She moved tentatively, as if nursing an ageing hip. In fact, as her father backed away, his expression less confusion, more frustration, he moved quicker than his daughter, despite his great age and his stick.

'Thank you.' Frank allowed Gerry in first.

Once they were in and the door closed, Frank regarded Julie on the bottom step.

Her eyes and face were red and blotchy.

'Is everything all right?'

'Yes... fine... I...'

'Hungover.' Arnold snorted. 'Might be better if you came back later?'

Frank stared up at the towering man. 'Is it okay if we talk to your daughter alone, sir? Then we can talk to you.'

'Curious,' he said. 'Is it not best she's someone with her? Aren't there rules about this kind of thing?'

'Your daughter is fifty-five. It is perfectly acceptable to interview her without her father present,' Gerry said.

Frank regarded the DI he'd warned off speaking. He then looked back at the red face of Arnold.

All right, Frank thought, *I'll let that one slide. It was rather funny.*

Chapter Sixty-Three

JULIE SCRATCHED at the frayed arm of her sofa.

'We're here about a discovery that was made several nights ago, up near the whalebone arch on West Cliff.'

She nodded. 'It was on the news. Who was it?'

'An eighteen-year-old girl that went missing on the September 18th, 1987. Charlotte Wilson?'

Julie abandoned the sofa arm, took a sharp intake of breath, and leaned forward. 'I know who she is.' She squeezed her eyes shut and lowered her head.

'Take a moment,' Frank said.

Julie nodded.

He didn't give her long. 'How did you know her, Julie?'

Eyes still shut, she shook her head. 'When I read about the remains, I never imagined... never thought... *couldn't believe...* it'd be her.' She sobbed.

Frank glanced at Gerry, who was taking notes frenetically. *About what? She's said nothing yet.*

Julie opened her eyes. 'I thought she'd just upped and left. *Gone.* God, I never imagined that she...' She rubbed at her eyes with her sleeve.

'She was your friend, then?'

'Yes.'

'Close?'

'Yes. Although we only knew each other for a short time.'

'When exactly?'

Sniffing, she slumped back in the sofa chair, and returned to destroying the sofa arm. 'Christ, it was years ago. I was eighteen. It was just after Christmas. I remember thinking it was mid-Jan, and they still had the Christmas tree up in the Mariner's Lantern. Thought that was weird. That was the first night she played. We were friends until about August.'

August? Why not September? Frank made his first note.

'Your name never made its way into the investigation in 1987. Did you speak to the police?'

She shook her head. 'No.'

'Why not?'

She shrugged. 'The police never came to me.'

'Why didn't you go to them?'

'Why would I have done?'

Frank purposefully looked at Gerry to show that Julie's behaviour confused him. He wanted Julie to see his act of confusion, but it was pointless because Gerry was busy note taking. He turned back. 'A close friend vanishes from your life... a public appeal... and no attempt to speak to the police? Sorry, but that confuses me.'

She picked harder at the arm of the sofa. 'I didn't know, all right? It must have been a year before someone told me she'd disappeared. If there were a public appeal, it never found its way to me.'

'Ah,' Frank said, feigning surprise. He looked at Gerry. 'DI Carver, did the public appeal stretch to Whitby?'

'Yes,' Gerry said. 'Although primarily focused on Scarborough, it reached out around North Yorkshire.'

'I think you overestimate the airtime it got here, DCI.' Her persistent picking of the sofa's arm was getting louder. 'I don't recall it.'

Frank made a note. 'Still, your friend stops visiting Whitby, and you didn't notice?'

'Yes, of course I noticed.'

'Right... So?'

'So what?'

'You didn't think to call her mother, or maybe ask after her?'

Julie sighed. 'Well, I didn't know her mother, *but* I hear what you're saying. Look... we had an argument. A big one. Although, looking back, it was childish. But when you're eighteen, shit happens, eh? I assumed she was angry. Weeks turned into months, and I just figured she'd moved on from our friendship. I wasn't losing face by chasing after her. At least that's how my brain worked then. As a kid, you think differently, don't you?'

'What was the argument about?'

'Silly things. A lad she fancied played a set before hers. I chatted with him. She was annoyed. Thought I was bloody flirting. Told her where to go, that I had a boyfriend.' She shrugged. 'And that was that. I never saw her again.'

'But she knew you had a boyfriend already?'

'Yes.'

'So, what made her behave so irrationally?'

Her finger disappeared into the now-enlarged hole in the sofa arm. 'I don't know. But she was pissed off and that was that.'

'All right, who was the lad she fancied?'

Julie shrugged. 'I don't know.'

Frank stared at her.

'Shit! You serious? I mean, how many years ago was this?'

'Thirty-seven,' Frank said.

'I'd never seen him before and never saw him again.' She closed her eyes, clicked her fingers. 'Daz... no, that was someone else... Mike... no... look, wow, I couldn't be sure. I only spoke to him for about five minutes, and that was just me fawning all over him. *Apparently.*'

Frank wrote *Daz* and *Mike* anyway, but suspected there was little in it.

Frank raised an eyebrow. 'This argument was on the night of her disappearance?'

She shook her head. 'It can't have been. I last saw her in August.'

'How certain are you about that?'

'I split with Paul in August, and that was after she'd gone.'

Frank wrote it down. He was struggling with her denial that she hadn't known until a year later. But then media wasn't what it is now. There'd have been no Facebook appeal. And Whitby was a relatively small seaside town that kept itself to itself. It was sad to imagine his predecessors approaching it so weakly. Maybe the case file was an accurate reflection, after all. An all-round pathetic investigation?

'Look, I wish I'd known. I think, if I had have done, I would've been first in the queue to look for her. But I was eighteen. All I did was listen to records and drink with my boyfriend. When I wasn't doing that, I was playing the guitar. I wasn't watching *Crimewatch* on the TV. It just wasn't me.'

'Aye, I remember the eighties,' Frank said. 'People used

to talk a lot, not sit glued to their phones. Still, it's strange that no one thought to say – hey, Julie, you know that good friend of yours—'

'Well, no one did,' Julie said. 'People I knocked about were more like me. They probably didn't know.'

'How did you eventually find out?'

'The one who owns that pub now... what's his name?'

'Marvin Hails?'

'Yep. Him. It was about a year later. I'd split up with Paul, my boyfriend, and Marvin tried his luck. He was slimy, and always preying on every girl that came in! You should probably talk to him. He started talking about Charlotte. He told me a friend of his from Scarborough, who'd once seen Charlotte play in the Mariner's Lantern, had filled him on the sad news that Charotte had gone missing in Scarborough a while back and had never been found.'

'How did you feel?'

'Gutted. Obviously. I went home at this moment. Marvin didn't look too happy! He should have chosen a better choice of conversation. Idiot. Mind you, sure he got over it. That man was never short of a shag or two! He used to take bookings and man the free drinks for the acts. Was always using that to his advantage, I can tell you. Mind you, he was loaded. Still is. Money talks anyway, I guess.'

Frank made a note to pursue the Marvin Hails angle.

'So you were gutted? Did you do anything at *this* point?'

'Look. What is this? Are you suspicious of me?' Julie asked.

'Why would you say that?'

'Your tone. It's almost as if you don't believe me.'

'Not at all,' Frank said. 'I'm simply gathering information. She'd other acquaintances, including your ex-boyfriend, Paul, and Marvin. They'll get some of the same questions. I'm just hoping you can shed some light on that part of Charlotte's life, being that you were close to her. Sorry, the closest person to her. Is that fair? During your time in Whitby, you were her closest acquaintance?'

'I dunno... maybe.'

'And you'll be surprised, Julie. Even the smallest detail can spark a fire.'

'I understand.'

Arnold came in, holding a tray. He wasn't using his walking stick.

Frank stood to assist, but Arnold shook his head. 'I'm fine. Thank you.' He leaned over at the hips and placed the tray on the central table. He did it nimbly and with no discomfort on his face.

Frank felt a twinge of jealousy. If an eighty-five-year-old man could keep himself supple and lean, he really had no excuse over the state of himself.

Arnold attempted to linger, but Frank was patient, and eventually Julie's father gave up and left.

'Could you talk through exactly how you met Charlotte?'

'In the Mariner's.' She looked off into the distance, nursing her tea. She'd just played an open mic. 'Her voice. It was like... well... Incredible. I mean, the quality was never high in the Mariner's, but she had something special. She was going places. I saw her sitting alone afterwards. I approached. And that were that. We just hit it off. Me and her. Loved all the same music. Janis Joplin, Jim Morrison... We became close.' Sadness filled her expression. There'd been very few genuine moments, but this one was convincing.

Sadness doesn't make you innocent, though.

'Who would hurt her?' Julie stared at Frank. 'Leave her buried there? How did she even die?'

'Someone hit her on the back of her head.' He watched her face, looking for the shock. 'Smashed her skull.'

She flinched. Although, to be fair, his gruesome choice of words would probably make most people flinch, even if they were the killer.

Julie took her fingers from the hole and rubbed at her eyes again. 'Sorry…' She took several deep breaths. 'Charlotte taught me to play the guitar. I've kept it up. Even now, after all these years, I'm not a patch on her, but that's all right, few people are.'

'I know,' Frank said. 'I've heard her.'

She straightened up on the sofa. 'How?'

'*Your* demo tape.'

She regarded Frank. Her brow was creased. 'Sorry, I…'

'"Broken". And two other recorded songs.'

'Christ… really? How?'

'I'll get to where we found them in a minute. What can you tell me about the time when it was recorded?'

'Well, it certainly wasn't *our* demo. I did the backing vocals, and I think my voice was turned right down on the final copy!'

'Do you have *your* tape?' Frank asked.

She shook her head. 'No. I lost mine. A long time ago, during a move…'

'That's sad,' Frank said.

'Yes,' Julie said. 'Maybe I could have a copy?'

'We can discuss that another time, okay? I'll make a note.'

Frank made a show of scribbling in his book, but really, he was considering his next question. Every part of the interview at this stage was key; he didn't want to walk away, like Reggie had done yesterday from Marvin without getting him to look at a photo like a daft pillock. He glanced over at Gerry, who was still diligently making notes. *What are you writing? A full-on psychological profile?*

'After you met, how did your relationship develop? Did you see each other a lot?'

Julie shared details that certainly suggested the relationship was close. Regular meet-ups day and evenings; music concerts; rehearsing in Ron's studio.

He interjected with questions to build a fuller picture. They'd spent a lot of time together in 1987, in Whitby. However, she claimed not to know Laura Wilson. 'She didn't talk about her mother often, but she spoke about her father all the time. She was in adoration of him.'

'John Asante?'

'Yes. She said he'd been very talented. That he'd passed it to her. Sometimes, she became overwhelmed by the gratitude.'

'Overwhelmed how?'

'I remember her breaking down a few times when she talked about him. He was never out of her thoughts. Her song lyrics seemed to be all about him.'

'And did she meet your parents?'

Julie shook her head. 'My father wasn't happy that I suddenly went all in with the music and wasn't interested in training for a profession. Big council man.' She sneered. 'Wouldn't do to have an artistic layabout. He certainly was no John Asante! No encouragement there, I can tell you. I thought it best just to keep Charlotte away. How embarrassing would it have been if he'd said something? I was eighteen, remember? And bloody concerned about what people thought. Self-conscious times. Not sure I'd care less these days.' She lowered her voice. 'In retrospect, he was probably right, eh? Music never amounted to much for little old Julie and now look at me! I'm a suspended checkout girl on a common assault charge, facing six months in jail.'

Frank felt pity for her. A broken life was not something that went unnoticed by a man who'd spent his life in the force helping people, but right now, his focus was on another kind of 'broken' life – one that left the individual with no second chance. 'Would you say you were a violent person, Julie?'

'And what does that mean?' She rolled her eyes. 'That bitch, Cassie, deliberately got me sacked. All I did was pull her hair.'

'How about the argument with Charlotte?'

'Wasn't violent.'

'But you've a temper?'

'Wouldn't I be some kind of robot if I didn't? What happened with Cassie was an anomaly.' She leaned forward. 'Ask anyone. I get on with people. And that's the *truth*.'

The way she emphasised the truth made Frank wonder if she was drawing attention to the fact that some of the other parts of this interview had been deceitful.

Frank made some notes. 'Paul has done well for himself, hasn't he?'

'He has, yes. I take it you've been to his restaurant?'

'I can't spend that kind of money on food.' He laughed. 'Part of my nature. My wife used to say it was an illness.'

'Fairly common in these parts, I imagine.' Julie smiled. 'My father has never been one for spending money, either. You two would get on well.'

Frank recalled their chat at the door. *Somehow, I doubt that*.

'Are you and Paul still in touch?'

'No... of course not. I mean, we'll say hi if we pass one another, but we split up not long after Charlotte left. August. Caught him snogging another lass. Polly Howe. Ended up treating her like shit for a year or two before moving on again. He was all right. Just in his nature, you know? Can't settle. Always consumed by the next big thing. Me and Pol are excellent friends now! Something good came out of that shit show. Promiscuous times, eh?' She smiled.

Frank nodded and made some notes. His youth had been pedestrian in comparison. He'd only ever had one partner. Mary. He didn't expect to have another. He noticed a button had popped on his shirt around his waistline. *Jesus.* Make that a certainty that he'd never have another partner.

'Paul and Charlotte. Were the two of them friends also?'

'Of course. Yes... for a time, anyway. Summer was a blast. Strange how those happiest times suddenly come to a shuddering halt, eh?'

'Anything between them?'

'No. Charlotte wouldn't have done that to me. I knew that. Guess that's why it made me so sad when she thought I'd do it to her. Like she was the only one with a moral compass!'

Frank nodded. 'Did she have any boyfriends that you can remember?'

Julie thought about this and shook her head. 'Not that I recall. A lot tried it on, like... but I never saw her disappear off with anyone.'

He took notes.

'All right, a few more things,' Frank said. 'Did Charlotte ever stay over in Whitby?'

She shrugged. 'Not that I know of. She often had to get the last bus home.'

'Her mother claimed she sometimes contacted her from a payphone on East Terrace.'

'Sorry... I know nothing about that. I always had to be home. I mean, I never told my parents about her, so I never attempted to bring her home to stay.' She nodded towards the lounge door, clearly referencing her father. 'Imagine. Poor girl would've been told straight she was wasting her life, and that she needed to abandon her dreams, immediately.'

'We believe she may have stayed at North Sea Nook Beach Huts. Did you know anything about that?'

'Sorry... what? Beach huts? Sounds odd. Can you even sleep in them?'

'Well, it's not what they're designed for, but if you've a key...' Frank said. *Not sure that it'd do my back the world of good sleeping in one like...* 'At the beach huts, we found her guitar.' He showed her a picture of a guitar.

'I remember it. It was a nice guitar. She often let me use it.'

'We also found this.' He showed her the image of David Roberts and Charlotte by the bar. 'Do you know who that is?'

'David Roberts? The landlord's son at the Mariners.'

'How well did you know him?'

'Not well.'

Frank made a note. 'He's the same age as you? You probably went to school with him?'

'Never had much to do with him to be honest.'

'Have you seen him in recent years?'

'No. Not heard anything about him. Not since the Mariner's burned down.'

'He lives in Scarborough now,' Frank said. 'They seem close on that photo, don't you think? Charlotte and David.'

'Let me see again?'

Frank turned the phone around.

'I guess. Polaroid?'

Frank nodded.

'An instant camera,' Julie said. 'It was revolutionary, but people didn't want to waste a shot. It was expensive. People often tried too hard with photos and so came across as too excitable.'

'True enough, I was there. But still...' Frank returned to his seat. 'Excitable or not. She must have thought something of him to mark the picture with his initials. That was a memory she wanted to keep.'

Chapter Sixty-Four

'You barely said anything.' Frank closed his car door.

'Yes,' Gerry said. 'On your instruction.'

'That wasn't what I meant.'

'What did you mean?'

'I meant for you to stay silent while I led, but if you noticed anything essential to question it.'

'You didn't make that clear whatsoever. Your words were "watch closely, analyse her reactions."' She held up her notebook. 'So I did.'

'Oh, I saw.' He rolled his eyes. 'Next time, you can ask some questions then, okay? I was just worried about putting Julie on the defensive too early, you know?'

She nodded.

'So, what did you think?' Frank asked.

'You were very thorough. Direct. In fact, I think our styles are rather similar.'

'Not about me! What did you think of Julie?'

'Well, I got what I needed.'

Frank shook his head. 'You got what you needed... and

what was that? Do share please! I'm feeling rather uninformed here!'

'You're not being truthful, Frank. I could tell from your tone of voice and questioning that you were picking up on the same elements as me.'

He smirked. 'Are those elements written in the manuscript?' He nodded at the book in her hands.

'I was analysing her body movements, facial expressions, tone, choice of syntax, etc. Every single reaction.'

'All of them! Bloody hell. Do you reckon you reached the same conclusion as me then?'

'Yes.'

Even though I haven't even told you my conclusion... oh, yeah... you just read me like a book, too. I remember.

'She's lying,' Frank said. 'I'm certain she will have known about Charlotte's disappearance long before Marvin Hails filled her in.'

He didn't need an expert on facial expressions for that. Nothing could be more blindingly obvious. If you were friends, you didn't sever all contact, forever, over a childish argument.

'But it wasn't all deceit,' Gerry said.

'Go on.'

'She did care about Charlotte deeply. Her affection to her was, and still is, genuine.'

Frank nodded. 'And whatever happened to that poor lass has plagued her to this very day.'

'She's emotionally fragile. The signs of heavy drinking are clear. I wondered if we should speak to her father.'

'What? To monitor her? Look at him! I think he's already doing that!'

'I don't get the sense, though, that she's responsible for Charlotte's death.'

'Me neither.' He nodded at the book. 'But why not tell us the truth? Innocence and lying do not a match make.'

His phone rang. It was Reggie. 'Okay, as requested, I've prepped the public appeal. I've got the beach huts in there, as well as the times she was last sighted in Scarborough at the train station.'

'It's a long shot,' Frank said. 'So long ago. But memories about significant things exist. Let's be positive. More so than our predecessors were, anyway.' He hung up and turned to Gerry again. 'Okay, next up. Who do we need to see more urgently? A doctor or a chef?'

'I'm not hungry, so the doctor?' She glanced at him and smiled.

He made a point of laughing at her attempted humour. 'Well, Gerry, I'm hungry... always am... but I like your call. Better for my health not to eat and see the doc.' He started the engine, indicated and moved out.

Chapter Sixty-Five

Julie dealt with the shock over the visit in the only way she knew how.

While her father pounded on her door, demanding that she explain what the hell the police had wanted, she set fire to her anxiety with alcohol.

Eventually, once her father had given up, she slumped down on the wall beside her old guitar. Her phone rang. She answered it, half-expecting the police again, but getting the receptionist at her son's secondary school.

The receptionist sounded distraught. It sent a shiver running down her spine. She stood and stumbled around the room, pissed. She couldn't believe what she was hearing. *Tom...*

The receptionist was apologising over and over.

'How could you? How could you let this happen?' She hung up, threw some clothes on, snatched her car keys from beside the bed and swung open her door, staggered down the stairs, out the front door, and after falling twice – the second time ripping her trousers – she clambered into the car.

The world spinning around her, she started the engine.

She thought she glimpsed her father at the lounge window but didn't take a second look. Keeping the car on the road was going to take all of her focus.

Tom?

Where the bloody hell have you gone?

Chapter Sixty-Six

They parked outside a plush business complex on the outskirts of Scarborough.

The visitor parking spots were pushed very far back, so Frank circled the staff parking until he found a bay marked Best Life Therapy. A sleek jag occupied one of the two slots. He snorted. 'Should have trained to be a psychiatrist.'

'I don't think you possess the right attributes for that career path,' Gerry said.

He parked. 'You're right. I'm too warm and fluffy.'

Gerry pointed up to a sign. 'They may clamp you.'

'It's not my car.' Frank climbed out.

He buzzed the receptionist from the entrance on the ground floor to access the complex.

While Frank made a beeline for the lift, Gerry pointed out the stairs. 'It's only two floors.'

Followed by a heart attack. 'Not for me.'

Predictably, the lift was out of order.

That's God that is, old man, Frank thought, *telling you to get your arse in gear. Let's have this!*

Motivated, he followed Gerry up the steps with vigour.

By the time he reached the second floor, his language was so obscene that people were staring out at him from glass-fronted office windows.

The receptionist in *Best Life Therapy* pointed out some comfortable seats behind a flowerpot and told them David Roberts still had twenty minutes of an appointment to go.

He considered pissing David off by calling an abrupt end to the appointment, but then decided it was only twenty minutes, and would be quite harsh to the person in there who was chasing this elusive "best life" promised by the countless leaflets and posters strewn around the place.

He used the time to review David's history from the notebook. Married to Hanna Goodall… childhood sweetheart… no children… no priors… Oxford educated… psychiatrist for some top London institutions… a return to North Yorkshire in 2010… Best Life set up… accolades, etc.

Pleasant life, eh, fella? Quite a contrast from Julie with her washed-up life.

Paul Harrison would slip in nicely alongside David, no? Two successful men… power-hungry…

Charlotte and Julie vs David and Paul.

Bloody hell… a real man's world back then, eh?

He looked over at Gerry. It'd have been difficult for her to fly up the ranks in 1987. And yet… he'd never come across someone so adept at swooping for a single needle in a haystack before emerging with two.

The world was moving on, and rightly so. He hoped it wasn't too late for Maddie to dig out something for herself as well.

The office door opened, and they heard David's booming voice before they saw him.

Here was a man who liked to have his presence felt.

Over his career, Frank had endured a boatload of people like this.

David swaggered out. Even at fifty-five, he still possessed the same boyish good looks and the fine wavy blond hair he'd had in 1987 in that polaroid. He didn't look over at the two detectives sitting in his waiting room.

It could have been because he was so engrossed in his own voice with the thirty-something petite brunette who was looking up at him, nodding her head, hanging off every word. Or he could just have been ignoring them. Either obnoxiously or possibly, because he'd something to hide.

David's hand was on the small of the woman's back as he guided her towards reception.

Frank wondered if David's physical touch intimidated his patient.

Most of the modern world wouldn't accept it any more, and for good reason. Not that this had ever been an issue for Frank. He'd always kept his hands to himself. He didn't have to be taught what 'appropriate touch' meant; unfortunately, the same hadn't applied to some of his male colleagues, especially in the earlier years of his career.

Many of these colleagues had been forced into early retirement. Deservedly so.

Gerry was about to rise to prepare for his greeting, when Frank whispered, 'Don't. Let the obnoxious idiot acknowledge us first.' In his experience, the more sophisticated and entitled the male believed himself to be, the more likely he'd respond to a traditional pissing contest. Frank picked up a magazine and thumbed through it to an article. He stopped on an article pretending to be non-fiction, about a young man who'd accidentally married the mother who gave him up for adoption. According to the headline, the truth came out on their second wedding anniversary. Frank wondered as to the integrity of the article's fact-checkers before a shadow fell over him. He put the magazine down and looked up.

'Mr David Roberts.' He rose. 'I'm DCI Black. This is DI Carver. Thank you for seeing us on short notice.'

'Or with no notice, as the case may be.' David smiled.

Frank returned the smile. 'It's very important. We need to ask you a few questions. Can we go into your office?'

'Can't it wait? The thing is, I've got another appointment in less than an hour.'

'Not really.'

'Can we be quick then?'

Frank didn't respond.

'Okay, come with me.'

It'll take as long as it takes, Frank thought as they followed him into his office. *And then some, you arrogant pillock.*

When in the office, Frank looked around the walls at the certificates and accolades. Then he took a seat opposite him at the desk.

'What's this about?' David asked.

Frank took out his phone, scrolled to the polaroid taken in the Mariner's in 1987 and slid it over the table.

David smiled. 'Wow. Where did you get that?'

'So, you can verify that this is you in that photo?'

David pushed the phone back over the table. 'Well, unless I've got a doppelgänger roaming wild, then yes' – he touched his chest – 'that is *I*.'

Frank recognised that smirk. He'd seen it countless times. The smirk of the arrogant. Of those who thought themselves untouchable.

'I was quite the looker.' He winked at Gerry.

Aye... among other things.

'Who's that in the photo with you?' Gerry asked.

Frank was glad she was having a go now. His attempt to rein her in, which had ultimately silenced her, had made him feel guilty.

'Who?' David reached back for Frank's phone and drew it back towards him. 'Let me see again... hmm... it doesn't ring too many bells.'

This was bullshit. If his detached attitude carried on for much longer, Frank would have to sit on his hands or risk pushing the boundaries. He glanced at Gerry. *I'll give you two questions to unlock him. Otherwise, I'm going in.*

'But it was a long time ago,' David continued. He massaged his forehead as he stared down at the phone.

'There were some initials on the back. C and DR. 1987. DR is you,' Gerry said. 'David Roberts. So, the C could help?'

'Well, let me think. It's a musician... that's a given, because I took a lot of these. Open mic, 1987. Bloody hell! There were so many. Everyone wanted to be a pop star. I would've been seventeen... eighteen? I took photos with loads of them in case any of them became famous later, you know? Silly boyish naivety, I suppose. I don't think any of them ever made it to the big time! Ha! Not that I kept up with the music scene. More of a classical man myself.' He leaned back in his chair. 'They were happy days though, them... the landlord's son! Old enough to drink.' He winked at Frank. 'You can imagine. Living above a pub... living the dream, eh?' David crossed his arms.

He was trying to lead them off-piste.

'Her name was Charlotte Wilson,' Gerry said. 'She played many times in that pub. Marvin Hails, current owner of the Saltwick Sailor, knew you and your family well back then. He knew who she was. Unforgettable is how she's being described by many. Seems strange that you can't remember her? Maybe look again.' She had David fixed in a piercing stare.

So, this is what you save the eye contact for, Gerry!

David touched his lips and thought. He lifted his eyes.

Bloody hell, this isn't for the Oscars, man.

'Charlotte... Charlotte...' He clicked his fingers. He leaned over and looked at the picture on the phone for the third time. 'Yes, of course! She played a few times at our place.'

'She went missing,' Gerry said. 'In 1987, do you remember?'

He nodded. He clearly knew there was no point in denying it any longer. 'Yes... I recall now.'

Frank's turn. 'I assume you contacted the police?'

'My father took care of all that.'

'All of what? Reporting missing people?' Frank asked.

David's eyes widened; he caught Frank's tone full on. '*Everything*. Look, if I remember correctly, my father told me she had gone missing, and that he'd phone it in.'

'You said "remember correctly"? Why aren't you positive?'

'Memory is untrustworthy. You know this was a long time ago, right?'

'Thirty-seven years,' Gerry said.

'Very precise.' David smirked.

'And there's no record of your father making a report in the missing person's file,' Frank said.

David shrugged. 'He said he did. Unfortunately, you can't ask him. He's dead, you see.'

The fact is, his father could have made contact. After all, not everything had made it into the wafer-thin report.

Frank mentally sighed when he considered the incompetence of his predecessors again.

'Tell me what you remember about Charlotte,' Frank said.

David shrugged and folded his arms. 'I didn't *bloody* know her! Look, you've triggered vague memories of her playing. She was good... I think. I genuinely can't remember taking that photo *because* I took a lot of photos. In fact, that was Hanna's camera. Yes,' he nodded, smiling, 'Hanna's. My spoiled wife! Her parents have a lot of money, you see.' He chortled. 'I mean, how many eighteen-year-olds had one of those cameras back then?'

'Does she still have it?' Gerry asked.

David snorted. 'Are you serious? I might dig up an old digital camera from ten years back, but if I still had that camera, it'd be on eBay! Reckon it'd be worth a fortune. Nope. Sorry. But it was hers. As I just said. Ask her. She took photos of me with these musicians. Just, you know, in case the next Eric Clapton showed up. He didn't. I was eighteen and my head was in the clouds. Like any other eighteen-year-old!'

'Did you take photos for all the musicians to take away with them, too?'

'Ha! They were musicians. Rebelling against the system. I was a well-to-do lad about to shoot off to Oxford. Not sure I would've taken pride of place in their memorabilia.'

'But isn't that strange?' Gerry asked.

'Come again?'

'We found this photo in Charlotte's possessions with your initials on the back... You already suggested you hadn't written them. You weren't a potential rockstar so why did she want a photo of you?'

David paled for the first time.

Bullseye Gerry. 'Were you friends, perhaps? Lovers?' Frank asked.

'Don't be ridiculous!' There was a flash of anger in his eyes now. 'Hanna was my girlfriend. It was hardly the best way to sneak about behind her back, eh? Have her take photos of me? Maybe, Hanna took a second photograph and gave it to her? Or, this girl stole my original?'

'Before you were adamant that a musician wouldn't want one of you,' Frank said.

He shook his head, appearing rattled. 'I really couldn't tell you why.'

Gerry said, 'Maybe you could dig out these old polaroids and see if there isn't another version, after all.'

'Ah,' he said. 'That'll be difficult.'

Surprise surprise… 'Why?'

'All those polaroids burned along with the Mariner.'

Frank sighed.

Gerry asked, 'Aren't you curious as to why we're asking about Charlotte?'

'You haven't allowed me a second to ask yet.' He fixed Gerry with narrow eyes.

Gerry continued making eye contact, looking completely unfazed. Frank liked how she slipped into these different zones. He much preferred this no-nonsense approach to the frenetic scribbling of body movements she'd adopted when interviewing Julie. No need for any observation to know this man was completely and utterly full of shit.

'My colleague has a point,' Frank said. 'Surely, you'd be curious.'

'I assumed it was about those remains discovered by the whalebones.'

'Why would you do that?' Frank asked. 'Assume?'

'Because I saw it on the news earlier... because things like that rarely happen around here.'

'Huh,' Frank said and then made a point of scribbling down some notes.

'I mean what else is going to bring two high-ranking detectives swanning into my humble life?' David asked.

Frank glanced around the room again. *Nothing humble, here. You're displaying every qualification and every achievement like a medal in here.*

'So, am I right? Do the remains belong to the person in that picture?' David asked.

'Charlotte?'

'Yes... Charlotte.'

Frank nodded.

David shook his head. 'Look. It's clear we've rubbed each up the wrong way, here. Honestly, now, if I remembered this Charlotte, I mean *really* remembered her, I'd tell you more, I would. Whoever did that and put her in the ground was obviously a monster. How did she die, anyway?'

'A blow to the back of the head,' Frank said.

'Animal.'

'Have you ever used a beach hut on West Cliff, Mr Roberts?'

His eyes widened. 'A beach hut? One of those multi-coloured things people get changed in? What a strange question. No!'

'Ever heard of the North Sea Nook Beach Huts?'

'Can't say I have.'

'Do you know if Charlotte had a boyfriend?'

He rolled his eyes and slowed his voice down to show frustration. 'I didn't know her.'

'But we've established that you did,' Gerry said.

'It took me three bloody looks at the picture before my synapses fired up and I remembered her singing. Honestly, this is a lifetime ago and frankly, ridiculous.'

Frank put his hands on the table and leaned in. He looked David up and down. 'Is it? How would you feel if that was your child recovered?'

David snorted. 'What a thing to say. It isn't my child. I don't have children, either. Still, I sympathise with the mother. I hope you catch him.'

'Two things,' Gerry said. 'First, you said mother. We never told you that Charlotte only had a mother. Why not say parents or father?'

David flinched but then steeled himself and leaned forward. 'Ha! So that'll be part of your argument in court, will it? That I pictured a crying mother instead of a crying father?'

Smartarse.

'You also said *him*. What makes you think it was a man?' Gerry continued, undeterred.

David sighed loudly. 'I don't know. Isn't it always?'

'No,' Frank said. 'So, search the synapses. Did she have a boyfriend? Friends?'

'I don't know. And if she had friends, she probably had more than me. I liked to keep myself to myself.'

'Apart from when taking photos with potential stars?' Gerry asked.

'Something like that,' David said.

'Do you know Julie Fletcher?' Frank asked.

'Vaguely... I remember chatting to her a few times back in the day.'

'When was the last time you saw her?'

'God! Decades!'

'Did you know she was good friends with Charlotte?

Close friends.'

'Was she?' He scrunched his brow. 'I might have some flashes of them together. It's difficult, you know, memory. Sometimes we create memories based on suggestions. But right now, I've a vague image of them laughing together.'

'And Paul Harrison? Know him?'

'Paul. The chef?' David asked. 'I know him. I've eaten at his restaurant. So?'

'He was Julie's boyfriend. He knew Charlotte too.'

'Let me think. Yes, he's sitting there alongside them, but I can't tell if you put it there, DCI?' He shrugged and raised the palms of his hands. 'You can't trust memories.'

We certainly can't trust yours.

'But I remember that Julie dated Paul, if that helps.'

Gerry asked, 'You said your father told you about Charlotte's disappearance.'

'That's right. My father told me about it on the phone when I was away at Oxford.'

'I see. Can you be more specific on dates?'

David said. 'Sometime near Christmas? When did she go missing?'

'September 18th.'

'Ha!' He slammed his palm down on the table. 'I was away. Oxford. Term would have started. So there we have it!'

'There we have what?' Frank asked.

'My innocence.'

'We've not been discussing your innocence,' Frank said.

'Nonsense.'

'No,' Gerry said. 'My superior is correct. We levelled no accusations.'

His face was growing redder. 'You came in waving that photo like OJ Simpson's glove!'

'I think you're misreading the situation,' Frank said. 'We're trying to build a picture.'

'Nonsense,' he said again. His face was glowing. 'And I've had enough. I want a solicitor—'

His phone rang. He snatched it up. 'What?' His face grew redder and screwed tighter as he listened. 'But they're already here!'

Who's already here? Is he referring to us?

'Different...? How...? What've they said...? *What?* Okay, one moment.' He put the phone down and stared at it, confused.

'What's happening?' Frank said.

'The police.' He pointed at Frank. 'You lot,' – he swung his finger at the door – 'out there. You planning to arrest me? I'll have you for—'

'Eh?' Frank interrupted. 'Nothing to do with me.'

'They're in uniform.' David stood.

'Then it's not about this. What have you been up to, Mr Roberts?' Frank stood.

'Nothing, I...'

'Wait here,' Frank said. He pointed at the chair. 'I'll go.'

Frank went out into the waiting room. Two officers, male and female, were standing over at the desk.

Over on the sofa, a young lady – *was everyone who came here a young lady?* – was pretending to read the magazine Frank had been reading, while casting furtive glances.

He went over to the officers and identified himself. They did the same. He asked them why they were here.

The young police constable, Louise Harris, said, 'To arrest him, sir.'

Frank asked, 'What for?'

The two younger officers looked at each other.

'Do I have to get my ID out again?'

'Sorry, it's not that. I just didn't want to say it out loud,' Louise said.

'You're about to take him out in cuffs, Constable. That'll ruin him. Doesn't matter what the lady over there pretending to read hears, but whisper to me if you'd prefer.'

She did whisper, but it was the kind of whisper that would surely be heard.

'He assaulted his wife, sir. Day before yesterday. She admitted herself to hospital early the next morning feeling sick. They suspected a minor concussion. About an hour ago, she gave a full statement to the police. He's been doing it for years.'

'Bloody hell,' Frank said.

The office door opened. He turned to see David emerging. Behind him, Gerry followed.

'What's going on?' the psychiatrist asked.

'They'll have to tell you about that, Mr Roberts, but one's things for certain. I now know where to find you when I need you again. Come on, Detective Inspector.' As they were leaving, he turned. He looked over at the patient, then at the receptionist, and finally at the officers. 'Make sure you remind him of exactly what he's under arrest for. Spare no details. He'll appreciate that, what with his rather dicky memory. What was it you said, Mr Roberts? Takes a while to fire up the synapses? Maybe, read him his rights twice. That'll get them very warm.'

Frank turned, smirked and left the office, thinking, *Enjoy your impending nightmare, you savage bastard, I'll see you soon...*

Chapter Sixty-Seven

Julie tore down the road towards Tom's school.

Other drivers pounded their horns, but it didn't slow her, or stop her from taking on the amber lights before they turned red.

Her phone buzzed on the passenger seat.

Tom?

She grabbed her phone. Her eyes left the road as she fumbled with it. Another horn blared. She looked up to see she was straying into the other lane. She corrected herself before colliding with the panicking motorist who'd been too close to stop.

Eventually, after conceding this was suicide, she pulled over to read the message.

Thank God.

She knew where he was.

Although, it still wasn't the best news.

Needing to go in the other direction, she headed down a side street to swing the car around.

What the hell had he gone there for?

Sneaking out of school, scaring the living shit out of her was one thing, but *that? Going there?*

That was a whole new level of dissent.

It wasn't long before the fury pushed her past the speed limit again.

Chapter Sixty-Eight

HAVING SURVIVED THE JOURNEY, Julie pounded on the door.

No one answered.

She pounded again; then she turned full circle, noticing she'd left her car door ajar on the road after exiting her vehicle in haste.

A pair of middle-aged women watched wide-eyed from the other side of the road.

'Fuck off!'

She turned again, knelt, pushed open the letter box and shouted in. 'Tom! Get your arse out here now. *Tom!*'

'Wait a moment, Julie, for heaven's sake, I'm coming...'

Sylvia.

'You better, you stupid cow, or I'll kick—'

The door swung open.

Sylvia stood there, looking, to her credit, far healthier than she'd done the last time Julie had seen her two years back. Extreme weight loss, purple rinse and a change of wardrobe suited the sixty-eight-year-old well.

'Where's Tom?' Julie asked.

'I'm here, Mum.' Tom emerged from the lounge door in the hallway just behind Sylvia.

'Get your arse out of here *now*.' She pointed at the car.

Sylvia took a step towards Julie, holding out the palms of her hands. 'There's no need for—'

'*Don't.*' She narrowed her eyes. Then, she glanced in Tom's direction again. '*Now.*'

He mumbled something, lowered his head, and slipped past Sylvia.

Sylvia took her thirteen-year-old grandson by the shoulders and kissed the back of his head.

'Get your hands off him,' Julie said.

'You're being ridiculous, Mum,' Tom said. 'I told Nan not to text you. Said you'd react like this. She's kind. You're not.'

Julie grabbed the front of her son's jacket. 'Kind, eh? You don't know the first thing. And I'll tell you what's ridiculous. Your bloody school phoning me and telling me you'd pissed off somewhere! That's ridiculous. And that's not kind. To me. Now get in the car before I completely lose it.'

Tom marched towards the car. 'You already have lost it.'

'What the hell do you think you're playing at?' Julie turned to Sylvia.

'He just came round.'

'Why didn't you let me know?'

'I did.'

'No!' Julie pointed inside the house. 'He doesn't go in there.'

'You want me to turn him away? Make him wait outside? He's thirteen. And you know what he's like. He's vulnerable. He could end up in trouble.'

Forgotten Bones

'I know what he's like, *Sylvia*. He's my son.' She thumbed her chest. 'My *fucking* son!'

'And he's my grandson. I was trying to help. Come in, Julie. Come in, calm down and we can talk?'

'Calm down.' She shook her head and looked off to the right. Some more locals were throwing inquisitive glances from two doors down. 'You can fuck off too!'

Sylvia reached a hand out. Julie batted it away. 'Stay back.'

'Whatever happens,' Sylvia said. 'I'm still his family. He won't forget me.'

She glared. 'Guess what? I can't forget you either. What you did... what you didn't do.'

'But it's different now. Why don't you let me explain how?'

'Why should I? He has a family. He doesn't need anyone else.' She turned around to see that Tom had climbed into the car. He'd left the door open so he could eavesdrop. 'Shut the bloody door!'

He closed it.

'Look.... he told me,' Sylvia said. 'About the bed wetting, about the nightmares—'

Julie swung back. 'Jesus... this is why I didn't want him here.'

'And the bullies.'

'What bullies?'

'That's not even the worst of it. For him, anyway. You know what's concerning him most. You. Julie. You.'

The words came at her like a blade, cutting her. She flinched and took a step back. 'You sanctimonious old cow. You're a fine one to talk!'

'I'm not judging, Julie. I'm not the same person. Since they've left, I've woken up.'

Julie took another step back. She felt off-guard. This wasn't the right time for this. 'I can take care of my son just fine.'

'I'm sure you can, but it's not a bad thing to get help. I did.'

Julie shook her head. Did she look that bad? What had Tom been saying? 'It's bullshit. All of it. I'm fine!'

Sylvia sighed.

'I'm fine!' Julie said.

'Are you?'

Pissed out of my face. Driving. Ranting and raving on a doorstep. Swearing at your neighbours. But apart from that, fine, yes!

A tear ran down Sylvia's cheek. 'I want to help. I do. I miss Tom so much... he's been texting me, and I'll be honest, I've been texting him back.'

Shit ... shit!

Julie pointed at Sylvia. 'You *know* I don't want that. Can't have that.'

'But why? It's *so* different. I swear on everything.'

'But I can't forgive you, don't you fucking get that? Any of you.'

'But Phil's gone. Three years. It's not the same here. I'm my own person, again. Who I was before. So long ago. That bastard doesn't control me, believe me. The person standing in front of you will do anything for Tom... and you, too, Julie, if you believe me.'

'But I don't. How can I?'

'You should. I'm not trapped... I'm not sick any more.'

'You never stood up to him. You never stood up to either of them. Phil or Carl. When I needed you, when *he* needed you.'

Sylvia wiped at her tears. 'I know... and I'm sorry. I

couldn't see the woods for the trees. I was scared of my own shadow. Phil's heart attack was the best thing that ever happened to me.'

Julie snorted. 'Well, I admit, you look a damn sight better for it. But then, who wouldn't? Phil was a fucking animal.'

Sylvia nodded and looked down. More tears ran down her face. 'Think I finally realised that when I saw how many people turned up to the funeral. You could count them on one hand.'

'You reap what you sow.'

'I should never have taken his side,' Sylvia said.

When Tom had been nine, he'd accidentally broken a window with a football and that angry dickhead, Phil, had knocked the living daylights out of him.

'No, you shouldn't have.'

The song 'Stand by Your Man' was playing through Julie's drunken mind; it also made her consider her own father, someone she'd stood by over the years, despite *his* controlling nature.

'I'm sorry. Please believe me.' Sylvia was crying harder now.

Julie stared at the ground. *Why is it me that always ends up feeling guilty? For God's sake!* She looked up. 'You were always good with him. I get that. I can see why he wants to come back and see you, but his father, Carl, I can't risk it.'

'Carl is overseas. Married in Thailand. He won't ever be coming back.'

'You can't know that. Not for sure.'

'No, I can't, but I promise you it isn't the same. Carl never had power over me like his father. Carl is too weak. Too...'

'Pathetic?'

Sylvia nodded. 'If he ever came back, I'd tell you.'

Julie looked down again, shaking her head.

'Please, Julie.' Sylvia stepped out of the door and onto the path. 'Let me see him. Let me help you.'

Julie looked up, shaking her head. *What was happening here?*

A moment ago, she'd been full of rage and now she was being talked round.

Why do you always crumble so easily? Get a grip on yourself, woman! 'Look, I don't think—'

'*Please...* let's just get a coffee together. All of us. Talk.'

'I can't. I *just* can't.' Deep down, Julie knew Sylvia was harmless. That she'd experienced dreadful treatment and had lived in a state of fear. 'I can't even think right now!' She turned and headed back to the car.

'Please,' Sylvia called after her. 'I'm not too old to help!'

As opposed to my old man, is that what you're implying?

She jumped in the car and slammed the door.

Outside, Sylvia stood on her doorstep, hand pressed to her chest.

She looked at Tom, who was glaring at her. 'Don't,' she said. 'Just don't. I'll give you two minutes to think about who just bloody caused this and then we'll talk about it.'

Chapter Sixty-Nine

Two minutes quickly became three, and even more rapidly, became five.

She glanced at him, her frustration mounting. He was looking out the window, seemingly indifferent. 'You walked out of school! Without permission. That's the issue here. What were you thinking?'

He didn't turn.

Why can't he understand the gravity of the situation?

'To hear your child has disappeared... do you know what that does to a mother?' Her voice was cracking.

Nothing.

'I know you're not selfish, Tom, but that was thoughtless.' She tried to keep her tone even.

He turned and glared. 'Thoughtless. Nan is harmless. And you know it.'

'I *know* she stuck up for the person who almost broke your neck.' The memory sent a chill down her spine.

'He's dead.'

'As far as I'm concerned, he's very much alive in that house, and I don't know her as well as I thought I did.'

'Well, I do.'

'Really?'

'Yes. I've been texting her for months. This is also the third time I've visited.'

'Shit!' She slammed the steering wheel. *How could he keep this from me?*

'And you know what? She's more in control of herself than you are!'

His accusation hung in the air.

'And what's that supposed to mean, young man?' Her heart raced, dreading his response.

He mimed drinking. 'This... all the time...' He wiped tears away. 'Ian says it will kill you. He says it killed his dad.' Ian was his best friend at school.

Julie felt her heart sink, guilt washing over her. 'Honey, I...' She looked at him, taking in his red eyes and vulnerable expression. *Still, so much like a baby. My baby. How could I do this to him? Subject him to this?*

He shook his head and broke eye contact with her and looked forwards, his body language closing off.

Suddenly, his whole body tensed up, his eyes widened and his mouth fell open in horror. '*Mum...* the lights!'

She glanced ahead as she passed through the red light, realisation dawning too late. *Shit!* Her body froze over and she didn't even have time to consider the brake before she heard the loud horn, glanced right and saw the front of the oncoming bus.

Chapter Seventy

From his bedroom window, Paul watched the two suited individuals approaching his house. They looked quite the pair. The female was fresh-faced, tall, lean and smartly dressed; the other was... well, the complete opposite in all regards.

Not that any of that was important.

An icy claw of anxiety clutched his heart, and he steadied himself against the windowsill, fearful he might take another turn.

'What's wrong?' Jess asked.

Paul closed his eyes, turned, leaned back against the wall, and as he exhaled, said, 'They're here.' He opened his eyes and regarded her lying beneath the covers of his bed.

She sat up; the covers dropped away, revealing her breasts. She was beautiful.

His heart dropped over the certainty that this was surely the last time they'd be together.

The doorbell sounded and he saw her flinch.

'See?' He said.

She shook her head. 'But how...? You said she gave you twenty-four hours to get your affairs in order?'

He shrugged. 'Maybe she panicked about me running?' He went across the room and slipped on his dressing gown.

'Wait... don't—'

'What's the point?' Paul asked. The doorbell sounded again. 'It's over.' He walked over, leaned in, and kissed her. *Why are you still here, anyway? After everything I told you last night. There's too much goodness in you for that, Jess.*

'Remember what we talked about,' Jess said. 'You give your side of the story. You plead for leniency.'

He smiled. 'After this, I don't want you involved. I don't want you taking my side. You've your family to think about.'

Jess had tears in her eyes. She clutched his arm. 'Don't go. Maybe they'll leave. Give us some more time. Think up a better plan.'

The doorbell sounded a third time, and Paul turned away. 'No, Jess. Time's up.'

Chapter Seventy One

After introductions and identification, Paul gestured down at his fastened dressing gown. 'I haven't just got up. Just been on the exercise bike and was about to hop in the shower.'

Frank glanced to his right at Gerry, who was observing Paul's face – something she seemed to do well in a professional context, despite social contexts providing her with a seemingly unscalable mountain.

He bet she was thinking the same thing as him: *A lingering smile? Anxiety. Also, exercise? Where's the red face, the damp hair, the shimmering brow?*

We've another liar.

'What's this concerning?' Paul asked.

'Best we come in and explain,' Frank said.

'I won't lie...'

Well, that would be a good start.

Paul looked upward and shrugged. 'I've company. Could we maybe make an appointment? I'll come to the station?'

'It's pressing, Mr Harrison. We'll be discreet. Whoever is upstairs will barely notice we're here.'

Paul's eyes flicked between the detectives.

'Okay?' Frank considered probing into why he was so paranoid about having them anywhere near him. His date would be none the wiser about the visit's purpose if they stayed upstairs.

Paul nodded but looked far from okay. Granted, he was working hard to maintain a stony demeanour, but Frank was long enough in the tooth to know that here was a man crumbling inside.

Not the super-confident chef renowned for wowing the rich of North Yorkshire.

Paul led them in.

If the size of the townhouse on Mulgrave Place hadn't already demonstrated that he was well-off, then the interior certainly would.

Expensive dark rich woods met the caress of deep blue fabrics. A nod to the relentless waves of the North Sea, perhaps? The fireplace was expansive and full of grandeur, but it was the oil paintings above it that caught Frank's attention. Moonlit abbey ruins. Tumultuous seascapes. The paintings that drew you off the street into an artist's gallery, before repelling you with their dangling price tags.

Paul offered them a seat, which they accepted, but then didn't sit himself. Frank insisted and then took out his notebook.

Paul leaned forward in his chair, tapping one foot, desperate to remain calm, although Frank would warrant that his blood pressure was currently reaching record levels.

'Mr Harrison, are you aware that someone discovered human remains close to the old whalebone arch several nights back?'

Paul nodded. 'Yes, of course. It's in the news. And a stone's throw from here... I was aware of the commotion. I had to find other routes around it.'

Commotion? Sorry if it put you out... 'The recovered remains belonged to Charlotte Wilson. Did you know her?' He paused and waited for Paul's response.

Paul's eyes darted between the two detectives as they had done on the doorstep.

Denial wouldn't be your best move, Paul – just ask David...

Eventually, he dropped his eyes. 'I knew her, yes. And that's sad to hear. She'd a wonderful singing voice and was a lovely girl.'

'We're hearing that a lot,' Frank said. 'What was your relationship with Charlotte?'

'Friends. *Just* friends.'

'Close friends?' Frank asked.

'I wouldn't say close. She was closer to Julie Fletcher, my girlfriend, at the time.'

Frank nodded at Gerry. He was interested in hearing her go again.

'Can you remember when you and Charlotte first met?'

Paul rubbed his forehead. 'It was an age ago. When was it? Late eighties? I met Charlotte with Julie. To be honest, I wasn't with Julie all that long. Let me think. I celebrated my eighteenth birthday with Julie in December 1986' – he clucked his tongue – 'and we weren't together for my nineteenth birthday in December 1987.'

'Charlotte disappeared on September 18th, 1987. You and Julie were friends with her in the time leading up to then. Julie seems to think it was sometime around January that you both met Charlotte.'

'You've spoken to Julie?' Paul raised an eyebrow.

'Yes,' Frank said. 'She was very helpful. Anyway, do all those dates make sense to you, Mr Roberts?'

He nodded. 'It fits, I guess. In my head. Hazy, though... I'm fifty-five now!'

'Hazy?' Frank asked. 'I'm surprised it's not clearer for you, Mr Harrison?'

'Sorry, what do you mean?'

'I mean, wasn't it a turbulent time?'

He paled. 'What're you getting at exactly?'

'We'll get to that in a moment,' Gerry said. 'Let's stay focused on Charlotte in the meantime.'

Frank didn't mind waiting. Let Gerry call it. She'd done a good job before with David. The discovery of Paul's 'turbulent' time in 1987 was down to Gerry. Let her unleash it later in the interview.

'Can you recall how you and Charlotte met exactly?' Gerry asked.

'Through Julie... that's what I recall. Charlotte started playing the open mic at the Mariner's Lantern. Julie was into her music, and they struck up a friendship. They became practically inseparable. Julie could tell you a lot more about that time than I could, that's for sure.'

'Aye... like I said, she was very helpful,' Frank said. 'But as you just said, it was an age ago... so the more that contribute information, the merrier. Tell me about your relationship with Charlotte.'

Paul leaned back in his chair. 'Brief. I was working every night as a dishwasher at the Captain Cook's Galley. So, I only ever saw her in the pub once, to be honest. A rare evening off from work. Over the next months, Julie and Charlotte used to attend a recording studio regularly. You know. The one that Ron Michaels used to run?'

Frank nodded.

Forgotten Bones

'Did you attend many sessions with them?' Gerry asked.

Paul shrugged, his brow furrowing as he thought. 'I can't recall. A reasonable amount, I guess. It was during the day, so I wasn't working. You know, if anything, I remember becoming irritated towards the end of our relationship. Julie became less and less interested in spending time with me, and more obsessive with Charlotte and their band – or at least, they thought it was a band.' He shook his head. 'To be honest, it was just Charlotte with the talent. Most of the time, they just played in the rehearsal room for free. Ron only charged for the recording. Nobody was flush with cash then, and they weren't having any of mine. I was earning a bloody pittance for washing dishes!'

'Aye... you've done well for yourself.' Frank nodded. 'From washing dishes to local celebrity chef, eh?'

Paul waved his hand dismissively. 'Hardly a celebrity!'

Frank raised both eyebrows. 'No need to be modest, sir. You're well known around these parts.'

'I just love to cook. Anything else is just a bonus... or, rather, sometimes, an inconvenience.' Paul sighed, his expression turning pensive.

'How so?' Frank tilted his head slightly.

'People stopping you in the street to compliment you on your food was fun at first, but as you'd expect, it gets tiresome.' Paul's shoulders sagged a little.

Wouldn't know, Frank said. *I've never been popular. And those that knew me well enough just steered clear.* 'Well, seems a small price to pay.' Frank made a point of looking around the room. 'Like an art gallery in here.'

Paul nodded. 'I like art. Look, is there anything else I can help you with? My memory of Charlotte is rather vague. And I wasn't as close to her as Julie, so—'

'Were you not concerned on September 18th when she vanished from your life?' Gerry asked.

He shrugged. 'Not really. My memories of it are vague to be honest.' He looked upwards, trying to make out he was racking his brain. Eventually, he lowered his gaze and said, 'I recall Julie telling me she'd had some sort of argument with her and that she was sulking. I don't think I saw her again after that.'

'You didn't ask what the argument was about?' Frank asked.

'I think so. Who wouldn't be curious? But she wouldn't tell me. Julie was stubborn like that.'

'Julie said it was over some musician she fancied?' Frank asked.

Paul shrugged. 'Sounds familiar. But I can't remember the details. We were eighteen. Julie never told me much, anyway. We weren't right, me and her. First girlfriend, first sexual partner, you think it's everything, but it's not. Best to play the field, I guess?' He looked at Frank as he said this.

Frank, himself, had only ever had one sexual partner. Another had never been a consideration. He'd been happy. But this wasn't his conversation, and he certainly didn't want to throw a retort that was going to make this interview any ickier than it was becoming. Plus, the fact that Frank hadn't been Mary's only sexual partner suddenly raised its ugly head, which was never a warm, fuzzy thought.

'So, even when news of Charlotte's disappearance hit the press and appeals were made, you didn't think to say anything?' Frank asked.

'I genuinely heard nothing at the time. A few months later, possibly. But by then, it was all rather too late. Plus, what could I offer? Like I said, I wasn't the one close to her.'

'Also, I imagine you were very distracted around then...' Gerry said.

It was only the second mention of the situation that Gerry had uncovered, but it seemed to have a large impact on Paul. He paled and crossed his arms. 'If you're referring to what happened at the Captain Cook's Galley, it wasn't my situation, okay?'

'So, are you happy to talk about it?' Gerry asked.

'Not happy, no, but I've nothing to hide.'

Frank made a note. 'You do seem uneasy, Mr Harrison?'

'Well! Who wouldn't be? This is all rather out of the blue! Do I need a solicitor?'

Frank shrugged. 'From what you've told me so far, there doesn't seem to be any reason to be uneasy or concerned. Assuming we're hearing the truth?'

'Of course you are! But why's Captain Cook's Galley relevant?'

Frank made a show of looking back at the previous page in his notebook. 'You said that you were always working when Charlotte was playing in the Mariner's, but that can't be the case. Captain Cook's Galley closed on August third, 1987, because of the awful events that transpired there. In fact, it never reopened. So, you could have visited the pub between then and up to September 18th when she disappeared?'

'I could have done. But I genuinely didn't. You know what happened, I assume? Believe me, I didn't feel like going out around then. Plus, there was no job, so I obviously had no money.'

'It must have been an unsettling period. It's a tragic story.'

'It was. Arthur Barclay was my mentor. I've a lot to be grateful for.'

'Strange,' Frank said. 'But why did he mentor you? You were the dishwasher?'

'I was there for years. Some nights he was down on staff, and I helped. Guess he liked what he saw... we sort of just cracked on from there.'

Frank nodded. 'But he still paid you as his dishwasher?'

Paul shrugged. 'I was a kid. He was teaching me things I couldn't have learned anywhere else. I caught the bug from him. And who better to catch the bug from? The man was a master. It was hard not to worship him. And, well, as you pointed out before, I've done okay out of it long term.'

Just okay?

'Did you know he died recently?' Frank said.

Paul gave a swift nod.

'You didn't go to the funeral... Any reason?'

Paul looked down.

'Mr Harrison?'

Paul raised his head, glaring. 'I've been busy. *Unbelievably* busy.'

'But you just said you worshipped him?' Frank asked.

'I did. But this is what he wanted. He deliberately stayed out of touch with me. It was his wish. He didn't want me to be tarnished by his reputation. I only found out about his death through a mutual acquaintance.'

'Who?'

'A customer at the restaurant told me. Someone who kept in touch with him.'

'Must have been heartbreaking.'

He nodded.

'So, just to confirm, you didn't get an invitation to the funeral?'

Paul looked away. 'Correct.'

'Can my detective inspector go through the details of

what happened on August third, 1987? Just so we're clear on what distracted you from Charlotte's reported disappearance. Then we're on the same page?'

'If you must, but I think it's fairly black and white.'

Frank gave a gentle laugh. 'If only it was in this job, Mr Harrison. If only.'

Paul gave a swift nod.

'Thank you,' Frank said. 'Every little helps.'

Gerry began. 'Ellis Bramwell was thirteen years old when he died on August third, 1987, from tachycardia brought on by myristicin poisoning—'

'He died of a heart condition,' Paul said.

'The coroner identifies the primary cause as myristicin poisoning or nutmeg intoxication,' Gerry insisted.

'But Ellis had a heart defect, did he not?' Paul asked.

'Yes, he did,' Gerry broke off. 'But he still suffered from poisoning, so the coroner is content with that as the cause of death. Ellis could have lived with an undetected heart condition for the rest of his life.'

'Or he could have had a heart attack playing football on a Saturday. Would they have attributed the cause of death to football then?'

'I'm not in a position to answer questions like that,' Gerry said. 'Myristicin poisoning is rare. During the trial, the jury took the heart defect into consideration as a mitigating circumstance. They didn't buy in.'

'Well, in my opinion it's mitigating.'

And in my opinion, it isn't, Frank thought. *He wouldn't have died if not for the restaurant's negligence.* 'Please continue, DI Carver.'

'Experts deemed the spiced nutmeg rice pudding to have contained levels of nutmeg beyond safety standards. Head Chef Arthur Barclay claimed responsibility, not simply because it was his kitchen, but because he prepared the dish. Because of the loss of life, the investigation was big news in Whitby.'

'Yes... as you said earlier, it was turbulent,' Paul said.

'And you provided a statement saying that you witnessed Arthur preparing the rice pudding?'

'Unnecessary, as he'd confessed, anyway. But Arthur wanted me to make a statement. He *asked* me to. Desperate to make sure none of his other staff took the blame. He was a good man.'

Do you think Ellis Bramwell's family considered him a good man? Frank thought.

'But you saw Arthur making the pudding?' Frank raised an eyebrow.

'Of course.' Paul narrowed his eyes. 'He was showing me how to make it.'

'Did you not spot the mistake as it was happening?'

'Of course not! I was an untrained chef! That was the point of Arthur showing me. I was interested.'

'Please conclude, DI Carver,' Frank said.

Gerry said, 'The levels were toxic, and Arthur's severe departure from the standard of care expected to his customers led to him being charged with gross negligence manslaughter. He served five years in prison. The court also imposed a banning order as part of his sentence, preventing him from working in the food industry again.'

'He was very unlucky that the boy died.' Paul shook his head and sighed.

'Not as unlucky as that boy,' Frank said.

Paul rubbed his forehead. 'Well, yes, you can see why I was otherwise distracted around then.'

'For a while and then you built a brilliant career,' Frank said.

Paul straightened in his chair. 'What're you implying?'

'Just that you've done well.' *You're rather snappy, Paul. Too snappy for my liking.* 'A couple more things? Do you know David Roberts?'

'David? What's he got to do with anything?' Paul's brows knitted together. 'We went to school together but were never friends. A landlord's son... a psychiatrist now, I believe. He's eaten in my restaurant and said hello. Nothing beyond that. Why?'

Frank showed the image of the polaroid on his phone. 'Charlotte and David looked close here.'

Paul shrugged. 'Honestly, that means nothing to me.'

'Have you ever used a beach hut down on the West beach?' Frank pressed on.

'Sorry?' His eyes widened. 'A beach hut?'

'Aye.'

'At some point, yes.'

'When?'

'I don't know. A while back. Decades possibly.' He rubbed his chin.

'Did you ever stay at North Sea Nook Beach Huts?'

Paul shook his head. 'Never heard of it.'

'They were around in the eighties.'

'When I was a kid, I never used a beach hut. It was much later on. Nineties perhaps?' Paul's leg bounced. He was becoming more agitated.

'Okay.' Frank took a note. 'We suspected Charlotte may have used one... did she ever mention it to you? During those rehearsal sessions, perhaps?' He leaned forward, probing with his gaze.

'Not that I recall.'

'How about Julie? Do you know if she used one?'

'Look... I'm really at a loss.' Paul threw his hands up.

Frank looked the man up and down. Not only did he look exhausted, but he looked at his wit's end. 'You seem so edgy, Mr Roberts.'

He sighed. 'I'm burned out if you must know.'

'Why?'

Frank listened to him explain his audition for the Thomas brothers.

'Well, it sounds exciting,' Frank said.

'We'll see.' Paul's tone was flat.

'Any more questions, Detective Inspector Carver?' Frank asked Gerry.

'Yes, you never married or had children and—'

Paul cut her off, his voice rising. 'Not a crime, is it?'

Gerry continued, unfazed. 'You've no siblings, *but* your mother is still alive.'

He nodded. 'So?'

'Why don't you go to see her in the nursing home that you pay for?'

Gerry's question hung in the air.

Eventually, Paul's face reddened. 'How do you know about that?'

Good question, Frank thought, *news to me, too.* 'It's our job to know as much as we can.'

'Is it relevant?' Paul asked.

'We don't know. Enlighten us and we'll tell you,' Frank said.

Paul grunted. His shoulders sagged in defeat. 'She wasn't kind to me as a child, okay? But I don't want to go into it. I'll do what's right with her. Pay for her care, but beyond that, we've little to say. I'd rather you didn't get her involved. I assure you... she knows nothing about Charlotte Wilson.' His voice cracked slightly, a hint of pain seeping through.

'Okay, thank you,' Frank said.

After handing Paul a card in case he should recall anything of importance, Frank and Gerry made their way to the car.

Once they were in the vehicle, and the doors closed, Frank nodded down at the book in her hands. 'What did you discover in your deconstruction?'

'That he's lying.' Gerry's tone was matter-of-fact.

'That's three in three. We're on a roll.' He glanced back at the house. 'Nice place. What do you think?' He drummed his fingers on the steering wheel.

'Yes, it's nice.'

'No. Not the house. Him? Other than the lying?'

'I think he was struggling emotionally before we arrived at the door.'

'Aye, bottling something, wasn't he? Wonder what's tearing him up? Something to do with his mother, perhaps? He got cagey around that topic.'

'Possibly. Shall we see her?'

'Not just yet. Let's phone it in. Get some background on his childhood and his parents. Might be nothing, might be something. First, I must meet Charlotte's mother at the whalebones. She's getting a taxi. I haven't got time to drop you back, I'm afraid. Shall I get you a taxi?'

'I don't mind coming with you.'

Gerry's response was quick, surprising Frank.

'This isn't part of the investigation,' he said. 'It's just something I feel she needs. You could stay in the car, catch up with research and—'

'No.'

It was the first time she'd interrupted him this abruptly, and he was rather stunned.

'I want to come,' she said.

Chapter Seventy-Two

Having collected Charlotte's mother from her taxi on East Terrace, Frank and Gerry walked alongside her.

She'd arrived dressed in a smart black outfit. It would be fitting for a funeral.

Frank figured Laura had kept this dress on standby for when this day to say goodbye arrived. Keeping it hidden, just in case, one day, Charlotte made an unexpected return.

As they neared the whalebones, Frank saw the long shadows from their silhouettes on the cobbled ground and sensed the day reaching an end. He felt Laura's arm hooking his, a sensation he hadn't experienced for many years since he'd lost Mary. He smiled at her, wondering if she'd done that so she could get support for weariness, or whether it came from a need for warmth and connectedness in so emotional a moment.

He glanced at Gerry, who stared stony-faced ahead, wondering why she'd come.

Is this how you learn, Gerry? Observing situations around you? Feeding your knowledge bank of emotions, responses and behaviour? To read people? To learn how to behave in certain situations?

Frank led Laura behind the Captain Cook memorial, and then over the grass towards Pavilion Drive car park. They then veered off through the broken fence to where Charlotte had been recovered. Forensics had taken away the large stone that had tripped Sam Farnsworth as evidence. There was still police tape in a two metre by two metre square around the hole. There was also still a warning sign. It wasn't being manned any longer because no one believed there was anything more to be taken from this burial site. In a few days, the hole would be filled.

Laura pulled away from Frank and edged towards the hole, looking down.

Frank stood back, respectfully, but warned her, 'Not too close please, Laura. It's not safe.'

Frank looked back at Gerry, who was half a metre behind them both. Her expression remained serious, but her eyes focused on the event playing out.

As he watched Laura for ten minutes, he felt his phone, on silent, buzzing in his pocket. Of course, he wanted to answer it. Who knew what his team had discovered regarding the individuals he'd spent most of the day talking to? Their shield of lies may be tough, but he knew from experience that a single discovery could turn their defence brittle.

But he didn't answer. This was a moment for quiet reflection. Or, at least, Laura's reflection.

He expected she was talking to Charlotte now, in her head. In a similar way to how he talked to Mary at her gravestone.

Eventually, she turned and came back towards Frank.

Her eyes were bloodshot, but she smiled and took his arm again. 'Thank you.'

'Don't thank me.'

The sun was dipping towards the horizon now; the purple in the sky was darkening.

She turned and gazed out over the North Sea. Frank turned, too, joining her in her reverie. Nature was strong. Right down to the tumultuous waves, and the whipping cold sea breeze. Untameable. But this loss. This *unspeakable* loss hadn't been natural.

Frank was no stranger to tragedy. He'd seen enough in his sixty-four years. *Experienced* enough. But you could never become indifferent.

Well, at least he couldn't.

Laura dropped her arm and clutched his hand instead. It didn't feel uncomfortable.

He was happy to share her grief.

In a way, she was sharing his, even if she didn't realise it.

∽

Afterwards, once Laura had left in the taxi which Frank had paid to wait for them, he sat alongside Gerry in the car.

He looked at her, surprised to notice that her eyes were a little red, and her cheeks a little damp.

He started the engine, wondering if Gerry had displayed a rare moment of emotion. It'd take the hardest of hearts not to empathise with that woman and her loss.

When she answered the phone to Reggie, he heard her usual matter-of-fact tone of voice, and wondered if, in fact, it had been the biting wind up on the cliff that'd caused her to tear up.

Chapter Seventy-Three

DAVID POUNDED on the cell door and shouted.

It'd been a while now. Both his hand and his throat were sore.

Dickheads... ignorant dickheads...

He tried kicking instead.

When that didn't work, he opted for something he knew they couldn't turn a blind eye to. 'Open this door, or I'll top myself. I swear I—'

The door swung open almost immediately.

Two officers stood there, staring in.

He sneered at them. 'Wouldn't want that on your watch, would you?'

The largest of the two officers grunted. 'If we're concerned, then we could restrain you—'

'Listen... I just want to get this over with. What's the delay? Interview me, charge me, and let's get bail organised.'

The officer looked back at the other. 'We're waiting on your solicitor.'

'What? He's not here yet?'

The officer shrugged. 'Seems not.'

'Bloody hell...' He shook his head. 'On what I pay him?'

The officer shrugged again. 'So, is that all? Are you a threat to yourself? Do you need to be restrained?'

David took a step back, folded his arms, and sneered. 'I was bluffing.'

'That's better.' The officer smiled and slammed the cell door.

David sat down in the cell's corner, closing his eyes and taking deep breaths. He tried to take his mind somewhere else, but eventually, he opened them, cursed loudly, rose to his feet and started pacing.

Despite his proficiency in mediation, this current weight of anxiety was impenetrable.

What the hell are you playing at, Hanna?

I thought we understood each other.

I can't have been wrong. Not all this time. I wouldn't have stayed with you, otherwise.

He looked down at his clenched fists. He thought of his mother's glare, her wagging finger. 'One day... one day, David... your aggression, your need to control everything to the nth degree, it's going to get you into trouble.'

I guess you were right, after all, Mother.

It's got me in trouble.

Again.

Except. There's always a way out, isn't there, Mother? He unclenched his fists and smiled. *Just like last time, and all those times before.*

I'll be fine.

Just fine.

Chapter Seventy-Four

'WHAT THE HELL *do you think you're playing at?'* Julie *turned to Sylvia.*

'He just came round.'

'Why didn't you let me know?'

'I did.'

'No!' Julie *pointed inside the house.* '*He doesn't go in there.'*

'You want me to turn him away? Make him wait outside? He's thirteen. And you know what he's like. He's vulnerable. He could end up in trouble.'

'I know what he's like, Sylvia. He's my son.' She *thumbed her chest.* '*My fucking son!'*

Her son.

Tom.

But I'm not on Sylvia's doorstep... not any more...

God, where the hell am I?

She opened her eyes. The light burned. There was movement around her. Yet, everything was so unclear. She closed them again.

Her son.

'Tom?'

She heard a loud horn.

Someone was holding her down. 'Julie... please... you need to be calm.'

She saw the front of an oncoming bus.

'Tom,' she shouted. 'Tom!'

'Julie, listen, *please*. It's your father. Your father!'

She opened her eyes again. Her father's face emerged, momentarily, from the swirl. 'You're in hospital—'

'Dad? Let go of me!'

How was her father, in his eighties, strong enough to keep her down?

She shut her eyes again; the light was agony.

'Please, Julie.' Another voice. Female. Someone else restraining her.

'Sedate her.'

Another female voice. Three of them.

'What's happened? Where's Tom?'

She felt a prick on her arm. She opened her eyes to the pain. Everything remained blurred.

'Take a deep breath, Julie,' her father said. 'When you're still, I'll explain.'

The deep breath made her moan in pain. 'It hurts...'

'It's your ribs, Julie,' one of the female voices said. 'You've broken some ribs. Once you're calmer, I can get some more pain relief for—'

Julie scrunched up her face and bit down. She fought through the pain before forcing open her eyes to look at the three looming faces. 'Tom, where's my son? Where the hell—'

But then the sound of the horn came from nowhere

again, as did the sight of the oncoming bus, and a sudden pressure on her chest...

She screamed her son's name as loud as she could into the chaos.

Chapter Seventy-Five

Unbeknownst to Fiona Barclay, Paul already had her address in Redcar, having paid a visit there back in 1992.

Fiona and Arthur had remained in touch with people in Whitby. It hadn't taken a great deal of effort for Paul to gain his former employer's new address.

So, following Arthur's release from prison in 1992, Paul had tried to speak to him.

Paul hadn't made it further than the doorstep.

Not because of Fiona. He'd ensured she was out before his visit. Arthur had told him to leave and never come back.

His reason was simple. Fiona couldn't forgive. *Would never forgive.*

The look on Fiona's face when she opened the door to Paul suggested that Arthur had never told her about the visit in 1992.

'How do you know where I live?'

'I've known for a long time.' He tried to sound assertive despite the obvious slur in his words; he'd spent the afternoon on the whisky again. 'My turn to pay an impromptu visit.'

She folded her arms, the surprise clearly dissipating. She looked him up and down and sighed. 'Wasn't I clear enough last night?'

'Yes. It's just taken me a while to digest it.'

She nodded. 'Okay. Well, what's changed? You seemed resigned to everything yesterday. To be honest, I was surprised. A man like you. I expected more.'

'A man like me! What's a man like me?'

'Where to start? A liar? A murderer?'

He pointed at her and edged closer to the open front door. 'Liar? That's rich, going against Arthur's wishes now that he's passed.'

'Arthur was confused.'

Paul shook his head. 'No. He knew what he wanted. Everything that happened. It was always *his* decision.'

'We've already been through this. He never knew what he wanted. He was never in sound mind after what happened. He ruined his life. Our lives. For you. And now, he's at rest, I can assure I can right wrongs without causing him stress.'

Paul looked at his watch. 'Why all this waiting around? What's the delay?'

'I told you it'd be this evening.'

'Why not in the morning?'

Fiona sighed and shook her head. 'I made it clear to take the day. Get your affairs in order. You get that opportunity because of him... not because of me.'

'Nonsense,' Paul said. 'You're doing this to make me suffer... and dread what's coming.'

Fiona shrugged. 'Sounds familiar. Sounds like what we had to endure. Go away. Take advantage of the little time I've afforded you.'

'Little time! Who the fuck do you think you are? You're a bitch, Fiona, always have been.'

'I'm in control, Paul, and that's all that matters.'

He grinned. 'Are you? I'm here for that recording.'

'Go home.' She reached forward and thrust the door. He wedged his foot in to stop it slamming shut. After glancing both ways, ensuring that no one was watching, he threw his weight against the door, which sent her backwards. She remained on her feet and, wide eyed, she turned to run. He followed her in, closed the door behind him and turned the lock.

Then he swung back to see her partway down the hall, towards the door at the end. Paul stalked after her. 'I only need the recording... *Just* the recording. Then, I'll go.'

She went through the door at the end of the hallway and into a kitchen.

It was a different kitchen, but the memories were raw, and he couldn't prevent them from making an appearance. He recalled the moment he was down on the floor, while Fiona, far younger, sliced the air with the knife, lost to despair over the sacrifices her husband was about to make.

The memory caused him a moment's disorientation, and when he resumed his focus, he saw her fiddling with a mobile phone. Making two steps, he extended his arm and snatched it from her. He slipped the phone in his trouser pocket.

He regarded her. She was pale. Her irritating confidence gone.

He sighed and sat down at the kitchen table. He rubbed his temples. 'Everything I built... I built as a tribute to him. Why would you tear it down?'

It took her a while to respond. 'That's a lie. You built it for yourself.'

He dropped his hand from his head and glared up at her. 'Not true.'

'He never recovered,' Fiona continued. 'It wasn't just going to prison; it was the loss of nearly everything he ever loved. Even you. Ironically. Being a chef was everything to him. If not for me, I dread to think what he would've done.'

'But what purpose does all this serve now?' Paul asked.

'It's right that you take responsibility.'

'Where's that tape and the Dictaphone?'

'Gone,' Fiona said. 'I've sent it already.'

'You're lying. You wouldn't risk losing it in the post. You'd hand deliver it. Did he even know you had it? Did he know there was a recording?'

She flinched.

He stood and pointed at her. 'So, you tricked him? Recorded him without his permission?'

'It needed to happen.'

'Against his wishes. Maybe it's you who should take some responsibility.'

She turned, opened the kitchen drawer and swung back, holding a knife.

He felt like he was back in 1987. 'Are you serious?'

'If I have to be.'

'I always wondered, Fiona. What would you have done if Arthur hadn't stopped you?'

'I'd never have killed you. Now get out of my house!' She waved the knife and edged towards him.

He took a step back, narrowing his eyes. 'No. You would've done. There's something unpleasant in you, Fiona. He may not have seen it, but I do.'

She swung the knife. He took another step back with his palms out.

'Get. Out.'

'Admit it, Fiona. Admit you would've killed me.'

She took another step, her confidence growing. 'You're a monster. I *always* knew. He wouldn't have it. But *I* know. You ruined my husband on purpose. And I've watched you over the years, too, Paul, while Arthur was still alive. Checking on you. Waiting for you to slip up again.'

'And, surprise, surprise, I haven't! Because you're a paranoid old—'

'*No*... you and that Jess... I know what you two are up to. That poor husband and child. About to have their lives ruined, and all because of you. You're at it again.'

His adrenaline surged. He didn't want Jess involved in this. 'You're deluded.' He reached out to grab her.

She swung again. It narrowly missed his hand.

'I'll be telling her husband,' Fiona said. 'He doesn't deserve that. He deserves the truth about her... about you... I won't let you destroy any more lives.'

His stomach turned. 'You do that, Fiona, you'll destroy that family.'

'Not true,' she snorted. 'If I leave it, it'll fester. I know all about the festering. Clear the air now and they can refresh, restart. There's only so long you can live a lie before it becomes destructive.'

'You're going too far.' His hand flew out and seized her wrist. 'You leave Jess out of this.' He squeezed her wrist until she cried out in pain and her hand opened. The knife hit the floor. He released her and looked down at the weapon.

He bent down and picked it up. When he looked up, she was sliding away along the work surface. 'We need to get something straight, right now. You aren't to involve yourself in Jess's life.'

'I make the rules.' She slid away.

'Not any more.'

She pulled a rolling pin out from behind her back. 'Get out.' She must have swooped for it while he was retrieving a knife.

'This has gone on long enough. I'm not leaving until you tell me where the tape is, and I get a guarantee that you won't wreck my friend's marriage.'

She snorted. 'Over my dead body.' Then she raised the rolling pin and went for him.

Chapter Seventy-Six

AFTER HEARING the news about Julie and her son from Reggie, Frank was in no mood for any conversation on the way back to HQ.

Gerry was happy to think. He'd lost count of the number of times she opened her notebook and scribbled something down. Cerebrally, his colleague never seemed to slow.

Back in the incident room, Frank watched Gerry reunited with Rylan. She pressed her cheek to his crown and closed her eyes.

It was warming to see this moment. It made him feel guilty for his considerations on her emotional deficit, which made him wonder if he'd been totally off the mark when assuming it was the wind that had caused those tears before.

Just before leading the briefing, he received a message. His daughter from her new phone:

> Going to see Mum. I know it's late. Going over the fence.

Bloody hell. Like father, like daughter.

Unfortunately.

He sighed. Well, at least she'd let him know she was going out this time, rather than leaving him in a state of complete panic.

He already had a clear idea of what tomorrow held and so was determined to wrap up the briefing quickly. 'This morning, we had three very relevant names.' He turned to look at the line of photographs on the board. 'This evening, those names are no less relevant. Paul Harrison, David Roberts and Julie Fletcher are all hiding something.' He then went through his notes from the three interviews, pausing periodically to allow Gerry to fill in any gaps.

Nobody asked any questions. The room felt very subdued. News of the car accident had shaken everyone up. Tom, Julie's son, was still undergoing emergency surgery because of internal bleeding. Julie had escaped with broken ribs but was currently inconsolable.

Regardless of whatever else happened in this investigation now, irrespective of who may be guilty and who may not be, the life of a thirteen-year-old boy was in the balance.

A completely innocent boy.

Focusing was going to be hard until he was out of the woods. *If* he came out of the woods.

Frank had already asked Sharon to monitor the developing situation regarding David Roberts. The charge was ABH. His wife Hanna had a damning medical report. 'There's evidence of a sustained period of abuse,' Sharon said. 'And this from a man who gives therapy to people with abuse-related trauma. I've never known irony like it! David is on bail but under the court's order to stay away from his wife. She's staying with her sister, Briony Goodall. I can't see him being stupid enough to go around. Hanna has agreed to talk to us tomorrow.'

Frank nodded. 'Good. I'll look forward to speaking to him again tomorrow, too.' *Pompous, aggressive dickhead.* 'However, we'll have to play talking to Julie again by ear. It'd be better if we saw some improvement in her son first. We also need another run at Paul. There were question marks over the others, but nothing like the ones we had over this man! A complete bag of bloody nerves. Not what I expected from some kind of confident celebrity chef supposedly at the top of his game! And I think we need to find out what fractured his relationship with his mother. Sean, could you get me some more on his family history before I chat to him again?'

'Yes, sir.'

They spent the next thirty minutes hypothesising over how any of these three could be responsible for Charlotte's death, before Frank called it a day. 'Now, I think we should rest.' He looked off into the distance, avoiding eye contact with his team. 'I took Laura to where her daughter was thrown away today. So long ago, yet the pain feels fresher than ever. We need to get to the bottom of this.' He turned and looked at the three faces again.

I'm listening, Charlotte. It's one of them, isn't it? Don't stop singing. We're getting there.

Chapter Seventy-Seven

Frank accidentally left his coat in HQ, but he couldn't be bothered to return for it. Instead, he drove rattling old Bertha directly to the graveyard.

After scaling the fence with more elegance than last time, he wondered, briefly, if he may have possibly shed some weight in the last couple of days from knocking booze on the head.

Absolute bollocks, of course, but at least he was looking for some encouragement in what was sure to be a torturous period of abstinence.

By the time he'd worked his way through the graveyard in the dark, he was cold, but he didn't mind one bit. Seeing his daughter standing with her mother warmed his heart and filled him with hope.

'Mads?'

She turned from Mary's gravestone and smiled at her father. It was dim, but he was certain he could see vitality and life returning to her cheeks, following their last two weeks of hell. He actually recognised his daughter again.

'Mads,' she said. 'You haven't called me that since I was a child.'

'Sorry, I... are you okay with that?'

She smiled. 'Don't be ridiculous, Dad.'

He felt his cheeks redden. Then, he felt her arm slip around his shoulders, and as he raised his head again, he panned his gaze over his wife's headstone.

He imagined Mary there – as he always imagined her. *She came back to us, love.*

To the backdrop of squawking seagulls, Maddie recalled her favourite childhood memories with Frank and Mary. This included Max, their beloved Jack Russell. Max was long gone now, but the memories burned bright. Max woke up Frank every day by saturating his nostrils with his tongue. Experiences like that certainly never left you.

When they entered a period of silence, and tears crept into the corners of Maddie's eyes, Frank sensed that the conversation was about to take a serious turn. He was an expert at sensing this, so he tried to pre-empt it with, 'I think we should head—'

'We've never spoken about what happened, Dad.'

Frank sucked in air through his nostrils. He looked away.

'I still don't fully understand what happened between you and Mum,' Maddie pressed.

Frank exhaled. 'Now isn't the time, Mads.' He gazed at Mary's headstone again. 'She wouldn't want us to. Not now, anyway. Let's go.'

'You're so... forgiving, Dad. Too forgiving.'

He turned, grunting. 'There's nothing to forgive.'

'That's not true though, is it?'

He swung towards her. 'Listen up...' Recognising the

aggression in his voice, he broke off quickly. 'There's *nothing* to forgive. Please just trust me on that!'

'No.' Maddie, as had always been her way to be fair, wouldn't be silenced.

Like father, like daughter, he thought again.

She pointed at her mother's grave. 'How could she do that to you?'

He shook his head. 'Please don't, Mads. Don't do that.' He reached out and pushed her hand down. 'I was partly responsible.' *As was Nigel Wainwright.*

How he'd like to piss on that man's grave again, tonight!

Of course, with Maddie in attendance, that wouldn't be happening.

Maddie put her hand on his shoulder. 'She was the one who had an affair. Surely it's impossible to blame yourself completely?'

Oh, not really, Mads. It's actually quite easy.

'If you make her responsible, then you can stop blaming yourself so much. You'll realise that she does need to be forgiven. I think it would do you good. Accept she needs your forgiveness—'

He shrugged his shoulder away and took a step back from her. 'I can't. I brought it on myself. I was never there for her. And, after what happened with...' He broke off. Involving his daughter's behaviour in this would only widen the guilty net, and make Maddie feel worse.

He took another deep breath, moved in, and put his hand on her arm. 'Look... honey... Mads... I promise to talk about it *all* with you. All of it. Not talking is wrong. After everything that happened with your mum, I know that now. But I can't do it this moment. This second. Not here. Not where it's so raw.'

'I understand.' Maddie moved in and embraced him.

They hugged for a time.

After a while, she backed away. She still had tears in her eyes. He kissed her on the forehead.

'Dad?'

'Yes?'

'I need you to do something for me.'

'Anything, Mads.' *As long as it's not talking about* this. Here.

'I'd a friend on the street. I told you about her last night. Sarah? Sarah Tyler?'

'Aye... I remember.'

'Sarah was like a daughter to me. I took care of her.'

Frank nodded, feeling nauseous. There was a problem here. One that wasn't going away.

'And she was in trouble. Or at least had been. Before she was on the streets. She had an ex who was violent. I mean... very violent, Dad. He broke her arm once.'

Frank's instinct was to narrow his eyes, pass comment, potentially growl. His behaviour when confronted with the behaviour of animals such as this could often be animalistic itself. However, for his daughter, he kept himself in check.

'She won't know where I am. And I don't know where she is. Last time I saw her was in Leeds...'

'Leeds? You ended up in Leeds?'

Maddie nodded. 'Among other places. Look, I *could* find her. Ask about. Check on her—'

'No, that's not happening.'

Maddie nodded. 'I know you don't want that but listen. I'm done with that life, the drugs, but I can't just leave her.'

'No. Absolutely not.' *I'll lock you up again if I must. No. You're not going there.* He held his breath, keeping his terror locked inside.

'Dad—'

'I'll sort it, okay?'

She creased her brow. 'How?'

'Just trust me. I'll find Sarah Tyler. Check on her, and then I'll make sure this man never touches her again.'

'But can you? Is that a promise?'

Not really, but... 'For you, yes.'

She hugged him again. 'Thanks.'

Taking on this task was certainly inappropriate considering his position, and what he was currently doing, but his thoughts drifted to Laura Wilson looking into her daughter's shallow grave earlier.

If she could turn back time, Laura would've done anything for Charlotte, but now she couldn't.

Frank had already left it too late with his wife, Mary.

Time to learn from the past.

This was on him.

Chapter Seventy-Eight

After being released on bail the previous evening, with an order not to go within spitting distance of Hanna – and oh, how he wished he could spit on her right now – David had headed back to Tate Hill Pier and spent the entire night by their wooden post. The one that both he and Charlotte had carved their initials into all those moons ago.

The initials that had been scooped clean away by Hanna in that jealous rage.

Initially, his long padded coat kept him warm, but over the night, he'd become more and more damp.

But he never moved. Not once.

A normal man would've broken in the early hours, and run for warmth... but was he a normal man?

Of course he wasn't.

His mother had been right.

His wife was right.

And he'd known it from a very early age.

How could you ignore the fact that you lacked empathy? Especially when everyone around you was so bloody consumed by it!

Still, he prided himself on being different.

Look Mother, Hanna... look what I've achieved without it!

How often are writers told to write what they know?

By such reasoning, shouldn't he have struggled with compassion, empathy and relationships? Yet, not only had he written countless bestselling self-help manuals, but he'd made a small fortune as a psychiatrist!

You could become well-versed in anything if you put your mind to it.

You didn't *actually* have to experience it.

Yes, okay, some would argue that he was, after all, an emotional being. He was, clearly, privy to anger and frustration. But there was a reason behind this. A mother who never attached self-worth to her child. A perpetual, developing bitterness. Call it what you will.

There was something else, though. Something significant, and rather inexplicable.

He stroked the post.

She'd provoked a feeling in him.

Charlotte.

And he still thought of her.

Had he ever felt anything like this with Hanna, or anyone else for that matter?

No.

It wasn't love. He was well-versed in the feelings that went with love, and its physiological, chemical explosions in the brain.

This was different.

It was like being drawn to something, like a moth to a flame.

A fascination, perhaps? An interest, a focus, which engaged his mind and wouldn't let go.

Like being hypnotised.

He closed his eyes, now, as he'd done many times throughout this long, bitter evening, and took himself back to the Mariner's Lantern. There he sat at the bar, watching. The delicate strokes of her hand over the strings of the guitar; her eyes gazing off, seeing past the physical, searching; her mouth opening and closing, producing sounds very few other humans could produce...

She'd been a work of art.

One to be admired and studied.

And she'd accepted that from him... for a time...

He opened his eyes, took a deep breath, and listened to the sea, which had been gentle this evening, but seemed to liven now with daybreak. Along with the cries of the seagulls.

He breathed in the salty sea air and thought now about how his anger and his sudden emotional outburst had ruined that time with Charlotte.

Despite being well-versed in psychiatry, his unique make-up made it so difficult to put his finger on why he always moved to sabotage.

Yes, his link to his mother had something to do with it.

As was his sudden innate desire to release.

But for him to allow his restraint and inhibitions to melt away so quickly? There just had to be something else. But no amount of self-hypnosis would reveal the answer.

He always felt that another outburst was close to hand.

And now, more than ever, he felt it.

Rising to his feet, he acknowledged what needed to be done.

Hanna was the source of this build-up.

So, it was her responsibility to prevent the explosion.

And he knew where she was.
Briony's.

Chapter Seventy-Nine

Frank may have been getting more sleep now, but it wasn't perfect.

He'd only just been coming to terms with having Charlotte and Maddie on his mind, constantly, and now he had Sarah Tyler, a fifteen-year-old homeless lass, there too.

He must have woken five or six times.

At least he'd had Charlotte's songs to help him back off each time. He'd usually drift by the end of her second number on the three-track demo.

It was remarkable that these songs had this impact on him.

He knew that the possessor of that voice was no more because of foul play. It maybe should have left him wide awake, propelled him up and out of bed to wrap up the investigation. But it did nothing of the sort. Instead, it just took his frayed mind to a gentler place.

At 5 a.m., he went into the kitchen drawer, rustled around behind some old receipts and bills, and took out Maddie's old phone, relieved that he'd still not got rid of it.

That would've been a disaster. The information he needed was on it.

He switched on the phone and entered the new passcode he'd created the last time he'd broken into it with her fingerprint.

Then, he scrolled through the contacts to S, hoping and praying.

Sarah Tyler.

Brilliant!

He wrote the number down, switched the phone off, chucked it back into the drawer, checked in on his sleeping daughter, and went to work.

He'd planned to contact Sarah Taylor after briefing, but Gerry had put in a late one, and an *early* one, as per usual, and had thrown up a significant discovery. They cut the briefing short and, before the caffeine from his coffee could kick in, they were breathlessly on their way to Redcar.

Chapter Eighty

The tighter Julie gripped her father's hand, the more her own injuries hurt, but when your thirteen-year-old son's surgeon was standing at your hospital bed with the verdict, then it was hard to care about your own discomfort.

The surgeon had started with a smile. She wanted to take that as a good sign, but as he dragged up a chair, she thought, *He's hardly going to come into the room crying, is he?*

As the surgeon sat down, he said, 'I'm confident that it went as well as it could.'

What does that even mean? 'Is he going to be okay?'

'We're off to a positive start. No question of that. We got the internal bleeding which was in the spleen. My first thoughts were removal, but we managed a splenorrhaphy. Successfully. So, we're hopeful he can make a good recovery from this. He lost blood, but transfusions have kept him in check. With no sign of head trauma or paralysis, we can be positive.'

She felt a warm sensation starting in her stomach. The

ignition of positivity. This caused her to well up. 'So, he's going to make it... he's going to come home... with me.'

The surgeon smiled. 'I don't want to get too ahead of ourselves. He's going to be in a lot of discomfort for a while. He's multiple fractures in his arms and legs.'

Multiple. The word made her freeze all over again. 'But he'll be okay?'

'As I said, positive start. He's out of immediate danger, but his injuries were severe and exhausting. He has a period of recovery, and potentially, rehabilitation, ahead of him.'

'But he's not going to die? Just tell me that. He's going to live?'

He looked around the room, as if concerned that someone would observe him giving assurances he probably shouldn't be giving, and then nodded. 'He's young and strong.'

'A fighter.' Tears ran down Julie's face.

'Thank God.' Arnold kissed the side of his daughter's head. 'Thank God.'

Chapter Eighty-One

AFTER HIS KNOCK went unanswered for the third time, Frank stepped back, leaving Gerry on the doorstep. He surveyed the front of the house. Someone had drawn all the curtains. Not unusual, considering the early hour.

A quick glance left and right informed him that the adjacent houses also had their curtains drawn.

He took his phone out and tried Fiona Barclay's number again, but was sent straight to voicemail. He didn't bother leaving a message this time. It was his third try.

He tried her landline for the first time since pulling up.

'I can hear her phone ringing inside,' Gerry said.

'It's me,' Frank said. He let it ring until he was certain that no one was going to answer. 'Shit. Do we have a list of relatives that Fiona could be staying with? Phone numbers?'

'There was no one else,' Gerry said. 'The only other living relative of Arthur Barclay is Paul himself.'

This was the reason they were here.

Gerry, working tirelessly, had made the discovery late last night.

Paul Harrison was adopted.

The mother who raised him, his adoptive mother, was in a home, while his birth mother, Cathleen Holmes, had passed decades earlier. The actual birth certificate didn't record any information about the father. Gerry had taken on the challenge of finding the birth father with her usual gusto. It was unbelievable to think that Gerry discovered something in one night that the investigators into the Captain Cook's Galley restaurant incident weren't able to discover in three months! Gerry found Cathleen had worked alongside trainee chef Arthur Barclay in 1969. The year he'd married Fiona. Gerry then tracked payments made into Cathleen's bank account over the next seventeen years until her death. The payments had come from Arthur.

It all fit perfectly.

Paul had been born in 1969.

So Arthur slept with Cathleen around the time he was going to marry Fiona. It'd been an expensive fling. He'd paid Cathleen off to protect his reputation and his marriage until her death. Maybe he'd told her to give Paul up for adoption? Maybe she did it because she was still very young?

Their discussions earlier, in the briefing, had revolved around this.

Had Paul somehow discovered Arthur to be his father? If so, how had Arthur felt about this? Had he offered him these life-changing chef training opportunities because of more extortion, or from a sense of duty to his own flesh and blood? And what had really gone on with the death of Ellis Bramwell? Why had Paul made that statement which effectively sealed his father's fate? Paul had said that Arthur wanted him to make that statement – had that been true? Maybe Arthur had sacrificed himself for the son he'd abandoned as a baby...

But, most importantly, how did all this connect to Charlotte?

Earlier in the incident room, Frank had thrown out a possibility. 'Say Paul had been responsible for Ellis's death rather than Arthur. Could Charlotte have known somehow and been silenced? By Paul, or even Arthur?'

Frank looked up at Fiona's house. He was absolutely certain that the answer lay within those four walls, but, frustratingly, no one was home... or, at least, answering.

'I'm going around the back,' Frank said. 'Please stay here, Gerry. In case she finally makes an appearance.'

'That's not a good idea, Frank,' Gerry said.

'I know, but that's how it's going to play. Anyway, don't worry, I won't break in. Unless I see that she's in danger, of course...'

'The sensible choice is to speak to the neighbours first, to see if they saw her return. Then, trace her mobile and—'

'Totally agree.' Frank unlocked the side gate. 'Yours is the sensible option.'

He worked his way down the side of the house, pausing at a window that didn't have its curtain drawn for once. He cupped his hands to shield the glare of the morning sun and peered in. A bog-standard utility room, but it looked to be getting more use than his own back in Whitby. There was an ironing board set up, and a pile of freshly pressed clothing. The door to the utility room was half-open. He caught movement. The shape of someone slipping past the doorway. His heart kicked into overdrive.

Looking ahead, tunnel vision narrowed his sight and the garden – surprisingly floral considering the time of year – faded into the periphery. He hurried, but not too fast to put him out of breath—

He turned at the end of the wall and saw Paul standing close to the back door holding a spade.

Blood running cold, Frank took a deep breath. 'Now, there's a greeting I wasn't expecting.'

'What the hell are you doing here?' Paul asked.

Frank straightened up, trying to calculate if he was within swinging distance of Paul's spade. It was possible, so he shuffled a step back; unfortunately, Paul took a step towards him at the same time.

Frank held up his hands. 'It's not too late to put an end to this...' *Whatever this is.*

'I agree.' Paul's eyes were darting, and the knuckles on his hands that gripped the spade handle were bright white.

He'd looked out of sorts the previous day, but he'd now taken it to a whole new level.

Threatening a police officer was ambitious, but Frank was certain from looking into his eyes that he was capable of much more.

'If you sling that onto the grass, fella' – Frank nodded at the garden – 'then I'll just assume you were here to dig up the weeds.'

Paul raised the spade slightly higher. This may end up hurting... a lot... or...

He took a deep breath.

...killing him?

He guessed it wouldn't be the first time someone had died from being hit by a spade.

Frank sighed. 'Yeah. I get it. I noticed that there were no weeds, too. Look... I suggest you listen, Paul. This is going to get a lot worse before it gets better if you don't put that down, you know that?'

Paul narrowed his eyes. 'Ball's in your court. Go back to the front of the house.'

'And then what? You run?'

'Yes.'

'Bloody hell. Why? What's gone so wrong?'

Paul snorted. 'Everything.'

'You won't get away.'

Paul nodded to the fence at the back of the garden and then nodded back at Frank. 'You won't be able to catch me.'

Fair point. 'Would you believe me if I said I'm fitter than I look?'

'No... now go. Fuck off.'

Shit! 'Have you hurt Fiona Barclay?'

Paul flinched, but then steadied his eyes and moved in closer with the spade. 'She brought this all on herself.'

Frank edged back.

Christ... this isn't looking good...

Paul feigned a swing. 'I will.' He did it again. 'You know I will.'

'But you must know I can't just walk away.'

'I can't go to jail for the rest of my life...'

Rest of his life? Was he admitting to murder?

Fiona Barclay? Charlotte Wilson? Ellis Bramwell?

Which one?

All of them?

'Tell me what you've done and let me be the judge of what happens next.' Frank chanced a small step forward, despite entering striking range again. 'I'll listen, I promise.' Frank moved his left hand roughly in line with the handle just beneath the spade head, so he'd be able to parry or grab when the time came; meanwhile, he readied his other hand into a fist.

Frank pounced, but Paul had already swung.

Chapter Eighty-Two

DC Sharon Miller's jaw clenched tightly, the absurd claim grating on her last nerve.

She'd had enough.

Scoring a position on Frank's operation had seemed like the crowning moment in her fledgling career. Even when Chief Constable Oxley had spoken to her, Reggie and Sean in his office, assigning them the task with a tired expression and an apologetic tone, she'd remained positive.

After all, Frank Black, despite his infamous grumpiness and reputation as being difficult to work with, had been involved in many well-known investigations over the years, and his success rate spoke volumes. Many of her contemporaries would happily swerve such an assignment, preferring to work investigations in the more modern, more measured, more technologically driven way, rather than in an instinctive, primitive fashion prone to human errors, which had inevitably become obsolete long ago.

But Sharon had been raised by a father obsessed with BBC crime dramas. She'd sat through her fair share too. She liked the old ways and pined for them despite never having experienced them firsthand.

She wanted to be pounding the streets, not sitting behind a desk, answering the phone and taking notes like an overpaid receptionist.

It seemed Donald Oxley had been right all along. Working for Frank Black was like drawing the short straw.

She was on her fiftieth phone call today. Someone claimed to have seen Charlotte Wilson playing guitar the other night in a bar around the corner. Sharon had explained that Charlotte would be in her fifties by now and, given that they'd recovered her bones, she was dead, making this scientifically impossible. The polite man on the call didn't see that as a potential stumbling block to his intel. 'Her daughter, then. This has to be her daughter.'

After this call, she sighed and rubbed her forehead. People would do anything for attention. That was the be all and end all. Yet, how on earth could people consider *this* attention worth having? Calling a police hotline with information that meant absolutely nothing? What was the endgame here? Getting lucky with a completely fabricated story? That, somehow, the conjuring of a needy mind could, just by magic, become the new reality? Throw them into the spotlight as a case breaker?

'Give me strength.'

She couldn't remember John Thaw or Dennis Waterman spending two days taking calls from cranks in an episode of *The Sweeney*.

Also, since the number of calls had intensified, they'd forced Sean to work on a landline as well. At least she was trying to sound enthusiastic when taking calls, Sean wasn't hiding his boredom from the callers. If something came up, then he'd certainly fluff it. She wondered if Sean had a specific skill-set that she wasn't privy to yet. After all, someone had thought him suitable for a detective role, and it wasn't down to confidence, assertiveness or a rabid attention to detail.

She watched him nod as he talked with the caller. 'I don't understand; you've phoned this in before? When?' He made a note, his pen scratching against the paper. 'In person? Really? Can you remember the date?'

Her interest was piqued, she sat up straight behind her desk. She caught his gaze. He looked at her sleepily. She sighed, shaking her head. *He was such a sloth!*

'Are you all right?' She mouthed her question.

He nodded and pointed at the receiver in his hands. 'Another crank,' he mouthed back and shrugged.

Probably, she thought. *Still, show some backbone, Sean, and dig just to be sure.*

After he said thank you, she went around behind him. He was turning to a fresh page in his notebook and awaiting the next call, his posture slumped.

'What was that one about?' she asked.

He shook his head, his eyes still on the notebook. 'More bollocks.'

She turned away, disappointed. *So many dead ends...*

'Just a retired taxi driver claiming to have given Charlotte a lift,' he said.

She swung back, her eyebrow raised. 'Eh?'

'As I said, it's bollocks. For a start, he said 1986, not 1987, so he's clearly confused.' He leaned back in his chair, his arms crossed.

She nodded, considering his words. 'People make mistakes, though. It *was* almost forty years ago.'

'The date was in the public appeal.'

'Hmm... How old is this taxi driver?'

'Eighty.'

'*Eighty?*' She echoed. 'That's unusual.'

'Yeah ... why?' He looked at her, puzzled.

'Well, I mean who calls up with nonsense at eighty?'

Sean shrugged. 'Someone who is losing it?'

'No.' Sharon started to pace. 'Something must have struck a chord with him. Calling that in is a lot of effort for a man of eighty.'

'Guess it depends on how fit he is, I guess.'

'Where did he claim to have driven Charlotte from?' She stopped pacing, her attention fully on Sean.

'Scarborough station...'

'Woah, hang on there, fella.' She put her hand on his desk and leaned in, her eyes wide. 'The station where she was last seen?'

'Again, it was on the public appeal... He was just regurgitating what he'd read.' He waved his hand dismissively.

'This is already more interesting than anything I've had today. You should be grateful.'

'Are you really buying this?'

'Did he say why he didn't report it at the time?' She pressed on, undeterred.

'He said he did. Someone looked into it, apparently, and got back to him to tell him it'd come to nothing. We've read the file back and forth and there is no report of this lead.' He was looking more and more frustrated.

She shook her head. *Wake up, man!* 'Why do you find that hard to believe? We know they were lax on recording information. Can he remember who he spoke to back then?'

'He can't remember.'

'Shit.' She bit her lip.

'It's bullshit, *Sharon*. He made little sense.' He rubbed his temples.

'Where did he say he took her? From Scarborough station?'

He looked down at his notebook and read from it. 'Pleasanton Road.'

'May I?' She held out her hand, gesturing for the book.

He leaned over, tore the page out, and handed it to her, his jaw clenched. 'That way I can get on with my bloody job.'

She took the notepaper from the dipstick and went back to her computer. She searched the road out on Google Maps but couldn't find it, her brow furrowing in confusion.

'Anything?' He looked over at her, grinning. *Smug bastard.*

She was about to screw up the paper when she decided instead to whack the road name into the Google bar, accompanied by Scarborough.

There were hits.

Many hits.

She read, wide eyed.

'Listen... Sean... In 1988, they assimilated parts of Pleasanton Road into a new shopping centre. The complex continued to expand. By 1993, the new centre had wiped out most of the road and the former shopping district. God bless capitalism!' She smirked at him.

His face was impassive. 'So?'

'So, where did our taxi driver take her on Pleasanton Road?'

'He *never* bloody took her anywhere, so I didn't ask.' He raised his voice. This was the first genuine display of emotion she'd seen from him.

She liked it.

She played around until she got a list of businesses that traded on that road until the huge capitalist machine swallowed them. There were over forty, ranging from shoe stores to a family dental practice.

She stood and grabbed her coat. 'I assume you logged his address on the database?'

'Of course, this may be a waste of time, but I don't want Black pulling me up for not logging every caller.'

'Good. Grab the address and let's go then.' She grinned.

'And why would—'

'Why wouldn't you?' She cut him off, her tone brooking no argument. 'This is the most interesting thing I've heard in over one hundred phone calls. If anything, you get to stretch your legs.'

He stood up and yawned, reaching for his jacket. 'If it comes to anything, you get me a coffee.'

'Yes... I'll get you one anyway... anything to wake you from hibernation.'

He mumbled as he followed her out of the door. 'That's good, because it won't come to anything.'

Smug bastard.

Chapter Eighty-Three

Frank tilted his head back, a blood-soaked tissue pressed against his nose.

Despite her own ordeal of being tied up all evening, Fiona Barclay fussed over him, taking the drenched tissue from him and presenting him with a fresh one.

'I'll be fine.' His words were nasal. 'Was sick of the way it sloped to the left anyway. This'll save me a fortune on corrective surgery – I can use my pension for a cruise instead.'

He glanced at Gerry, sitting with her arms folded at the table. Since helping him to his feet by the back door, she'd only uttered three words, repeated twice, 'That was stupid.'

Verdict delivered. She felt no need to elaborate further. She'd already made the call to control to apprehend Paul. As their fugitive had opted for the back garden wall, he'd abandoned his car outside the front of Fiona's home, which could make the task easier; however, the possibility that he could grab another vehicle remained. Still, in that instance, they'd ANPR...

Gerry had also called an ambulance.

Being checked over was the last thing Frank wanted. The investigation had never felt so urgent. He'd consent to a quick going over, but if they asked him to come with them in the back of the ambulance, they'd have to wrestle him into it.

'How are you feeling, Mrs Barclay?' Frank asked.

'I'm fine. He was all puff and no pastry.'

Frank smiled, then winced at the stab of pain. He wondered if she used that expression because her husband had been a chef. Frank himself favoured the phrase 'all froth and no beer', so what did that say about him?

'Although, to his credit, he kept disarming me. First the knife, then that.' Fiona nodded toward the rolling pin on the floor. 'Not what I once was. There was a time when I'd have...' She paused, thinking better of what she was about to say. 'Anyway, he roughly handled me into a chair and tied me up. He told me that unless I produced the tape, he'd stay until we both starved to death. Told him I was quite happy with that if it meant he would face justice. When you turned up at the door, he taped my mouth and took a spade from the utility cupboard.'

'He must have seen me peering in.' He shook his head, irritated with himself. 'Anyway, Mrs Barclay, is it possible we could get everything clear before I borrow that rolling pin to fend off the oncoming paramedics? We believe Arthur is, *well*, this may be surprising news to you, but—'

'Paul's father?'

His eyes widened. 'Okay, so you know?'

'Of course I know! It was a mistake to keep it quiet. That, among many other things. Arthur knew my views. Not that the pig-headed bugger ever listened. Look... what happened with Cathleen hurt me. I was rather old-fashioned, and we hadn't slept together – we were waiting for the wedding. Seems I was the only one doing the waiting! Cathleen targeted Arthur when he was drunk one night. Offered him something he wasn't getting at home. I don't think she expected to get pregnant, but she did rather well out of it while she was alive.' She sighed and gazed off into the distance. 'It's unbelievable that our marriage even got going. But when he told me the truth and begged for my forgiveness, I knew, deep down, he adored me. So, I gave him another chance. He was too ashamed for people to know about the baby, and he was also worried about embarrassing me.' She turned her eyes back to Frank. 'I told him I thought it was best to just come clean and get it all over with. But he didn't listen. It cost him a lot of money over the years until Cathleen died. And, eventually, his freedom and career. To think, if he'd just followed my sodding advice, we may not be sitting here.'

Frank winced as he lifted the tissue away from his nose. He reached for a fresh one. 'And how did Paul find out the truth?'

'Another of Arthur's silly bloody moves! You must think I'm crazy for suffering so much. And you're probably right! You know, if that man hadn't had a heart of gold and loved me so much for over fifty years... well... I'd have got shot of it all! Arthur went out of his way to find out who Paul was adopted by. He then watched Paul throughout his childhood, and when his adopted mother, Margaret Fielding, who I believe is still alive and kicking, threw him out at sixteen when he had nothing, Arthur made his move.'

'Why did Margaret throw him out?' Gerry asked.

Frank was glad to see her emerging from the sullen mood.

'You'll have to ask her that!' Fiona snorted. 'If you can get sense out of her. She was as mad as a box of frogs, that one! Drinking, arguing... off the rails. Arthur, being the man he was, couldn't bear to see his own child suffering. He rented Paul an apartment and gave him a job. Saved his life in a way, I guess. Ironic really, as eventually it cost him his own. But he felt that was his obligation, and I didn't stand in his way. So, I stood by and watched their relationship blossom. I always knew something was up with that Paul... long before all this happened. I just knew. Too distant. Too self-absorbed. Measured in everything he said. He was using Arthur for everything he could. A real plotter. Yes, the money was important, but he saw an opportunity for a trade, to be a chef, and where most would've had to join some kind of queue, he jumped right to the front, for obvious reasons. And not just any old queue. My husband was one of the greatest ever chefs from around here. I can tell you that for a fact. No wonder Paul turned out to be so bloody good. He's a thief.'

Fiona looked down at her hands, solemnly. 'Look, I expect you're thinking, well, Arthur was his father and, in a way, should show responsibility. Why shouldn't he have supported Paul? I get all of that, I do. And I could live with it just fine. But when Paul made that mistake in the kitchen, tipped a load of nutmeg into a spiced pudding despite Arthur's simple instructions, then he should have held his hands up. But he didn't, did he? He cowered, terrified, and hid behind Arthur! And Arthur, bless the foolish old sod, did what he believed any father should do in that situation. Protect his son.' She sighed. Her eyes filled with tears. 'But what a cost, eh? What a cost! When he came out of prison, he was a shell of the man he was.'

She reached over for one of the tissues and soaked up her tears. Then, she nodded, and her eyes grew fierce. 'My view has never changed. The truth is everything. With his reputation ruined, Arthur would never chef again. Still, he'd never budge, and, over the years, he watched on, with some pride, admittedly, as his son became more and more successful.' Fiona's expression started to soften again. 'I'd never have betrayed him by exposing the truth. Not while he lived. I loved him so much. But now, he's gone, his legacy in ruins… well, I'm not having it, you hear? Not having it. I want him to be remembered for the honourable man he was.'

She placed a digital Dictaphone on the table. 'I'm going to play an audio of a conversation recorded between me and my husband without his knowledge. In it, he admits to what happened, admits he still believes it to be the right decision. I knew that if he ever died before me, then this recording would find an audience. I wanted Paul to believe that I was a doddering old woman, and I only had a single copy, just in case he came looking for it, and took it, which he almost did. To be honest, I could have given it to him before he hit you, DCI Black, and I'm sorry for that, but I didn't want to make out I was giving it up too easily. I didn't want him to suspect I had other copies. You see, I'm old, but not doddering, and I know how a cloud works.' She winked and pressed play.

Together, Frank and Gerry listened to the damning audio recording.

While Arthur's voice was frail, the recording left no doubt he was fully lucid and in control of his faculties. The admissions were clear, viable, and credible – evidence that could undoubtedly be used in court. Whether it'd ultimately prove successful was another matter; Frank knew all too well how fickle the judicial system could be these days when it came to evidence.

One thing, however, was certain – Paul Harrison was well and truly buggered, no matter how you sliced it.

Assault, kidnapping, evading arrest, perjury regarding the nutmeg poisoning... even without a manslaughter charge, his reputation would be decimated and his career over.

As for Arthur's role, he may have been the head chef, the one in charge, but he'd still wilfully lied, shielding his son's mishap. Would this recording truly restore his tarnished legacy? Frank harboured doubts, but he wasn't about to voice them aloud. Let Fiona cling to that hope for now. She'd sat on this dark family secret for the better part of her life. To have it all potentially amount to nothing would be devastating.

Frank explained the investigation into Charlotte's murder. He showed the picture of her in the Mariner's.

'I remember her,' Fiona said.

Frank took a deep breath.

Fiona continued, 'Because I remember Paul's girlfriend, Julie. Before the incident involving that poor boy, Ellis, I used to help at the restaurant. Obviously, Julie used to pop into see Paul. She seemed nice. Sometimes, she brought Charlotte with her. Now, the reason I remember it so well is that Charlotte turned up on her own, quite a number of times, in those last few weeks before Captain Cook's Galley closed. It was clear they got on well. He used to smoke outside with her. At one point, I just assumed that he'd moved on from Julie to Charlotte, but I couldn't confirm or deny that.'

'Did they ever look affectionate with one another?' Gerry asked.

She thought and shook her head. 'Not that I remember, but listen, it was a long time ago. I know what you're thinking, still... *look*, I know I'm not his biggest fan, and I'm happy to see him pay big for what he's done, but I can't see him killing that young lady. Unless it was an accident, like it was with that boy, Ellis. No. He's not a good person by any stretch; I think that's clear as day. But brutal murder? Like I say, he's all puff and no pastry!'

Still, Frank thought, *he neglected to tell us about a deepening relationship with Charlotte.*

Fiona rubbed her temples and then looked between the two detectives. 'To hell with it. I'll tell you something. There was a time, long ago, when I had that bastard at knifepoint. I was close. So *very* close. You know when you can feel despair making your every move? It was like that! You know, if not for Arthur turning up, things may have turned out differently... who knows? But, it didn't, and I couldn't tell you, genuinely, if I'd have done it. However, I've sat here, with Paul, all night, while he demanded this' – she pointed at the Dictaphone – 'and I never believed he'd actually hurt me. He's a bastard... that's true... but the killer you're looking for? I don't think so. Unless it was an accident I guess.'

'Even if she'd known about his mistake with the nutmeg?' Frank asked.

She thought and shook her head. 'No, I don't see it. Even then. He's just not a violent individual.'

Could have fooled me! Frank though, dabbing his nostrils.

Frank heard the wail of the ambulance.

Taking Fiona's directions to the toilet, he ducked away to clean away the dried blood caking his nostrils. He examined his battered reflection in the mirror as the paramedics pounded insistently at the door. A bit bent... would likely look worse tomorrow... but a medical emergency?

No.

Confident he could fend off their ministrations, Frank

nodded at his reflection... only for his nose to begin pissing blood again.

Great.

Cursing under his breath, he grabbed a wad of toilet paper and resigned himself to enduring the paramedics' fussing after all.

Chapter Eighty-Four

Clifford Moorhouse adjusted his glasses, peering up at the two detectives from his wheelchair as they stood at the door. Sharon had already shown her identification and explained they were following up on his phone call.

'Blimey! Feels like I only just put the bloody phone down! This is my daughter, Eileen,' Clifford said.

The middle-aged woman gripping the wheelchair's handles offered a warm smile. 'I knew it was worth phoning.'

'She badgered me into it.' Clifford snorted. 'Told her it was pointless. After all, I reported this over forty years ago to you lot... heard back once! They said it'd come to nothing. Never heard another peep after that.'

Sharon exchanged a glance with her partner, Sean. He arched a sceptical brow, his expression betraying his doubt about the old man's claim. Well, if it turned out to be nothing, at least they'd taken the opportunity to enjoy the fresh air instead of being cooped up behind those godforsaken desks!

Sharon wheeled her father backwards to make way. 'Come in, please. I've got a pot of Yorkshire brewing.'

Once settled in the cosy living room, Sharon asked, 'Can you remember who you spoke to initially, Clifford?'

'It was a young woman, and then an older gentleman, a DI of some sort, called me back.'

'Maybe if I read out some names, it might jog your memory.' Sharon consulted her notes, reciting the list of officers who'd been involved with the case.

Clifford's eyes widened at the third name. 'DI Roger Roland. Yep, that's the one! I remember now – Sharon here was just a bairn, watching Roland Rat on the telly while he rang me back.' He chuckled, tapping his temple. 'Strange how little things like that stick out in here, you know? DI Roland, Roland Rat – a weird little coincidence, eh?'

Sharon stole another sidelong glance at Sean, catching his arched brow. She could tell he still wasn't buying it. Roland had ultimately dismissed Clifford's lead. Now, it seemed her cynical partner wanted to do likewise.

But at least Sean had logged it. Roland hadn't even bothered!

Sharon fully got procedures were laxer back then. She doubted the Flying Squad in *The Sweeney* would have documented every scrap of information. But surely *this* called for a bullet point or two somewhere in that file?

'Okay, could you walk us through again what you told DI Roland and my colleague, DC Groves, earlier, please?' Sharon asked.

Out of the corner of her eye, she caught Sean checking his watch, barely suppressing an eye roll. *Prick.*

A steaming mug of Yorkshire tea found its way into her hands as Clifford launched into his recounting. 'Not much to say, really. This lass jumped into my cab around 11 a.m. – I know it was eleven because the train from Middlesbrough had just pulled in, always a guaranteed fare there. She wasn't too talkative, seemed a mite nervous about something. I remember she had a guitar case, so I asked her to play me a tune.' He tapped his temple with a rueful smile. 'Just thought she was one of those serious musician types, you know, lost in her head.'

The fact that he knew about the guitar case didn't give any credibility to his story, either. It'd been on both press releases.

Clifford explained how he drove her to Pleasanton Road.

Sharon said, 'I read that since then, developers have transformed most of the road into a shopping centre.'

'Aye,' Clifford said. 'Bloody unrecognisable. A right eyesore.'

'So, she paid and left the cab? Did she say where she was going?'

'No, but I assumed she was going to get her teeth looked at?'

Sharon took a deep breath and furrowed her brow. 'You dropped her at a dentist?'

'Didn't I mention that? I'm sure I did.'

'You didn't,' Sean said. He sounded irritated.

'Sorry, well, I definitely mentioned it to that Roland fella, back then.' He rapped his knuckles against his skull with a self-deprecating chuckle. 'Sorry, maybe this old nut isn't what it used to be.' He closed his eyes. 'But I do recall it. The place she approached looked more like a private residence, rather than the other shops on that street. She knocked, and a young fella let her right in.'

'But you're certain it was a dentist?' Sharon pressed.

He opened his eyes. 'Oh aye, no doubt about it. It had a standing sign out front with teeth on it and everything.'

'Can you remember the name?'

'Afraid not. Only that it was a dentist.'

'Did your customer say anything before she left your vehicle?'

'Not that I recall. Maybe she was nervous about getting some dental work done? That's the long and short of it, I'm afraid.'

'And you gave DI Roland all these details?'

'Positive. Aye. He got back to me and said it'd come to nothing. But it always kind of stuck with me, you know? I was positive it was the girl in the picture.'

As they headed back to their vehicle, Sharon tapped away on her phone, searching for dentists operating on that street during the timeframe in question. At one point, Sean's hand landed on her shoulder. She glared at him briefly until realising his intent. He was guiding her around a lamppost before she walked straight into it. She offered him a grudging nod of thanks.

'Come on,' Sean said. 'This *was* investigated... just not written up. We already know how it worked with them back then.'

'Ever heard the expression: If someone tells you it's raining, go out to check?'

He sighed.

She continued searching on her phone and discovered two dental practices: Peasholm Dental Partners and Robinson's Dental Practice.

After informing Sean, she said, 'We should go back and ask Clifford which one—'

Images of the shopfronts in the eighties appeared on the screen before she could finish. A grainy photograph depicted Peasholm as an ambitious affair with oral products displayed in the window, while Robinson's was unmistakably the residential-style building Clifford described, complete with a cheap sign standing out front.

'Bingo!' She showed Sean the image.

He regarded it with a resigned shake of his head. 'Still won't be anything. When do I get this coffee?'

Then, she googled the practice name properly and nearly dropped her phone in shock.

'Not yet,' she said. 'Definitely not yet.'

Chapter Eighty-Five

As PREDICTED, the paramedics tried to badger Frank into the ambulance.

Unsurprisingly, his abrupt tone in 'it's only a bloody nosebleed, man!' didn't help matters.

'Actually,' Gerry had unhelpfully added, 'it's *definitely* broken. I can see a slight curve—'

At that point, he'd declared to all those bothering him, 'I wasn't knocked out. I'm not concussed. And I've got shit to do.' Then, he walked away, holding his hand up in farewell.

He waited for Gerry to get in the car. She crossed her arms like she'd done before in Fiona's home.

Give me strength... Sighing, he reached for the ignition key.

'It isn't safe to drive with that injury,' Gerry said. 'Can you say, with all certainly, it isn't affecting your vision?'

'Well, I can see you.'

'You need to be assessed.'

'Look, Gerry... I can't deny that I'm a rather old-fashioned dickhead who just wants to crack on. But you're going to have to believe me when I tell you, for the last time, all is good. I'm not bloody concussed!' He turned the key and the car lurched sharply. He'd left it in gear.

'Say nothing!' He held his finger up. 'That's because you're distracting me.'

They drove in silence for ten minutes until he received a phone call from Reggie. They were in the vehicle from the carpool, so he could pump his voice through the speakers. After the good news that Julie's son was out of the woods, he received the bad news that there was no sign of Paul. His phone was switched off and there'd be no reports of any stolen cars, which scuppered the ANPR angle. *Shit. You should have got off your fat arse, scaled that fence and chased him.* He shook his head. *And most certainly dropped dead...*

'Also, I got something back on David Roberts' claim that he was away at Oxford during the time of Charlotte's disappearance,' Reggie said.

'Are you about to tell me he wasn't?'

'Exactly that. He had his tonsils removed at the end of August, and so didn't leave for Oxford until September 21st. I've a signed copy of the enrolment details in my inbox.'

'Lying bastard,' he said. 'That's three days after her disappearance.' He gritted his teeth.

'Are you okay, boss?' Reggie asked.

'Aye. Why do you ask?'

'You sound a bit funny... and I heard you took a battering.'

Frank squeezed the steering wheel. 'Hardly a battering.'

'Heard it were a spade. Nothing you could do about it, boss.'

Ha. You sound as genuine as a three-pound note. 'You think I don't know that?'

'Just saying... in case—'

'In case what? In case my pride is hurt? It's fine, Reggie.'
We're not all vain little bollocks like you.

Feeling irritated, Frank hung up on him. He looked at Gerry. 'If he asks, tell him the reception cut out.'

'I wouldn't feel comfortable lying.'

'Okay, don't lie. Just don't bloody talk to him.'

Then, he remembered his daughter's request, which had completely slipped his mind.

Sarah Tyler.

Maybe the spade had shaken something loose in his head, after all.

He pulled over to the side of the road. 'Going to make a private phone call.'

Met with silence from his passenger, Frank exited, drawing in a sharp breath of cold air that stung his throbbing nose.

Irritation simmered beneath his skin, that ever-present cantankerous temper he was infamous for threatening to boil over. Grumpy old Frank Black.

Taking a few deep breaths, he willed himself to regain control before continuing with the day. Losing his cool now would only complicate matters further.

He took his phone out of his suit pocket.

Chapter Eighty-Six

AFTER DISCOVERING that Sarah Tyler's phone was disconnected, Frank's mood darkened further. Without that point of contact, his chances of contacting her became very limited.

He sighed. It'd be necessary to call in old favours. The methods would be questionable.

Not great, now they were in this grand age of accountability and whistleblowing. But he'd have to give it a whirl. And, if all else failed, he'd go super old school and hit the homeless shelters in Leeds, waving photographs.

This wasn't what he needed right now.

Desperate to get his head back to Charlotte, he engaged Gerry on the subject on the way back. 'What do you think of that glowing character reference from Fiona Barclay about Paul?'

'Glowing as in positive? It wasn't positive.'

'I was being sarcastic. Look, her praise only stretched as far as claiming that he was too weak to be a stone-cold killer. Maybe there's something in that. It'd take a real dark streak to murder Charlotte. Aye, Charlotte may have known the truth about who really poisoned that lad, Ellis, and that there is a strong motive for Paul, but still... everything points to him being more concerned about concealing the truth regarding his role in Ellis' death in 1987, *not* Charlotte's murder. I mean, if it were you, which one would you be more worried about? One will cost him, but the other is going to put him in jail for the rest of his days. Chasing around after Fiona's Dictaphone wouldn't be my priority.'

'I see your point.' Gerry nodded. 'But it seems he still lied about how close he became to Charlotte. And maybe he believes that the truth behind Ellis might set off a chain of events that eventually connects him to Charlotte's murder?'

'But if that was the case, *and* he was prepared to kill Charlotte over knowing the truth, then why the hell hasn't he the guts to kill Fiona? Surely, he'd been better off silencing her a few years back?'

'I agree. Although Fiona never betrayed Arthur, Paul wasn't to know she'd never waver – and she's done just that. He must have lived with the fear of this for a long time. If he'd killed Charlotte before, then why hesitate to kill again? Honestly, I've never considered him a major suspect.'

Frank raised an eyebrow. 'So with a line through Paul, albeit a faint one, where next? The all-round vicious bastard who lied about being away? Dr David? He was stiff at our interview. *Cold.* People like that have no empathy. Makes them dangerous.'

Gerry unfolded her arms. 'I, too, struggle with empathy.'

His face reddened. *Shit...* 'Sorry... I didn't mean it like that.'

She glanced at him for the first time in a while. 'Why are you sorry?'

'Because... well...' *Oh bloody hell, here goes the hole digging!* 'You're different. You're kind, good-natured...'

'Am I?'

'Aye!' *Bloody hell.* 'Of course.'

'My parents taught me how to behave, how to act.'

'That's like everyone, isn't it?'

'No, most people assimilate. I constructed my behaviours with guidance from my parents.'

You're not a bloody robot, Gerry. 'Look, I can't buy that. You must feel the need to help people. Otherwise, why join the police?'

'Because I love puzzles. They soothe my mind. Rylan, too, of course, focuses me. Without them, I can be quite different.'

'How so?'

'We discussed this before. Agitated. Distracted.'

Frank shook his head. 'I don't believe you've no empathy. You care. I know you do.'

'I never said I don't have any empathy; I said, I struggle with it.'

He indicated to change lane. 'No. Still not sold. It's not just about doing puzzles. If so, buy a bloody *Puzzler*! You don't sleep four hours a night to solve puzzles! You sleep four hours a night because you give a shit.' He waited for a break in the lane alongside him and moved his car over.

'You've read my file... that's compiled by professionals. Experts. You should use it to better understand my needs.'

Sod experts. 'Of course.' *Now, enough of this.* 'Your thoughts on the all-round vicious bastard then?'

The question hung in the air a while before she answered. 'He's capable. Yes. But what's his motive?'

'Does he need motive?'

'I think so... yes. The man is very intelligent. Successful. I can't see him taking risks without very good reason.'

Frank glanced at her. 'According to his wife, he can be angry and aggressive. That could lead to impulsive behaviour, and fatal accidents.'

Gerry's nod was swift. 'It's possible.'

He tried to breathe through his nose, but it was clogged with blood. Instead, he inhaled through his mouth and sighed. 'How about Julie?'

'Charlotte's best friend,' Gerry said. 'She feels that loss, deeply. I can't see why she'd intentionally kill her.'

'Any other suspects?'

Gerry's silence confirmed what he was already thinking. That there weren't any yet.

He growled as he changed gear forcefully. 'Thirty-seven years, Gerry! We need something else. A catalyst, something...' He clenched his teeth and shook his head. Eventually, he said, 'Okay... let's speak to Hanna now regarding David. He clearly is our best fit so far.'

His phone rang. Sharon's name appeared on the handsfree. 'Sir, I have something... something *big*.' Her voice was filled with enthusiasm; it was unusual, but very welcome.

His mouth dropped open as he listened to her discovery from an old ignored lead that had resurfaced. *Bloody Roland. If you weren't dead, I'd kill you myself.* He indicated to come off the carriageway so he could turn the car around.

'Okay, Hanna will have to wait a while. This is more pressing. Also, Gerry, could you reach into the glove compartment and chuck us two paracetamol, please? My nose feels like it's on fucking fire.'

Chapter Eighty-Seven

WHEN FRANK SAW the picture of DI Roger Roland on his incident board with the words *DI ROLAND RAT* written below it, a wave of irritation washed over him. 'Who did this?'

'I did.' Reggie shrank into his chair. 'I thought—'

'You thought it'd make everyone laugh?'

Reggie flushed. Everyone else in the room, apart from Gerry, dropped their heads.

'Not exactly... but he was a bastard, boss. Look at the investigation.'

'You don't have to tell me. I worked with the man.'

Reggie shrugged. 'What's the problem, then?'

'The problem, Reggie, is that he's dead. Where do we draw the line? Mocking a dead man? Doesn't that make us a bunch of bastards too?' He rubbed out *RAT*. 'It certainly doesn't make us bloody professional.'

'Boss,' Sharon said. 'In Reggie's defence, it was actually our witness, Clifford Moorhouse, who called him Roland Rat. I told him, and so I gave him the idea.'

Frank narrowed his eyes and looked between Sharon

and Reggie. 'I'm *full* of ideas. Thankfully, for some of you in this room, they'll remain that forever more. Ideas.' He tapped his head. 'Locked away.' His stare froze on Reggie. 'God forbid they ever get out.'

'Sorry, boss,' Reggie said.

'Okay,' Frank said. 'We move on.' He turned and looked at DI Roland again, the idiot he'd once had the misfortune of brushing shoulders with. Just another self-obsessed, lazy and sneaky officer in a time of many. When Roland went, many sighed with relief. His death from a heart attack a year later barely featured on anyone's radar.

Frank looked down at his gut again. *Be you if you're not careful. Dead months after retirement. And probably unnoticed, too.* 'Okay, Sharon, talk us through everything in detail, please.'

Sharon had already handed pictures out. The first image showed Pleasanton Road in the years prior to its redevelopment. A property was circled with red ink. Robinson's Dental Practice. 'Clifford dropped her off here around 11.15 a.m. About twelve minutes from the station. She had her guitar case with her.'

Frank nodded, picturing Laura Wilson chasing her daughter down the street with her lucky pink plectrum signed by Bob Marley. It was incredible to Frank how a young woman's last movements from so long ago could grow into something so vivid in his mind.

'He said she came across as nervous, but he wrote it off to her being a brooding musician, and the visit to the dentist. Of course, Clifford didn't know what was really happening at Robinson's Dental Practice. Nervous was an understatement.'

Frank looked down at the printed newspaper report provided by Sharon. Together, they read through it.

Archibald Robinson wouldn't be the first successful individual to descend into shadiness driven by greed, and he certainly wouldn't be the last. But that didn't make the situation any less curious.

A prosperous dentist, born into wealth far exceeding that of most, chasing an extra buck through unsavoury means.

Frank could only suppose it was about wielding power, seduced by the intoxicating thrill of getting away with more than the ordinary person could.

In 1987, the Abortion Act had been in effect for nineteen years, allowing women in England to access safe abortion services under regulated conditions. It was a success in largely eliminating the underground market for unsafe, unsanitary, and often dangerous illegal procedures. However, a fringe market persisted – some women were concerned about confidentiality and were willing to pay exorbitant prices, while others still avoided the NHS out of fear of judgement or refusal. Many were concerned about their parents finding out, because of religion or other firm beliefs, so preferred to head under the radar.

Parasites like Archibald Robinson had preyed upon such weaknesses, capitalising on desperation.

In 1988, the law exposed Robinson's underbelly operation, shut it down, and imprisoned him.

Sharon was very vocal about these discoveries, while Sean stayed his usual subdued self; he couldn't help suspecting that it was Sharon, herself, who'd gone to town on this one.

He considered the fact that he'd underestimated her. It certainly wasn't intentional. Was he simply a product of the time he'd learned his trade in? Gerry and Sharon were knocking it out of the park, more so than any male colleague he'd ever had alongside him, and yet he'd been so tentative with them at the outset.

It bothered him.

He didn't feel narrow-minded, and hoped that wasn't the case, but he knew, with his background, that it was certainly possible.

He made a resolution there and then. As well as improving his health, he'd also work on his attitudes.

Sharon was now explaining how this lead had then developed. 'Archibald's daughter Jenny, a successful feminist author, has written at lengths about her father's behaviour and abuse of power in the seventies and eighties. When I contacted her, she was very determined to help. Within the hour, she'd got back to me. She owns copies of her father's own records. The courts used the originals in his trial and archived them, but she obtained hard copies for her own research after submitting an application. Archibald had used the same ledger for all of his dental appointments and his illegal abortions, and had simply added an extra code, "TE", alongside the abortion appointment. "TE". *Termination.* Charlotte Wilson had an appointment at 11.30 a.m. on September 18th, 1987. Alongside her name was the code, "TE".'

Frank put his hands on the table and lowered his head. He could already see it all. Playing out in his mind.

DI Roland following up on the lead and Archibald, rolling in it, paying him for silence. What other explanation could there be for this damning lead being omitted from official reports? Roland was no fool. Archibald's illicit activities would've been glaringly obvious after a cursory investigation. Yet he dismissed Clifford's tip, not even bothering to jot it down in some forgotten notebook.

The powerful and rich always got what they wanted,

then and now. *Always.* This was just another bloody example of the privileged abusing their status. A surge of anger rushed through Frank. The spike in blood pressure caused his battered nose to throb painfully.

Both Archibald and Roland were long dead. Frank felt disappointed that he could never confront either, look them in the eye, and condemn them for failing a vulnerable eighteen-year-old with a kind heart and a bright future. Yes, he imagined they wouldn't have cared less, but they would still have heard his condemnation. Every word. On behalf of Charlotte. And who knows? Weighting their dark souls that little more may hopefully have taken them further towards damnation.

'So, who do we think the father of this baby was?' Frank asked his team.

Sharon looked up. Her wide eyes and straight posture spoke volumes about her enthusiasm, showing that she hadn't finished. 'She paid with a cheque, boss.'

Charlotte didn't have a bank account... He leaned on the table again, his nose now throbbing to high heaven.

'Hanna Goodall signed the cheque,' Sharon said. 'Goodall was Hanna Roberts' maiden name.'

Heart thrashing, Frank swung around and glared at the picture of David Roberts. His nose was in agony, but he no longer cared.

He was on the precipice of the truth...

'Fancy that, eh? And to think we were already on our way to see her,' he said.

Chapter Eighty-Eight

Frank pulled into the driveway and turned to face Gerry, who was reaching behind her seat to stroke Rylan's head. Before leaving, she'd approached Frank, requesting that Rylan accompany them because of her feeling of unease.

Frank had pressed her for more detail on her concerns, but she couldn't provide any. 'Often there's no identifiable cause. It'll pass, but I know from previous experience it is better to have Rylan with me.'

Now that they'd reached their destination, Frank asked, 'Are you feeling any better?'

'No, sorry... still uneasy. I'll stay in the car with Rylan—'

'Should I ask if Rylan can come in?' Even as he asked it, Frank knew how ridiculous that sounded.

'That wouldn't be appropriate. And we know that Hanna is hiding something. It is better to approach without asking favours first.'

'I wouldn't feel indebted,' he said, but he agreed that it was inappropriate. 'Well, if you feel better, come in. Otherwise, I'll see you shortly.'

With a sigh, Frank exited the vehicle and made his way to the front door of Briony Goodall's home.

Chapter Eighty-Nine

As DAVID WALKED the ginnel connecting the street where he'd parked with the one where Briony lived, he ran through options, again and again, in his head.

Briony was unmarried, childless, and lived alone. Earlier, he'd phoned her work and asked for her, hanging up when he heard her voice.

Hanna would be alone.

This was a risk, yes, because a phone call to the police for coming too close to his wife would see him back in the nick.

But he was confident it wouldn't come to that.

Words were his strength. With them, he could reassure and calm.

Manipulate.

Rarely did he fail with patients. And this was Hanna, too. His wife! He knew her inside out.

Before the afternoon was through, this would be over and done with.

And if talking failed? Well, there was another approach...

Forgotten Bones

But it would have to be a last resort. If he could mend the situation without resorting to frustration and anger, then he must do.

Reaching your boiling point wasn't something you planned for.

He stopped dead at the end of the ginnel opposite Briony's house when he saw that cocksure fat DCI from the other day approaching her front door. He edged backwards behind some low-hanging tree foliage drooping over the path walls.

Now, what did he want? David sucked in a deep breath. *Surely not? Hanna wouldn't, would she? Give that fat idiot the truth?*

He exhaled, knowing he'd be stupid to take anything off the table.

Had he thought Hanna capable of having him arrested? *No.*

Did he think Hanna would betray him regarding 1987? *No.*

The rules of the game were changing.

His stomach stirred with irritation.

Soon, it'd become frustration. And, well, after that...

Boiling point.

Craning his head around the foliage, he saw that someone else was in the plush new VW that Frank had arrived in.

He also recognised her from the interview at his office.

DI Gerry Carver.

Why was she staying back?

Chapter Ninety

Frank showed Hanna his ID, but didn't explain the reason behind his visit until they were both sitting in the lounge. She didn't ask. Undoubtably, she assumed it to be about David assaulting her.

Before arriving, he'd planned to wait in order to settle her and take her off-guard; however, after seeing Hanna's black eye; her pale, worn out features; and the shaking in her hands, he did it purely from sympathy. She'd been through it big time, and he wanted to keep everything calm for her as long as possible.

Tea sounded appealing when offered, but he declined, not wishing to trouble her.

'Your nose looks painful,' she said.

Back at HQ, he'd tried to make it less of an eyesore with a plaster, but had probably only succeeded in drawing more attention to it. He waved it away. 'I'm on the mend.' A complete lie, as it'd only just happened, but at least his eyes had stopped watering.

'How did it happen?'

'Disagreed with a door.'

The gentle nod of her head spoke volumes.

How often had Hanna used a similar excuse for her own injuries?

He suddenly felt rather untactful and so set the record straight. 'A disagreement with a suspect. He lashed out before we could compromise. Never a dull moment.'

Now she nodded her head with conviction. 'You need to be more careful.'

Don't I just know it? Frank hoped he wouldn't have to tear into her. The levels of trauma she must have endured in thirty-six years of marriage were inconceivable.

Still, Hanna had signed a cheque to a dentist, not for dental work, but for an illegal abortion. *Whatever your current plight, you must be accountable for such behaviours.* 'I'm not here about the assault charge against your husband, Mrs Roberts.' He sighed. 'Have you heard about the remains recovered by the whalebone arch?'

Hanna nodded.

'They belonged to Charlotte Wilson. She died late in 1987, more than likely on September 18th.'

Hanna stared downwards; she chewed on her nails.

'Did you know her?' Frank asked.

She chewed for a moment longer, before looking up. 'I think you know I did. Otherwise' – she sighed – 'why would you be here? I knew Charlotte. Not very well. But I knew her. Yes.'

'In what regard?'

She shrugged. 'She was having sex with my husband. Or rather, boyfriend at the time.'

Frank hadn't expected so blunt a response, but he kept his surprise in check. 'So, you knew David was cheating on you?'

'Oh yes. It wasn't his first sexual relationship behind my

back, and it *certainly* wasn't his last.' She snorted. 'He doesn't always tell me, but I always know. You could smell it on him. He never worked that hard to conceal it.'

A sign of true arrogance, Frank thought.

She stared, sadly, at Frank. 'Are any of Charlotte's family still alive?'

'Just her mother.'

Hanna sighed. 'I can only imagine. All that time. The pain. Although, I wouldn't pretend to understand that anguish fully. I never had children, you see.'

Frank nodded.

'I'm sorry for her loss,' she added.

'It's taken its toll, aye, but she'll make peace with it,' Frank said. 'She's strong.'

'It's important to be strong in this life.' She pointed at her black eye. 'If you aren't strong, you risk becoming someone like me.'

Frank looked at her sympathetically. 'I wouldn't be hard on yourself, Mrs Roberts. Unfortunately, in this career, I've encountered this many times. Sometimes the stronger you are, the worse it can be. I met people who believed that they could beat it, that they could weather it, actually *help* the other person. That, to me, is a sign of strength, too.'

'Still foolish though, eh? No matter how you dress it up?'

'I think you've to know when to give it up.'

'It's taken me thirty-eight years of being with him to work it out. Don't pretend that's strength, DCI Black.'

Frank didn't want to continue down this track. He didn't feel qualified to provide opinions on so sensitive a matter, but he tried to close it off with something obvious, something he respected in her. 'You're doing the *right* thing now, Mrs Roberts. That's what matters. Not for how long it took. You're trying to stop him from hurting anyone else.'

She smiled. 'Thank you, DCI Black.'

Anyway, back to it. 'So, what happened regarding Charlotte?'

'The inevitable, I guess. He got her pregnant. I'm surprised it hadn't happened before with one of his other flings.'

His phone rang. 'Sorry...' He took his phone out, regarded the unknown number, switched on *silent*, and put the phone on the left arm of the chair. 'David was adamant he had very little to do with Charlotte.'

'Not only is my husband a born liar, but he doesn't deal very well with shame. All to do with his mother, you see. Not that I'd bore you with that.'

This is far from boring.

'Still,' she continued. 'There're no excuses for being a mean bastard.'

Frank plucked his phone from the arm and showed her the picture of Charlotte and David together in 1987. She stared for a time, tears pricking at the corners of her eyes. Then he placed his phone back on the arm of the chair.

'I took that photograph, you know,' she said.

'Aye. He told us.'

'I already *suspected* they were at it, too. They were so flirty.'

'He said that he took photos with all the open mic acts.'

'Did he now?' She laughed. 'I don't recall ever taking photographs of him with any other performers, and that was my camera.'

'How did you find out for certain?'

'Followed them one night to Tate Hill Pier. *Disgusting.*

They were all over each other. Carving their names into the wood. Revolting. He's revolting.'

Frank took a deep breath. Although he'd suspected this before now, he'd never considered the fact that it gave Hanna a significant motive.

Did you kill Charlotte, Hanna?

Until this point, the thought hadn't crossed his mind; now, suddenly, it was burning bright like a beacon.

'Did you confront him *then?*'

'No! God, I was as weak then, as I am now! To think if I'd done that then! My life, oh my, my life! It could've been completely different!' The tears in the corners of her eyes ran down her face. 'I've nothing, DCI, *nothing*. I'm fifty-five and I've no children. But what do I do now? Adopt? Would they let me? I'm too old, surely, and alone. So, what happens now? Do I just live with this regret for whatever time I've left?'

Frank looked at her, sympathetically. He allowed her a moment and then redirected the conversation. 'How did he find out you knew about Charlotte?'

'Who's saying he ever found out?' She smiled. 'I know so much about him and what he's been up to over the years. To be honest, it's the only power I've ever had. When I know and he's unaware that I know. Pathetic, eh? Amazing what we hold on to when deluded.'

Come now, Hanna. Enough is enough. Tell me everything. 'You must have confronted him.'

'What makes you say that?'

He sighed. He opened his mouth to say, *because of the abortion you paid for*, but she got in there first. 'She told me, okay? Charlotte felt guilty, and she confessed to me what had been going on. Charlotte ended it. They were clearly not a good match, were they? He was more the intellectual snob, or at least thought he was. She was the laid-back rock girl. Knowing that I'd been told, he came crawling back for forgiveness. And I forgave him. Because that's what I do. What I've always done.'

She folded back in the chair as if she was done, and at the end of the tale. She sighed, clearly exhausted.

But that isn't everything, Hanna. Not at all. I understand your pain, your trauma, but someone didn't just rob Charlotte of her dignity and happiness. They robbed her of her entire life.

'I need you to tell me about Charlotte's abortion,' he said.

Hanna leaned forward, her eyes wide, her mouth hanging half-open.

Frank waited, but when it became obvious that she wouldn't speak, he said, 'We know you signed the cheque to Archibald Robinson to pay for Charlotte's abortion—'

'I did not.' Her eyes widened even further. 'I *did* not.'

Frank nodded, choking back a sigh. 'I'm sorry, but we—'

'It was *him*. It was that idiot. David took my cheque book and signed a cheque. He forged my signature.'

Frank raised an eyebrow. 'Is that what happened?'

'Yes, of course, why wouldn't it be... you think I'd pay for *that*? A problem that I didn't cause?'

'How did it happen then?'

'It's straightforward. At first, Charlotte refused an abortion. She didn't want to upset her mother. Her mother was Catholic and didn't believe in them. But it turned out that Catholicism wasn't the main reason. Apparently, and I learned this much later, she simply felt guilty because her mother had given birth at fifteen, and Charlotte now felt that refusing to raise a child at eighteen would devalue the sacrifices her mother had made for her. But Charlotte had no money. David's parents may have been loaded, but there was no way he was asking them. They'd have been horrified! They were funding his adventure to Oxford. So, he stole a cheque from the drawer in my room, and only admitted to what he'd done after it was cashed, so I wasn't stunned when I checked my account. I didn't know what to do. Challenge him? Tell his parents? It didn't help he'd just had his tonsils out and wasn't feeling great. And then, well then, I don't know... everything seemed to stop. The problem kind of went away. He went to Oxford, we kept up a relationship long distance, and Charlotte, well, she never returned.'

'Because she was dead, Mrs Roberts.'

She pointed at her chest. 'And I didn't know that! You think I haven't felt guilty... awful... about what happened with that abortion, but I just didn't know what the best thing was to do, so I did nothing.' She put her hands over her face.

Yes, David was surely banking on that.

She dropped her hands away and regarded Frank tearfully. 'Genuinely, there were so many times in which I believed I should say something. I heard about the fact that she was missing. I knew that September 18th was the date of the abortion... but... I also believed I *needed* David. He has this way. Always has done. Makes you feel you *need* him. Briony, my sister, sees through him, and I'm committed to changing. To seeing through him too. I'm a fool... an idiot... but I've got my desserts. Unbeknownst to me, I ended up paying for an abortion for a vulnerable girl. I mean, was that what she even wanted? David said so, but how do I know he didn't just make her like he makes everyone do things? Is it any wonder I've no children? Karma.' Her eyes widened. 'Will I go to jail?'

Frank doubted the charges would have legs. This woman had been bullied and manipulated into such behaviour for decades. Would the CPS really want to bother trying to prove otherwise?

Frank leaned forward in the chair, so he was closer to her. 'Hanna, did David kill Charlotte?'

She looked deep in thought. 'I won't lie, I've thought so before now. You see, I know what kind of man he is. He'd had his tonsils out and he wasn't the best, but he could have done something. He wasn't bedridden. But I just convinced myself, every time, that no, even for an emotionless control freak like my husband, murdering that girl would just be one step too far. Unthinkable.'

'Do you still think that?'

'I don't know what I think. If you asked Briony, she'd tell you straight. That man is capable of anything.'

Frank took a deep breath. He didn't wish to go to the next level, but the truth demanded it. Charlotte demanded it. 'You know, Hanna, how this looks? Others may say the relationship she was having with David infuriated you; or, that Charlotte may have tried to blackmail you with the fact that you paid for an illegal abortion?'

Hanna shook her head, touching her chest. 'Really? Is that what *you* think?'

'I said others,' Frank said. 'They'd see motive.'

'If that's what you think, then take me in. I'm exhausted. If you want to waste your time.'

'But see it from our perspective,' Frank pushed. 'She had an abortion. She told you it was over, but were you convinced? Did you really believe that she was done with

David? That they wouldn't reunite? It could have pushed you to act in—'

'*No!* I'd never. That isn't me. No. Never!'

Frank nodded. 'Okay, I—'

'*Besides,* I knew it was over, because I confronted her. She told me she wouldn't go near David again, and I believed her.'

Chapter Ninety-One

David was sick of standing in the ginnel.

It must have looked suspicious to those passing by.

So, when someone approached either from behind or in front, he'd take his mobile out, and pretend to have stopped dead in his tracks to text someone. It was that, or he'd look like some kind of stalker!

Finally – *thank God* – Briony's door opened, and the DCI waddled his fat carcass back to the VW.

Once the two detectives had departed, he sprinted over the street to the front door.

Back at home, Hanna was notoriously bad at leaving the front door unlocked when she was home. So, rather than knock, he tried the handle first.

It seemed she was no more vigilant at her sister's!

The gods were finally smiling down on him and giving him a long overdue piece of luck.

The door glided open.

Chapter Ninety-Two

Frank drove away from Hanna's sister's house, his mind awhirl with the contents of the interview. 'Charlotte informed Hanna that the relationship with David was dead. She didn't feel there was any reason not to believe her. She never gave the consent to the subsequent abortion. David stole the money from her and...' He cut his eyes sideways to Gerry, trying to gauge her reaction. She was just staring ahead, as impassive as ever. Frank shook his head. 'Aren't you finding this curious?'

Gerry's features remained stubbornly blank. 'Of course. It's intriguing.'

Frank huffed out an incredulous laugh. 'Intriguing? Is that it? C'mon, what's whirring away in that brain of yours, Gerry?'

'I'm processing.' Her voice was devoid of inflection.

'Right, of course you are.' Frank tamped down a surge of exasperation. 'Well, while you chew it over, I reckon it's high time we loop the rest of the squad in. Maybe they'll demonstrate a smidge more enthusiasm.'

Gerry swivelled her head to face him, brows pinched. 'Is that sarcasm I'm detecting?'

Frank blew out a gusty sigh. 'Look, would it be too much for a little excitement? We're finally getting somewhere.'

'Someone has died. Any excitement feels misplaced.'

Frank reached for the car's touchscreen to dial HQ. He growled when he clocked the 'No Connection' error message glaring back at him. 'Where's my bloody mobile?'

Keeping one hand on the steering wheel, he patted his pockets with the other. *Nothing.*

Then he remembered his phone sitting on the arm of Hanna's chair.

It was like a smack to the forehead.

Buggering hell!

He shot Gerry a pained grimace. 'Ruddy thing's still at Hanna's.'

Making sure the road was clear, swung the car around in a tight U-turn, tyres squealing their protest.

Chapter Ninety-Three

DAVID CORNERED Hanna in one of Briony's upstairs bedrooms and tried his best to talk her round.

After five minutes, he realised he was at a dead end.

And it wasn't something he was used to.

In five minutes, he could talk the most pained patient around. Take them into an agreeable state. One in which his suggestions and *manipulation* would carry weight.

He recalled one instance in which it'd taken him less than five minutes to talk a married patient into sexual intercourse with him.

Five minutes was a good measuring stick.

Yes. There really was a problem here.

The frustration growing within him must have been clear to Hanna. She pressed herself against the wall on the far side of the king-sized bed, while he surveyed the posh bedroom, considering his next move. The bedroom had its own fireplace. Briony, a silver-tongued lawyer, was well-off.

Silver-tongued... like me.

She'd obviously talked Hanna round to her way of thinking. Succeeding where he was failing.

His eyes settled on the rack of silver pokers by the fire. They looked threatening. Taking a deep breath, he closed his eyes. *Keep control. Hurting her before has backfired on you.*

He tried talking to Hanna again, but it was useless. Her eyes were full of condemnation. She even started ridiculing him! Accusing him of being a control freak; that he lacked empathy and compassion; that he always treated the people who loved him like puppets in his world.

He saw his mother standing where Hanna was. Pointing… judging… *'You're too controlling, David. Expecting us, everyone, to do what you say. You must change. You can't live like this. You can't keep hurting others.'*

Adrenaline spiking, his gaze panned to the pokers again. *No… stay in control…*

He looked back, held up a finger and said, 'There's still time, Hanna, for us to work this out.'

Then, she confessed to what she'd told the fat carcass of a DCI.

His heart thrashed in his chest. 'Why would you want to destroy me?'

'You did that all by yourself.' Her voice was cold.

He moved to the fireplace, reached down for a silver poker, held it up, regarded it for a moment, then circled the bed, switching it from hand to hand.

'Please,' she said. 'Please… you'll only make it worse.'

'Worse?' He grunted, regarding her terrified eyes. '*Worse?* I think we're past that, don't you?' He struck her across the head.

Chapter Ninety-Four

'WAIT HERE,' Frank told Gerry as he heaved himself out of the car, trying to ignore a twinge in his hip. *Christ, when did everything start to ache so much?* He felt sixty-four going on eighty!

He made his way up Briony's path at a half-jog, already feeling the burn in his lungs from minimal exertion.

Unease settled over him when he saw the door was ajar. His mind raced back to when he'd left, replaying the scene. Hanna had shut the door behind him, hadn't she?

He raised his finger to the doorbell, but paused, thinking back through his exit again.

Yes, she'd closed it.

He dropped his finger and pushed the door open.

Silence greeted him.

He stepped cautiously over the threshold and paused in the entryway, his pulse thrumming in his ears. He eased the front door closed behind him, but didn't let it latch. To his left, the lounge door stood open – he could just make out his mobile lying on the armchair where he'd left it. Straight ahead was a closed door, and to his right, a staircase leading to the upper floor.

'Hanna?'

He waited a moment, but the silence persisted.

His instincts screamed at him to grab Gerry for backup, to get the cavalry on their way ASAP. So, he opted to retrieve the phone first.

He crept into the lounge, his pulse now causing agonising throbbing in his bust nose. After confirming the room was empty, he grabbed his phone. He saw several missed calls and a voicemail notification.

A sudden squeak of floorboards from above made him freeze.

'Hanna?' He called again.

Nothing. The hairs at the nape of his neck prickled.

Time to call for back up...

Footsteps thundered down the stairs.

Shit!

Shoving the mobile into his pocket, he scanned the room, desperate to arm himself. His wild gaze landed on the TV remote lying on the coffee table. He swiped it and surged out of the lounge in time to see a tall figure opening the front door.

David Roberts!

Frank charged towards David. 'What the hell are you doing, Mr Roberts?'

David spun to face him, teeth bared in a feral snarl, a wicked-looking fireplace poker clutched in his fist. Frank's stomach turned a somersault. *Christ, not again.* The universe had a sick sense of humour, putting him on the wrong end of a lunatic with a blunt instrument for the second time today.

'Put that down.' Frank held up the remote control as if it was a deadly weapon.

David advanced on him.

The other day, David's eyes had been cool and calculating.

Today, there was no reason or restraint. Only the uncaged glint of a man with nothing left to lose. 'You shouldn't have come here. Hanna shouldn't have talked to you.'

Frank's eyes widened. 'Where is Hanna?' *If you've laid a finger on her...* 'Where is she?'

'Too late.' David flicked his gaze toward the ceiling. 'This is your fault.'

As David raised the poker, Frank chucked the remote at him. The plastic cracked against his nose. While David yelped, Frank used the split-second advantage to lunge forward.

Unfortunately, David recovered too quickly. The poker whooshed through the air in a deadly arc.

Frank scrambled backward, narrowly avoiding getting his ribs staved in. His shoulders slammed into the kitchen door as he pressed himself flat, chest heaving. The metal tip of the poker glinted cruelly, inches from his face.

This was it. Cornered by a maniac with murder in his eyes, no weapon, no backup. Frank's mind scrabbled uselessly for a way out, for some flash of inspiration or a surge of heroic strength. But he was painfully mortal. Just a knackered old copper with more bollocks than sense, about to die a pointless death in some suburban semi with not even that bloody TV remote for protection any more.

Then, the bark of a dog split the charged air, followed by the scrabble of claws on hardwood.

Rylan came bounding in through the half-open front door.

David swung.

Frank felt his adrenaline surge. 'That's a boy!'

Rylan stopped a metre from David, hackles raised, standing his ground but keeping out of range of the poker. Buoyed, Frank rammed his palms into the man's shoulders, sending him staggering.

Rylan skipped out of the way.

David caught himself on the stair banister, his face maroon with rage as he rounded on Frank again.

Frank hunched his shoulders and prepared to bulldoze forward. It'd been a lifetime since he'd played rugby, but he prayed muscle memory and desperation would be enough.

Before Frank launched, Gerry appeared at the door like an avenging angel, snapping a kick at the back of David's leg. He crumpled with an agonised howl. Quick as a flash, Gerry wrenched his arm up behind his back and planted her knee between his shoulder blades, pinning him neatly to the floor.

Frank stared at her, heart stuttering. *Christ, you really are something else.*

'Nice one.' He steadied himself against the wall.

Gerry glanced up at him. He waited for a sassy quip, a wry half-smile, anything to acknowledge the wild magic of the moment. But she just gave him a brisk nod and returned her attention to the squirming suspect.

Before Frank could gather his wits, a low moan drifted down from upstairs. Frank's blood turned to ice in his veins.

Hanna.

Without a word, he pelted for the staircase, terror and fury warring for dominance in his gut. *Hold on, lass,* he thought. *I'm coming. And God help that bastard if he's hurt you.*

Chapter Ninety Five

Hanna had crawled to the top of the stairs.

She sat upright against the wall, shivering. Her head was bleeding.

'One moment.' Frank ran into a bedroom and grabbed a blanket and towel. He returned and laid the blanket over her. He gave her a towel to help with her bleeding head. 'You've had a shock and need checking over. But it's over now.' He phoned in for support and an ambulance. 'It's all over. Help will be here soon. Please wait here.'

Back downstairs, he saw that David was struggling against being restrained. 'Let me.' Frank relieved his colleague by taking hold of the wrist locked behind the idiot's back. 'Please fetch the cuffs from the car, Gerry.'

Sweat trickling down his brow, Frank held David's wrist. He used a very firm grip. The blighter had come at him with a bloody poker! 'Well, that was ridiculous, Mr Fletcher.'

'Fuck off.'

A gust of frigid wind whistled through the open door, raising gooseflesh on Frank's arms. He noticed his sweat-soaked shirt clinging to his back, the salty tang sharp in his nostrils. Christ, he was getting too old for this!

'Hanna?' Frank called out, pitching his voice to carry up the stairs. 'You still all right, love?'

'Yes... I think so. My head hurts but I'm not dizzy.'

'Just stay there, okay? The cavalry can't be far away. I don't want you on those stairs.'

With Rylan at her side, Gerry reappeared, cuffs in hand. Frank hauled David's other wrist behind his back, none too gently, allowing her to snap the restraints on.

David hissed in pain. 'Police brutality, eh?'

Frank snorted. 'Brutality? Mate, you're lucky I didn't introduce your bollocks to my size elevens, the stunt you just pulled.'

David squirmed.

'If you want me off your back, save your energy.'

He stopped.

Frank stood. 'But stay face down.'

'Whatever. Now what?'

'Now, you're nicked. Assaulting your wife, attempted assault on a police officer – you'll be calling Armley nick home sweet home for the foreseeable.' He read him his rights.

'You're making a mistake.'

'Oh, I reckon I'm finally putting it right. Gerry, please go and sit with Hanna until the ambulance gets here. I'll babysit this one.'

As Gerry headed upstairs, Rylan alongside her, Frank blew out a breath, trying to slow his racing pulse.

David twisted his neck to sneer up at Frank. 'You think you're so fucking clever, don't you? Hate to burst your bubble, but this is far from over.'

'How do you figure that?'

'Because I didn't kill Charlotte, shit for brains.'

Frank snorted. 'Even if that's true – and I've my doubts – you're still a nasty little shit. I'll rest easy knowing you're behind bars, regardless.'

'Won't last.' The measured confidence in his voice from the other day was returning and his wild side disappearing. 'Any halfway competent brief will have this tossed. Argue that my crazy wife provoked me, that you lot roughed me up. I'll walk.'

Anger surged in Frank's chest, hot and acrid on the back of his tongue. 'Listen up. I've watched bigger idiots than you fall and fall hard. Arrogant fools who thought they were untouchable. But the law catches up to everyone, eventually. Your time's up, and good riddance to bad rubbish.'

'You don't know the half of it.' David snorted. 'You don't know what Hanna's really like. The woman's obsessed with me! Has been for years. Paranoid. Delusional. She's the one who needs locking up.'

From upstairs, Hanna's voice rang out, thin but fierce. 'Only because you made me this way. Your years of abuse, your twisted mind games.'

'Ha! You're no saint, love. I should have bashed your fucking skull in harder, you harpy.'

Frank's blood ran cold. This bastard had ice water in his veins. 'One more word and I'll add threatening a witness to your charge sheet. Wind your foul neck in.'

David barked out a laugh, undeterred. 'You seem so determined, Hanna, to tell them what happened! Air our dirty laundry. Well, don't leave any gaps! Have you told them how you stalked me like some lovesick schoolgirl while I was with Charlotte? Pathetic, eh?'

'Yes, I agree. You made me this way.' Hanna cried, anguish ringing in every word. 'I saw the way Charlotte sent you packing. She saw right through you. I wish I'd done the same. Found someone who treated me better. Like she did.'

Frank's head snapped up, homing in on Hanna's words like a bloodhound scenting a trail. 'Hanna. What do you mean? Found someone nicer? Who did Charlotte find?'

A pregnant pause stretched out, ripe with unspoken secrets.

David laughed. 'I knew my wife would leave that out. Anything to keep herself smelling of fucking roses. Charlotte was a dyke. A rug-muncher. She shagged that silly bint Julie!'

Frank's heart pounded, pieces slowly clicking into sickening place. 'Is this true?' He looked towards the stairs, willing Hanna to confirm.

'Yes.' Hanna's answer was soft, laced with old pain. 'I saw them together. Charlotte and Julie. They were... intimate.'

'When?' Frank demanded. 'Where?'

'At the beach. In one of those huts. I followed Charlotte one day, and I heard them both in there...'

'Why didn't you tell me?' Frank asked.

David laughed again. 'Because she's a meddling cow, DCI Black!' Triumph ringing in his tone.

Frank could hear Hanna sobbing.

David continued. 'She rang Julie's dad up. Spilled those beans! Brutal, eh? You're no rose garden are you, honey?'

Frank's eyes widened. 'Hanna? Is that true? Did you tell Julie's father about her and Charlotte?'

Hanna's sobs were ragged and raw.

'Hanna?' Frank pressed.

Between mouthfuls of tears, she said, 'I did... God help me, I did. I wanted to hurt Charlotte... Punish her for what she'd done with David. I thought... I thought she'd lose her job, her reputation. But I never dreamed... God, I was just a kid!' She dissolved into tears again.

Frank's mind was reeling, the landscape of the case shifting and warping around him.

Julie's conservative father, a councillor, a man of influence learning of his daughter's affair, a controversial affair for the era. A potentially fatal threat for a man of such standing...

Frank reached for his mobile with clumsy fingers, desperate to relay this earth-shattering new lead to HQ. His scattered mind barely registered the paramedics coming into the house.

All he could focus on was the yawning chasm of possibilities that had just cracked wide open. A disappearance reframed as something potentially far darker. The taste of ugly secrets turned to ashes on his tongue.

After an officer secured David, he put in a very specific request with Reggie at HQ, and returned to the VW. Gerry was already in there, making a phone call.

After he sat, he felt Rylan prodding his arm. He turned to see the Lab standing on the back seat facing him. He leaned in and kissed him on his furry forehead. 'Therapy is one of your skills, young man, but when it comes to saving lives, well, you excel.'

Gerry hung up and turned to him. 'Arnold Fletcher isn't with Julie at the hospital. He went home over an hour ago.'

Frank nodded and drove to Julie's home.

After parking, he glanced at Gerry. 'He's old... he almost lost his entire family in an accident... I imagine he's going to be weak and flaky.' He sighed. 'I think the trick is to keep him ticking over long enough to understand what really went off. Slowly... slowly... okay?'

Gerry nodded.

He looked at the house and sighed a second time. 'What do you think? Is this it? You always seem to have a sense for it.'

'I think that this is the next best move.'

'Agreed.' Frank nodded and opened the door. 'So, let's make it.'

Chapter Ninety-Six

THE DEMEANOUR of this eighty-five-year-old man had changed since the previous day. Events, as Frank had predicted, had taken their toll. His height and stature had been impressive yesterday. Now he was hunching, and his walking stick was taking most of the strain.

'Julie is still not home.' He sighed. 'I thought you'd be aware?'

'We are, and we were sorry to hear about what happened, Mr Fletcher,' Frank said.

'Please, call me Arnold. What happened to your nose, anyway?'

'Long story. It looks worse than it is.'

'I'd get it looked at, DCI. Your voice has altered somewhat. Anyway, regarding Julie, even if you went to the hospital, I'm not sure she's well enough to talk to you either. She almost lost Tom.' He put the back of his left hand to his mouth and took a deep breath through his nose. There was a silence. 'I almost lost them.'

'Once again, we're sorry, Arnold. But we're here to speak to you. If that's okay.'

'Really?' He furrowed his brow. 'Can't fathom why.' He shrugged and turned. 'Come on in, then.'

Even with the weight of the world on his hunched shoulders, he still impressed Frank with his mobility and speed, and he wondered briefly if he'd be in any such state in twenty-one years.

He doubted it very much.

They sat in the same seats as their previous visit, Arnold taking Julie's position on the single sofa with the hole in the arm opposite the detectives. He had a guitar alongside him, propped up against the wall, a plectrum weaved between the strings on the fretboard. Frank couldn't recall seeing the guitar there the previous day.

Frank nodded at the guitar. 'Do you play?'

Arnold looked at it and gave a half-hearted grin. 'Aye.' He waggled his fingers. 'Used to be better, though. Arthritic fingers slow you down. I suggest keeping the practice up if you play DCI, keep the fingers limber. My daughter plays too.'

Hearing the word daughter reminded him momentarily of the fact that he'd missed an unknown call earlier at Hanna's and had still not checked his voicemails. *Shit.* What if it'd been his own daughter? He opened his notebook and scribbled a reminder for him to check his messages after this interview. Looking down caused the pain in his nose to flare up again. He felt some relief when he looked up.

'Arnold, some information has come to our attention, and we'd like to get your take on it. I'd like to apologise in advance if this is news to you, and proves distressing—'

'Are you going to tell me Julie killed that lass?' Arnold leaned forward, eyes wide.

Frank straightened up. 'I wasn't planning to. Is there any reason you'd say that?'

He shrugged. 'Well, why else would you be here? You're investigating the girl's death, aren't you?'

'Gathering intel takes a wider form than the issuing of accusations,' Gerry said.

Arnold regarded her, silently, for a few seconds before smiling. 'Fair enough, dear.'

'I'd prefer it if you wouldn't address me as dear.'

Frank winced.

'I didn't mean to offend,' Arnold said, touching his chest.

'I'm not offended,' Gerry said. 'I'd just prefer it if you didn't address me that way.'

This was awkward. Frank cut in to move it on. 'Were you aware that Julie and Charlotte were in a relationship?'

Arnold cocked an eyebrow. 'Relationship? As in friends?'

'A sexual relationship,' Gerry said.

Arnold's eyebrow didn't return to its normal position. Silence hung there for a moment before he managed a smile. 'Ha! You almost had me there.'

'Actually,' Frank said. 'We've a statement that suggests that Charlotte and Julie were romantically involved, and that they spent time alone at North Sea Nook Beach Huts.'

'Poppycock. She's not gay. No. Not my girl. Bloody hell! If only she were, it may stop this endless parade of men through the bloody house!' He guffawed. 'She has a son, too!' He lifted his hands up. 'What more do you need?'

'Having a child and having heterosexual relationships doesn't exclude other sexual interests,' Gerry said.

'And this was a long time ago,' Frank said. 'It could have

been experimentation. She could be bisexual. There're a few explanations.'

'This all sounds bloody ridiculous to me. I think you should double check your source.'

'Do you know Hanna Roberts?' Frank asked.

He thought for a moment. 'No, should I?'

'She claims to have contacted you by phone in 1987 to make you aware that your daughter was in a relationship with Charlotte Wilson. Can you recall that phone call? Hanna Roberts is her married name. Her name then was Hanna Goodall.'

Frank caught Arnold's eyes darting left and right as he straightened in the chair. To Frank, it didn't look like bewilderment. It looked more like a response to a physical blow to the stomach. 'I've no idea what you're talking about. A phone call? 1987? Who can remember a phone call from that far back?'

'If the call was significant,' Gerry said, 'which we believe it *was*, then it's very reasonable you'd remember.'

'Just think a moment, Arnold, before you answer,' Frank said.

His eyes continued darting. He was floundering.

He crossed his arms. 'Think about what? I'm not likely to forget this, am I? How absurd!'

Frank had seen nothing in this response to suggest that Hanna's claim hadn't been true.

'Would it have bothered you if your daughter was engaged in a sexual relationship with another female?' Gerry asked.

Arnold uncrossed his arms and puffed his chest out. 'A ridiculous question, as it never happened.'

'It was a very different time.' Frank nodded. 'It'd be understandable if such a discovery would bother you.'

'I've nothing against gay people now, nor did I then!' Arnold gave a swift nod.

'So, in answer to my question, "*no*, it wouldn't bother you"?'

'Yes. That's what I'm saying.'

'How about your colleagues? Others on the council... in your political party?' Frank asked.

Arnold gritted his teeth and shook his head. 'Where the hell is all this going?'

'Just flagging up that you had a prominent position in the council. Look, this was a very different time. How would the idea of your eighteen-year-old daughter conducting a love affair with another young girl have been viewed by—'

'That's enough!' Arnold hissed. 'I mean it, *enough*.' His face was now red. 'The last couple of days have been hell enough without all this...' He waved a hand. 'Poppycock! I've never heard the like, but...' He took a deep breath. He looked down for a moment and exhaled, trying to take back control of himself. Eventually, he looked back up. 'I understand that you're only doing your job and responding to crank tip offs.' He touched his neck. 'But my throat is burning. I may look good for my age, but I'm not used to fighting my corner against an interrogation! At least not since retirement. Will you excuse me while I get a glass of water?'

'Of course,' Frank said.

Arnold exited the room.

Frank looked over his shoulder and saw that Arnold had left the door ajar. So, he didn't tell Gerry what he was thinking in case he was listening in. Instead, he wrote it down on a page in his notebook and showed her.

He's lying.

She nodded.

Warrant to search?

She nodded again.

'Let's wrap this up for now, then.' Frank rose to his feet.

He approached the acoustic guitar. A Yamaha. Nothing too special, but it had a pleasant sound. He ran his fingers down the fretboard and—

His blood froze.

He closed his eyes. The image of Laura Wilson running down the road after Charlotte on the morning of December 18th, 1987.

A lucky plectrum in her hand.

Pink. Signed by Bob Marley.

'What're you doing?' Arnold was at the doorway.

Frank's eyes snapped open. He narrowed them momentarily, but then widened them as he turned. 'Just admiring the guitar.'

'Yes... okay.'

'I notice you've a distinctive plectrum.'

He nodded.

'Signed by Bob Marley. I mean, wow... don't come across that often!' He looked over at Gerry, who'd stiffened, and looked, unusually, engaged by his sudden announcement.

Arnold paled. 'Yes, well, I—'

'Where did you get it, Arnold?'

He shook his head and widened his eyes again. 'Come on... I've had it years! I could have picked it up anywhere.'

'A Bob Marley-signed plectrum? Wish I could find something like that in an old drawer! Bet it'd fetch a small fortune on eBay!'

'Haven't thought to look.'

Frank nodded. 'Can you remember where you were on the night of September 18th, 1987, Arnold?'

'That's a joke isn't it, DCI?'

'No sir. It's not. Charlotte owned a plectrum just like this.'

'What? Forty-odd years ago? Seriously? A coincidence. Not likely to be the only one in existence, is it?'

A pretty big coincidence!

Still, he needed more... the more he could feed the CPS, the better.

He wanted to make sure that the threshold for arrest and charging him was well and truly breached. Still, there was enough for a search.

His phone started ringing. He looked at the screen. It was Reggie. 'Sorry, Arnold. I'll take this outside. And then we'll get this wrapped up.' *And then I'll get a warrant to come back.*

He answered outside. Reggie was responding to his earlier request for information.

He listened, shaking his head with disbelief. 'Reggie, this time you've delivered.'

'Thank you.' He sounded close to tears! Frank, feeling uneasy over having made the pillock feel good, quickly hung up.

While Gerry continued inside with Arnold, he made enquiries with the CPS.

But even with the plectrum and Reggie's discovery, CPS still wanted more.

Greedy buggers!

Chapter Ninety-Seven

Arnold down at the station, under caution, being recorded, was the dream.

The card in Frank's possession, provided by Reggie, could cause a seismic wobble in Arnold and bring this dream to fruition.

The other option was to wait for the warrant.

No.

Time to go for broke and bring it on home.

Frank came in, deliberately looking buoyant but not overdoing it. Frank Black, looking buoyant, would be a peculiar sight in itself; best not to push it.

In the same way that Julie had done, Arnold was now fiddling with the hole in the arm of the sofa.

Frank looked at Gerry. 'We need to head off now, DI Carver. The intel we requested is through.'

Gerry looked at him. 'Which intel?'

'The phone and bank logs.' He glanced at Arnold. 'It's all coming together.'

Arnold raised an eyebrow. 'How so?'

'Long story short, there was a payphone near the whalebone arch back then on East Terrace... do you recall?'

'No, of course not—'

'Well, we've accessed all the calls made on September 18th, 1987.' This was fabrication. BT hadn't kept records this far back. 'And you know, there was an ATM on East Terrace, too. I know back in '87, eh? They've been around a while! But yeah, there was one of the first round there. Bank has supplied us with all the transactions made.' This was the information that Reggie had recovered. It showed that Arnold had withdrawn fifty pounds on August 18th, 1987.'

Arnold picked harder at the sofa arm.

Frank's card was working! He grinned. 'I always said *that* would be the last piece in this jigsaw, if we could get it. And woe behold, we did. So we'll head back to HQ and check it out. Thanks for your time, Arnold, we'll... oh wait...'

Frank slipped his specs down from his head over his eyes and made a show of looking down at his phone again. He pretended to open and read a message.

He creased his brow, and let his buoyant demeanour quickly slip away. Eventually, with a stony expression – far less of a challenge for Frank to manage – he pulled off his specs and looked up at Arnold again.

Frank heard a ripping sound from the arm of the sofa. 'What is it?' Arnold asked.

'Arnold, it might be best for us, at this stage, to head to the station and discuss—'

Arnold rose to his feet. '*What* is it?'

'I find a formal setting helps with clarity. I imagine having the conversation in this house can be rather disconcerting and—'

'Whatever you think you have, it's wrong...' Arnold looked terrified.

Frank looked down at Gerry, hoping that, for once, she'd understand the impact of actually making eye contact with him.

She did!

He nodded at her, and she nodded back. She rose to her feet.

'No, Arnold,' Frank said. 'We believe this evidence is—'

'Okay, okay... She phoned me! Okay? That Hanna lass *phoned* me.'

Frank's heart rate surged. Arnold's sudden admission was clear. And to be honest, all Frank had suggested was that they chat down the station – he'd not offered him any false evidence, arrested him, or anything of the like.

'I see. When?'

'A couple of days before... before... well, you know!'

'Before the eighteenth of August?'

'Aye,' he sighed.

'And what did she tell you?'

Arnold waved his hand at Frank. 'What you said! Before. About the hut.'

'And what happened?'

He sat back down and sighed. 'I confronted Julie, obviously. Told her enough was enough. It was inappropriate.' He didn't make eye contact with either of them. Frank suspected he would know his views would seem outdated.

'And?' Frank pressed, continuing to stand.

'Ha! You've met my daughter, haven't you? She confessed everything, but it didn't stop her. I tried everything to turn her round. Nothing worked. Eventually, I told her, you want to stay here, you don't get up to activities like that. Fell on deaf ears.'

'What happened on September 18th, 1987?' Frank

asked. 'You withdrew fifty pounds from the ATM on East Terrace., didn't you?'

Arnold rolled his eyes and returned to the hole in the sofa arm. 'For that girl. Charlotte. To pay that young lass to go. Leave Whitby and never come back. I thought fifty quid would cover it, too. Youngsters then were fickle... that relationship, as you call it... how was that a relationship? They both liked music, so what? Played guitar? That meant they had to frolic? *Disgusting*. It was a flash in the pan for Julie. She was always an attention seeker. Nothing gay about her! So, the fifty quid was to put a stop to it.'

'And what did Julie have to say about it?' Frank asked. 'Paying off her girlfriend to leave her be?'

'Girlfriend?' He glared up at Frank. 'Stop it with this horseshit! She. Was. Attention-seeking! Julie likes men. Too many men, if you ask me! But at least they're men! I could make peace with that.'

Frank wasn't about to be offended by homophobic attitudes in an eighty-five-year-old man, but he wanted to keep up his serious pretence, so he shook his head. 'But what did Julie think of this?'

'We've never discussed it!'

'Why not?'

He narrowed his eyes. 'Well, if you let me finish?'

Frank nodded.

'I followed Julie out that night. I saw them at the whalebones together, so I came up with the idea and went to get the money. Well, when I got back, I offered that girl the money, and she refused. She said she loved my daughter. Poppycock!' He broke off to rub his temples.

Frank allowed him a moment before saying, 'Please go on.'

Nothing.

'Arnold? What happened *next?*'

Arnold dropped his hands from his temples and fixed Frank with a stare. 'I think you know.'

Frank stared back. 'Finish the story, please.'

Arnold crossed his arms. 'Well, they both stood there arguing with me, winding me up, talking to me like shit on their shoes, and when that young lass... the cheek of her... told me that she was proud of what she had with Julie, that they would tell the world, well, I picked up a stone and... you know... hit her.'

Frank forced back a sigh of relief.

The threshold was breached.

'Arnold Fletcher, I'm arresting you on suspicion of murder. You do not have to say anything—'

'But I didn't mean for her to die!'

Frank continued reading him his rights.

'Listen!'

When it was clear that Frank had heard enough, Arnold started to cry.

Chapter Ninety-Eight

WHILE ARNOLD WAS GETTING ACQUAINTED with his solicitor, Frank's adrenaline subsided. He recalled the missed calls and voicemails. He stepped outside the nick to investigate.

The voicemail was from Maddie. 'How could you, Dad? After everything I told you... how could you?'

So why hadn't Maddie's number shown up on his phone? Had she blocked her caller ID?

Frank's stomach dropped. The panic rose in his throat like bile as her words sank in. *What have I done?* He tried calling her back on her new number, filled with dread, but the phone was off. He was sent through to her voicemail. He begged her to call him back.

Thoughts spiralled through his mind. If she was having one of her low moments again... then, God... *no! Could she lose control?* He made for his car and, while driving, he contacted Gerry. 'I'm sorry to leave you with it all, but I have to go.'

'Why Frank?'

'It's personal. Sorry. You'll have to handle Arnold's interview. I trust you.'

'Are you sure?'

'Yes. You're one of the best I've ever come across.' He hung up and peeled out of the station car park in the VW.

The journey home passed in a blur of dread. When he burst through the front door and glanced into his kitchen, the answer smacked him square between the eyes. Scattered bills and receipts on the kitchen counter... the half-open drawer in which he'd been storing Maddie's phone open...

He yanked the drawer fully open.

Of course, her mobile wasn't there.

He groaned and put his head against the fridge.

You dickhead, Frank... you absolute dickhead...

He hit the fridge door with his bare hands.

After glancing down at the drawer, he groaned again, trying to work out what had happened.

Earlier, he'd replaced the phone but had become distracted by the sound of her coming out of her room to go to the toilet. He must have put the phone back in the drawer and closed it, but, idiotically, left the bills and receipts out on top.

Maddie, seeing the loose paper, must have opened the drawer and—

He yanked the drawer out and threw it across the kitchen. It crashed into the sink, and two glasses on the draining board paid the price, tumbling and smashing.

He ran through to her bedroom. No belongings. An empty wardrobe.

Maddie, like that infernal phone, was also gone.

Chest heaving, he cradled his head in his hands as the gravity of his actions crashed over him in waves. He'd driven his own daughter away with his well-intentioned deception.

Think, man, think!

If this was an investigation, he'd be lightning quick. He'd have a solution, or a plan of action, in a heartbeat or two.

No dust could settle.

But this wasn't an investigation.

This was personal.

Dropping to his knees, he moaned and buried his face in his hands...

His ringing phone brought him out of the fog.

He quickly grabbed it from his pocket. 'Maddie?'

'No, Frank, it's Gerry.'

'Not now... please, not now.'

'I thought you'd want to know. To be honest, Frank, you need to know—'

'Spit it out, Gerry.'

'He didn't do it.'

'What? Who? Gerry, what's this—'

'Arnold didn't do it.'

'He confessed. I was there!'

'I know, but it doesn't tally up. He's just been through it again. It's in the description of how he killed Charlotte. He says he struck her on the crown, near her forehead. Face on. We know the blunt-force trauma came from behind. Also, think about it... The case? A spade to dig the hole? He claimed he went back home for these things first, but then he'd have to leave the body, out there, exposed; or, take the body with him—'

'And if he took the body with him,' Frank continued, nausea sweeping over him. 'Why bother bringing it back to an iconic location?'

And then the truth hit him like a steam train.

'Frank?'

He closed his eyes. Despite his mind swirling now in panic over Maddie, he could still see Charlotte's face in the chaos, and he could hear that voice. That angelic voice. Tinged with self-loathing, torment and loss.

Just like him.

Just like Maddie.

And just like—

'You're right, Gerry, it wasn't him.'

'But why lie?' Gerry asked.

The same reason I lied about this bloody phone!

'To protect the people we love.'

Chapter Ninety-Nine

So, Charlotte, I can hear now, loud and clear.

Frank sat beside Julie's hospital bed, the sterile white walls pressing in around them. Her face was a mess of mottled bruises, her chest swathed in stark bandages.

She certainly looked as if she'd been to hell and back.

While he waited for Julie to wake, he tried to keep his mind off Maddie, and focused on Charlotte. This was *her* finale. Her young life, so full of promise, snatched away in an instant. It was high time to find out the truth of what happened, once and for all.

No more would Charlotte simply be a beautiful voice confined to a tape and a pile of abandoned bones; now it was time for her to truly sing.

And it'd come through Julie. Another broken soul.

Don't fret, Charlotte, I'll go easy. You loved her, didn't you?

Julie's eyes fluttered open, blinking against the harsh fluorescent light.

And I suspect she loved you fiercely, too.

Julie coughed and then winced over the pain.

'You want me to fetch someone?' Frank asked.

'No,' Julie said, tears suddenly welling up and spilling down her cheeks.

Frank made no effort to stop her. He instead held her hand, and she squeezed it in return.

When her sobs eased, she mumbled, 'Sorry.'

'It's all right,' Frank said. 'Nothing to be sorry for.'

She nodded down at his hand clinging to hers.

'Oh, aye, you want me to...?' He loosened his grip, ready to pull away.

'No. It's nice. It makes me feel... I don't know. Comforted? My dad struggles with that sort of thing.'

Frank nodded and kept his hand in place.

'Maybe I'm being unfair to him. I know he loves me. He always has. So much. But folk show it differently, don't they?'

'They do. Aye, they do.'

'I can tell you're the type of man who's always there for those he loves. Dependable, like.'

Frank thought of Maddie and Mary, shame coiling in his gut. *It wasn't always that way.* 'You're right about your father. He loves you rotten. Make no mistake.' *If nothing else is clear in this whole mess, that one thing is shining through bright as daylight.*

'Why are you here, then?' Julie finally met his eyes. 'Why now?'

I reckon you know, lass. He drew in a deep breath, letting it out slow. 'Julie, I—'

She yanked her hand from his grasp as if she'd been scalded. He folded both of his in his lap, fighting the urge to reach for her again.

'You're being nice to me just to get me to spill my guts, is that it?'

He shook his head firmly. 'Nothing like that.'

'Men have always been like that! Trying to get what they want from me.'

'I'm here in an official capacity, but I'm not trying to pull the wool over your eyes, Julie. I'm after the truth, plain and simple.'

'About Charlotte?'

'Aye.'

Her lips trembled; fresh tears threatened to fall. 'What we had was real. More real than anything.'

'I believe you.'

Julie turned her face to the ceiling, blinking back tears. 'And now she's gone, just... gone.'

'Aye, too young by far.' He scrubbed a hand over his stubbled jaw, heartsick and weary. 'But I reckon it's time. Time for you to tell me the whole story.'

'Yes.' Another tear ran down her face. 'It's a shame Charlotte can't tell you. She'd the most beautiful voice.'

'I can't deny it,' Frank said. 'But in a way, I can hear her. Do you know your father confessed to her murder?'

Julie closed her eyes. 'He's a bloody old fool for sacrificing himself like that.'

'Maybe that's how it should be. Between parents and their bairns. Wouldn't you do the same for Tom?'

'No question,' she said.

Julie winced, pain etching fresh lines around her mouth. The sickly sweet stench of antiseptic stung Frank's nose, mingling with the coppery tang of blood that clung to her.

'I can get a nurse in here, no bother.'

'No... the stuff they give me, it knocks me out. I need to keep my head straight, even if it hurts. Anyway... I was ready to tell the truth. I think the moment they told me my son would live, I knew it was time. I've spent my whole life trying to survive with the lie, and the pain of losing her, and do you know... can you understand... how agonising that is?'

Frank nodded. 'I can imagine.'

'Tom will be fine... better off without me...'

'He'll still have you, Julie. You're his mum.'

Julie's laugh was bitter and broken. 'Will he?'

'Of course he will. He's a smart lad. He'll understand, in time, that you did the right thing, coming clean like this.'

She searched his face, her bruise-blackened eyes pleading. 'So, will you believe me if I told you it was all an accident?'

'I'll try my best. But I've got to caution you first, official like. So, you know what you're getting into.'

At Julie's jerky nod, he recited the caution, the formal words strange and heavy on his tongue. She didn't flinch or look away, just stared at him with glassy eyes.

'North Sea Nook Beach Hut was our special spot,' she said, her voice roughened with pain and memory. 'I was chuffed with the deal I wrangled from the owner. I remember him being old, past retirement. He gave me a good price. I scraped up what I could working Saturdays, and Charlotte would bring in a bit here and there from gigs and whatnot.' Julie picked at a loose thread on the thin hospital blanket. 'Those tight bastards, the Roberts, at Mariner's Lantern, never paid her anything, but she'd get some from other pubs around Scarborough way. Decent tips, too, when punters were feeling generous. The owner didn't know Charlotte from Adam, and I gave him a false name for myself. I don't know if he ever witnessed Charlotte coming and going; if he did, he never questioned it.' A ghost of a smile flickered across Julie's face. 'It wasn't always like that between us. We were mates first, for a few months.

Practising guitar together at Ron's, that sort of thing. But there was something more there, right from the start.

'I was still with Paul then, and Charlotte was mucking about with that wanker David, but any fool could see it was each other we wanted. Once we got up the bottle to do something about it, we'd meet at the hut three, four times a week. Had to be dead sly about it, though. A councillor's daughter with another woman? In 1987? Can you imagine the uproar?'

Frank nodded. 'I understand it must have been tough. So, what happened regarding David and Paul?'

Julie sighed. 'Me and Paul, we'd been on the rocks practically since we got together. Just a poor fit, really. Best friends, but a bad couple. Charlotte, bless her, only took up with David to get a rise out of me. She told me once, dead casual like, that she'd never had a thing for blokes. Well, David ended up knocking her up. Treated her like shit, as I knew he would.' Julie's voice cracked. 'When she found out she was pregnant, we'd been together for a month already. One more on top of that before that bastard started badgering her to get rid of the baby.' She dragged a shaking hand over her face, smearing the tears. 'We'd talked about keeping it, Charlotte and me. Raising the bairn together. I'd have done it in a heartbeat, Frank. I loved Charlotte more than anything, I swear I did. Wanted to say fuck the lot of them and just be a proper family.' A bitter laugh tore from her throat, devolving into a hacking cough.

Frank winced at the wet, bubbly sound of it.

'But then, David, manipulative as he was, put his foot down. Scared her. Told her he'd speak to her mother, and my parents, and she went and did as he asked. I never even knew until I saw her that evening.' She broke off and shook her head. 'It broke my heart.'

A moment of silence lingered.

'Is that why it happened, Julie?' Frank asked. 'Is that why Charlotte died?'

'No!' Julie shook her head vehemently, despite the pain etched into every line of her face. 'It wasn't that. Her mess with David was nothing compared to the baggage that came with Paul.' She shot Frank a searching look. 'You know Hanna Fletcher blabbed to my dad about us?'

Frank nodded.

'Worst barney me and my dad ever had. Slapped me, called me all sorts. A dirty lezzer, unnatural, disgusting. Said if he ever caught me with Charlotte again, he'd chuck me out on my ear.' Julie paused, chest heaving, face a sickly greyish white. 'I was terrified. Told him I'd stop seeing her. Didn't mean a word of it, of course. But he didn't believe me anyhow.'

She trailed off, blinking rapidly. Visibly steeling herself to go on.

'Take your time,' Frank said. 'We can stop if you need to. Get the doc to give you something for the pain.'

'No!' She sucked in a shuddery breath. Let it out slow. When she spoke again, her voice was leaden with exhaustion and grief. 'It was September 18th.'

The way Julie said it, all heavy with meaning, sent a chill skittering down Frank's spine.

'It started with my dad saying I wasn't to go out that night. Of course, I slipped out anyway like.'

'And he followed you?'

'Is that what he told you?'

'Aye. To catch you with Charlotte and try to bribe her.'

Julie snorted. 'Load of old bollocks! He never followed! She'd never have taken his money, anyway.' She shifted on the thin hospital mattress, trying to find a comfortable position. 'I went to meet Charlotte at the hut. She confessed about going behind my back for the abortion. I felt like she'd kicked me in the gut.' Julie swallowed hard, her voice dropping to a hoarse whisper. 'But that wasn't even the worst of it...'

Frank leaned forward, hands clasped between his knees, listening intently.

'We went for a walk out to the whalebones. That's when she dropped the bombshell that Paul had blabbed to her about his issues. About poisoning that poor lad, Ellis.' Julie narrowed her eyes. 'Two things about that got right up my nose. First off, Charlotte being all pally with Paul without telling me. Seemed that they'd taken a shine to one another during the time we spent mucking about at Ron's. And second...' She trailed off, working at her bottom lip with her teeth. 'Well, I might have lost interest in Paul in *that* way, but I still cared about the daft 'apeth! He was like a brother. An annoying little brother, you know?' She grinned. 'I didn't want to see him banged up! And he'd only gone and confessed *everything* to Charlotte. What a fucking idiot! She told me she couldn't keep quiet about it. Said it was eating her up inside. She'd been trying for ages to convince him to confess to the police, but he wasn't having none of it.'

Julie's red-rimmed eyes glazed over as she stared into the middle distance, lost in painful memory. 'Charlotte was too bloody good for this world. She'd a heart of gold.' A wistful smile flickered across Julie's battered face, there and gone in an instant. 'Always talking about her dad. What a top bloke he was. Gentle and kind. She wanted to be just like him. And I loved her for it, I truly did, but...' She closed her eyes and took a deep breath.

Frank waited through a long pause before asking, 'But you didn't want her dropping Paul in it?'

'Too bloody right I didn't!' Julie's eyes snapped opened. She winced. 'Christ!' She clutched her ribs, breathing carefully through her nose until the pain eased.

'I'm calling someone—'

'No! Let me finish.' She fixed Frank with a stare. 'I swear on Tom's life, Frank, it was an accident. But Charlotte finding out about Paul, that's what lit the fuse. Part of me thought it was Arthur Barclay's fault. His kitchen, wasn't it? And he was supposed to be teaching Paul the ropes. He should've done a better job of it, the pillock. But Charlotte, she couldn't let it lie. And we had a right set-to over it.'

'This was while you were out by the whalebones on the night of the eighteenth?' Frank clarified.

'Yes.' Tears tracked through the bruises that mottled her skin. 'After the argument, I thought I'd talked her round. We walked a way, sneaked over the fence, so we could get closer to the cliff's edge, and...' She closed her eyes again. 'I can feel it all now – the crash of the waves, the smell of salt and cold on the wind...' Her voice dropped to a thready whisper. 'She took my hand as we stood there, looking out over the ocean. Kissed me, soft and sweet. And just when I thought it was all smoothed over... she pulled out this letter.' She opened her eyes. 'She told me she was going to post it to the coppers. *Anonymous*. Everything Paul had told her. Paul... he was my best mate long before Charlotte came along. I'd known him since primary school, Frank; our relationship may not have been going anywhere, but we'd always been thick as thieves. The thought of his life being ruined, it made me nauseous.' A shudder rippled through Julie, rattling the bed frame.

'And that was it. The moment. When everything went to shite.'

Frank stayed silent, giving her space to gather herself. The harsh fluorescent light threw the planes and angles of her face into sharp relief, highlighting every cut and bruise.

Julie drew in a shaky breath. Let it out slow. 'I've relived that moment a thousand times. More.' She scrubbed a hand over her face, wincing when she hit a tender spot. 'So sometimes, when I'm going back over it all, I change what happens next. I come to my senses, agree with Charlotte that the truth needs outing, no matter how much it hurts. That Paul's got to face up to what he's done.' A bitter little laugh escaped her. 'Reckon me and him had more in common than I ever realised. Two peas in a fucking pod.'

She broke off to play with the loose thread on the bed sheet again.

'Julie?' Frank prompted.

'I wish I could change it but I can't, can I? We rowed and rowed...' She mimed grabbing the letter, her movements sharp and jerky. 'I got hold of the letter. It tore. Let half of the bloody thing blow away while we screamed at each other.' Julie shuddered again, so violently this time that the bed creaked. 'We got physical with each other, shoving and grappling about. And then... it was over, just like that.'

The room was tomb quiet. Julie stared blankly up at the ceiling, her chest hitching with silent sobs.

'She fell?' Frank asked.

'I pushed her,' Julie choked out, the words thickened by tears and mucus. 'I pushed her too hard. There was a rock. And so much blood. I tried to wake her up, begged her to open her eyes... but she wouldn't...' A moan tore from Julie's throat.

Frank allowed her a couple of minutes to cry while he

held her hand tightly. When she'd finished, she slipped her hand away.

'And what happened next after the accident?'

She rubbed at her eyes with the back of her hand. 'I legged it to the nearest payphone. Called my dad in a right panic. Amazing how we just turn into that dependent little child when the world turns upside down, eh? Told him his precious girl wasn't just a lesbian now, she was a murderer, too! Gave him the details. He told me to leave, but I didn't. I stayed beside her body for a while, holding her hand. Within ten minutes, he was in the Pavilion Drive car park, which was empty, and heading towards me with a suitcase in one hand and a spade in the other.' Julie sucked in a breath and let it out slow. The bruises scattered over her skin stood out like spilled ink against her sickly pale flesh. 'I'll never forget his face. He looked possessed. Wide eyed. Desperate. He thrust fifty quid in my hand, told me to push it under the owner's door at Nook's with a note saying I was off, *and* told me to get all of Charlotte's stuff from the hut and dispose of it on the way home.'

'But you didn't grab her stuff?'

She shook her head. 'No. I was too stunned. I couldn't bear to go back to that hut. See the place where we'd been together, in happiness, so many times...'

'Did you tell your father?'

'No. I did go back a few days later to post the fifty quid and the note though. The owner of that place never knew Charlotte's name, and I'd given him a fake one for myself anyway. When news came out that she was missing, I got paranoid that he may have recognised her from the photo. But nothing ever happened. Maybe he'd never seen her? Maybe he was just happy to keep fifty quid and stay quiet.

God, if that was the case, it says a lot about human greed, eh?'

I've experienced my fair share of that, Frank thought, forcing back a scowl.

'Dad never said anything about what he'd done with Charlotte. Even though he had the suitcase and the spade, I reckoned maybe he'd thrown her off the cliff. I used to have these nightmares of her just floating out to sea, all pale and bloated. I'd wake up choking on my own screams, the bed soaked through... But, no, turns out he took his time to dig up the soil.

'Him and me, we never spoke of it after. I tried to bring it up a time or two. He'd storm off, slamming doors fit to shake the house down. There isn't a day goes by I don't miss her something rotten. That I don't hate myself for what I did. I try to numb it out with booze, but the pain just keeps dragging me under, over and over.' She wiped at her now streaming nose. 'I was rat arsed when I crashed the other day. You can add that to my list of sins. I'm nothing but a disgrace. Our Tom, he's the only thing what's kept me going. But I've been useless to him. Choosing the bottle over my own bairn more times than I can count. I'm a piss-poor excuse for a mother.'

Frank looked at her steadily, no judgement in his care-worn face, only a bone-deep weariness and sorrow. 'You're still his mum, no matter what. Nothing will ever change that.'

Julie shook her head. 'Tom's best shot of me. Especially now the truth's coming out. You'll see I swing for this, yeah? My father shouldn't have helped me cover it up, but this is on me. Okay?' Her lips twisted. 'I put him through some grief, I did. Poor old bastard.' Julie eyed Frank. 'And Tom will be fine. I know someone who can take care of him.

Someone who loves him very much. Don't go feeling sorry for me, DCI. I'm getting nothing I don't deserve.' A ghost of a smile flickered across her ravaged face. 'It's Charlotte's time now. To have her story told properly.'

Frank bowed his head, a lump rising in his throat. He reached out, covering Julie's cold hand with his own. 'Aye,' he said. 'It is that. You rest now. I'll make sure Charlotte's voice is heard, loud and clear. I promise you that.'

Julie's eyes drifted closed, tears still leaking steadily from beneath bruise-blackened lids. 'Sing for us, Charlotte,' she breathed. 'Reckon it's a grand day for it.'

And in the hush that followed, broken only by the soft hitch of Julie's breathing and the distant squeak of the nurse's shoes in the corridor, he imagined he could hear it at last: Charlotte's sweet voice, rising in a final glorious crescendo.

Singing her truth for all the world to hear, at long, long last.

Chapter One Hundred

Once an officer had arrived to stand watch over Julie, Frank contacted Gerry.

'Aren't you heading back to HQ to wrap things up?' Gerry said.

'I've something to do...' He broke off, knowing how mysterious this sounded, but knowing that elaborating on his dilemma was not an option.

After hanging up, he realised he'd no idea what his play was.

All he could think of was heading home.

That was where Maddie had disappeared from.

And not for the first time in her life.

～

Back home, he paced the kitchen, chain smoking, wondering if coming here was just wasting more time.

His brain had never felt so empty of options.

After three roll-ups, he tore through her bedroom for the third time, throwing the duvet on the floor and taking the drawers all the way out of the chest and slinging them aside.

Nothing.

It was as if she'd never been here.

Back in the kitchen, on his fourth roll-up, he looked at a picture of Mary above the sink.

The shame was debilitating.

I'm sorry, love... I'm so sorry.

The kitchen was full of smoke; he cracked the kitchen door to release it.

Then, despite not wearing his jacket, he headed outside.

It'd been an unusually dry day considering the time of year, and the sinking sun cast a fierce orange hue.

He noticed something at his feet. He bent and picked a small piece of rolled cardboard from the ground. Yellowed with tar and resin. A roach. He lifted it to his nose for confirmation. The stench of marijuana was strong.

He regarded it in the palm of his hand.

Dry and undamaged.

It'd rained heavily last night, meaning it was from today.

He took a deep breath, closed his eyes and recalled Rez Sterling in his garden, hood up, looking through the window.

You came back, you little fucking scrote.

Chapter One Hundred One

Paul Harrison started the climb up the 199 steps.

He didn't count them. Didn't need to. Millions had counted the steps before him.

He looked down at the roman numeral on the twentieth step. There'd be one on the thirtieth, too.

Yes, 199 steps.

It was a matter of fact.

Just like this ending, now.

A matter of fact.

As a young man, he'd have taken on all the steps without a breather. But he wasn't a young man. He was fifty-five. He'd also been awake for days and drunk a hell of a lot.

But there was no need to worry. Not any more.

So, he stopped on a coffin step. A wide step that allowed those carrying the dead to pause for air on their ascent to the church.

Far ahead, the sun was setting over the west. The cliffs. The whalebones.

He thought of Charlotte then, of the strange, sad bond

they'd shared. Those luminous threads of connection, so rare in his life. So precious.

And from Charlotte, his mind wandered to Jess. His Jess. The only other soul who'd ever truly touched his own, however briefly. Another shimmering cord severed too soon. Paul looked out over the water, watching the low sun set the harbour aflame. The hazy smudge of the East pier cloaked the newer, shinier sections of Whitby from view. He stood suspended between the ancient town and the endless sea, straddling the boundary between past and present.

Before he reached the top, and the staggering ruins of the Benedictine abbey, he switched on his phone for the first time since leaving Fiona's home. He scrolled through to Jess' name. His finger hovered over the call button for a whole ten steps before he reached 199 steps. A seagull screamed overhead, harsh and mocking.

No. He couldn't. All that sorrow in her voice. He couldn't bear it.

On the last step, he searched out another name and punched in his message.

He sent it.

Not bothering to turn his phone off, he pocketed it. Let them trace it. He'd be beyond their reach soon enough.

At the top of the steps, Paul paused again. To his left stretched the churchyard, a jumble of lichen-spotted stones pitching drunkenly atop one another. Cracked and weathered by centuries of salt-scoured wind, the inscription on some nearly worn away entirely.

He knew a good many of those stones marked empty graves. Monuments to those lost at sea, their bones consigned to the deeps. A shiver crawled up his spine despite the muggy air. The sour stink of his own stale sweat filled his nostrils, laced with the phantom reek of briny depths.

Gravel crunched beneath his feet as he walked on the left-hand path alongside St Mary's. He stared out at the vast expanse of grey-blue water as the sun sank lower, its dying rays painting the world in shades of blood and bruise. Light bled away, the taste of night rising cool and crisp in the breeze.

Eventually, he broke free of the path and moved to the cliff edge. He leaned over the wire to see the rocks below.

As he watched the sun complete its descent over the West Side, and darkness enveloped all, he thought of the child, Ellis, taken too young; Arthur, the father he'd hung out to dry; Fiona, the woman he'd tortured; Charlotte, the girl who'd become lost.

But most of all, he thought of Jess. The only woman he'd ever loved. The only bit of softness in his miserable sodding life.

I'm sorry.

Behind him, the church bells tolled. Once, twice, the peals shivering through his bones. Calling the faithful to prayer. Calling him home.

Paul sucked in one last salt-tinged breath. Closed his eyes. Thought of Charlotte, Ellis, Arthur and Jess.

Then he looped one leg over the safety railing and stepped into the emptiness beyond.

∽

Roy Thomas opened the text message.

> Everything I own is going to Jess. That includes my shares in the restaurant. I want you to know that she's more talented than me and has phenomenal room to grow. I hope you can give her the chance you were willing to give to me. Thanks. Paul.

Chapter One Hundred Two

Frank pounded on the door of a shithole just south of Barrowcliff park in Scarborough. The sour stench of piss and stale beer made his eyes water.

The door swung open. It took barely a second for recognition to spread over Rez's mug. Then, another second for a shit-eating grin to split his horrible little face. 'Well, if it isn't Fat Daddy.'

The coppery taste of rage filled Frank's mouth. 'Where's Maddie?'

Rez sneered. 'I'm sure I told you to fuck off the other day on the phone, Fat Daddy.'

Frank sucked in a deep breath through his nose, the lad's rank body odour made his stomach churn. 'I told you to stay away.' He dug in his pocket, yanked out the roach and shoved it under Rez's nose. 'You've been round again.'

'Free country, ain't it, Fat Daddy?'

Frank flicked the roach away. 'Your words don't mean nothing to me, lad... but your whole bastard existence does my head in.' He pointed at Rez. 'One last time, where's Maddie?'

'Just fuck off pig—'

The red mist descended in a rush. Frank snatched Rez up by his shirt collar, slamming him back into the dingy hallway.

'Get off—'

Frank cut him off with a stinging slap.

'I'll fucking kill—'

He slapped him again.

Rez's fists flailed. One blow connected with Frank's already busted nose. Sharp pain bloomed. He struck the scrote a third time before kicking his feet out from under him.

Rez crashed to his knees with a yelp. Frank seized a fistful of greasy hair, wrenching the lad's head back to glare into his eyes. 'Where. Is. She?'

'I don't fucking know, all right? I don't!'

Frank gritted his teeth. The urge to pummel the drug-pushing wanker into a smear on the carpet was intoxicating. He pulled on his hair harder making him squeal. 'Why did you come back to my house today?'

'I didn't.'

Frank backhanded him viciously. He closed his fist to show him that next time would be worse.

'You're a fucking pig, you wouldn't.'

Frank drew his fist back.

'Okay... okay... she called me.'

Frank took a deep breath. 'And?'

'You're too late. She's gone again. Fucking gone.'

Frank snarled. 'Where?'

'Leeds, I think? Where her mate Sarah was? Fuck! That's all I know, I swear.'

Frank shoved Rez away in disgust, staggering back to slump against the wall. He dragged in ragged breaths, heart hammering, sweat trickling down his spine. 'Why did she call you? Drugs?'

'No. She wanted a few quid to get herself moving.'

'And you gave it her out of the goodness of your heart?'

'Something like that.' Rez looked away, a ghost of a smile on his face.

'Fucking animal.'

Rez shrugged.

Frank straightened up again and glared.

Rez's face fell. He held his palms up. 'Look. I never treated her badly.'

He moved closer to the kneeling drug dealer. 'Apart from selling her drugs? Anyway, if I find this Sarah, I find Maddie? Is that right?'

Rez stared up at him. 'Shit, you don't know?'

'Know what?' Frank loomed over Rez, his heart rate picking up again.

Rez paled. 'Fuck...'

'*Know what?*'

Rez's eyes widened. 'Sarah's dead, okay? Nothing to do with me. *That* psycho boyfriend of hers beat her to death the other night.'

Frank clutched at his head, the words slamming into him.

In that moment, Frank felt his daughter's despair. It crashed over him in a drowning wave. His legs buckled, and he backed against the wall again; this time, he slid down it, bile scorching his throat.

'She took it badly,' Rez said.

Frank pinned Rez with a venomous glare. 'So, it was you that told Maddie about Sarah?'

'Well, yeah. But how was I to know she hadn't heard?

But it makes sense. No one could get in touch with her. You took her fucking phone off her, man.'

Frank looked down at the floor, shaking his head. *The phone. This is all because of the phone.*

Rez said, 'When she found it, she tried ringing Sarah, got no answer. So then she—'

'Rang you instead,' Frank finished, each word ash on his tongue.

Rez was clambering to his feet, not wishing to remain a sitting duck. 'And after I told her, she asked me to come round with some money.'

Frank looked up. 'And you went out of the goodness of your heart.'

'This is the fucking world we live in, man. Don't get anything for nothing.'

'Did you give her drugs?'

He shook his head. 'No.'

Frank narrowed his eyes.

'I fucking swear. She wanted cash not drugs. She wanted to get herself back out there.'

'But it won't be long, will it?' Frank shook his head.

Rez shrugged. 'Look, it's my fucking job, all right? They ask, I deliver. Simple as.'

'You're an animal.'

Rez snorted. 'You're the one what took her mobile, Daddy! Bad move. She reckons if she'd got hold of Sarah sooner, she might've—'

'So it's my fault she's gone?'

The twist of Rez's mouth said it all. *Aye, he absolutely thought that!*

Frank stood again, trying to slow his breathing, but his heart was going so fast.

'You should have stopped her,' Frank said.

'She was desperate to get away from you.'

Frank clutched his chest, his breathing accelerating, but he couldn't seem to get in enough oxygen. The air reeked of old fags and stale misery. Of failure and loss.

He was being choked by the urge to beat Rez into a smear of blood and teeth.

But it wouldn't change anything. *Couldn't* change anything.

'Maybe you're right,' Frank said, each word a leaden weight on his tongue. 'Maybe this is all my fault, God help me.'

He turned but almost instantly spun back. He stabbed a finger in Rez's direction. Tears burned his eyes but he didn't give a toss. Let the little prick see how close to shattering he was. Might make him take this warning to heart.

'If anything happens to Maddie, as a result of drugs, and the world that you service,' he said, his voice a rough scrape of grief and fury, 'I'll come back and fucking end you, get me? A father with nothing left to lose? You think that's something you can step away from?'

Rez swallowed hard.

'So, my advice to you is that if she gets in touch with you again, contact me, *immediately*.'

Without waiting for a response, Frank turned and stumbled out into the night.

As he walked away, the yawning void that lived behind his ribs seemed to pulse and spread, devouring everything in its path.

It was just like before. A raw, weeping wound where his heart used to be.

Just a sad, lonely old man and his missing daughter, lost in the dark once more.

Chapter One Hundred Three

Using tongs, Gerry lifted the chicken breast from the griddle, and double-checked that both sides were a perfect, even shade of bronze. The sharp, peppery scent of charred meat filled her nostrils as she slid the chicken onto a waiting plate and began to slice and dice, the knife clinking rhythmically against the ceramic. She spooned a portion into a fresh bowl for Rylan and placed it beside the one that she'd already prepped for kibble. The earthy aroma of dry dog food mingled oddly with the savoury notes wafting from the fresh meat. Unlike most pet owners, Gerry never mixed the two. Something about combining different foods on a single plate unsettled her, set her teeth on edge.

Rylan sauntered over for his two courses.

Gerry carried her own plate to the table where a neat mound of boiled potatoes and a tidy serving of green beans awaited. She sat, fork in hand, and stared at the food with a strange sense of detachment. Her stomach felt leaden.

This was, of course, strange, and it made her check her watch.

Exactly 6 p.m. Depending on how long the food took to

prepare, she always ate within at least ten minutes of that time.

In fact, she always carried a box of nuts around with her in case she got waylaid at work.

Hunger was irrelevant. When the designated hour arrived, Gerry ate. Like clockwork.

But now, confronted with a perfectly cooked dinner, the urge to push it away overwhelmed her. She sighed, resigned. The reason was painfully apparent, wasn't it?

Her brain, at least on a subconscious level, was expecting something of her.

Which, in a roundabout way, meant society expected something of her.

Because society still had its own sly way of trying to penetrate her mind and force her to doubt the way she approached life.

With a grimace, she stood, and with Rylan padding beside her, went into her lounge.

She sat and looked up at the picture of her parents on the mantlepiece.

Reaching for Rylan, she drew him close. She rarely smothered him like this unless the need arose. But the need was there.

Her parents smiled at her from the image, forever frozen in a moment of joy.

It was a copy of the same photo she'd taken to the office with her. A daily reminder of who – and what – she'd lost. And a shield of sorts, projecting an illusion of normality. To remind her coworkers that she wasn't completely defective, no matter how alien she seemed to them.

Yes, here was concrete proof that Gerry *was* capable of human connection.

Of love. In a fashion.

It was two years to the day since a freak storm had shattered her world.

Two years since her father's frantic shouts and the howling wind swallowed her mother's choked screams. Since Gerry had plunged into the churning waves, salt stinging her eyes, the cloying taste of brine and terror thick on her tongue. Since she'd bobbed helplessly, lungs burning and limbs leaden, as the yacht crumpled against the rocks.

Two years since she'd walked away from an accident that her parents hadn't.

With her eyes closed, she recalled it vividly, as if it were happening right now. Gerry, at her father's instruction, had jumped from the yacht wearing a life jacket, while he and her mother tried to steer the boat away. They'd failed. Until the very end, she'd heard her father demanding that her mother jump, too. But she'd refused, believing, incorrectly, that the only way to save the yacht was if they both remained on board.

Despite the visceral nature of the memory, Gerry's heart didn't pick up tempo.

It couldn't.

Her mind was too rational and rigid to know it as anything but a memory, and so her adrenal glands would never respond.

She had grieved, of course. The experience had been traumatic, and so it'd bitten deep for a while. Saying farewell to those who championed her above everyone else had also taken a savage toll. But she'd recovered, or at least *appeared* to recover quicker than most.

Rigid routine was her treatment, and functionality her end goal. Her parents weren't coming back, and she'd needed to get back on her feet. So, she had done. Quickly.

Forgotten Bones

Some of her parents' close friends had suggested it was rather quick, and Gerry had tried to explain to them why that was so. They were confused, as people often were confused by her, so she added that if they'd genuinely been true friends of her parents, they would accept this, because as they well knew, Gerry was different, and to disrespect that was to disrespect her parents.

She'd be lying now if she said she thought of her parents often. She didn't. It was just her nature. She lived now. In the moment. Always had done. Looking back wasn't a genuine part of her nature, and looking forward was only relevant to her when setting goals, like becoming a police officer, or finding someone who'd broken the law.

But she tried. She really did. Because she knew that her parents would've liked that, in a way, and she'd always liked what her parents had liked.

So, every now and again, she'd sit, look at the picture of them, smile, and force herself to recall a memory of their time together. Sometimes she'd rub the scratchy wool of her mother's favourite cardigan against her cheek to try to invoke something. Other times, she'd light a pipe, and use tobacco scent to help conjure up her father. Whereas, sometimes, she'd simply sit and stare at this image.

Her parents had provided her with a good life. She'd been well looked after, her condition understood; they'd taken her on holiday regularly, yachting; they'd wished to evolve her, and they had.

She often found after the initial period of forcing herself to remember and mourn, there were rewards. She felt something. A moment of nostalgia. Enough for a smile, and occasionally, a tear.

Staring at the photo, she recalled her father's booming

laugh and her mother's exasperated eye roll as they played ruthless rounds of Scrabble.

In fact, she'd seen something similar the other day when Laura had visited the whalebones and gazed at the hole in which her daughter had been buried. She saw, in Laura's eyes, the nostalgia as she revisited happier memories.

Gerry had a problem with empathy. It was true. Understanding others had always required a steady process of learning and observation. Hardly the most romantic approach to empathy and understanding.

But this was one area in which she seemed to have stumbled on something.

The sudden, piercing ache of nostalgia. The shattering knowledge that some vital piece of yourself was gone, scattered like ashes on the tides of memory.

Gerry would forever struggle with many of empathy's finer nuances, but this nostalgia, she now understood on a bone-deep level.

And sometimes it made her cry.

And, in a way, she liked to cry.

It made her feel more part of this world.

Yet today was frustrating because on one level, a two-year anniversary made little sense to her. Whereas everyone would see it as a time to lament, pay tribute and reflect with immense sorrow, and happiness. And deem it *bittersweet*.

And she'd tried, but failed, to ignore it. Her mind, her body, had demanded her attention by taking away her hunger.

She stood and approached the picture.

But now, in this moment, she didn't mind so much. In fact, she didn't resent it at all. She was happy to take the moment to remember.

She reached out and touched each of their faces.

Because, in her own way, she'd always miss them.

And even blunted and faltering, that grief was the most human thing about her.

Epilogue

Two months later

DAVID MADE Hanna wait two weeks before he consented to see her, wishing her to know who still had the power in their relationship.

Concealed behind a glass partition, usually reserved for the most dangerous prisoners, David watched as the guard led her into the room.

He didn't recognise her dress. More vibrant and colourful than anything he'd ever seen her wear before.

Unacceptable.

He grinned at her.

She appeared taller. As she neared, he recognised this was the effect of a straighter, firmer posture.

A new handbag, clearly worth a few quid, hung over her shoulder.

'No need to put on a show on my account.'

Hanna sat in a plastic chair. 'Thank you for seeing me.'

'You're welcome.' He pointed at her through the partition. 'I took time out of my busy day just for you.'

Forcing back his irritation, David leaned forward. He pressed his hand to the glass.

Now, to work my magic.

He looked at her long and hard and even forced a tear into his eye. He brushed it away. 'I've missed you.'

'Please take your hand off the glass,' the guard on his side said.

He pulled his palm away. 'I keep thinking about that holiday we were going to have.'

'The skiing trip? The one that you booked?'

He shook his head. 'No, the other one. Somewhere hot. Where—'

'The one you asked me to book?'

He leaned back in his chair. His eyes wanted to narrow, but he didn't allow them. 'You need to listen, Hanna, please. I really need you to listen—'

'No, David. I won't listen and I never will again. I found a psychiatrist. He's helping me understand my experiences. He's helping me heal.'

The irony. 'Are you having me on?'

She shook her head.

He opened his palms in her direction. 'This is all intentional and staged, isn't it?'

'No, David—'

'Whatever possessed me to put up with you so long?' He leaned forward. 'Bitch.'

'Because I suffered you. Most people, like your mother, would just call you out long before the poison—'

'Watch it,' he hissed, pointing at her through the glass. 'My mother is nothing to do with anything.'

The guard came up alongside. 'If you raise your voice again, then the meeting will have to end.'

He smiled. 'Noted.' He regarded his wife, turning his smile on her. 'Do you feel any guilt over the whole Charlotte situation?'

'That's between me and the therapist.' She returned his smile.

He raised an eyebrow. 'Still... you must feel partly responsible?'

'Her father didn't kill Charlotte.'

He shrugged. 'One way of looking at it. But if you hadn't told Julie's father, then she mightn't have contacted him for help that night. She may not have gone missing for thirty-seven years. Lost to her mother...'

'Maybe. Maybe not. Like I said, that's between me and my therapist.' She reached into her bag. 'Anyway, the reason I came.'

'You didn't come because you missed me?'

She pulled out some papers. 'These are divorce papers.'

He narrowed his eyes. 'Which I won't be signing. Big believer in until death do us part.'

'I'm afraid it doesn't work like that,' Hanna said. 'I want a divorce.'

'Fine, but I can still delay it for a long, long time.' He gestured around himself. 'Not like I've much else to do, honey!'

'You could have done before, yes. Made it a long tedious process, but the law changed in April 2022, *honey*.' She couldn't resist a smile. 'The "no-fault" divorce law. I mean, don't get me wrong, you're very much *at fault* here, but there's no need for me to present the case. All I have to do is supply the application.' She held it up. 'The waiting period is twenty weeks. If you respond, agree, then great. If not... then the move to divorce will only take an additional six weeks.'

Shit! He took a deep breath. 'Six months to be free of me, eh?'

'Yes.'

He smirked. 'We best enjoy every second then, hadn't we?'

'I'm okay with that... I'll be enjoying those seconds with...' She broke off and smiled again. 'Gary.'

His eyes widened. 'Gary?'

She stood and put the papers down on the chair. 'The guards will serve as witnesses that you—'

'*Who's* Gary?' He was on his feet now.

'—received them.' She turned.

He slammed both fists into the partition. Behind him, the guard shouted a warning.

'I'm talking to you, woman. Who the fuck is Gary?'

She turned. 'I've been speaking to a solicitor. All that money that you've invested into that pension, too. This is going to be done, fairly.'

'Bitch!' He hit the partition again. 'Just try it! I'll fucking kill you!'

Behind him, the guard was shouting into his walkie-talkie.

He pounded the glass over and over...

A multitude of hands descended on him and dragged him to the floor.

∼

Julie stood and watched as her son approached on crutches.

She placed the back of her hand to her mouth, willing herself not to cry, because it'd make Tom emotional, too.

But he hadn't visited in four weeks because of surgeries, and appointments, and to her, it'd felt like four years.

She wiped the tears away before he reached the table, but she doubted that would hide the evidence. She was in a low-category prison, so she swooped around the table and embraced him.

'Not too hard,' he said.

'Sorry.' Forcing back tears, she kissed him on the forehead and stood back, regarding him. 'What *have* you been eating?'

'What do you mean?'

'You're a foot taller!'

'Well, it has to go somewhere,' Sylvia said, approaching from behind. 'He's eating me out of house and home.'

'I'm sorry... Do you need more money? I've got a little still in savings—'

'No, Julie, that's not what I meant. My pension covers us both. I've no mortgage. It's fine.'

'Still. I've been told probate will take another five months. Dad left a sizeable amount.'

Arnold had died of a stroke five weeks before. The car accident, followed by the emerging truth, had sent him on a rapid spiral.

'You'll need that in the future, when you're no longer in here,' Sylvia said.

Julie reached out and put her hand on Sylvia's arm. 'Thank you...'

'For what?'

'I treated you like shite.'

She noticed that Sylvia now had tears in her eyes. 'Maybe I deserved it.'

'You didn't. The men in your life. That's what caused it.'

'Well, Tom's welcome to stay with me as long as he needs to. And we've started to put a few quid away, haven't we, Tom? For the future.'

'Nan wants me to go to University,' Tom said.

Julie smiled. 'Does she?'

'You're a bright lad,' Sylvia said, ruffling his hair. 'We're not letting that go to waste.'

Julie moved around the table, sat down, and they all talked as if there wasn't a care in the world.

Despite the situation, Julie realised she was happier than she'd been in many, many years.

'How are the guitar lessons going?' Julie asked.

Tom shrugged. 'They're going well. Kind of. Grandad would be happy with how much use it's getting. I recorded something for you on my mobile, but they wouldn't let me bring my phone in. However, they said I could share digital content, and then you'd be allowed to listen to it, alone, during your rec time.'

Julie smiled. 'I'd like that very much.'

～

Frank heard the knock at his door and peered through the peephole.

Bloody hell! Unexpected.

He ran back through into the lounge and regarded the pizza box and seven empty beer cans from last night.

He hadn't done his teeth today, and the bitter, hoppy taste still lingered at the back of his mouth. 'Bugger it!' He'd have to keep his distance!

He quickly chucked the cans into the pizza box, not giving a toss about the dregs of beer that ran onto the cardboard and seeped through the corners.

He hurled it onto the kitchen worktop, slammed the door shut, and went to let Laura Wilson in. Only when he moved into a shaft of light coming through the small window did he notice spots of beer staining his trousers.

'Bugger it!' he said again, before opening the door, hoping that she wouldn't catch a whiff of last night's indulgences.

Laura looked nervous but smiled. 'Hello Frank, I'm sorry to be a bother—'

'Eh? Nothing to worry about. You aren't bothering anyone. Come in.'

'Are you sure it's a good time?'

A good time? Here? In the Black residence?

He almost laughed out loud at the absurdity of the question but put on a friendly face and smiled. 'Come on in.'

While she seated herself in his lounge, he glanced around, hoping he'd got rid of the worst of the mess. He was still paranoid over the smell though. 'Bit stuffy in here.' He crossed over and cracked a window, letting in a breath of crisp air.

He sat opposite her. 'How's everything going with you?'

'Good. Lots happening at the church, keeps me busy, you know. The funeral was grand...' Her words trailed off as she took a deep breath. 'I reckon it gave me the closure I needed.'

'I can imagine.'

'I wished you'd have come.'

'It was for you, and Charlotte; I'd have been surplus to requirements.'

'Nonsense, you were the most important part of it all! Without you, there wouldn't have been a funeral.'

'It was a team effort. And if we hadn't sorted it, some other lot would have. No need to be putting me on a pedestal.'

'I like a modest man.' She smiled, her eyes twinkling.

He blushed. 'You aren't flirting with me, are you?'

She put a hand to her chest in mock indignation. 'A good Catholic lass like me?'

He grinned and nodded towards the kitchen. 'Fancy a brew?'

'I can't stay long.'

'That's a shame. You're always welcome.'

'Thank you.' She looked around.

'Yes, the place could do with a spring clean.'

She regarded him. 'I seem to remember you saying you lived with your daughter. Is she not about?'

'Not at the minute, no,' he replied. No need to mention he hadn't clapped eyes on her for two months now, even after taking leave and searching high and low, desperate to find her.

Truth was, it'd all gone back to the way it was before. Him with no bloody clue if his daughter was even still breathing, or if he'd ever see her again.

Who better to understand that kind of heartache than Laura?

Still, Frank wasn't in the habit of spilling his guts about stuff like that.

He had beer, roll-ups and crap food to keep him company and drive him into an early grave. And it's what he bloody well deserved, seeing as it was clearly his fault she'd done a runner again.

'Pity that. I wanted to say hello, let her know what a wonderful dad she has.'

Frank nodded, thinking to himself that Maddie might not be so quick to agree if she were here…

'Anyway. I came to give you something.' Laura rummaged in her handbag. She pulled out a CD case. 'I know CDs are a bit old school, but better than nothing!' She held it out to him. 'And it looks professional, doesn't it?'

He took it from her. The cover was a rather artistic black-and-white photo of Charlotte and her father. She looked about eleven or twelve, guitar slung over her shoulder. Her dad stood next to her, looking proud in his fedora and denim, proper bohemian folk singer style.

Printed below it in large font was: *Broken by Charlotte Wilson*.

He gazed down at the image of the lass who'd sung to him across the years and felt a smile tug at his lips, realising that only now, facing his own demons, could he feel some kind of peace that he'd heard her. That he'd listened.

'Cheers Laura, I'll treasure it.'

'What're you thanking me for?'

He glanced down again.

Makes sense.

Thank you, Charlotte.

~

Julie waited while the guard operated a computer in a small office.

Eventually, when it was all set up, the guard looked back at her. 'I have to stay.'

'I understand.'

The guard hit play.

It was Tom's voice. 'I hope this is all right, Mum. Not how I sound... I mean, what I've chosen. Nan has tried to help me understand everything, and I think I get it. I know it was an accident, and I know you were young and scared. I also know...' He broke off. 'I know you loved her.'

Julie put her hand to her mouth.

Her son played the guitar.

She closed her eyes and was back in the Mariner's

Lantern. 1987. Someone new was taking the open mic. Beautiful brown skin. Piercing eyes. Her fingers moving eloquently over the strings.

Every eye was on her.

There wasn't a voice to be heard in the place.

After Julie opened her eyes, she wiped tears away with the back of her hand. She saw the guard reach over for a Kleenex as her son continuing playing so perfectly... so magnificently.

But he wasn't singing.

Which, in a way, was good.

Because no one could ever sing like Charlotte Wilson.

Still, right now, with a Kleenex crumpled in her hand, and tears running down her face, Julie Fletcher gave it her best shot for the girl on that open mic she'd always love.

Continue the series to discover the dark secrets of Whitby's Forgotten Victims. DCI Frank Black and DI Gerry Carver return in *Forgotten Lives*...

Detective Chief Inspector Frank Black has always believed that no life should be forgotten.
While consumed by the search for his missing daughter, Frank is called to the North York Moors when a decades-old body is discovered behind the cellar wall of the derelict Rusty Anchor pub.

With the help of unconventional Detective Inspector Gerry Carver, Frank delves into seedy past of the pub and its notorious poker nights, where the town's most notorious locals gathered. But as they uncover the truth, they find themselves in a dangerous game with desperate individuals who have all experienced unimaginable trauma.

As the case become more complex, Frank starts to question if he's been wrong all along. Could it be that not everyone deserves justice? And are some lives better off forgotten?

Scan the QR to Order!

Free and Exclusive read

Delve deeper into the world of Wes Markin with the **FREE** and **EXCLUSIVE** read, *A Lesson in Crime*

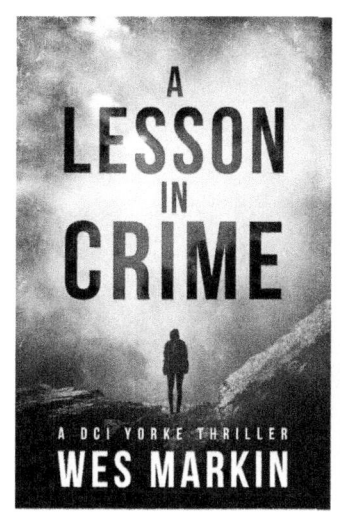

Scan the QR to READ NOW!

JOIN DCI EMMA GARDNER AS SHE RELOCATES TO KNARESBOROUGH, HARROGATE IN THE NORTH YORKSHIRE MURDERS ...

Still grieving from the tragic death of her colleague, DCI Emma Gardner continues to blame herself and is struggling to focus. So, when she is seconded to the wilds of Yorkshire, Emma hopes she'll be able to get her mind back on the job, doing what she does best - putting killers behind bars.

But when she is immediately thrown into another violent murder, Emma has no time to rest. Desperate to get answers and find the killer, Emma needs all the help she can. But her new partner, DI Paul Riddick, has demons and issues of his own.

And when this new murder reveals links to an old case Riddick was involved with, Emma fears that history might be about to repeat itself...

Don't miss the brand-new gripping crime series by bestselling British crime author Wes Markin!

What people are saying about Wes Markin...

JOIN DCI EMMA GARDNER AS SHE RELOCATES TO KNA...

'Cracking start to an exciting new series. Twist and turns, thrills and kills. I loved it.'

Bestselling author **Ross Greenwood**

'Markin stuns with his latest offering... Mind-bendingly dark and deep, you know it's not for the faint hearted from page one. Intricate plotting, devious twists and excellent characterisation take this tale to a whole new level. Any serious crime fan will love it!'

Bestselling author **Owen Mullen**

Scan the QR to READ NOW!

Also by Wes Markin
ONE LAST PRAYER

"An explosive and visceral debut with the most terrifying of killers. Wes Markin is a new name to watch out for in crime fiction, and I can't wait to see more of Detective Yorke." – *Bestselling Crime Author Stephen Booth*

The disappearance of a young boy. An investigation paved with depravity and death. Can DCI Michael Yorke survive with his body and soul intact?

With Yorke's small town in the grip of a destructive snowstorm, the relentless detective uncovers a missing boy's connection to a deranged family whose history is steeped in violence. But when all seems lost, Yorke refuses to give in, and journeys deep into the heart of this sinister family for the truth.

And what he discovers there will tear his world apart.

The Rays are here. It's time to start praying.

The shocking and exhilarating new crime thriller will have you turning the pages late into the night.

"**A pool of blood, an abduction, swirling blizzards, a haunting mystery, yes, Wes Markin's One Last Prayer for the Rays has all the makings of an absorbing thriller. I recommend that you give it a go.**" – *Alan Gibbons, Bestselling Author*

One Last Prayer is a shocking and compulsive crime thriller.

Scan the QR to READ NOW!

Acknowledgments

North Yorkshire is my home, and relocating my writing here has been both exciting and fulfilling. This is my first, but certainly not my last, journey to the Northern seaside town of Whitby, a location I remember fondly from my youth, and a place that has become a firm favourite with my young family.

I am immensely grateful to my support network who expressed enthusiasm and motivation for this new adventure. Their unwavering belief in this project has been invaluable, and I hope I have managed to give it justice.

Starting with new characters always feels like embarking on an uncharted expedition, but Frank has felt different from anyone I have written about before. He has already lived a full life, making me feel like an intruder! Frank has certainly charted his own course through the pages of this book, and I find myself listening to him, rather than telling him what to do. I am in awe of his developing relationship with Gerry, a character so different from his own, and I hope that you are, too.

I owe enormous gratitude to my family: Jo, Hugo and Bea, who continue to support all of my ambitions, keep me laughing, and remain incredibly patient with me.

I am deeply grateful to every reader who has taken the time to delve into my work and engage with my stories, and to the amazing bloggers who have done so much to support me along this journey.

Lastly, thank you Whitby, for being a mysterious, captivating seaside town that offers not just a wonderful backdrop for these intriguing tales, but a wealth of inspiration. Your winding streets, ancient abbey, and windswept cliffs have become as much a character in these stories as the detectives themselves.

I will see you in the next instalment, where bones found in the cellar of an old public house will lead us down another dark path...

Review

If you enjoyed reading ***Forgotten Bones***, please take a few moments to leave a review on Amazon, Goodreads or BookBub.

Printed in Great Britain
by Amazon